Praise for the Awakening Novels

Visions of Skyfire

"Hastings continues with the second book in her witchy, alternate universe series with great success. While building upon the expertly woven foundation of *Visions of Magic*, the new characters presented here are exciting and the sexual tension between them sizzles off the page. Waiting for the next installment of the Awakening saga won't be easy!"
— *Romantic Times*

Visions of Magic

"Magic, passion, and immortal warriors—this fabulous new series has it all."
— *New York Times* bestselling author Christina Dodd

"Hastings launches a troubling and darkly riveting new Awakening series. . . . This series starter begins laying the foundation of an intricate mythos that promises exciting future exploration. Good stuff indeed!" — *Romantic Times*

"Regan Hastings provides a powerful but dark thriller. The story line is fast-paced, with deep characterizations that make the Awakening of magic seem real. However, it is the underlying social issue of burning the Bill of Rights that makes this a terrific cautionary tale." — Alternative Worlds

"A nice addition to the paranormal genre."
— Romance Reviews Today

"I really, really like the world setup that the author created." — Fiction Vixen Book Reviews

"This book has it all: romance, adventure, witches, magic, and immortal hunks." — Jennifer Lyon, author of *Night Magic*

D0974010

Also by Regan Hastings

Visions of Magic
Visions of Skyfire

VISIONS OF CHAINS

AN AWAKENING NOVEL

REGAN HASTINGS

A SIGNET ECLIPSE BOOK

SIGNET ECLIPSE
Published by New American Library, a division of
Penguin Group (USA) Inc., 375 Hudson Street,
New York, New York 10014, USA
Penguin Group (Canada), 90 Eglinton Avenue East, Suite 700, Toronto,
Ontario M4P 2Y3, Canada (a division of Pearson Penguin Canada Inc.)
Penguin Books Ltd., 80 Strand, London WC2R 0RL, England
Penguin Ireland, 25 St. Stephen's Green, Dublin 2,
Ireland (a division of Penguin Books Ltd.)
Penguin Group (Australia), 250 Camberwell Road, Camberwell, Victoria 3124,
Australia (a division of Pearson Australia Group Pty. Ltd.)
Penguin Books India Pvt. Ltd., 11 Community Centre, Panchsheel Park,
New Delhi - 110 017, India
Penguin Group (NZ), 67 Apollo Drive, Rosedale, Auckland 0632,
New Zealand (a division of Pearson New Zealand Ltd.)
Penguin Books (South Africa) (Pty.) Ltd., 24 Sturdee Avenue,
Rosebank, Johannesburg 2196, South Africa

Penguin Books Ltd., Registered Offices:
80 Strand, London WC2R 0RL, England

First published by Signet Eclipse, an imprint of New American Library,
a division of Penguin Group (USA) Inc.

First Printing, June 2012
10 9 8 7 6 5 4 3 2 1

ALWAYS LEARNING   PEARSON

To my kids, Jason and Sarah
For all the love, all the laughs
I'm so proud of both of you
And couldn't love you more.

ACKNOWLEDGMENTS

A big thank-you to my ever-amazing plot group, Susan Mallery, Kate Carlisle, Christine Rimmer and Teresa Southwick. Without you guys, this book would have had way more holes than plot.

Thanks to Jennifer Lyon and, again, Kate Carlisle for always being willing to listen while I obsess. I really owe you guys. Lattes on me next time.

Thanks to my agent, Donna Bagdasarian, for her incredibly hard work, tenacity and incredible wells of patience.

Thanks to my editor, Kerry Donovan, for brainstorming and for her insights in all the right places.

A huge thanks to my family—they never seem to begrudge the craziness.

And again, thanks to the Wiccans I spoke with along the writing journey of this book. I appreciate your help more than I can say.

Chapter 1

Deidre Sterling was used to being followed. Secret Service. Reporters. Paparazzi. But giant black dogs? That was new.

She peeled back the edge of the drapes and looked out the window of her friend's apartment. Her heart was hammering in her chest and her stomach was tumbling like an Olympic gymnast. If she had any sense, she'd leave before things got worse. But then, if she had any sense, she wouldn't have been there in the first place.

Three floors below, the street lay in complete darkness, but for the puddles of light from the streetlamps gleaming on wet asphalt. Cars were parked along the curb. A newspaper hurtled down the street, tossed by the wind. Lamplight shone from a few other apartments across the street and directly below her stood two men in black overcoats. Her Secret Service protection.

Hell of a thing to be a grown woman and not be able to take a walk without at least two armed guys following behind her. But since her mother was the president of the United States, Deidre didn't really get to make that call.

Still, here she was, planning to ditch her guards, just to do what she had to do. Her gaze moved on, checking every shadow, every slice of darkness that could hold— *there*. Just outside a pool of lamplight. The dog. It moved with a stealthy sort of grace that gave Deidre cold chills. Its head was huge and its paws were the size of saucers. What the hell was it? Great Dane? Pony?

"What are you looking at?" Shauna Jackson walked into the room and slipped beside Deidre at the window.

"A dog," she answered, feeling stupid. But she could have sworn over the last few days that the damn thing had been following her. Everywhere she went, she felt its presence, even though she'd caught a glimpse of it only once or twice.

Shauna took a quick look and shrugged. "Don't see anything except your two human guard dogs in overcoats."

"It's there. At the mouth of the alley across the street."

Shauna looked again. "Nope."

Okay, why couldn't her friend see the dog? It was huge. Deidre wondered if maybe PTSD was becoming an issue for her. Was she seeing things? And if she was, why wasn't she imagining fluffy kittens? Why a dog that looked as though it could—and wanted to—swallow her whole?

Deidre shivered as the huge animal tipped its wide head up and fixed its dark eyes on her. Okay, she was really freaking over this. The dog that her friend couldn't see could not be staring at her. How would it know what apartment she was in? At that thought, she almost laughed. Crazy much? She let the draperies fall and told herself she was getting way too paranoid.

"You're not trying to back out, are you?"

Deidre turned to face her friend. Shauna's hair was clipped short, the tight, black curls trimmed close to her head. Her chocolate brown eyes were narrowed. "Dee, the execution is in the morning. How could you think about walking away? You agreed that rescuing the witches is the right thing to do."

"I know." Five women were scheduled for the fires first thing in the morning. She didn't know if they were witches or not. And she didn't care. State-approved executions of witches and suspected witches were happening more and more frequently, despite her mother's attempts to rein them in. The general public was scared. And when scared people came together they usually became bloodthirsty.

She ran her hands up and down her arms, trying to dispel the cold that had been with her since the previous raid she had gone on, two weeks before.

But the cold wouldn't lift any more than the memories would dissipate. She remembered everything from that awful night. She saw it all over and over again whenever she closed her eyes. Her group, the RFW, Rights for Witches, had infiltrated an internment camp to free the captive women inside. But something had gone wrong. Somehow the alarms had been sounded and guards had fired on them and men had been killed.

She hadn't pulled the trigger herself, but she may as well have. And that night, she had made the decision to step away from the RFW. She had joined to stop the violence, not to perpetrate it. Yet here she was, drawn back in. But how could she sit back and do nothing when the Bill of Rights was being crushed under the heel of angry mobs? How could she let innocent women be imprisoned or executed without trials?

"You're having second thoughts again. You in? Or out?" The expression on Shauna's face was impatient and her eyes glinted with determination.

She took a breath, then reached down for the black jacket on the couch beside her. "I'm in. I shouldn't be, but I'm in."

"Of course you should," Shauna told her, slipping into her own black jacket. She picked up a revolver, checked to make sure it was loaded, then tucked it into the waistband of her black jeans.

Deidre frowned, remembering that last rescue gone bad. "I thought we agreed no guns."

"We agreed *you* weren't going to carry one. But, honey, if somebody shoots at me, I'm going to shoot back."

"This is nuts. The whole world is nuts," Deidre muttered.

"It's always been crazy," Shauna said quietly. "It's just now, the whole crazy-ass world is on a mission."

A mission to kill witches and rid the world of magic. Which was why Deidre was here, ready to go on another raid. It was unjust. "There has to be a better way to end this."

"Well, if there is, we haven't found it," Shauna said flatly. "Besides, if anyone could do something about this, it's *you*."

Deidre laughed briefly, gathered up her blond hair and quickly braided the mass to keep it out of her way. "Right."

"Your *mother* is the president of the United States."

"Yeah, and she won't be pleased to know I'm back in the RFW." Deidre didn't even want to think about her mother's reaction. She had been delighted to hear that Deidre was stepping back from the RFW. As president,

Cora Sterling walked a fine line between the citizens who wanted magic stamped out—along with the witches who wielded the power—and protecting the witches, who—hello?—were also citizens and had rights.

But then, every leader in the world was on that tightrope. Magic was out in the open now and those with power were being hunted down like rats by the very governments that should have been protecting them. At least her mom had shown some sympathy for the women being swept up and jailed. Or so Deidre had thought until she discovered that this execution was going ahead as planned *without* any intervention from the president of the United States.

So when Shauna called asking her to help, Deidre had immediately agreed. How could she not? She had seen firsthand the women who were tortured in prison. The women who were so broken by the time they were rescued they would never recover. And that didn't even take into account the women who had *died*. No, as much as Deidre wanted to be able to turn her back, she couldn't.

"Anyway," she said, jerking her head toward the window and the two men—not to mention maybe that dog—standing in the street, "I still don't see how we're supposed to get past the Secret Service guys."

Shauna grinned. "They'll never know we're gone."

Chapter 2

Twelve hours until the execution.

Finn leaned one shoulder against the doorjamb and watched his lieutenants prepare for battle. There was no talking, only the occasional whispered comment. This group had been together less than three months and trust was still building. They worked on a first-name basis only—that way if one of them was captured they wouldn't be able to give anyone else up. Danger was a constant companion with Death hovering around every corner and still they came to fight.

He wondered if it was for love of freedom as they claimed—or if it was just that some people always needed something to rage against.

The lights were dim and seemed to soak into the dank rock walls rather than reflect off of them. It smelled like old liquor and cats down here in the chamber below the apartment building's basement. High aboveground, buildings sent spires skyward; down here, there was a labyrinth of tunnels and rooms long forgotten by those on the surface.

Scowling, Finn looked at the people busily strapping

weapons to their bodies, getting ready for the raid. Mortals. Willing to risk their already too-short lives in the hopes of saving innocents.

He had spent centuries avoiding contact with humans. He hated cities. The noise. The crush of humanity. The relentless reminders of just how alone he really was. Yet here he stood now. In the heart of a city, surrounded by humans.

War made for strange alliances.

And they were definitely at war.

Finn pushed away from the wall and lifted one hand to his second-in-command, Joe. A former Navy SEAL, Joe was, like Finn, a born warrior.

"Everyone ready?"

Joe glanced at the others as they checked pistols, stuffed knives into scabbards. "As ready as they can be."

Finn nodded and reached for the curve-bladed sword he had carried for eons. He slid it into the sheath that ran along his spine. "We'll leave as soon as she gets here."

"Whatever you say, boss."

Boss. How the hell had his existence come to this? Joe took orders from Finn because he agreed with the missions. He wouldn't blindly follow anyone for long and for that, Finn respected him. Trusted him. He didn't trust many, either. His brothers, of course, but humans? They were too fragile. Too easily broken or swayed by whatever popular opinion was in fashion. They lived foolishly and died too soon. What was the point of knowing them? To an immortal like Finn, a human's existence was equivalent to a fruit fly.

He checked his knives, then tucked a few extra throwing stars into the pockets of his black leather jacket. Although he was not accustomed to caring for humans, there was one who was different.

At least he hoped to hell she was different. And he would fight to protect her.

Deidre took another look out the draperies, to make sure the two men in black overcoats were still standing guard in front of the building. They were. Silent, stalwart sentinels. She almost felt bad about sneaking out on them. Almost.

They left Shauna's apartment and in seconds they were crossing the hall and slipping into the stairwell. They moved quickly, but carefully, trying to muffle the sounds of their footsteps, yet the hollow echo in the deserted space seemed to thrum around them. The fluorescent lights threw weird shadows on the walls as they passed and danger seemed to crouch around every turn. Deidre's stomach twisted into knots and her breathing was short and sharp.

She couldn't believe it had come to this. Sneaking away from her guards. Going on a *very* illegal rescue mission. She'd be lucky if her mother didn't have her imprisoned for treason. But she couldn't let those women die without at least trying to save them. These days, the Salem witch trials weren't just history; they were looked on more as a how-to manual for dealing with the supernatural.

They opened the door to the basement and slipped inside. It smelled bad in there. Like mildew and old socks with a hint of cigarette smoke layered over the top. Shauna didn't hit the lights, so the darkness was fairly absolute, but for the hint of moonlight slipping through the narrow casement windows. The basement was big but crowded with crap. No surprise. The tenants used the area for storage, she guessed, since towers of cardboard boxes lined the walls.

When she looked around and didn't see an exit, Deidre's stomach took another sharp lurch. "What are we doing down here?"

"You'll see," Shauna whispered as she walked quickly across the cement floor to a metal storage rack filled with all kinds of useless stuff. Broken appliances, boxes of old toys, tools.

"Help me move this." Shauna stood at one side of the shelving unit and pushed but hardly moved the rack an inch.

Looked like the whole thing weighed a couple hundred pounds. Deidre placed both hands on the cold metal and felt an icy burn in her palms. She let go quickly and shook her fingers to dispel the tingling sensation.

"Hey," Shauna complained. "A little help, here?"

"Right." Frowning, Deidre laid her hands on the metal again and felt that same pulse of something . . . different. This time she ignored it though and pushed at the shelving unit. It swept across the cement floor as if it were on wheels.

Shauna flashed her another grin, then tugged at a length of rope that had been hidden behind the shelving. With a whisper of sound, a panel slid open and Shauna stepped through into shadows. "Follow me."

Deidre's hands were still tingling. She clenched her fingers into fists. "Where are we going?"

"Almost there," Shauna said.

Not really an answer.

Deidre didn't like any of this, but she was in too far to go back. Besides, the scheduled execution was going to happen unless they got those women out of the internment center. She followed her friend and tried not to panic when the panel behind her closed, sealing her into the dark.

Ahead, another panel slid open and Shauna stepped through, swallowed by a deeper darkness on the other side. A cold knot formed in the center of Deidre's chest. Weird, but she had the distinct impression she shouldn't take another step. It was as if every cell in her body was screaming *go back*. She scrubbed both hands over her face, and noticed the tingling in her hands was nearly gone now. This whole night was getting weirder and weirder.

But her being creeped out wasn't reason enough to leave. Not when five women were due to die in a few hours. They needed someone to rescue them. Telling herself it was all just nerves, she followed gamely after Shauna. Every step was tentative though, as if she expected to fall down a rabbit hole and disappear forever.

Shaking her head, she ignored that screaming warning voice inside her head and stepped through the second panel behind her friend. Instantly, she walked straight into a cold, damp rock wall, stubbed her toe and said softly, "We can't have a light?"

No answer.

That sense of foreboding grew but the second door had closed behind her, just like the first, and there was no way to go but forward. God, she hated this. She couldn't see a damn thing. Shauna wasn't talking and what was that noise? Were there rats down here? Oh, she really hated rats.

"Shauna? Where are you?" Her voice was a frantic whisper that went unanswered. Holding one hand against the wall on her right, she crept ahead, wondering where the hell her friend had gone. Then she rounded a corner and was blinded by a sudden brilliant stab of light.

One hand over her eyes, she yelped, "Shauna!"

"What the hell is *she* doing here?"

"Oh my God. Is that who I think it is?"

More voices joined in, at least five or six of them, all shouting questions. She lowered her arm and blinked warily at the people staring at her. When her vision was clear again, she saw that the light wasn't as bright as it seemed in comparison to the inky darkness behind her. But that wasn't important. What was important was the people looking at her as if she had three heads, two of them breathing fire.

The *armed* people staring at her, she corrected silently. They were all carrying guns and those guns were trained on *Deidre*.

Had she somehow crossed over into an alternate dimension or something? Breathing fast, she tried to get her bearings. Then Deidre scanned the faces, found Shauna's and asked, "What's going on?"

Before her friend could answer, another woman shouted, "I can't believe you brought the president's daughter here. What the hell were you thinking?"

"Jesus, we're all toast now," someone else commented just loud enough to be heard.

"She's gonna get us all killed."

Everyone there was arguing, shouting at each other, but their weapons stayed trained on their target. The gun barrels looked damned serious so if this was some kind of weird joke, Deidre wasn't getting it.

Which meant that she had been betrayed.

Her gaze fixed on Shauna. Her friend stared back, chin lifted, defiance glittering in her dark eyes.

Great. Perfect. She'd been handed over to some terrorist group and her friend didn't even have the decency to feel badly about it.

"Shauna—" Deidre said, raising her voice to be heard over the others. "What's this all about?"

"Yeah, Shauna," another voice asked, tone mocking. "What the fuck are you up to? Bringing her here? Right before a raid?"

"Shut up, Tomas," Shauna said.

"Don't tell her my *name*," he countered, eyes wild.

"I don't care who you are," Deidre shouted.

"Your mother would," he snapped. "So she can have us all burned at the stake."

Insult and fury mingled inside her chest, dispensing the cold fear and trepidation that had been nestled there. "My mother is doing everything she can to protect witches."

Laughter met that statement and Deidre's anger pumped even hotter. But bottom line, she didn't give a damn what these people thought. She sent a sharp look at Shauna. "I just want to know what's going on."

Shauna picked up a semiautomatic weapon from a nearby shelf and briskly checked the loads before slinging the strap over one shoulder. When she was finished, she held the gun to her like a teddy bear and shrugged. "Sorry, Dee. I was told to get you here."

"Told?" she countered, scanning the furious faces surrounding her. "By who?"

"By me."

A deep, dark voice cut through the tumult of frantic conversation. There was power in the voice. Enough so that the room quieted as two men walked in.

One was tall, with cool blue eyes and long blond hair pulled into a ponytail. She hardly noticed him. But the other man, she couldn't take her eyes off of him. He was even taller than the blond. Black hair cut military short, he wore unrelieved black and carried enough weapons strapped to him to start a war and win it single-handedly. But it wasn't the blank expression on his face that worried her. It was his eyes. Pale gray, they locked on her and Deidre watched them swirl, shifting color and emotion. Like . . . magic. She knew those eyes.

She'd seen them on the night of the last raid.

When he had killed a man to save her life.

"Congratulations," he said quietly, pale eyes fixed on her, deep voice booming into the silence. "You've just joined the WLF."

Panic reared up and gathered inside her throat. Deidre's gaze swept the others, whose expressions ran from proud to downright threatening. Shauna stepped forward then and said, "I couldn't tell you, Dee."

"Well, you should have," she snapped, feeling the last of her control begin to unravel. She knew the WLF. Everyone did. They were on every most-wanted list in the country. Shaking her head, she said, "No, I won't do this."

"No choice, babe," the leader said, folding his arms across a massive chest. "You've seen us. So you're in."

"I don't belong here. I *thought*," she said with a glare for Shauna, "that I was going to an RFW meeting."

He laughed and she fumed.

"Rights for Witches is a 'write your congressman' organization. Witch Liberation Front is more the blow-shit-up-and-demand-change sort of group."

The others laughed in appreciation, but Deidre didn't see a damn thing funny. "Yeah? And how's that workin' for you?"

Probably not smart to argue with armed wackos but she couldn't seem to shut up. "Every time you guys kill some civilian it only makes the people that much more determined to exterminate you and witches along with you."

"They don't need an excuse," one of the other men in the group said. "They're on a damn holy mission and the only thing they pay attention to is gunfire."

"Try selling that to yourself if you have to," Deidre shot back, "but it won't convince me. You can call yourselves whatever you want. It doesn't change anything. I know what you are. You're terrorists. And I won't help you."

"This is nuts," someone argued. "She's the president's daughter, Finn."

Finn. She turned her head to face the dark-haired man. His features were sharp, his eyes now a flat, cool gray as he watched her. His name struck a chord somewhere in her memory, but damned if Deidre could figure out why. She didn't know him. Had seen him only once before. The recurring dreams of him and those mesmerizing eyes certainly didn't count. So why . . .

"What better way to keep us from execution than to have Sterling's girl in our group?" A half smile curved his mouth.

She felt as if she'd been slapped. She was insurance, plain and simple. Well, why not? All of her life, Deidre had been used by people. As a child, when her father died, Dee watched as her mother went into politics. Dee had been the appendage that looked good for the cameras. The brave, beautiful daughter, soldiering on without the guidance of a father, holding fast to the hand of her strong, brilliant mother. Growing up, Deidre had never had a friend who wasn't secretly trying to get to her mother through Deidre. As an adult, every guy she'd dated turned out to be using her to get close to her mother—hoping for a position in her cabinet or some other high-up government job. Even the RFW had recruited her because, as the president's daughter, she made an impact statement. Now, a terrorist group wanted her for the same reason.

Her stomach churned and her eyes stung briefly as she turned her gaze on Shauna. *"Why?"*

Still holding her semiautomatic weapon close to her chest, Shauna stepped toward her. "Wish there'd been another way, Dee. I really do. But I'm a witch."

Deidre took a shocked breath and held it. She'd had no idea.

Shauna was still talking. "Me and the others like me? We don't have a choice. There are bounties on our heads. If I so much as do a locator spell to find my *keys*, I could be burned at the stake. So forgive me for doing whatever I have to do to protect myself."

Okay, she could understand Shauna's motivation. Being a witch was dangerous. But bottom line, Dee had been used again. By someone she'd trusted as a friend. "You could have told me."

Shauna shook her head. "Couldn't risk it. If you had turned me in, I might have broken under torture and then"—she waved a hand at the people behind her—"that would have put all of them and more at risk."

"Get your gear," Finn said quietly into the sudden stillness.

Deidre looked at him and felt the power of his gaze burrow inside her where it set up shop and started a buzzing reaction that raced through her like a swarm of killer bees. She didn't like it. Didn't want to feel an attraction to an admitted terrorist. And hell, he was as good as kidnapping her, wasn't he? Dragging her into his own private army?

"I won't help," she said.

"Not your call," he countered, then crossed the room to her side. He took hold of her upper arm and a blast wave of heat shot down her arm to dazzle at her fingertips.

He seemed unaffected by it though as he tugged her along in his wake. "Let's get this party started."

Chapter 3

The tunnels were narrow, and the ceiling was low enough that both Finn and Joe had to hunch over to prevent knocking themselves out. The rock walls on either side of the passageway were damp and mildewed with age. November in DC was damn cold and these tunnels, carved out of the rock below the city, seemed to radiate that cold outward. The rebels' breath puffed in front of their faces in tiny clouds.

Candles were tucked in ledges sporadically along the wall, and a few flaming torches threw what little light there was to be had. And Joe's flashlight beam danced from side to side as he guided the group following Finn through the labyrinth.

Finn didn't need the light. Hell, most of the group wouldn't need it, he thought, keeping a tight grip on Deidre's upper arm. The WLF had used these tunnels for months now and each member of his small group knew the way through the mazelike structure. But Deidre was another story. He felt tension coming off of her in waves.

He also felt the heat burning between them. But this was business. Payback. Call it a kiss to karma. He would do what they had to do to make things right. But after that, they would go their separate ways.

He could smell her fear.

That was good. Her fear would engender the change in her. But he needed more than her fear. He needed her sharp. Ready to fight. He needed . . . Well, he expected he needed too much from her.

Deidre Sterling, though she didn't realize it, was his witch and her powers were quickening. He felt it. The hum of magic just beneath her skin. She felt it too—he knew it. She just didn't know what it was yet.

She would soon.

He would explain everything to her. Eventually. First, though, he had to force her power to awaken and to do that, she had to be in danger. Which was why she was here on this raid.

While his mind worked at a furious pace, he kept his gaze fixed on the winding path ahead. As an Eternal, an immortal, his eyesight was profoundly better than a human's. He didn't need the flashlight beam bouncing around the rock walls to guide him any more than he needed the guttering candles. Besides, he thought with a silent chuckle, if he *did* need light all he'd have to do was call on the flames that lay within him and he could light up this place in a blink.

"I never knew these tunnels were down here," Deidre murmured and stumbled on an outcropping of rock. She righted herself before he had to help.

"No one knows about them," Shauna said from behind him. "Except Finn. He knew they were here. Showed us around a few months ago and we've been using them to strike our targets secretively ever since."

"And how did the Great and Powerful Finn know about them?" Deidre muttered.

Finn smiled to himself. Good to know she wasn't cowed. She'd need that flash and spirit before they were finished.

"Does it matter?" Joe asked, in a tone that clearly indicated he didn't need or want an answer.

Finn nodded approvingly. He would answer Deidre's questions. When *he* chose to and he wouldn't be doing it in front of an audience. Even though he had led this small tactical squad for months, none of them knew him for what he really was. And he planned to keep it that way.

Deidre tried again to tug her arm free, but Finn only tightened his hold. He wondered if the buzz of magic and heat pouring back and forth between their bodies was getting to her as it was to him. He'd find out soon enough.

"It smells old down here."

He laughed at that. After all, he was as old as time. What was *he* supposed to smell like?

"No one knows for sure how old they are," Joe told her, "but the tunnels predate the Civil War at least. Parts of them were used as a chain in the Underground Railroad."

She absorbed that information and kept quiet for a few seconds so that the only sound in the tunnel was the scuffing of their feet against the rock.

"Where are we going?" Deidre asked suddenly.

"To an old jailhouse. It's been decommissioned, stands empty most of the time." Joe's voice echoed slightly. "There will only be a few guards because they're trying to keep the women's location a secret. It's close to the site of tomorrow's public execution."

"Yeah," someone behind them sneered. "Want the witches to be fresh for their TV debut. Nothing worse than burning a witch alive on television and having her look tired from that long trip down from prison."

Fury erupted inside Finn at the thought. Down through the centuries he had been witness to the persecution of women of power. He'd saved those he could and mourned the loss of the others. Humanity hadn't changed. Hadn't evolved. They were still willing to kill what they didn't understand. Still eager to wipe out what they feared.

Idiots. All of them. They had no idea the witchcraft they sought to stamp out could save them in the end. He wondered if that knowledge would make a difference. Would they embrace the craft and the women who practiced it? Would witches finally be honored and accepted for the gifts they carried?

He doubted it. He had witnessed too many struggles for power.

Voices washed over him as his crew muttered back and forth in whispered bursts. Finn scowled and thought about telling them all to shut up. But he knew that tension had to be blown off somehow. They were only human, after all. And they were gearing up for a major fight.

He slowed, lifted one hand and then stopped. Turning to Joe, he said, "We're below the old jailhouse now, so, the rest of you, keep it down. We'll wait here for a while, give them all time to settle in up there, relax their guard a bit. Then we'll hit the jail, grab the witches and disappear into the tunnels again."

The small group eased down to sit on the damp rock, cradling their guns, mentally preparing for what was coming. Finn watched them all and felt another small stirring of respect for these few humans.

Joe sent the beam of his flashlight across the ceiling and smiled when he hit on the indentation that indicated an opening in the tunnel. He shifted his gaze to Finn. "I went through last night. Cleared the path outside the tunnel entrance." He half turned to face the others and grinned. "The entrance is so well hidden, they'll never find it once we get away. Hell, I knew it was there and only just managed to see it myself. We've got a little cover up there. Some bushes, and a half wall. The opening is situated behind the jail, so we'll get through the back door, take out the guards and fight our way down to the cells."

Several nods to this statement.

"We've got the key to the cell doors," Finn told them. He didn't tell them that he had used his own magic to flash into the jailhouse last night so he could steal the damn thing. He'd even thought about getting the women out at the same time, but he never would have been able to get *all* of them out and he couldn't risk tipping the guards to their plan. "We retrieve the accused women and get back into the tunnels as fast as possible. Joe and I will cover the rest of you. You bunch concentrate on the witches."

"Got it," Shauna said, her fingertips caressing the cold black gun she held so familiarly.

"How do you get them away?" Deidre asked and Finn looked at her. "Are you taking them back the way we came?"

"You don't need to know," Joe blurted.

"Right." She nodded. "Can't trust the kidnap victim."

"We'll send them through the tunnels to the closest Sanctuary," Finn said, ignoring the heated look Joe sent him. He knew none of them was happy about Deidre's presence but they'd just have to get over it. She was here now and he wouldn't let her go.

"Where's the Sanctuary?" she asked.

"Virginia."

"We're *walking* to Virginia?"

"We're walking to the Key Bridge. Then we'll drive."

"That's like three miles from here."

"Don't think they'll mind the walk," Shauna told her hotly. "Not when the alternative is being burned to death."

Someone muttered in the darkness but Finn paid no attention. He caught her eyes and spoke softly. "You don't need to approve of what we're doing."

"Right. I'm just ballast on this little op, aren't I? Your insurance policy."

Even in the darkness, her blue eyes shone like beacons. At least to him. He could see her soul in them. The same soul he had known in many different incarnations over the last eight hundred years. She was scared, and her power was closer to the surface than ever. Her own fear was going to make her magic erupt.

Finn knew the "rules." He'd been playing by them for eight centuries. He couldn't tell Deidre who she was until her powers had Awakened. But nowhere was it written he couldn't help that Awakening along a little. That's why she was here. He didn't need "insurance" for his little band of marauders. He needed Deidre's life to be endangered enough that her magic would rise as she protected herself.

Tonight, she was going to wake up in more ways than one. Tonight they'd finally start the damned quest that had been awaiting their attention for all these long centuries.

Yeah, she was pissed, but Deidre stayed close to him, as if something inside her already knew that was where she belonged. Well, he mused, either that or she was too scared to move away.

"And what do I do while you're all busy? Wait here?"

Joe huffed out a short laugh and she shot him a murderous look.

"Yeah," Finn said, sarcasm dripping from the words. "Because you'd stay put and wait around for us to get back. Not a chance, blondie. You'll be with us. Just do what I tell you *when* I tell you and everything will be fine."

"And I'm supposed to trust you? My kidnapper?"

"Technically, Shauna's your kidnapper," he pointed out.

"Thanks," that woman muttered.

"She did it on your orders," Deidre argued.

"Seems to me most women in your position would be a little more concerned about pissing me off."

"Screw you. Be pissed off. What do I care?" Her pupils were wide, the black almost swallowing the blue of her irises as she focused in the darkness. But Finn saw that her expression was mutinous. Good. She'd need fire in her belly if they were going to pull this off.

She was part of the last great coven and he had waited eight hundred years to be Mated with her. The first two Eternals and their Witches had completed their tasks and were now back at the coven's sanctuary in Wales. He knew those two couples had faced a lot of trials together and come out on top. He was determined that he and Deidre would do the same.

Deidre ran her hands up and down her arms and Finn watched her expression carefully. She was still mad, but she was also, from what he could tell, sympathetic to the situation. He suspected her devotion to the cause would only strengthen, as soon as she knew that *she* was one of the most powerful witches in the world.

Chapter 4

Deidre felt wound tight enough to give off sparks.
    Between her fury at her friend's betrayal and her
fear of being captured—or killed—her mind was in turmoil. And to make everything worse, Finn never left her
side. Stressed didn't even come close to describing what
she was feeling.

They came up through the tunnel into a parking area,
surrounded by ten-foot-high chain-link fencing. As promised there were a few scraggly bushes and a half wall, but
the wide, empty lot stood between them and the jailhouse. The light poles were dark. Those in charge were
no doubt trying to make it look like the building was still
empty. The darkness was nearly absolute, but for the
light of the waning moon overhead.

From a distance, voices came to her, what sounded
like a mob of people chanting, and it took Deidre a minute or two to understand what they were saying. When
she did, her blood went cold.

A crowd was repeating, *"Burn, witch, burn,"* over and
over again in a hypnotizing rhythm.

She looked at the others and saw their features twist

into expressions of disgust and anger. Shauna held her gun even tighter to her chest, as if she could find security there.

"The righteous," Finn murmured close to her ear. His breath was warm on her skin and his proximity made her shiver. "A few dozen of 'em are camped out down the street, in front of the TV station, waiting for tomorrow. Five witches burning at once? Don't want to miss that."

Deidre felt the bloodlust in the air and was sickened by it. How could she blame the WLF for terrorist tactics when this was what they were going up against? She had spent the last five years working for change within the RFW and had accomplished exactly squat. There were more internment camps than ever, executions were now televised and more and more women were being snatched off the streets every day on mere suspicion of magic.

Maybe Finn and these others were right. Maybe the only way to fight terror was with force. And she couldn't believe she was even thinking that.

In the next moment though, there was no more time for pondering her life's choices. She was on the move and struggling to keep up with Finn. His grip on her arm ensured she stayed right beside him. For a big man, he moved with surprising grace. He hardly made a sound as he ran through the darkness, headed for the steps of the building. The air was cold, but her blood pumped fast and furiously, keeping her warm.

Behind them, the others were spread out, heads down, running. Deidre was still watching them when the lights came on in a brilliant burst that briefly blinded her. The entire parking area was suddenly bright as day, outlining her and the others in the group as if they were on a stage beneath a white-hot spotlight.

Gunfire erupted.

Someone screamed.

"Down!" Finn threw her to one side and Deidre hit the icy asphalt hard, scraping her knees and the palms of her hands. She whipped her head up in time to see Tomas cut practically in half by a stream of automatic-weapons fire.

Horrified, Deidre shrieked and looked up and over her shoulder. Armed uniformed men were on the roof. An ambush? Or were they simply there in case someone tried to mount a rescue? Their weapons fired in staggered volleys, creating a stream of noise that sounded like World War III. They must have been lying flat in wait, until the WLF came into the open. Now, they were standing, with a perfect view of the parking lot, empty but for the handful of would-be witch rescuers.

Someone screamed as another volley of gunfire erupted. Deidre hunched her shoulders and tried to make as small a target as possible as she looked around. Shauna fell to the ground nearby, writhing in pain as blood streamed from her shoulder and arm. Panic and rage jolted Deidre into action. She crawled to her friend's side, wincing and ducking with every new outburst of gunfire.

"Hurts. God, it hurts." Shauna's voice, mumbling, praying, chanting.

"Hold still," Deidre ordered, tearing off her jacket to bunch on top of Shauna's wound. She held the fabric there, applying pressure, feeling a different sort of pressure building inside her.

Finn was standing over her, throwing knives as fast as

bullets could fly. His big hands were a blur of motion and still it wasn't enough to stop the attack. More gunfire chattered and the noise was tremendous. Horrifying.

Joe was lying flat on the ground, his weapon cradled in his arms as he coolly returned fire. A couple of the others were shooting too, but the men on the roof definitely had the advantage.

Bullets slammed into Finn. She heard them hit, but he never wavered. Like a superhero or something, he stood his ground and continued to throw what seemed like an endless supply of knives and throwing stars.

Deidre's fear surged into fury as she watched another of the WLF team go down in a hail of bullets. Something elemental shifted inside her, fed by the injustice of it all. At the stark realization that these men and women were putting their lives on the line to rescue witches and being slaughtered for it. If something didn't change soon, they'd all be wiped out.

"Dee—look out!" Shauna's voice was hardly more than a strangled whisper, but Deidre heard it and reacted.

Before she could think about what she was doing, she stood up, spun around and lifted both hands in an instinctive attempt to stop the next round of bullets. A corner of her brain shrieked at her to run. To hide. That she was being an idiot and what good would holding up her hands possibly do?

But something inside her urged her on. The movements felt familiar. Welcome. Like an old friend dropping in after a long absence. The swell of an amazing sensation within pushed her forward. Deidre felt a surge of something hot and fierce and . . . almost primordial rush through her.

"What the hell?"

Someone behind her asked the question but Deidre didn't have an answer. She was as stunned as he clearly was.

Bullets stopped midflight. She blinked and looked again, just to make sure of what she was seeing. They hung in the air in front of their targets like brass snow-flakes. The men on the roof were helpless. Their guns had been pulled from their grasps and were dangling in the air fifteen feet in front of them.

"Deidre!"

Finn's voice reached her even as she stared unbeliev-ingly at what was happening. Was she doing this? Had she ripped the guns from the hands of the men trying to kill them? Was it *her* strength of will holding those guns in midair? How? *How?*

"Use your magic, Deidre. Feel the power in it and give it free rein. Trust it." It was Finn again. His voice was loud. Demanding. And something in her responded to it. As if she had been waiting all of her life to hear that voice. She turned both palms skyward then clenched her fists as her mind directed the weapons. And suddenly the barrels of those guns swung around to train on the men who only moments ago had been in complete control of the situation.

"Holy shit." One of the WLF came up behind her. "You're a witch."

She choked out a harsh, nearly hysterical laugh that scraped at her throat. "Apparently."

Her gaze trained on the guns and the men on the roof. Shock rattled her and fear came rushing in behind it. Was she really a witch? She fought against that even as the evidence was right in front of her. How else was she doing what she was doing?

The guns she controlled wavered and dipped as if in response to her own inner turmoil. She took a breath, held it and then released it when it didn't help. Something inside her bubbled and frothed and she fought to control it and the emotions churning at the same wild pace.

A hand suddenly came down on her shoulder and Finn's voice whispered, "*Focus* your power."

His voice steadied her. Like oil poured on churning water. She didn't know why and didn't question it further. Nodding to herself, she reached for the wellspring inside her and let it flow from her hands. The guns she still held control over straightened, steadied, barrels aimed at their owners.

Witch.

The realization of who and what she was slammed into her, but she couldn't really take the time to think about it now. There would be opportunity later—if they lived—to come to grips with what was happening to her. For now, all that was important was survival.

"Can you hold them?" Finn was still at her side. She felt him. The heat of him. A familiarity. The sense of tumblers in a lock clicking into place. As if she had finally arrived at a destination she hadn't been aware of until just that moment.

"Deirdre. Can you hold the guns and the men at bay?"

"I can," she said, with more determination than she felt. Power bubbled inside her again, rich and thick, and as if it was grateful to finally be acknowledged, it seemed only to grow with the passing minutes. She channeled it somehow, as if she had been born knowing how to do it. But how long would it last?

She wanted to admit she didn't know how long she

could keep it up. Fear took root again and it was over-powering. Too much was at stake here. The lives of the witches, their would-be liberators—not to mention Deidre's life. Refusing to fail, she risked a glance at the huge man still waiting at her side. "Go. I've got it. For now anyway. Get the witches."

He didn't hesitate. Didn't pepper her with more questions. He simply took her at her word, trusting her to do what was necessary. And for that, she was grateful. She felt his confidence in her and it fostered her own. Strength seemed to be pouring into her. She felt new. Reborn. Powerful. Her hands tingled as they had when she had touched the metal shelving what seemed like days ago now.

As the remaining members of the WLF disappeared inside the building, she half heard Shauna behind her whispering, "I don't believe this."

"I know. I can't either," Deidre said and flicked a weapon higher when the man in front of it tried to shift position. The gun barrel tracked him menacingly—with a simple twitch of a finger from her—and the man re-thought his position and stood still again.

The night was black, aside from the bright spotlights, now that what was left of the moon had slipped behind a bank of clouds. Icy winds plucked at her coat, tore at the braid hanging down her back and stung her eyes, making her vision water. But Deidre called on the new energy pulsing inside her and held her ground.

Until a different kind of chill invaded her body. It swept through her soul, crawled through her bones and sent the hair at the back of her neck standing straight up. *Evil.* It was here. With her. In the dark.

Her concentration dimmed and she fought to bring it

back, in spite of the screaming voice in the back of her mind urging her to run. Hide. Deidre dragged in an unsteady breath and, rather than give in to the cowardly impulse to run, swiveled her head slowly, trying to find the source of her fear.

It wasn't the men on the roof. They were merely humans. Vicious, but human. This was something . . . more.

There.

In the shadows.

It moved, black within the black and a flash of red that appeared and disappeared in a blink. But it was enough. She saw it. The dog.

The black dog that had been following her for days was here. Watching her. She felt a wave of revulsion wash over her and as her instincts cried out at her in warning, the dog slinked closer. Giant paws, stealthily planted, it dipped its head, then lifted it, sniffing the air. It must not have liked what it sensed because it stiffened, then turned and bolted back into the shadows that had borne it.

Deidre was shaking, swallowing hard past a tight knot in her throat and trying to quell the terror nearly choking her. What the hell kind of dog was that? The darkness inside it was absolute. And wanted nothing more than to envelop Deidre whole. Drag her into that darkness and keep her there for eternity.

How she knew that, she couldn't have said. But she felt the truth of it down to her bones.

Whipping her head back, she focused on the enemy she could control. The men on the roof who had caused so much destruction. Who worked for those who would burn a woman alive just on the suspicion that she might be different.

Her strength pulsed and wavered, but her determination was solid. She wouldn't give any ground. Wouldn't give them the chance to do more damage. She would hold them for as long as it took, no matter what.

It felt like forever but was probably only a few minutes before Finn and the others rushed from the building. Deidre spared a quick look in their direction, not really daring to take her eyes off what she was doing for long. Finn, Joe and two of the others half carried, half dragged five women who looked terrified and relieved all at the same time.

"Hold them there!" Finn's command came short and sharp.

Deidre nodded and saw him rush out to pick up Shauna, who groaned piteously at being moved. A fresh burst of fury erupted inside Deidre at the sound of her friend's pain. But she didn't react. What more was there to do, anyway? She'd stopped the carnage. Too late for Tomas and Shauna and another guy whose name she didn't even know. But no one else was getting hurt tonight, she told herself firmly, gathering her strength, molding it to the task at hand. She concentrated on the guards' weapons, kept the barrels pointed at them, following their slightest moves.

She heard Finn and the others leave and knew she was alone now in the bright lights. Could the guards make out her face? Would they recognize her? Finn had called her name, but there must be millions of other Deidres in the world, so that wouldn't give away her identity.

But if they did know her, then all hell was about to break loose. Her mother would be horrified and wouldn't be able to protect Deidre from the laws that would demand she be locked away.

"Oh, God," she muttered, and as her concentration

slipped, so did the gun barrels. One daring man jumped forward, but Deidre recovered in time to urge him back with a slap of the gun barrel against his head.

She had to concentrate and think only about what she was doing. If she let her mind wander, this would be over and she'd be dead before anyone could arrest her. She knew Finn and the others were headed for the tunnel entrance. The Magic Police would never find it, as skillfully hidden as it was. So Deidre knew that as soon as they were in the tunnels, they would all be safe.

Or as safe as witches could be.

"Time to go." Finn was back at her side and she almost laughed at just how sneaky the man was. She hadn't heard a thing. Hadn't seen him approach. He was just suddenly there.

"Right," she said, ready for this night to be over. "Just one more thing. No point in leaving them with full magazines of ammunition, is there?"

"Nope."

She felt his smile and shared it. Through the fear and anger and confusion, there was also a part of her that was really enjoying the sensation of magic in her veins. It was unlike anything she'd ever known and it was damn near overwhelming.

Flipping her hands over, she watched as the floating guns responded to her mental command and suddenly pointed downward, toward the ground and began firing. The guards shouted and bolted for cover, some of them sliding over the edge of the roof to drop two stories.

With the guns still rattling, bullets and sound tearing up the night, Deidre looked up at Finn and said, "I'm ready."

But she wasn't ready to be engulfed in flames.

Chapter 5

Haven, in Wales

Shea, Teresa and Mairi, three Awakened witches, gathered together in the heart of Haven to call on the magic.

They created a circle of power, kneeling around a silver bowl filled to the rim with crystal clear water. Behind them, in recessed niches carved into stone, living fire burned in flames of orange, yellow, gold and blue. Two of the recesses held cages magically constructed to contain pieces of Black Silver, returned to the coven by Shea and Teresa. A third recess waited for Deidre and Finn to complete their quest to retrieve the dangerous and ancient element.

The fire burned over the emptiness, around the cages. The flames snapped and hissed, casting dancing shadows across the witches and the room in which they worked.

Lines of silver threaded through the gray stone walls, flickering in the firelight, highlighting the ancient symbols of power carved there. The spiral, the Bindu, the snake that symbolized immortality and more. There were symbols from every known religion and some that had never been seen anywhere but in the sanctity of Haven. Here, the magic flowered. Here, power sang through the walls and the floors and enveloped the women who called this place home.

The Awakening was changing everything. The first three members of the last great coven of witches had completed their tasks and waited in Haven for the others to find their way home. Mairi, the once and future High Priestess of the Haven coven, looked at her sister-witches and, beneath her pride in their accomplishments, felt a tremor of worry snake through her. Until their task was complete, with every witch home and at peace with the past and the mistakes made, the world would be in danger.

Eight hundred years ago, she had led her sisters on a dangerous quest. They had turned their backs on their beliefs, their goddess, Danu, and even the Eternal warriors who were their destined other halves. They had embraced the dark, pushed too far in a search for more knowledge and power and in so doing, had ruined everything.

They had sought to open a portal to another dimension, focusing their immeasurable powers through the prism of a Black Silver Artifact. An Artifact that was born of blood and breath and fire a thousand years before the birth of Christ. The Black Silver was imbued with magic by its creators, the ancestors of the very witches who allowed it to be freed into the world.

A crest of interlinking knots, the Artifact, when whole, opened doorways into other dimensions and that was what had finally seduced the last great coven. They had hoped to grow their powers and their knowledge in other worlds, other times.

Instead, the gateway to Hell had swung wide and a horde of demons had rushed out, eager to claim this world for their own. When the doorway was finally closed again, despite the witches' efforts, the seal was incomplete. Dark energy had been leaking into this dimension ever since, creating havoc around the earth.

In atonement for what their greed had caused, a spell was cast and the witches' powers slept for eight hundred years. Now, the time of the Awakening was here and each witch would come into her power again—this time with the strength to turn their backs on the lure of dark power.

Finally the time had come, after generations of reincarnation, for the witches to at last secure that doorway. To gather up the pieces of the Black Silver and use it to ensure that Lucifer and his minions would never be able to use this gateway again.

But to achieve that, they would need *all* of their sisters and their Eternals to come home. And with one of the Eternals missing . . . that wasn't going to happen.

"Are you ready?" Mairi asked, her voice calm, in spite of the roiling emotions inside her.

"Yes," her niece Shea answered instantly.

"Sure." Teresa looked at the other women and shrugged. "But all we know is that Egan was trapped at the bottom of the sea. There's a lot of water on this planet . . ."

"True," Mairi agreed, letting her gaze sweep around the room. She didn't look at the power symbols, but at the faces carved into the stone walls. The faces of her sister-witches from so very long ago. Each of them was as familiar as her own features. Each of them dear. Each of them so very important to this cause.

And for this task, this locator spell, the three of them would draw on the magic that lived in this place. On the memory of those others, still far from home. Focusing their own knowledge and drawing on the gifts of the universe, they would try to find Egan.

"The best we can hope for," Mairi told them, "is a clue. A sense of place. To narrow it down enough that our Eternals will have a chance at finding him."

"If we had something of Egan's to focus the magic on . . ." Shea began, biting at her lower lip.

Mairi shook her head. "So far, there's nothing. His home in France had been cleaned out. Still, Damyn believes he knows of one more place Egan spent time in, so there's still hope."

She smiled at the thought of her Eternal, his bronzed skin stained with a Mating tattoo that matched her own, that of climbing roses. Damyn shared his strength with her, enhanced her magic and for a moment, she wished all three Eternals were with them, in the sacred circle. But this was work for the witches alone. They would have to draw strength from each other to make this work.

"Let's begin."

"Okay, but, *how*?" Teresa interrupted. She was the newest member to find her way home. She and her Eternal, Rune, had arrived only two days ago and her magic was still raw, untamed. As was Shea's, Mairi thought, since her niece had been here only a month longer than Teresa. But in this, they were all apace. They would remember together. They would align their magic and feed off each other's strengths and somehow, they'd pull it off.

"Link hands," Mairi said softly, holding her hands out to both Shea and Teresa. When they were joined, forming a living triangle, magic hummed in the air around them. The surface of the water stirred, as if someone had blown a breath across it. And in the tiny ripples, light and shadow formed and faded and formed again.

"Focus," Mairi whispered, her gaze locked on the water, waiting for a clear image to appear. The other two witches joined her, centering themselves, their gazes also on the churning water.

Mairi took a breath, let it slide from her lungs and softly chanted,

> *We seek the one lost*
> *To set him free*
> *Follow the magic*
> *And let us see.*

Shea and Teresa picked up the chant and repeated it with her. Their voices chimed together and became more than words, more than a chant. The essence of magic rushed through them, around them, wrapping the three of them in a blanket of warmth and the shimmer of power.

As the spell worked, the surface of the water began to twist itself into a spiral, as if it were churning to go down a drain that wasn't there. Faster and faster it spun, lapping over the edges of the crystal bowl, sprinkling the knees of the women kneeling before it. Then, as quickly as it began, it was over. The water stilled and an image formed.

Egan. Mairi took a sharp breath and stared at the haggard, tortured face of the Eternal. He was beneath the sea, trapped in a cage fronted by white gold bars. The flames of his magic coated his skin, but because of the water, burned faintly, more like the memory of fire than the living flame it should be.

But his eyes told the story of his suffering. His Eternal gray eyes, normally awash in shades of pewter and silver, were now black. As black as the treachery that had landed him there. As black as the deep ocean that held him.

Shea sighed and Mairi whispered, "Focus."

She reached for him, across the miles, sending her thoughts to the trapped Eternal. *Hear me, Egan. Feel the magic. Help us find you.*

Mairi held perfectly still, using every scrap of magic she possessed. She centered herself and drew on the reserves of strength provided by the connection to her Mate and by her sister-witches, now holding her hands in tight grips. Their magic flowed from their fingertips into Mairi's body until she felt herself expanding, blossoming, power filling her mind and heart and soul and then she tried again.

Egan!

She shivered, and beside her, Shea and Teresa gasped. As if he heard them, felt their presence, Egan stared out at them from the water's surface and shouted, "Mare Superum!"

The magic winked out. The women slumped in their places and struggled for air. After a few moments of recovery, Shea looked to her aunt and asked, "Mare Superum? What is that?"

Mairi shook her head, both exhilarated and bereft.

They had found him, but still didn't know where he was. "I have no idea."

Magic. He felt it. Dreamed it. Breathed it.

The dark water became lover and enemy. Surrounding him, invading, caressing him. Days and nights bled together. Weeks and months were links in a never-ending chain that stretched into eternity and beyond.

There was no change.

No light in his darkness.

There was only his rage.

And the rage was all consuming. All powerful.

He roared his fury and his voice was swallowed by the sea. He thought of the witches staring down at him and strangled the bead of hope that lay nestled in his chest near his unbeating heart.

Hope would change nothing.

Magic couldn't save him.

The white gold bars of his prison dampened his powers. The water surrounding him smothered the living flames that were the heart of him. He was immortal. Eternal.

And trapped at the bottom of the ocean by the female who should have been his Mate.

Egan grabbed the bars of his cage despite the cold ache that swept through him at the contact. As he had so many times before, he rattled and shook them with the waning strength left to him.

Nothing.

No change.

He fell against the heavy wood and white gold enclosure at his back and stared out at the watery grave she had caught him in. Fury roared through his veins, as hot and rich and pure as it had been the day Kellyn betrayed him. The day she had sealed her own fate.

Because he would get out, he promised himself as madness crept closer. And when he did, he would kill the witch himself and fuck the Awakening.

Chapter 6

"**W**hat the *hell* was that?"

Finn let Deidre go the minute they were in the tunnels, yet far enough from the rest of the team that no one else would see. As the flames on his skin slowly faded away, he caught Deidre's astonished expression. Eyes wide, she shook her head as if denying the whole thing had happened and took a quick step back. He read panic in her eyes and he couldn't allow it to take root. He knew he had to stop her from discounting what she'd been through. She was Awakened and she would damn well *stay* Awakened.

Whether she wanted to hear it or not, he was going to tell her the truth. About who she was. About who *they* were, together.

"Magic," he told her.

"Yeah," she countered, pushing a stray lock of hair out of her eyes. "I got that." She was still wild-eyed as if trying to figure out what she had done and coming up empty of explanations.

Finally though she said, "What I did back there ... with the guns, the guards. That was magic." She looked down at her hands as if she'd never seen them before. "I'm a witch. Sounds weird even saying it, but it's hard to dispute what happened out there. But you—" She looked up at him again. "Men aren't witches. And most men don't go up in flames and then zap themselves and a passenger anywhere they want to go. So what the hell are you?"

Finn glanced back down the tunnel. His hearing was far sharper than a human's and he had no problem discerning the scuffle of feet and the hushed whispers that defined his group's passage. They were headed for one of the main chambers off this section of the underground. The room they used as their headquarters. He didn't have enough time to go into a long explanation here, so he kept it short and less than sweet.

"What I am, is immortal. Who I am, is your Eternal. I'm here to help you Awaken your magic."

She scraped her hands up and down her arms. "Yeah, thanks, but I think I've done that already. Remember?"

He laughed and was startled himself by the sound. "There's more to it than the manipulation of metal."

"I'll bet," she said, then looked up at him with a shrewd gaze. "You weren't surprised at all by what I did. Everyone else was, me included, but not you. You knew. You knew that I was a witch when you told Shauna to bring me tonight."

"Yeah." He folded his arms across his chest and kept his eyes locked on her. He could almost see the wheels in her mind turning. "I've always known."

"Always? What's that mean?"

"It *means*," he said with more than a little impatience, "that I have known you for centuries. Eons of time stretching back far longer than even I want to remember.

It means you and I have what you could say, quite literally, *history*."

"Riiiiggghhhttt." She dragged that one word out so
long, it was a sentence in and of itself. Nodding as she
gave him a patronizing smile usually reserved for children. "Centuries. You and me. Sure. That makes as much
sense as anything else that's happened tonight."

Finn had expected disbelief. The sarcasm he could live
without. Down the tunnel, the group moved farther
away from them. "We don't have time for this right now."

"Yeah, well, make time," she said and folded her arms
across her chest, mimicking his position. "And try to
come up with some story that at least *sounds* real."

Unbelievable. Who would have guessed that she'd accept her magic so easily and still fight him? "You want
real? You got it. Bottom line? You're the reincarnation
of a powerful witch. I was your destined Mate. Your guardian."

She laughed shortly, but he just moved in closer and
started talking faster. "Back in the day, you and your
coven cast a dangerous spell that backfired big-time. It
opened a gateway to Hell, allowing demons through into
this dimension. Now, eight hundred years later, we have
to find an ancient Artifact that *you* hid back then. And if
we don't, the world is toast. Clear?"

"Oh yeah," she said after a long moment of silence.
"Way clear. You're nuts."

"Damn it." He grabbed her, pulled her in close and
kissed her, hard and long and deep. The connection between them simmered in her veins—he knew it. What he
had to do now was force her to remember. To feel the
draw between them, that bond that was never severed,
no matter how many lifetimes she had lived.

Their souls were bound. Always had been. If she wouldn't believe his words, then she would damn well believe what he made her feel.

She struggled for a second or two and then her instinctive pull to him kicked in and she kissed him back. Finn hadn't meant to give in to this; the kiss was simply a means to an end. But when she wrapped her arms around his neck and molded herself to his body, what the hell was he supposed to do? She had always been able to turn his blood to steam and his dick to stone. That hadn't changed. Tongues tangled, their breath merged and flames erupted over his body, devouring them both in a dancing, living flame that dazzled the darkness.

It had been too long, he told himself as he swept his hands up and down her body before cupping her behind and pressing her tightly to his groin. That's why he was instantly ready to find the closest flat surface and bury himself inside her. It had nothing to do with the Mating. Nothing to do with who she was or what they had once meant to each other.

She was female and he was more than ready for one. That's all it was. All it could be.

But even *he* knew that for the lie it was. So he let her go before he could give in to the urges choking him.

She stumbled backward and clapped one hand to her mouth. "Oh my God. I . . . *know* you. I mean, *I* don't, but something inside me recognizes you. The power surge when you kissed me was shattering."

In the soft glow of guttering candlelight, her skin looked pale and her eyes were even more blue than usual. Even through her shock and the residue of her fear, she was lovely. Enough to tempt him. But Finn pushed that thought aside. "That's the draw of a Mated pair. Our bodies, our souls, were meant to be together."

"That is probably the absolute weirdest thing you could have said."

Not the reaction he had expected.

"I'm supposed to believe we've known each other for *centuries*?" She shook her head and murmured. "No. No, this cannot be happening, that's all there is to it. This is some bizarre dream. Or a breakdown!" She said the last almost hopefully. "I'm in a locked ward somewhere, aren't I? And you're the gorgeous young doctor acting *really* unprofessionally with a patient. Yes. That's it."

Impressed with her imagination if nothing else, Finn said, "Okay. Whatever helps you deal with this."

"I don't have to deal. Breakdown," she reminded him.

"Right. Come on. I'll explain it all when we have more time. Right now, we don't have any time." He grabbed her arm and when she fought him he said, "It's either start walking or we take another fire ride. Your choice."

"Fine. I'll walk."

She started past him, muttering about medication and straitjackets and Finn took a quick second or two to admire the view. His gaze dropped to the curve of her behind and the long legs that were striding away from him. Black jeans hugged her body like cool night. Her blond braid was unraveling at the edges, but her chin was up, head held high.

Yeah, she was a beauty but she wasn't going to give him an easy time of it. His body was ready and aching and she was trying to dismiss him as a delusional dream.

The last couple of hours had been hard and fast. She'd held up to it, too, he told himself with a trickle of pride.

And now, her anger was leading the charge inside her instead of the fear and confusion he knew she was experiencing. Another point for her. She stalked down the tunnel ahead of him like a woman on a mission. And she was, he thought. A mission to put as much distance between them as possible.

"But that won't work, witch," he murmured. He'd felt her response to his kiss. Knew she was as stirred up as he was, she just didn't want to admit it. She'd have to deal, though. Now they were together and they were staying together until their job was done. Then he'd not only let her walk away—he'd make sure it happened.

Following after her, his boots not making a damn sound on the tunnel floor, Finn mentally geared up for the next month. They'd have thirty days, the cycle of the moon, to complete the quest that had been waiting for them for eight hundred years. They didn't have time for her to ease into this. To give her space to deal with her fear and the knowledge that she was a witch. They had to dive right in and make this work. Not just for their sakes—but for the world's.

Her fear stained the air. He could smell it as he took in her distinctive witch scent with every breath. Earth witches always smelled like nature. Earth and ocean and something else, specific to the witch. *His* witch smelled like cinnamon. Dark. Rich. Spicy. But the scent of fear almost overpowered it. It was alive and well and crouched deep inside her. Not surprising. She'd had a hell of a lot thrown at her in just a couple of hours. But he suspected that she was stronger than even *she* knew. At least he hoped so, because she was going to need every scrap of strength she could gather if they were to survive the coming trials.

Chapter 7

"Deidre."

Why did his voice vibrate on her skin like a damn tuning fork? She paused and looked back over her shoulder.

In the candlelight, his features looked harsh and sharp, as if they'd been carved from stone with an ax. How could she find that so appealing?

"The others don't know what I am," he said.

Deidre stopped, swept him up and down, taking in the scuffed black boots, the black jeans, the gray shirt and the short black leather jacket, before meeting his gaze again. "Well, then, I've got something in common with your terrorists after all, don't I?"

His mouth worked as if he were biting back words struggling to get out. "I *meant*, don't tell them. They won't understand."

They wouldn't understand? What? Like she did? None of this made any sense. He made fire come out of his skin. He zapped her from the parking lot to the tunnels in the blink of an eye. He kissed her and her body lit up like midnight on the strip in Vegas. That was so not her. *None* of this was.

"Ah." She gave him a look that should have made him wary of approaching her. "So I'm out of the magic closet and you get to stay neatly tucked away? Yeah, that's fair."

"All's fair in magic and war."

"That's *love* and war," she corrected.

"No such thing," he told her.

A flicker of disappointment flared inside her but was gone again in an instant. What did she care if this big, fiery guy didn't believe in love? Wasn't as if she was looking for a blind date, here. Even though that kiss had been amazing. She had way bigger things on her mind at the moment. "Fine. I won't say anything. But you've got *lots* of explaining to do."

"Agreed."

She turned back and hurried along the tunnel, hardly noticing that she wasn't as freaked by the underground passageway as she had been earlier. When you've suddenly become a witch and mentally ordered guns to fire themselves, a tunnel became no big deal. Up ahead, she heard hushed conversations, moaning and the soft, pitiful sound of weak sobs. Her steps hurried. Shauna. Shot. She had to try to help.

Walking into the candlelit chamber, she took it in at a glance. A wide room, there were a couple of chairs, several mattresses covered with blankets and a table with a camp light on top of it. No electricity in the underworld, she thought. Along one wall were stacked supplies. Bottles of water, canned food and a couple of coolers.

In a corner, huddled together for either comfort or warmth, the five freed witches stared out of haunted eyes.

None of them looked like they were ready for a trek to Virginia.

But it was the woman stretched out on one of the mattresses that had her attention.

Deidre crossed the room quickly, knelt down beside Shauna and reached for her. Instantly one of Finn's men lifted a weapon and trained it on her. "Back off, bitch. We don't need your help. I'll take care of Shauna."

Deidre hardly spared him a thought. She flicked her fingers at him and sent his gun scuttling out of the room into the tunnel. Amazing just how easily she was doing that now. She hadn't even had to think about it.

His eyes went wide.

"Forgot what I can do already, did you?" she asked, a tight smile on her face. "And yet you didn't mind my help a while ago. Oh. By the way, *don't* call me bitch."

Leaning over Shauna, Deidre let go of the sense of betrayal she had felt toward her friend. Hard to be mad at her when she was lying there bleeding.

Even in her pain the other woman managed a smile. "That is completely cool, Dee. I can barely light a candle with my magic."

Deidre forced a smile. "Lighting candles? Way more useful than gun throwing."

"Not tonight," Joe said from somewhere to her right.

She felt Finn come up behind her. Eerie. She didn't have to hear him. Or see him. She simply sensed his presence. What did that say? Heat from his body reached for hers and she was grateful for it. She felt as if she was frozen, like her blood must have ice crystals in it. Too much had happened too quickly. Being a witch. The cold night. The gunfire. The dog. Shauna being hurt. Being a witch. God, even thinking that twice didn't make it seem real.

All these years she'd had such empathy for the embattled witches—she had to wonder if her subconscious had somehow known what she was all along.

"The bullet's still in her shoulder, Finn." The man who'd called Deidre "bitch" spoke softly. "We've gotta get it out."

"Deidre will get it out, Mike."

"Me?" She turned her head around to look up at him. "She needs a *doctor*."

"No," Shauna muttered. "No doctors. Have to report bullet wounds. Might as well take me straight to jail, do not pass Go, do not collect two hundred dollars."

"Damn it, Shauna, this isn't a game." Deidre glared at her friend, then softened her tone because she'd already been shot. She didn't need to be yelled at. "You need a transfusion and antibiotics."

"We've got emergency medical equipment here," Joe said, walking up to stand alongside Finn. "We take care of our own."

"Just one big crazy family, how nice," Deidre snapped.

"You can get the bullet out, Deidre," Finn told her, going down on his haunches. He met her gaze and said, "Use your magic. Pull the metal from her shoulder. It will be less invasive than one of us using forceps to dig around in her flesh."

"Oh, God," Shauna moaned.

Deidre swallowed hard at that image and knew she'd have to try. She couldn't let Shauna suffer even more pain. Not if she could help it. "Fine. Just tell me what to do."

"You already know," Finn said. "Just do what you did outside. Direct your power with your mind."

"This is crazy," Mike muttered. "Just because she can throw guns doesn't mean she—"

Finn shot him a look that had the man shutting up fast. Deidre didn't blame him. Even with his features calm and blank, Finn was intimidating. A look of fury from him was bound to strike fear into the heart of anybody with a brain.

"Okay, just . . . back off," she said, looking at all of them in turn. "Shauna, I'm going to try to get the bullet out, okay?"

"Do it, Dee." She closed her eyes, and bit down hard on her bottom lip.

Hands sweaty, throat dry as dust, Deidre was half afraid she would have that meltdown she'd been joking about a few minutes ago. But like Finn had pointed out, there was no time for it now. She'd do that later. Indulge in a rant or a crying fit and then she'd demand some answers from the man kneeling right beside her.

Taking a deep breath, she laid her hands over Shauna's wound and felt the cold stickiness of congealing blood against her palms. She tried not to think about the fact that it was her friend's blood and instead concentrated on calling up that sparkling sense of power she had felt earlier.

She thought it would be hard.

It wasn't.

As soon as she reached for it, her magic was there. As if it had been hidden away in a locked chest for years and now was just eager to be used. To be needed. She smiled to herself as the shimmer of something wondrous spread from her heart, down her arms to her hands and then to her fingertips. Focusing on the shape and size of the bullet within her friend's body, Deidre *pulled* on it with her mind.

She felt it move. Felt it sliding from tissue and muscle

to edge past bone. While Shauna whimpered, Deidre concentrated, calling it forth, drawing on her magic, on the amazing thing she was doing until—

The bullet popped free and landed in Deidre's palm. It glittered in the candlelight, a shiny, blood-streaked brass piece of metal, smashed at the tip from its contact with Shauna's body. Astounding that something so small could do so much damage.

"Good job," Joe said and edged her out of the way. "I'll take over now."

He motioned to Mike to break open the medical supplies and then spared a smile for Shauna. "I'll have you stitched up in no time, cutie."

"Oh, God," Shauna moaned. "I've seen how you sew."

"Everybody's a critic . . ."

Still holding the bloody bullet in her palm, Deidre moved off, staring down at it as if she couldn't quite believe what she'd done. She wasn't even surprised to find Finn at her side.

"You did well."

"Yeah." She shook her head and closed her fist over the bullet. "It's been a great night."

"Deidre—"

"No more talk tonight," she said with a half laugh. "I don't think I can take much more. I just want to go home."

"No. I can't let you do that."

Chapter 8

Deidre stared at him, stunned speechless for about half a second. "You can't keep me here."

"Watch me."

"Oh, hell," Mike said under his breath, but just loud enough to be heard, "let her go."

"We have to talk." Finn grabbed her elbow and when Deidre tried to pull away, he simply tightened his grip. "Joe, we'll be in my chamber. No interruptions."

"Not even if Mike's bleeding from the eyes."

"Thanks," the other guy said.

"Dude," Joe told him with a slow shake of his head. "Learn when to shut your piehole."

Deidre wasn't really listening. Her mind was racing with the implications of what was happening. Not only was she a witch, but she was in an underground tunnel with a—whatever the hell he was. His "troops" weren't exactly on her side, either. There was no one to go to for help. And if the guards at the jail had recognized her, it wouldn't be safe to go home anyway. But she had to at least call her mother. Find out if those guards had said anything and if they had, she could try to explain.

Oh God, how would she explain this? And what could her mother do besides maybe find a place for Deidre to hide? Which, she told herself, she already had. Here in the bowels of the city with a man made of fire and his little band of terrorists.

Not to mention the escaped witches who weren't talking, just huddling together in a corner of the room.

She half ran to keep up with Finn's long strides and didn't complain because frankly, she didn't want to risk being enveloped by fire again. Down the tunnel, a right turn, a left, another right. Candles were lit here, too, but she sensed that she and Finn were all alone in this section. Great.

When he finally tugged her into another chamber and released his grip on her, she rubbed at her elbow and sent him a furious look. "Might have been easier to just club me over the head and drag me behind you."

"I considered it."

"No surprise there." Well, she thought, except for the room. It was bigger than the one they'd just left. Nicer, too. The ceiling was higher and there were crystals embedded in the rock walls. Finn waved his hand and torches hung from brass brackets around the room leaped into life, flames blazing, sending shards of light dancing from the hearts of the crystals.

Like prisms, they created slashes of color that moved around the room in rhythm with the dancing firelight. There was a huge bed in one corner, a table and chairs, and a screened-off alcove that led . . . she didn't know where. Not bad for camping out, she thought, though at that moment, she'd have given a lot for a hot shower.

"No shower, sorry," he said.

She whipped around and stared at him. "Didn't know I'd said that out loud."

"You didn't."

Horrified, she looked at him. "Oh God, *tell* me you can't read my mind."

"No, thank Belen," he muttered. "Just your expression. There's water in the far corner and towels. You can make do with those."

"Who's Belen and why can't I go home and take a shower?"

"Belen is my god, the lover of your goddess, Danu."

Danu? Witches, men of fire, now gods and goddesses. It was all too much. Deidre's head felt like it was about to explode and when it did, it wouldn't be pretty. "She's not *my* goddess. I've never heard of her."

"Yes, you have," he said with tired patience. "You've just forgotten."

Deidre nodded. "Right. Like I forgot you. And centuries of lifetimes."

"Exactly."

She lifted both hands and would have covered her ears, but stopped when she remembered the dried blood on her palms. Her friend's blood. She stared at the dried brown stains, took a breath and let it shudder from her lungs. Her stomach lurched and her vision blurred. "I have to wash up."

"Come on. Take a breath. No fainting."

"I don't faint."

"You look pale enough to keel over," he said as he led her across the room to the screened-off area. There was a wide basin cut out of a stone ledge. Several towels were folded neatly and stacked beside the basin. Above it, a pipe hung from the rock ceiling. The pipe was capped and pushed high and out of the way. As she watched, Finn pulled the pipe down, aimed it at the basin, removed the cap and fresh water poured out. When the makeshift sink was full, he recapped the pipe and pushed it higher again.

"I tapped into the city's water supply for the washroom." He nodded his head, indicating another cutaway in the stone. Deidre peeked around the edge and found what was probably a close relation to medieval garderobes.

"Really?" she asked nodding at it.

He smiled. "You'd prefer a bucket?"

"No, I'd prefer a room at the Ritz."

He shrugged. "Not happening. Here. Let me help you."

She pulled away from him and knew she sounded sulky when she snapped, "I don't need help. I'm not a child."

He took her hands in his as if he hadn't heard her. In spite of her declaration that she didn't need his help, Deidre was grateful for it. The night was suddenly catching up to her. She was shaking and a little weak in the knees. And remembering Shauna, lying on the ground, shot, made Deidre feel as if the world was tilting. Her stomach was iffy and her brain was full of all sorts of crazy information that she couldn't make sense of.

Finn pushed the sleeves of her shirt back, and dipped her hands into the icy water. Then he grabbed a bar of soap, worked up a lather and smoothed his fingers over hers, slowly, carefully. He rubbed her hands, her fingers, massaged her palms until she felt the tension inside her begin to unravel and a new kind of stress take its place.

She didn't *want* to feel anything for Finn. But it was as if her body and mind had two very different ideas.

His long, tanned fingers moved over hers. Soap bubbles popped and slid along her skin. She stared down at their joined hands—the hard bronze against the soft white—and felt something stir inside her. Something old. Something . . . *familiar*. They had done this before. She had marveled at the slide of his skin against hers before. She *knew* it, felt it, but couldn't understand how it was possible.

As if his touch, his nearness, had opened a door in her memories, she saw . . . pictures. They had washed each other many, many times. Flashes of images scatter shot through her mind. She and Finn, sitting in a tub together, laughing, unabashedly naked. She saw Finn's eyes as she moved over him in the water and slowly impaled herself on his hard, thick erection. She watched his eyes glaze over in passion and remembered a matching desire. She could almost feel the water slapping at her breasts. Almost feel the long length of him pushing into her body and how her own muscles clamped down on him, holding him deep.

She was breathing hard, heartbeat thundering in her chest. It was all so real. Too real. She swayed as the images dissolved. All she felt was *him*. Standing beside her.

Touching her.

Her heartbeat quickened even faster, jumping into an excited rhythm despite everything that had gone on that night. She tried to get a grip on her emotions, but all she really wanted to get a grip on was him. As she had in that blurred, hazy half memory. Finn the lover. Finn the mysterious. Finn the man of fire.

Finn the possibly crazed terrorist.

There was a jolt back to reality.

"Thanks," she said softly, reluctantly pulling her hands away from his. "I've got it now."

He took a step back as if he sensed her emotional withdrawal. "Fine then. When you're finished we'll talk."

She took her time, in no hurry to be alone with him again. If she was so tired that she was imagining sexy bathtub play with the guy who had nearly gotten her killed, then her judgment really couldn't be trusted at the moment. Still, even knowing all of that, she missed his stalwart presence when he moved off into the main room.

Laying both hands on the rim of the basin, she leaned forward and took a long, deep breath as she stared blankly down at the soap bubbles riding the surface of the water. Her life had taken such a wild turn she hardly knew what to think. And until she got more information, she wasn't going to even try to make sense of it all.

Chapter 9

"What do you mean she isn't there?" Cora Sterling, president of the United States, fixed a hard gaze on her new aide. God, she missed Parker. But her former aide and lover had met with an accident the month before. Stepping into the street, he had been run down by a speeding car and died only a day later.

A damn shame was what it was, Cora thought. Still there was something to be said for young, energetic blood. Even in her fury, she had to admit that her new aide, Darius, had stylishly cut blond hair, cool eyes and plenty of stamina. He also had the sense to keep his distance when delivering bad news.

It was just past dawn, an appalling time of day, in Cora's opinion. And starting off her morning with news of her daughter's disappearance wasn't making things easier. She had been awakened only a half hour ago. But now, she was dressed and sitting behind her desk, claiming her power as she faced whatever came next.

Darius clasped his hands in front of him and stood in the at-ease position. "After the WLF raid on the jailhouse last night, Deidre's Secret Service protection thought it would be a good idea to check on her. Agent Dante reported that they went to her friend's door, knocked and there was no answer. They let themselves in to find both women gone."

Cora frowned at the mention of the latest raid. The guards had been prepared for a possible rescue attempt and still they'd failed. Now the five witches were God knew where, two people were dead and several guards injured. She would have the press to deal with later and now she had to worry about Deidre, apparently missing.

"Just gone?"

"No sign of struggle; it was as if they simply left," Darius told her. "But the Secret Service had the front and back covered, so they couldn't have gotten past them unseen."

"Well, they didn't simply vanish," Cora snapped, then caught herself and took a deep, cleansing breath. She reached for her cup of coffee and took a long swallow, hoping the caffeine would jolt as well as soothe her system.

"They might as well have," he said now and she frowned in response. "There's no sign of either woman."

Darius was more than her aide. He was her newest lover and didn't know yet when to speak and when to keep quiet. He had better learn fast.

"Mind your tone with me, Darius." Her voice was soft, and carried enough ice in it that the temperature of the room dropped ten degrees. Darius noticed.

"I only meant—" He tried to backpedal.

She waved her hand in a dismissive gesture. "No explanations. No apologies. Do it right the first time. Are we understood?"

"Yes, ma'am."

"Good." She set down her coffee cup and muttered, "We have to find Deidre." Her nerves were jangling and a touch of panic oozed into her voice. "I don't care what it takes, Darius. We have to find my daughter. She could be in danger. What if the WLF captured her before their raid to use her as a bargaining chip?"

"The WLF? No one saw her with them. Though, from the witness reports, there was a witch among them."

"A witch?" Cora's gaze locked on him. "Why don't I have a copy of that report?"

"A copy is being made for you now, ma'am."

"What do we know about this witch?"

He frowned. "She is apparently fairly powerful. Snatched guns away from the guards and held them there while her friends got the prisoners out."

Cora's mind spun. A witch on a raiding party. A powerful witch.

"But ma'am, there's simply no evidence that Deidre was anywhere near the WLF last night and—"

"There's no evidence at all," she reminded him. "You just told me that. For all we know, Deidre's being held captive somewhere, waiting for *me* to find her."

"Madam President," he said softly. "We will find her. We've got men combing the grounds for clues. If there's anything there they'll find it."

They had better, Cora thought, hating the sense of helplessness that had her in its grip. She preferred *doing* to delegating. If she had her way she'd be on the streets herself right now finding Deidre. It was imperative that she be kept protected.

"See that they do. I want people on this around the clock until my daughter is found. Am I clear?" She tapped one finger against her desktop. The *Resolute* desk, commissioned by Queen Victoria and given as a gift to President Hayes, had been a favorite with Kennedy, Bush, Obama and Tucker. Now it was hers. Sitting behind this massive representation of the power of the presidency, Cora felt its strength imbue her. As the president, she had lines to tug on, and any number of favors to call in.

And she would use every tool at her disposal to find her daughter.

"Absolutely clear, ma'am."

"Get everyone on this," she said coolly, fighting to regain her composure. "Keep it from the media as long as you can. They're already frothing at the mouth because they've been denied the exclusive execution footage. We don't need to give them something else to chew on. Besides, if the world knows Deidre is missing, it could send radicals out looking for her. And, we have to consider something else. She may have been kidnapped. If she was, we can't afford to send those responsible into a panic."

"Yes, ma'am." He turned to go.

"And Darius?" She waited for him to look at her. "I want you taking center stage on this search. You find Deidre."

He nodded, then straightened his shoulders and met her gaze squarely. "I will. Count on it."

When he left, Cora stood up from behind the *Resolute* and walked to the wide windows. The sky was a palette of soft colors, gold and rose and violet. The world was barely awake and already there were crowds gathering outside the high fence surrounding the White House.

There were hastily scrawled placards being waved by the crowd. Some called for Death to Witches. Others proclaimed Freedom for All. She had two sides warring within her own people. And she wasn't the only leader in the world faced with these problems.

Witches. It all came down to the witches.

Some wanted them dead. Some wanted their powers and some wanted them treated just like any other citizen. The difficulty there was, they *weren't* like regular citizens. They had powers. Abilities. And as proven only last night by the WLF raid, witches were no longer afraid to use their power.

A protester threw something toward the White House and one of the armed guards shot it down. She flinched at the too-loud report of the rifle as red liquid exploded into the morning sky. Paint, she thought idly as her guards rushed the crowd to throw the man onto the street. Probably supposed to represent the blood of the innocents.

Just another day on the razor's edge of a new reality, she thought with a tired sigh. Turning from the window, she sat down to prepare her notes. She'd have to call a press conference to address the witch issue and wanted to make sure that several points were included in the speech already, no doubt, being written.

The witches' rescue was going to keep the media busy for the next few days, which was a good thing. If Deidre *was* missing, then they might be able to find her before the newspapers got wind of it.

The execution, if it had gone on without a hitch, wouldn't have taken more than one cycle on the twenty-four-hour news channels. But escaped witches would keep the newshounds busy for days. Of course, that wasn't the only reason Cora wasn't sorry the witches had been rescued. She didn't need another execution. Not when she was trying to bring a little common sense to the mob mentality ruling the world at the moment. The usually extremely liberal left was mostly quiet these days, except for a few strident voices wanting to protect *all* citizens' liberties. They were a small minority, though. Most Americans agreed with the rest of the world. They wanted suspected witches locked up and proven witches executed.

Odd, but for the first time in memory, the national media had left their liberal leanings in the dust. The majority of editorials were downright bloodthirsty, demanding more regularly scheduled executions in the name of "public safety."

"What they want," she muttered, "is a witch-death assembly line. Bonfires burning day and night, no waiting."

And in nearly every damn article the now most well-known line from the Bible was quoted: *Thou shalt not suffer a witch to live.*

Funny, not so long ago, those same newspapers hardly mentioned God. Now, they were all using Him as the weapon to kill witches.

People never ceased to amaze her.

Truth to tell though, Cora didn't give a good damn about the witch situation at the moment. All she could think about was her daughter.

She *had* to find her.

Chapter 10

Deidre walked back into the main chamber, and paused long enough to admire the torchlight pulsing through the crystals embedded in the walls. But soon enough, her gaze shifted to Finn—and locked there.

Her breath caught. He stood with his head down, his back to her. His shirt was off, displaying what looked like an acre of bronzed muscular skin. He wore a pair of daggers in a leather holster loosely hung from his hips. His legs looked impossibly long and as thick as tree trunks. But the sculpted muscles of his back were what caught and held her attention.

She felt a quick jolt of pure female admiration until she noticed the dark spots on his back. As she watched, something small and metallic fell from his body and clattered on the stone floor. It wasn't until just that moment that she remembered the battle and how she had heard bullets impacting his body.

"You were shot."

He glanced over his shoulder at her. "Yeah. Hurts like a bitch, too."

"Oh my God. Why didn't you say something?" She

hurried closer. "I can take the bullets out, like I did for Shauna."

Wow. She got used to that really fast, hadn't she? The strangeness of Deidre's night just kept compounding.

"No need." Another bullet popped free of his back and dropped to the floor. "Bastards weren't using white gold bullets, so I can take care of it myself."

"White gold." She repeated the words as she watched, transfixed, as he forced another bullet from his body. It was raining brass, she thought idly, examining his back and noting that the holes in his flesh had already sealed over, as if he'd never been wounded at all.

"They usually use white gold when they're expecting the magical kind of trouble," Finn told her, turning around and stretching as if just waking up from a nap.

Distraction alert, Deidre thought, watching the play of muscles across his broad chest and the sculpted beauty of his abs. The man could make a fortune as an underwear model.

"But, since they figured the WLF is all human, they didn't bother with the more expensive ammo." One shoulder lifted in a shrug. "Good for me. And Shauna."

"Right." She nodded and tried to get her mind back on matters at hand. Wasn't easy when looking at a half-naked Finn. "White gold debilitates a witch's power."

It was common knowledge, after all. Heck, the number-one-selling book on Amazon these days was *How to Kill a Witch*. Even a child knew that silver enhanced a witch's power and white gold drained it. People carried white gold antiwitch charms and the bottom had dropped out of the silver market years ago.

"White gold doesn't completely drain magic away, but it does dampen it. Makes it harder to reach your magic when you need to most." Finn pushed one hand across his short black hair and shrugged again. "That's why all those women we pulled out of the jailhouse last night were wearing white gold chains."

"Last night?" she repeated. She'd lost all sense of time and who wouldn't, being underground?

"It's early morning," he said. "Not dawn yet, but close."

Hours had passed and it felt like minutes. Yet at the same time, the night had seemed unending. Didn't make any sense at all, she knew. But then what had since leaving Shauna's apartment? She had walked into a brand-new world and there was no way out. Dealing with that was going to take some time.

Finn turned to pick up a leather holster of sorts with a long, curved scabbard attached. She took a deep breath and tried to steady nerves that felt like they were jangling all throughout her system. While she watched, he slipped his arms through the leather straps and tied them closed at the center of his chest.

"What's—"

He glanced at her, and picked up a wicked-looking sword with a curved blade that winked in the light.

"A sword?"

Staring at the blade, Finn smiled and then whipped the sword through the air a few times, in a deadly, elegant move that made the blade hum as it passed through the air. He shifted a look at her. "Been carrying it since 1357. Made for me by the best sword maker in the Ottoman Empire."

Deidre took that in, shook her head in stunned disbelief and watched as he slid the blade down his back into the scabbard. The handle of the blade rested just below the base of his neck. *The Ottoman Empire*, she thought wildly. 1357. Just how old *was* he?

Questions for later, she told herself, setting it aside. There was already too much going on in her brain. She really didn't need more.

When he turned to look at her again she went back to what they had been talking about. "The MPs and Bureau of Witchcraft will be looking for us now, won't they?"

"No doubt the hunt's already begun."

"The hunt," she repeated, realizing that now *she* was one of the hunted. No more standing on the sidelines trying to do her best for witches. Now she was one of them. Deidre took a breath and held it. How was any of this possible? How could she have *magic*?

"They'll scour the parking lot, look for clues, then try to track us. They'll fail."

She was almost sorry when he tugged the shirt on over his head and covered up that amazing body. He was a hell of a distraction. But it was better this way, she reminded herself, since she needed answers, not sex. Though sex . . . Never mind. "You sound so sure."

"This is not, as they say, my first barbecue."

Deidre stared at him, then laughed. "You don't talk like an immortal whatever."

"Yeah, well. Some of us hung on to the old ways," he said, stepping past her to grab two bottles of water off a nearby table. He tossed one to her. "A couple of my brothers avoided humans as much as possible, so they still talk as if it's the fifteenth century. Most of us don't."

"How many of you are there?"

He uncapped the water and took a long drink. "Interesting question. A few days ago, I would have said there was one Eternal for every member of your coven."

Her coven. She shivered as a wisp of memory floated through her mind. She couldn't catch it. Couldn't quite see it, but it was there. The word *coven* had triggered something inside her. Too bad she didn't know what the hell it was.

"And now?"

His gaze locked on hers. "Now we know that there are other immortals out there. Working against us. Against *you*."

She took a fast swallow of water and almost choked, since her throat was nearly closed by a knot of fear. "There are immortals after me as well as the MPs and BOW? Aren't I popular."

"Belle of the ball." He nodded. "And don't forget the Seekers and just your random psycho citizen, either."

"Oh, God." She had forgotten about the Seekers. They were a small but growing group whose mission was to capture known witches and find a way to leech off their magical powers. The head of that group, the notorious Dr. Fender, was a torture master. The few women Deidre had seen who had survived their time on Dr. Fender's table had wished they hadn't.

"This just gets worse and worse," she murmured.

"Yeah. And we're just getting started."

"Way to cheer me up," she snapped.

"I'm not here to pretend everything's shiny and rosy," he told her flatly. "I'm here to keep you alive. To help you reclaim your share of the Artifact."

"*What* Artifact?" Another drink of water and Lord how she wished it was vodka.

"Long story."

"Then don't tell me. I just want to go home."

"Already told you that you can't."

"Why *not*?" Fine. Stupid question and she knew it. She'd never be able to go home again. Because her life as she knew it was gone forever. Even if those guards hadn't recognized her, the members of Finn's happy little team here all knew who she was and weren't exactly big fans. Even knowing she was a witch didn't take away the inherent threat of her mother being the president.

And because she knew it wasn't possible, all she wanted in the world was to be curled up on her couch with a cup of hot tea and the stereo blasting out a little Led Zeppelin. She liked the new stuff fine, but when you wanted to relax, the key was classic rock.

Finn scowled at her and Deidre realized that in the few hours she'd known him, *this* was his most common expression.

"You're kidding, right? You just took center stage on a damn raid, Deidre."

She argued, because she didn't want to admit, even to herself, that he was right. "No one knows it was me."

"We don't know that." Shaking his head in pure frustration, he continued before she could argue. "Besides, even if they don't know about you, there are other things to worry about, remember? I just laid 'em all out for you—and that was just the tip of it, babe. Witches, in case you hadn't noticed, have become an endangered species."

They had. And she was one of them now. She capped her water bottle, then held on to it as if it were a lifeline tossed to her in a stormy sea. "I can't just hide. I have a life. People will be looking for me. Did you forget my mother is the president?"

"Hardly."

"Well, then, think about this," she said, words tumbling over each other in her rush to make her point. "There are

Secret Service men standing outside Shauna's apartment. When I don't come out this morning, they're going to go in and look for me. If I'm not there . . ."

"Can't be helped," he said, swirling gray eyes locked on her.

"Damn it, Finn, I can't just stay here."

Yes, she was scared. And overwhelmed and more than a little panicky. But she needed to get away from *here*. She needed something normal. Even if it was a lie, she needed to feel like nothing had changed. At least for a little while. Until she'd had time to think. To plan. To figure out how she was going to deal with her new reality.

"You will stay. As for your guards, they mean nothing."

"They mean something to *me*. And to my mother." She stopped and groaned. "God, what will I tell my mother?"

"Not a damn thing," Finn growled. "She's the president."

"Exactly," Deidre argued. "Who better to have on my side?"

He looked at her with what could have passed for sympathy on someone else. But Finn didn't strike Deidre as the feel-sorry-for-you type. A minute later, he proved her right by saying, "You don't know that she would be on your side. She's got a lot of people to answer to and if word gets out that you're a witch . . ."

He let his words trail off and Deidre was glad for it. Her mind was already wrestling with possibilities. Her mother hadn't been able to put a stop to witch executions. As president, she could suggest and advise, but the Congress and the Senate held the real power and they had already proved that they were all for what they called "cleansing." Plus, even if she had wanted to use a presidential pardon, she would turn the whole country on its ear. There would be even more violence than there was now, with riots and protests from the majority of the people who *wanted* the witches kept locked away or killed.

Finn was right. Her mother may not be able to protect her. And, if Deidre drew attention as a witch, what would happen to her mother? They might suspect *her* of witchcraft too. At the very least, she might be impeached. At the worst, imprisoned. Or tortured.

God, this was a nightmare. She couldn't go to her mother and couldn't not go.

"Deidre, you're not leaving." He held up one hand before she could argue.

"I can't stay locked down here forever." God, just the thought of being trapped belowground, looking up and seeing stone instead of sky, made her cringe. Glancing at the bottle of water in her hands, she watched the liquid slosh back and forth, trapped in its plastic cage. Suddenly, she knew what that felt like. "I'd rather take my chances topside."

"You don't get it. Without me, you've got no chance at survival." Finn tossed his water bottle down, stalked across the room and grabbed her shoulders. Jerking her in close to him, he stared down at her, his pale gray eyes nearly glowing.

"Let me go."

"Not gonna happen." His voice was low, tight. "I told you about the other immortals. We only just discovered their existence. They're the 'Forgotten' Eternals. They've got magical abilities and a serious rage on because they were ignored by our god, Belen. Now we think they're after you and the other members of the coven—"

"I'm not a member of a coven," she argued, though that word rippled inside her again.

"—the coven you once belonged to. These Forgotten want to take the witches and the Artifact and claim all the power for themselves." He looked at her, pale gray eyes swirling with secrets and powers she could barely understand. "We won't let that happen. So you're not going anywhere. Deal with it."

"Who the hell do you think you are to tell me what I can do and where I can go?" She pulled free of his grasp, and stumbled back a step or two.

"I told you before. I'm your Eternal."

This time, when he said it, it set off something inside her that felt oddly like champagne bubbles racing through her veins. Insane. All of it. Why would she feel *anything* for the guy who had had her *kidnapped*, for God's sake?

"Start dealing with this, Deidre. We don't have time to baby you."

"Baby me? You son of a bitch, I've been kidnapped, forced out on a raid, seen my friend *shot* and, oh yeah, found out I'm a *witch*. I think I'm doing pretty well on the dealing-with-it front."

He stepped in close, taking her upper arms in a hard grip. Heat poured from his body into hers in a steady, dizzying stream that made her feel as if her blood was about to boil. She felt something more too. A connection to him. As if tendrils of something mystical linked them together, tightening with every moment, every breath. She fought against that sensation. Deidre didn't want any of this. Didn't want anything from him.

Especially when she didn't see the slightest spark of warmth in his eyes.

"You're a witch of immeasurable power," Finn said, his voice a low roll of thunder that resonated inside her. "You have genetic memories stored in your mind. Once you find the key to open them, we'll have the information we need to do what we must."

"Which is *what* exactly?"

One corner of his mouth lifted into a mocking smile as he released her. "Save the world."

Chapter 11

"**D**o you know what Mare Superum means?"

Spell completed, the Eternals had returned to join their Mates. Now, Torin stared down at Shea. His witch wore the traditional one-shouldered white robe, her left breast uncovered, so that her Mating tattoo was bared to the room. Ordinarily, seeing the line of individual flames that began at her nipple, coiled around her breast to spread beneath her arm and up over her shoulder, was enough to make him hard as rock.

But her words stopped that thought dead in its tracks. "Mare Superum. Is that what Egan said?"

"Yes," Mairi answered him, stepping into the circle of her Mate Damyn's arms. Her left breast was stained with roses and Damyn carried a matching brand. As all Eternals did with their destined Mates. "It was awful. He's . . ."

"Crazed," Teresa finished for her. "Seriously crazed and half insane." She took Rune's hand as he helped her up from the floor. Then she stood, her back to his front, the lightning bolts of her tattoo clearly defined against her dusky skin. "Can't blame him, but he's not looking good, you guys."

"But he's alive," Torin insisted.

"Yes," Shea said, lifting one hand to lay it atop the matching branding tattoo on his chest. Beneath her palm, his heartbeat thundered. Another gift from his Mate. A heartbeat to measure out their eternity together. "He's alive, Torin, but—"

"If he's alive," Damyn said tightly, "that's all that matters. You're sure he said Mare Superum?"

"Definitely," Mairi told him. "Do you know where that is?"

"Yeah." Rune pulled Teresa in tight to him and wrapped one arm around her. "Egan always did prefer the ancient names for things. Claimed he couldn't get used to the way humans were always changing things up. Truth is, he was just stubborn."

"So where is he?" Shea asked the question.

Torin met the gazes of his fellow Eternals before looking back down at the woman who had claimed his heart and saved his soul. "Mare Superum is the Latin name for the Adriatic Sea. He must be there. Somewhere off the coast of Italy."

Shea wrapped her arms around Torin's waist and laid her head on his chest. "I was hoping for something a little less vague. That's a big sea, Torin. It won't be easy to find him."

"You guys narrowed it down for us," Rune pointed out, dropping a kiss on Teresa's forehead. "Without you three, we'd have had to search every ocean, lake and pond on the planet. One little sea? No problem."

Teresa slapped his flat abdomen. "Such a show-off."

"That's why you love me, baby."

"Teresa was right," Mairi said. "Egan was ... almost rabid. I *felt* his rage. All consuming. Terrifying. Madness is claiming him and I don't know that he will ever re-cover."

"Mairi . . ." Damyn's voice was a hush.

But his Mate shook her head and said aloud what they were all considering. "If Egan's mind is lost, the Awakening is over. If his Mate truly is the one who trapped him at the bottom of the sea, he won't be willing to complete the Mating with her. He's more likely to kill her on sight."

"We worry about the rest *after* we find him," Torin said quietly. Damyn and Rune both nodded solemnly. One of their own, one of their *brothers* was alive and in constant agony. No matter what else happened, they would free him.

"But if the Awakening isn't completed," Shea whispered, "we all lose and demons will overrun the earth."

"It won't happen," Rune said decisively, unconsciously shifting into a battle stance.

"Bring Egan here," Mairi said, leaning into her Mate. "Haven's strength will heal him. We'll all help."

Damyn smiled down at her, smoothing her red hair back from her face with a tender touch. "You are the heart of me, woman."

"Give us another day," Mairi said with a smile for Damyn. "We'll do another spell, try to narrow down the search a bit more."

Damyn nodded. "All right then, it's settled. We've got a starting point. Next we find Egan and bring him home."

Deidre staggered a little. "You're serious."

"Deadly."

Either he was completely batshit crazy or she was in serious trouble. Fighting down the wave of panic that rushed up from the pit of her stomach to clog her throat, she shook her head. "No. No way. I barely managed to help save a few witches. And you expected me to save the *world*?"

Looking down at the water bottle in her hands, Deidre thought about trying to focus this new power inside her and seeing whether she could actually turn the clear liquid into the vodka she really needed at the moment.

"Yes." He paced slowly around the circumference of the room and her gaze followed his every move.

"I've spent a lot of time in these tunnels over the last decade or so," he mused, shifting his gaze to encompass the ceiling and walls. "Once your mother brought you here to DC, I knew this was where you would Awaken. Knew we'd need a place."

She nodded as if she understood, but she so didn't. He'd spent a decade here? Waiting for her? Watching over her? God, could this get any more convoluted? She didn't know whether to be flattered, appreciative or pissed. He'd watched over her. In secret. Protecting her or waiting for his chance at her? Should she be *grateful*? No, Deidre didn't think she could go that far.

He waved one hand. "Brought in crystals for the walls."

"They're pretty," she said, barely giving them a glance.

"They're magical," he corrected, throwing a quick look at her. "While you're in this room, the crystals will strengthen your power. Help grow your magic."

She nodded, agreeing without comprehending. The situation was too strange and she still needed to find a way to get her bearings. But she could admit to feeling a buzz of sensation on her skin. She had since the moment she'd stepped into this chamber. At least now, she knew what it was.

"I built this place for you, Deidre."

"Thank you?" What the hell was she supposed to say to that? He'd been waiting for her for centuries? She was a witch? Destined to save the world? None of this made sense. None of it could be real.

Over the years, she'd listened to the stories of rescued witches. She'd heard time and again how the eruption of their power had totally surprised them. How they'd had no idea of who they were prior to that. And always, there had been a tiny kernel of doubt in Deidre's mind and heart.

She hadn't been able to understand how any woman could be caught off guard by something that was so inherently a part of them. How they could have been clueless about their true nature.

Man, she really owed those women a huge apology.

Her heartbeat was thundering in her ears. Down the tunnel somewhere her friend was bleeding and escaped witches were huddled together trying not to get too hopeful about a shot at freedom.

And Deidre Sterling was supposed to save the world? It was laughable.

So why did she want to scream?

As if she'd conjured the sound with her thoughts, an ear-piercing scream shattered the stillness. Deidre jolted and spun around to face the empty doorway. The scream seemed to echo over and over along the darkness of the snaking tunnels before being cut off, abruptly.

"Damn it!" A shout followed that all too brief scream.

Before Deidre could take a step, Finn shouted, "Stay here!" and bolted from the cave into the tunnels.

Sure, that was going to happen. No way was she staying in this crystal-studded magical cave by herself. Not that she trusted Finn or anything, but just the thought of being alone in the twisting labyrinth of these tunnels was enough to have her running after the man. Fear crawled up her throat and knotted there, but fear was almost becoming familiar now. Not a friend, but certainly not a stranger.

She heard him, far ahead of her, his heavy footsteps pounding against the dirt and rock. Deidre slapped her right hand onto the damp tunnel wall to guide her as she ran down the darkened passage. Her eyes struggled to adjust to the darkness, but all she could make out were lighter and darker patches of black. Right about now, she missed those dancing flashlight beams from earlier.

Deep, vicious growls rolled through the tunnels, echoing off the stone walls and even muffled as the sound was, the hairs at the back of her neck stood straight up. Her running steps faltered. Then two gunshots came so closely together it was one huge explosive noise.

Finn's pace sped up, his long legs making it impossible for her to catch up with him. The most she could hope for was to follow the sound of his passage, though that was bringing her closer to the growls and—another scream.

Ahead, a spill of pale light poured from the main chamber and she ran toward it like a soul aimed at the gates of heaven. She skidded at the entrance, the bottoms of her shoes sliding across the rough floor.

Deidre grabbed hold of both sides of the arched entrance and stared. Lanterns were lit and the small band of guerillas was spread around the room.

Joe was partially blocking the entrance, his arms stretched in front of him as he took aim at something Deidre couldn't see. Finn stood in the center of the chamber, legs braced, booted feet spread wide in a fighting stance. In the space of a single heartbeat, Deidre's gaze swept what she could see of the rest of the room.

Shauna, lying still on the floor, the cluster of rescued women a few feet away, hugging each other and squeezing themselves into as small a target as possible, but for one woman with defiant eyes, glaring at the far corner. Two of Finn's group, hiding their fear as they too aimed guns at the far corner. And, the man named Mike lay dead on the floor, blood welling from his torn-out throat.

Her stomach churned. She swallowed hard and fought to remain standing.

"Stay back," Finn ordered and she knew he was talking to her though he didn't so much as glance her way. His complete focus was on the source of the low growls emanating from the corner just out of her line of sight.

Deliberately, Deidre stepped farther into the room, moving past Joe so that she could see what stood in the darkened corner herself. A dog. Black, muscled. Huge, square head, burning red eyes. Lips peeled back from glistening white teeth that looked gigantic and very sharp, blood on its muzzle, dripping onto the floor with soft plops that sounded like gongs in the stillness.

Chapter 12

Deidre swayed in place. It was the dog she'd seen outside Shauna's apartment what felt like days ago. How had it found her?

"What the hell is that?" Joe muttered, his gaze and aim never wavering from the animal.

So she wasn't the only one in the dark here. Somehow that made her feel both better and worse.

A low growl rumbled up from deep in the beast's chest and rolled through the room like a sudden storm. The beast's eyes swept over all of them and in those burning red depths, a promise of pain glittered.

"Hellhound," Finn snapped. "Vicious. Strong. Under demon command."

"*Hellhound?*" Deidre's voice cracked on the words. The dog was even bigger than it had looked at a distance. Its head would reach her waist if she was stupid enough to get closer. Which she wasn't.

At the sound of her voice, the hound's head turned and those blistering red eyes locked on her as if she were the only one in the room. Its hackles lifted and the menacing growl took on a fevered pitch, becoming one long, continuous threat. She couldn't look away from those eyes. It was like staring into the yawning mouth of Hell itself. Waves of evil rolled off the huge dog, chilling the air in the enclosed space.

Something inside Deidre quickened and flickered to life. Ancient memories spilled through her mind in a rush of color, scent and sound. She didn't recognize any of them, but she *knew* them.

And they told her that this wasn't the first time she had faced a hellhound. As crazy as it sounded, even to her, Deidre's body knew exactly what to do. Instinct had her drawing on a well of power inside her, stretching out one arm toward the black dog and fisting her hand. The animal recoiled briefly, a growl cutting off as its throat squeezed closed under the magical assault. It shook its huge head as if dismissing her effort to stop it.

The dog shifted suddenly, lifting a saucer-sized paw edged with daggerlike claws before setting it down again. Finn stepped in front of Deidre. Fear and power rose up inside her, tangling together, creating a mess she couldn't make sense of. Whatever she had accessed before was gone now. Her instincts had dissolved as quickly as they'd arisen. What good was it to be a witch if she couldn't even save herself?

Forced to look around Finn's broad back to see what was happening, she saw the hellhound turn its burning gaze on Finn. The growl that was both challenge and threat deepened, became a thrum of sound that echoed off the walls and inside Deidre's mind.

"How the hell do we kill it?" Joe muttered.

"Silver." Moving in a blur of speed, Finn whipped a dagger from the holster he wore and threw it. It happened so fast, Deidre couldn't track it. The hellhound

howled in pain and fell back a step. Blood erupted from
the wound and even from across the room, Deidre saw
the dog's flesh begin to burn and char around the edges
of the blade. Dagger still embedded in its chest, the beast
gave another wild howl, then launched itself through the
air.

"Look out—" Finn pulled Deidre down, but she still
saw it all.

The massive hound sailed across the room, then
passed through the tunnel wall as if it weren't there. The
stunned silence it left behind was almost as terrifying as
the attack itself had been.

"What the *fuck*?"

Finn ignored the question whispered by one of the
others. He threw a hard look at Joe and said, "Gather
everyone. We're out of here. Now."

Frowning, Joe argued, "Shauna's shot and the others
aren't in any shape for a trek across the city. Besides that,
we're not supposed to deliver them until tomorrow
morning."

"We can't wait here. We'll go farther along the tunnels
and hole up closer to our target." Finn turned to look at
the huddled group of survivors and Deidre wondered
what was going through his mind. A second later, she
knew.

"Can you move?" he demanded.

One defiant woman looked at the others, then back to
Finn. "If it means staying alive? Yeah. We can make it."

Finn nodded and turned to Shauna. "You good to go?"

Deidre looked at her friend. Her caramel-colored
skin looked pale. Her brown eyes glittered with pain,
shock and fear. But she pushed herself up onto her elbows with only a wince to let them know how much the

movement cost her. "You think I'm going to stay here and wait for the puppy from Hell to come back? No, thanks. I'll make it."

"Good girl," Finn said, giving her an approving nod.

Leaving this place was okay by her, but Deidre glanced up at the rock wall where the hound had disappeared. "If it can pass right through walls . . . leaving's not going to do us much good."

"If we're moving, we're harder to track," Finn snapped. Then he looked at Joe. "Get ready. We move out in five."

"What about Mike?" Joe asked quietly.

Finn glanced at the fallen man, not a trace of regret or pity on his hard features. "Nothing we can do for him now."

"He's *dead*," Deidre said. She didn't look at the body again, but only minutes ago, he had been a part of Finn's fighting force. Now he was just so much trash?

"Yeah, he is, and long past our help. And if we don't move," he told her, "he won't be the only one dead."

Deidre looked away from the cold emptiness in his harsh gray eyes. One minute he was fierce and passionate and the next it was as if he'd turned to ice. His features gave nothing away and were as glacial as the frost in his eyes.

Joe spoke up softly to reassure her. "When the rest of our group shows up here in a day or two, they'll take care of Mike's body."

"The rest of you?"

Finn grunted. "Five of our guys were on another raid in Maryland—they had to skip tonight's festivities."

"How many of you are there?" she asked.

He ignored that and told Joe, "Gather up as much of the supplies as you can."

"On it."

"What if the others show up and there's a hellhound waiting for them?" Deidre demanded.

"No way to get hold of them now anyway," Joe said. "No phone reception in the tunnels."

"So they could just walk into a trap."

"They'll be prepared." Finn glanced around the chamber. "If that hellhound is coming back, it'll be tonight and when it finds us gone, there won't be a reason for it to return."

"But—"

"Enough talking," Finn muttered and turned to Joe. "The extra clothes I got for the women are in the far chamber."

Joe nodded at one of the other men and he quickly moved off on the task.

"Make sure you've got the silver too." Finn's gaze swept the room, as if he were half expecting to see the hound come crashing back in. "Especially now, we want to be ready."

"We will be."

Nodding, Finn said, "Five minutes."

Then he came toward her and grabbed her arm, tugging her toward the doorway. Deidre's heart was still galloping wildly in her chest and having Finn's hand on her didn't help the situation any. She threw a look over her shoulder at the spot where the hellhound had disappeared and wondered where it went. Would it need time to heal? Was it already crouched farther along the tunnel, waiting for another chance at them?

The others got busy, packing up supplies, stuffing backpacks with PowerBars, water and weapons. Shock was still running pretty hot. Not every day you got an up-close look at a hellhound. Even Shauna was on her feet, if a little wobbly. The freed prisoners stirred, with one of them seeming to take charge. Deidre finally swung her gaze back to Finn. She looked up at his profile as they left the light for the darkness.

His features were shadowed in the dim light and could have been carved out of bone with a hatchet. He looked hard and mean—and probably, she told herself honestly, was exactly what she needed right now to protect her.

Who the hell else did she know who could drive off a hellhound?

"Hurry up," he told her as he pulled her along in his wake. Once again, she found herself running through the blackness at his side.

"Up the tunnel, down the tunnel . . ." she muttered, hurrying to keep up with him.

"Just listen." His voice was low and rough and just barely carried over the sound of their footsteps. "That hellhound shouldn't have been able to pass through stone."

"Well, yeah, it's not something you see every day," she agreed, and winced when she stubbed her toe and still had to keep running alongside him.

"You don't get it," he said. "It *shouldn't* have been able to do what it did."

And, fear was back.

They made it to the crystal chamber and he released her. Moving around the room, he grabbed up his leather coat and slipped it on. Flipping open the lid of a trunk, he pulled out more knives, and throwing stars, then loaded up his pockets and hooked a new knife into the empty scabbard that had held the blade he lost on the hound. Then he picked up an automatic pistol. Briskly, he ejected the clip, checked to make sure it was full.

Deidre's gaze landed on the row of bullets. "Silver? Seriously? Silver bullets? Like for werewolves?"

"Werewolves and so much more."

"Werewolves are *real*?" Of course they were, Deidre told herself wildly. Why wouldn't they be? There were men made of fire and dogs from Hell. Why *not* werewolves?

"Welcome to a new world." He slanted a look at her. "Silver enhances white magic. Acts as poison to dark power. What do you think stopped that sucker a minute ago? That knife blade was pure silver."

Oh, God. She wrapped her arms around herself and hugged tight. She'd stepped into the rabbit hole and just like Alice, she was lost in a world that made no sense. For years, she had worked for witches. Trying to convince the world that magic itself wasn't dangerous. That power could be used for good to enhance everyone's life.

Now, she was discovering there was so much more to the situation than anyone knew.

Hellhounds, for God's sake.

Werewolves and who knew what else?

Dark magic.

Silver bullets.

She had spent years defending magic, but darker powers had never crossed her mind. And now it was all hitting way too close to home.

He slammed the clip home again, then tucked the pistol into his waistband. Grabbing a backpack, he tossed it to her. "Get some water. There are PowerBars in a box in the corner. Take as much as you can carry."

"Why don't you just catch on fire and zap us out of here?"

He paused to look at her. "Right. Great plan. Do I leave you here alone while I take the others first? Or maybe leave you alone at the river while I come back for them? One. At. A. Time."

"Oh. I didn't know—"

"Yeah," he grumbled. "The only way for all of us to get out of here is the human way. The *slow* way. Now fill that pack."

Chastened, Deidre curled her fingers into the rough canvas and squeezed tight before she moved off to do what he said. Why would she argue? He was right. They had to leave and frankly, anything that got her out of these tunnels would be okay with her.

Filling the pack as quickly as she could, she asked, "So how did the hound do it? Go through the wall?"

"Demons." He didn't say anything else.

"Demons?" Honestly, she didn't know how much more information she could handle. Wouldn't there be a tipping point where her brain just simply exploded?

He huffed out a disgusted breath. "Did I mention it's a *hellhound*? Lives in *Hell*? Where the demons are?"

"Great, sarcasm," she said, nodding as she grabbed two more bottles of water. "That's helpful."

He ignored that. "One of those demons—maybe more—have spelled that pup so that it can move through walls."

"Pup?" she asked, hands stilling as she stared at him. "That was a *puppy*?"

He snorted. "Full-grown hounds can reach the size of a buffalo. Or bigger."

"Holy crap."

"That about covers it," he said wryly. "Question is, how did it know we were down here?"

She had an idea about that. It had been settling over her for the last few minutes, like a cloak of ice. "Actually, I think it must have followed me."

"What?" Perfectly still, he stared at her as if she were speaking Greek.

She pushed another couple of PowerBars into the backpack. "I've been seeing it for the last couple of days."

"And you didn't think this was important enough to tell me?"

"I didn't know it was a dog from Hell, did I?" She zipped up the pack and swung it over one shoulder. The heavy weight made her stagger a bit. But she narrowed her eyes on him. "And just when did we have all this free time for a little heart-to-heart talk so I could tell you *anything*?"

He took a breath and the muscles in his jaw twitched as if he were grinding his teeth together. The fight for patience was written all over his face but when he spoke, the snap in his deep voice told her he'd lost that particular battle. "Where'd you see it?"

"Last time?" She shifted the weight of the pack, trying to make it comfortable. "When we saved the witches. It was in the parking lot when everything was getting shot to pieces."

"Fan-fucking-tastic." Grabbing a few more throwing stars and stuffing them into his coat pockets, he said, "Must have followed your scent. It's been on us all night probably."

Well, that completely creeped her out. "If that's true, why didn't it attack until now?"

"Who the hell knows why hellhounds do anything?"

"Great. Why would it follow me anyway?"

"Following demon orders. I told you that." He straightened up, crossed the room and took the backpack from her.

"I can carry it," she snapped and grabbed it from him.

"Fine." He slipped the straps over her arms, set the pack onto her back and didn't even laugh when the weight pushed her forward a step or two. "Let me know when it gets too heavy for you. Don't want you slowing us down."

"Charming. Do I get a weapon?" Not that she knew much about knife fighting, really—and she didn't know how to shoot, either. But damned if she wanted to go through those tunnels empty-handed, either.

He looked at her and frowned. "You are a weapon. Anybody throws a knife or points a gun, use your power to deflect it."

"Sure. No problem. Because I'm so used to doing that." She knew she was being unreasonable and didn't care. After the night she'd had, who had a better reason? "And if the hellhound attacks me? What am I supposed to do about that?"

She could see he didn't like the thought of that. Well, that made two of them. Finally, he pulled a knife with a five-inch blade from one of the pockets of his black leather coat and held it out, handle first. "Carry this, then. The blade's silver. Any hit you make will hurt him. If he gets too close, swipe it across his eyes."

Deidre swallowed hard at the image that brought up, but she nodded. Her fingers curled around the leather-wrapped hilt of the knife and as she got used to the feel and weight of it in her hand, she tried to get a grip on just how far out of orbit her world had slipped.

Shaking her head, she whispered, "Why is this happening? Why are demons sending their attack dogs after me?"

"Only one reason," he said and his voice dropped to a low rumble of sound that seemed to dance along every one of her frayed nerves. "The ante's gone up in this game."

Game. It was a game? Her life?

"Other Eternals and their Mates have completed their missions. Somebody somewhere's getting nervous. Looks like Hell is pulling out all the stops now to keep us from getting your piece of the damn Artifact."

There it went, she thought wildly. She could almost hear her brain reach its tipping point and start to snap. Frustration bubbled over and she wanted to tear at her own hair as she demanded, *"What freaking Artifact?"*

Those pale gray eyes of his swirled with secrets and promises that chilled her to the core as he looked at her. He seemed to be measuring her, judging how much she was ready for—and finding her wanting. He shook his head and said only, "Long story. No time. Get moving."

Chapter 13

Finn took the lead, holding his sword out in front of him. His right-hand man, Joe, brought up the rear and the others were grouped in the center. Deidre, he kept right beside him. He didn't want her falling behind or getting lost or getting a burr up her ass and trying to escape him.

He didn't think she would; she was too smart for that. But she'd also been pushed pretty damn close to the edge in the last few hours. He never had been able to figure out the female mind—and this female in particular had always been a damn mystery.

Centuries of time spent with her hadn't cleared up a thing for him. In every incarnation she'd experienced, her brain had always been one step ahead of everyone else's and obviously that hadn't changed a bit. He could practically hear the wheels in her mind turning, spinning as she searched her heart and soul for the answers only he could give her.

The tunnel twisted and turned on its way to the edge of DC. Too bad they had to cross the Potomac to get the witches to Virginia. He'd much rather keep the group belowground than risk the boat crossing—especially in November. But he didn't have a choice. Not only did the group not know he was an Eternal—but it would take too damn long and leave everyone at risk if he flashed them one at a time to safety.

This was way more involved than he would have preferred. He should have been able to take Deidre out of the tunnels and leave the group on their own. But now that demons were sending hellhounds after them, he couldn't risk it.

He hadn't counted on Hell getting involved so quickly in the action. But now that a hellhound was in the mix, Finn had no idea what to expect next. If there were sorcerers out there spinning demon magic and summoning hellhounds . . . he didn't want to think about it. With the dark energy still siphoning off into this world, there were all kinds of nasty things that could start cropping up.

His witch had to be ready to meet every threat.

Beside him, Deidre's breath huffed in and out of her lungs in visible streams. Clouds of vapor misted in front of her face as the cold air took her warm breath and froze it. Her scent caught in his chest and despite the situation, everything in him fisted with desire. This was his woman. His witch. And he wanted her. Bad.

First though, they had to survive.

Finn's gaze never stopped moving. The small, heavily armed group behind him was as quiet as possible, but speed was more important than stealth. The hellhound knew where they were. If it survived its wound long enough to report back to its demon masters, silence wasn't going to help them any.

Beside him, Deidre slowed down and that surprised him. She had kept up and hadn't complained about the heavy pack or their fast pace. Hadn't asked for help, either, and he admired that. Probably stubbornness as much as pride, but hell. She'd need both before they were done.

"Finn." She reached out and grabbed his arm, slowing him. "We have to stop for a while. Shauna needs to rest and so do the rest of us."

He came to a stop, turned and looked at the ragtag bunch behind him. Shauna was still pale and though she lifted her chin, he could see she was about ready to drop. And Deidre was right. The others weren't in much better shape. Especially the rescued women. They'd been on the march for more than an hour and the trek, along with the damp cold and the surrounding darkness, was seriously taking a toll.

"Fine. We'll rest for five minutes." While the others dropped to the chill, hard ground, Finn walked on, scouting ahead. The sting of icy, damp earth was all around him and the jagged rock walls radiated cold.

He reached out with his magic and when he was far enough away from the others, he allowed the flames to erupt on his skin. Shadows and light twisted and danced on the walls on either side of him, but he paid no attention. He closed his eyes, focused his power and mentally searched for danger. He didn't find any, but that could mean that their enemies weren't close enough to sense yet. Someone else was, though. He felt her before he heard her.

"That is so . . ."

He let the flames die as he turned to look at Deidre, coming up behind him. "Weird?"

"Beautiful," she said, surprising the hell out of him. "Weird too," she admitted with a shrug. "But beautiful."

He laughed. "There's a word no one's ever used to describe me before."

She continued her approach and everything in him lit up as she got closer. His dick went to stone, his chest felt tight and even his nonbeating heart felt a thrum of life. For centuries, he'd waited for her. For the Awakening. And now that it was here, it was all he could do to keep his hands off of her. He wasn't human. But he knew a male's need for his Mate.

She had been through a hellish few hours, but she was still standing. Her chin was lifted, her eyes blazed with worry, fear and determination and Finn wanted her more now, he thought, than he ever had.

"The fire's beautiful," she said, reaching up to touch his face. "You're not though. You're too *male* to be called that. You're too—"

Her fingers were feather soft as they smoothed over the hard ridge of his cheekbone and down to follow the stiff line of his jaw. He held perfectly still, not really trusting himself with her. The drive to Mate was overpowering, all consuming. He wanted her under him, over him. He wanted to taste and lick and nibble his way up and down her body. And then he wanted—needed—to bury himself inside her. To feel her muscles clench around him, to take all he had and then demand more.

He pulled back from her touch—not because he didn't want it, but because he wanted it too much.

Her gaze dropped when she let her hand fall to her side. "Okay, that was plain enough."

"You don't know what you're talking about."

She looked up at him again. "You don't want me touching you. That was fairly obvious."

"What I *want* is a hell of a lot more than a quick

touch." He moved in on her and something inside him ignited in an even stronger blaze when she didn't back up. She stood her ground, not realizing that the most dangerous predator in her world at the moment—*him*—was just a breath away.

He stabbed the tip of his sword into the ground beside him, then moved into her, his body aligning with hers. Her quick intake of breath told him that she felt the instant flash of heat that passed between them. He set his hands at her waist and absently noted just how small she really was. Small and fragile. And human. And all too easy for their enemies to kill. And he was all that stood between her and death.

He felt her breaths, heaving in and out of her lungs in response to his touch. Saw her lick her lips and felt his own body tighten in reaction. "What I want from you, Deidre, can't be had in a stolen moment or two in a damn tunnel. What I want will take hours."

She blinked at him, then sighed imperceptibly. "Hours?"

His gaze moved over her face, her eyes, her nose, her mouth, then down to the curve of her neck and the pounding of her pulse at the base of her throat. When his gaze finally met hers again, he added, "Or days."

"Oh, God."

He snorted. "That's not the name you'll be calling out. I guarantee it. When we come together, the only name on your lips will be *mine*."

He let the fire burst from his soul. Living flames of blue and red and orange and green danced from his hands to her body, licking at the curve of her waist, at the full roundness of her breasts. She gasped and arched into him, letting her head fall back as she sighed in deep pleasure.

"That's . . . oh my . . . Finn . . ."

Tempting, he thought desperately, watching her eyes close, her mouth part on another long sigh. The fire was him and he was the flames. He felt everything the flames touched. He knew the curve of her breasts and the pebbled tips of her nipples. He knew the sweet taste of her skin and the heat in her blood.

Hunger roared inside him and Finn surrendered to it for one brief, haunting moment.

Chapter 14

He bent his head and kissed her again, claiming her mouth because he simply couldn't do anything else. The taste of her had lingered with him through the years, taunting him, and now he found that it was so much more than the memory. The scent of cinnamon rose up around him as he pulled her in close. His tongue pushed into the warmth of her mouth and he swallowed the breath that rushed from her lungs. Their tongues tangled in a frenzied dance of desire that was so much more for having been denied for centuries. He felt every one of her frantic heartbeats and knew that if his own heart were able, it would be pounding in time with hers. And yet his heart would not beat until their Mating had been completed.

This was better than that first all too brief kiss. This was raw hunger being met by frantic need.

She wrapped her arms around his neck and held him to her. She leaned into him and he felt every delicious inch of her defined against his own body. The flames still flashing over his skin rippled and waved at the contact with her, enhancing their pleasure, entwining them in a heat that burned bright with magic. And it wasn't enough.

Would never be enough. Not until he had her naked and moaning and writhing beneath him.

The mission fell away. The tunnels, the group of fighters just down the passage from them. The threat of hellhounds and demons and the promise of a coming apocalypse if he and Deidre failed—it all fell away. All that mattered was this woman. This moment turning into the next and then the next.

His dick strained at the prison of his jeans and that ache in his balls ratcheted up to torturous levels. That pain was finally enough to remind him where they were, what they were supposed to be doing, and at last, to jolt him out of the moment.

Tearing his mouth away, he drew in one long, deep breath and let it slide slowly from his lungs as he rested his forehead against hers. He heard her struggling for air and while she did, he called the flames back within him. He cut off the connection between them as surely as if he'd taken an ax to it.

And even its absence was painful.

She fisted her hands into the lapels of his coat and hung on as if it meant her life. "What was that? What're you doing to me?"

He lifted his head and looked down at her. "That was the Mating magic flaring between us," he told her flatly. "And, babe, we're just getting started."

Her eyes were dazzled, her lips swollen. She licked them nervously and whispered, "If that's just the beginning, the ending might kill me."

Finn chuckled, lifted both hands and cupped her face in his palms. "Nobody's dying, Dee."

"Okay." She nodded. "I think I'm going to hold you to that."

"Deal." He let her go, and stepped back from her for his own comfort. Grabbing up his sword again, he asked, "Why'd you come to find me anyway?"

"Oh. Right." She shook her head and tossed the length of her braid behind one shoulder. "I just wanted to know how much farther we have to go."

He scraped one hand across his jaw, glanced down the snaking, dark tunnel ahead of them and said, "Another hour at least. Maybe more."

She sighed, but didn't complain and his opinion of her went up another notch. She was even stronger now than she had been in centuries past. She was so feminine, looked so damn girly, he hadn't really expected to find this spine of steel within her. He'd watched her from a distance the last few years and though she'd done her best to save witches, mostly, he had thought of her as a rich girl killing time. Now it seemed he had been wrong about that. So what else might he be wrong about?

She reached up with both hands and rubbed at her own shoulders.

"Sore?"

"I'll live," she said.

"Damn right you will." He returned his sword to the scabbard at his back. Reaching for her, he turned her around, then set both hands on her shoulders and massaged the muscles.

She stiffened at first. Then a groan of pleasure erupted from her and she slumped in his grip. Her head dropped and she kept up those soft moans as his thumbs and fingers dug into the tight knots in her muscles.

"You should have asked me to carry the damn thing."

"I don't need help," she mumbled. "Oh God, harder."

His dick twitched in his pants. She was going to kill him. No doubt.

"It's freezing down here," she whispered, the fog of her breath sighing out in front of her.

"Gonna be colder topside," he warned.

She frowned and rubbed at a spot between her eyebrows. "A Sanctuary is safe haven for witches, right?"

"Yeah. Run by witches for witches." He pulled his sword free and tested the balance automatically. "They're all over the world—small, magically enchanted safe houses. No human's going to find them and they're guarded well enough that even a magical attack wouldn't get far. I flashed over there a couple days ago. Warned them we'd have a few more guests for them and set up a spot for the hand-off."

"You've been busy."

He snorted. "You could say that."

"Okay, we get the women to Sanctuary. Then what?"

He fired a look at her. "Then you and I have some talking to do."

"And when do I get to talk to my mother, Finn?" she glanced back down the tunnel to make sure they couldn't be overheard. "I have to let her know I'm all right. She's probably got the Marines out looking for I by now."

He smirked at the thought. "You think I'm worried?"

She looked up at him, studying his eyes and in the darkness, he looked his fill of her. With his enhanced eyesight, he didn't need the light to see the depths of the blue of her eyes. Or the curve of her mouth or the arch of her eyebrows. Everything about her was lovely. Even her fury affected him like no other woman ever had.

Always, through the centuries, he had been drawn to her. She was the one woman who made him want. *Need*.

And never once had she needed him in return, he reminded himself. Which was just one reason why he wouldn't be doing the happily-ever-after thing. He'd Mate with her, complete their mission—then he'd be gone. He wasn't going to stick around and set himself up for an eternity of pain, thanks. Though the thought of leaving wasn't as enticing as it had seemed before he'd gotten to know her again.

Up until now, she had been his duty. The duty he'd been serving for eons. His honor demanded it. Just as his brother Eternals did, Finn protected witches, fought the rising tides of darkness and held the line that protected humanity from something most couldn't fathom. And through it all, his duty to Deidre in whatever incarnation she took, rang strong and true.

He would never turn his back on her—not just because honor demanded it—but because . . .

"If everyone in the country's looking for me," she pointed out with a calm, patient tone to her voice, "it's going to make your little quest harder to pull off, won't it?"

"*Our* quest."

"Whatever." She waved that away. "I'm just saying that if I can talk to my mother, I can get her to call off the search at least."

He shook his head. He wasn't calling her mother. Finn had no reason to mistrust Cora Sterling—he just didn't trust anyone but *him* to keep Deidre alive. Especially now that he knew hellhounds were on her trail.

"And what would your mother or the Marines do against a demon attack?"

"We can tell them about silver as a weapon against them."

"You think they don't know already?" He choked off a laugh. "Doc Fender, the MPs, BOW, they've all done enough 'research' and experiments on witches and anything else with a tinge of magic that they probably know plenty. Doesn't mean they can handle a full-grown hellhound."

"It was a puppy."

"Yeah, *that* one was. Next one probably won't be."

"She has to know I'm alive at least," Deidre argued.

He wasn't telling *anyone* that he had Deidre. Wouldn't risk losing her. Wouldn't risk her safety. "No."

"Just *no*?" She demanded. "That's it? We can't discuss it?"

"That's it." The buzz of desire was gone, and the mission was, as it should be, front and center in his mind. He walked a few feet back down the tunnel and shouted, "Break's over. Let's move."

"You're being a dick," she pointed out.

He smiled at her. "Thanks for noticing. Now go get your backpack. We're on the move."

She turned and stormed down the tunnel. He watched her go, held his sword in one clenched fist and waited, as he had for centuries, for Deidre.

Chapter 15

"Why not drive them across?" Deidre asked quietly, watching as the women were bundled into one of two boats drawn to the muddy riverbank. Wisps of early-morning fog drifted off the ground and twisted into ribbons.

"Because cops looking for escaped witches will be checking the cars on the bridge," Joe told her.

"And they won't notice boats?"

"Not *these* boats," he said, helping Shauna board.

The river raced past them, a rush of black churning water. Isolated chunks of ice bobbed and danced on the surface. The cars on the Key Bridge made a hum of sound off in the distance and their headlights streamed past, looking like a bright white streak in the night. The moon was behind a bank of clouds and the light was so dim, the world was shrouded in shades of gray.

After a whole day and most of two nights spent in a cold, damp tunnel, Deidre had been grateful to escape aboveground. She'd slept fitfully, as had everyone else but Finn. Every time she had opened her eyes, he was awake, alert, on guard. Now, Deidre felt bedraggled, exhausted and more on edge than she ever had been before.

And looking at the wild Potomac filled her with a new kind of dread. The two oversized rowboats Finn had had waiting for them looked too small, too insubstantial to withstand the raging river. As Shauna settled onto one of the seats, the boat rocked in a way that made Deidre's heart clench.

"What's so special about these boats?"

"Nothing yet," Finn said from behind her. "But once they're spelled magically, they'll be shrouded from sight."

"Well, I hope you know what you're doing." She whirled around to face him. She could hear the fear in her voice and there was no way to disguise it. "If you think I can work a spell, you're wrong. I've got no idea how to use magic."

"You do, but now's not the time to convince you. So we'll do it together." He stood behind her, took her hands and lifted them, aiming her open palms at the two small boats.

"Finn," she whispered low enough that the others wouldn't be able to hear her, "what if you're wrong? What if I'm not the witch you think I am?" The events of the last couple of days had been so surreal. How could any of this possibly be happening? Her magic had appeared so quickly, she half expected it to disappear.

He bent his head and his breath came warm and soft against her cheek. "You *are* my witch, Deidre. And you know it. I know you feel it, even though you're still fighting both me and yourself."

His witch.

Something deep within her trembled at those words. *Yes*, her mind whispered in response. *You are his and he is yours. Always and throughout time, we are linked by more than bone and blood—the kiss of magic unites us, makes us one.*

Deidre swayed in place as that internal voice forced her to realize the truth of all that was happening. Her body had known Finn even when she had tried to deny him. Now her mind called out to him and she couldn't pretend any longer that none of this was happening. Deep down she knew she couldn't escape it. Her life had taken a sharp turn and now the wisest thing to do would be to hold on tight so she didn't go spinning out of control.

He spoke again, whispering into her ear, sending a chill along her spine. "All you have to do is concentrate on what I'm saying. Feel your power within you and let it slide up and out of your palms."

Deidre laughed slightly. "That's all, huh?" She blew out a breath and shook her head. She'd had less than twenty-four hours to come to grips with this witchcraft legacy. She didn't know what it meant for her other than the obvious dangers every other witch in the world was facing. But she did know that she couldn't summon this mystical power at a whim. Not yet, anyway. "And just how do I do that?"

His hands tightened on hers as his deep, hushed voice came again. "You're a talented witch, Deidre. Believe it. Use it."

She hated that he knew more about her than she did. Hated that this new world had crashed down around her shoulders and she didn't have the choice of turning her back on it. Hated that she had power she couldn't use and *really* hated that having Finn standing pressed up against her felt so damn good.

With him that close to her, heat skittered through her

body, lighting up every dark corner within her and burning her up from the inside out. She looked at the faces of the people watching them and read the hope in their eyes. Even Marco and Tony, who had made no secret of their dislike for her, were now counting on her.

Then there was Shauna. Her friend, battered and still streaked with remnants of dried blood they hadn't had time to wash away. Her warm brown eyes shadowed with exhaustion, Shauna gave her a thumbs-up, and Joe, the tall blond warrior, looked completely confident in her abilities. She really hoped she didn't let them down. The pressure of everything that was riding on her magical abilities was almost too much to bear. The safety of those rescued women. Her friend's freedom—hell, her *own* freedom.

Finn remained behind her, a stalwart, stubborn presence. They were all so sure that she could do this that Deidre nodded and said softly, "Okay. I'll try."

"Just *do* it. Screw trying."

She almost laughed at the Yoda advice. But there was nothing funny about any of this. His hands on hers were warm and strong and steady. She drew in a deep breath of the icy November air and felt her feet slip a bit on the muddy ground, but Finn was there to steady her. The rushing river was a roar of sound that pushed every other thought from her mind.

She leaned her head back against Finn's chest, closed her eyes and listened as he murmured,

> *Hide from sight those we charm*
> *Keep them all from hurt and harm,*
> *We call the power from the night*
> *To aid us in the coming fight.*

Each word dropped into her mind and pinged against a wall that seemed to tremble and shake. She frowned because until meeting Finn, she hadn't even been aware of that wall and she worried about what she'd find when it finally came tumbling down. But now wasn't the time for those fears.

As she focused, she felt the magic rising inside her, as she had before in the jail parking lot. But this wasn't a wild, desperate pulse of something foreign.

This was a slow slide of a profound and deliciously familiar feeling moving through her. She recognized it. Knew it as well as she knew herself—which should have been funny, since as it turned out, she didn't know herself at all. But in this moment, the sensations coursing through her were so far beyond ordinary feelings that she couldn't laugh. Couldn't speak. Could hardly breathe as the sweep of elemental magic claimed her. It was *amazing*. Her body opened under the onslaught and welcomed that spill of power as a drought-stricken land responded to rain.

She fought to focus as Finn had told her to and experienced a new rush of something that was . . . indescribable. His hands tightened on hers and the link they shared deepened, spread, until it was connecting them almost on a molecular level. She felt him as a presence in her heart and soul. She sensed their energies merging, blending, twining together into an inseparable twist of power.

In her mind, she watched as it happened, her magic, represented by a ribbon of chains, each silver link shining bright as the sun. And his magic, a living lick of flame that wove in and out of every link as if searing the two together for all time.

She knew what was happening. It was their souls—
and their power—becoming one. She arched her back,
riding a swell of ecstasy that was nearly orgasmic. Her
body burned with desire for him. She stretched her
palms open farther and welcomed the magic. She concentrated on the feel of Finn's hands on hers, of focusing
their combined strength and power, then reached down
inside for what she needed. She trusted her instincts, let
her own magic guide her and it responded.

Something amazing was about to happen. She braced
for it and even then, was shocked to the bone by the
wonder of it. The power inside her burst, like a skyrocket
erupting into vivid color in the middle of a black sky. It
centered in her chest, then spread in a rush down her
body, firing her core, shaking her legs, then back up to
her arms, to her hands and out—

"Finn!" Deidre gasped and arched into him as the
magic pumped through her body and a jet of power shot
from her palms to encapsulate the two rowboats rocking
slowly on the frigid water. She opened her eyes wide and
saw the magic coalesce over the twin boats and the people within them.

What looked almost like a soap bubble, iridescent
color flickering over the surface around the boats, locking them into a magical circle. And then the power
within her evaporated as quickly as it had come.

She was left dazed, shaken, her body trembling in
Finn's grasp as her gaze fixed on the boats and the awed
faces turned toward her. Looking at them, Deidre shook
her head. No. That couldn't be right.

"I can still see the boats," she whispered. "It didn't
work."

"It worked," Finn told her, wrapping one brawny arm around her waist to steady her. "Humans won't see them. You can because you're part of the supernatural world."

She let those words sink in and surprisingly, it didn't terrify her as she may have expected it to. Maybe it was what had just happened. That rush of feeling, of tremendous power along with the soul-deep connection to the immortal who was still holding on to her. Then again, maybe she was growing numb to the whole situation? Or was it something more? Could her true nature have revealed itself? Had she finally been freed to be what she was always destined to be?

Finn's strength buoyed her. His hard body pressed to hers, offering strength, and Deidre felt more than magic whipping to life inside her. Her body was still thrumming with sensation. Desire blistered the chill air and filled her body with a need enflamed by the rush of magic swamping her. He felt it too. His body couldn't disguise his needs. The hard proof of his hunger for her pressed against her bottom and Deidre leaned back into him, deliberately increasing the pressure between them.

She heard him hiss in a breath and almost smiled. Good. She didn't want to be the only one suffering.

"You did it," he said, releasing her and stepping back. "Now we need to get moving. The Sanctuary witches will be waiting."

She turned and looked up at him and read the craven need etched into his features. A cold wind slapped at her as they separated. The river roared and one of the rescued women cried softly. It wasn't the time for what she was feeling. But judging by the look in his pale gray eyes, there would be time.

Soon.

"Let's get this show on the road," Joe whispered with a glance skyward. "It'll be light in a few hours."

"Right." Finn picked Deidre up and set her in one of the two boats. He climbed in behind her, picked up the oars and pushed off from shore. His powerful body leaned into the task and the rowboat shot out over the black water. Chunks of ice swept past them, bashing into the boat and then disappearing beneath the surface to bob up again later. The oars slipping in and out of the water took on a steady rhythm and became almost hypnotic.

Deidre looked at the boat alongside theirs and she shivered under an onslaught of fear that she knew everyone was feeling. Beaten women, still finding a reason to hope. Strangers brought together to fight against injustice. So many lives at risk, she thought and sent a quick prayer heavenward. It couldn't hurt and right now, Deidre felt as though she could use all the help she could get.

The cold bit deeper, and she shivered, hunching into the jacket Finn had provided her. Shifting her gaze away from the others, she found her friend watching her. The moon briefly peeked from behind a cloud and Shauna's familiar features were cast in strange shadows. Still, Deidre saw regret etch itself into Shauna's expression.

"I'm sorry, Dee," she said quietly.

Deidre gave her a half smile and a shrug. "What's a little kidnapping between friends?"

"That's not what I meant." She paused and nodded. "Although yeah, I should apologize for that too. No, I mean, I'm sorry I didn't tell you I was a witch."

The quiet was broken only by the sigh of the oars dipping in and out of the water and the continued weeping from the other boat.

"I guess I understand why you didn't," Deidre said finally. And she did. This wasn't a good time to be a woman of power. Hell, there were five women in the next boat who would not have escaped execution without their intervention. "But you could have trusted me."

"Yeah. I know." She winced, lifted one hand to her injured shoulder and patted it as if trying to ease the pain. "And if it had been just me, I probably would have. But I couldn't risk anyone else. If your mom had found out the truth, I'd have been in Doc Fender's torture chamber in a blink and—" She paused and gave a halfhearted smile. "I'm not that good with pain. I'd have given everyone I've ever known up to them."

Stunned, Deidre stiffened and instantly defended her mom. "My mother wouldn't have turned you over, Shauna. You're my friend."

"And she's the freaking president." She shook her head sadly, patiently. "Dee, I know you want to trust her and who can blame you? But you're a witch too—and judging by that spell I saw a few minutes ago, a damn powerful one." She reached out and caught Deidre's hand in her own. "You can't let your mother know."

Deidre looked down at their joined hands and internally denied everything Shauna was saying. She had to. Her mother wasn't the enemy. Okay, Cora Sterling could sometimes be cold and a little too focused on the big picture as she liked to call it, but she was still Deidre's mother. "Mom is doing everything she can to protect witches, Shauna. You know that."

"And yet we keep dying." Releasing her, Shauna sat back and gave a deep sigh. "Your mom's doing her best,

I suppose, but Deidre, nothing's changing for witches. Last year they executed more than five thousand witches in this country alone." She shook her head and turned her gaze out over the water, but not in time to hide the sheen of helpless tears in her eyes. "Worldwide, we're a dying breed, Dee. And there's no tree hugger out there making a Save the Witches documentary."

"So what?" Deidre asked quietly, bringing Shauna's gaze back to her. "We give up? We continue to hide? We trust no one? Not even the ones who might be able to help us?"

"Hiding keeps us alive. Fighting back gives us a chance." Eyes cold and hard now, Shauna added, "No offense, but the only one I trust my life to is *me*."

"What about Finn? You're here with him and Joe and the others . . ."

"Yeah. And now Tomas and Mike are dead along with Jermaine and Tori outside the jailhouse and the week before it was two others. We fight, we die. We don't fight, we die." Shauna smiled grimly. "I prefer to go down fighting."

It all seemed so useless. Was there really no hope of changing anything? Now that her life had been altered was Deidre looking forward to a lifetime spent in tunnels and caves, always waiting for the next attack to come? Never being able to trust anyone? She didn't think she could even consider that living.

"I don't accept that," Deidre said firmly. "Besides, she's my mother. She must already know I'm a witch."

"You know as well as I do, it's not always hereditary. Sure, the freaks and the MPs and the Seekers lock up whole families on the off chance they'll nab a coven in the making"—she sighed once again—"but there are witches from families that have never shown power before. Power just *is*. And by the looks of it, you've got a shitload of it."

"That wasn't all me," she confessed, though she remembered all too well the rush of something amazing and magical moving through her body. "Finn was right there, helping me."

"Bullshit. He was the conduit and hell," Shauna added, with a sly grin and a wink at Deidre, "who wouldn't want him as a conduit? But the power came from you. You didn't see your face, Dee. You were lit up from the inside. Your damn skin was glowing. Hell, for a minute there, you were the whitest white girl I've ever seen."

Deidre laughed, then clapped one hand across her mouth to stifle the sound.

"I know Finn's got power," Shauna said, solemn again as she looked from Deidre to him and back again. "He's never said anything, but I can feel it. But the power I saw a while ago? That was special. That was off-the-charts magic. And it came from you, Dee, whether you want to acknowledge it or not."

With that, Shauna sat back and slipped into silence as if the conversation had worn her out. Hugging herself to keep warm, Deidre thought about everything her friend had said and had to admit that she felt a little shaken about confiding in her mother. She knew she could believe in her mother, but could she trust the people surrounding President Sterling?

Deidre looked up at Finn. What did she really know about him? That he made her blood burn. That he had kidnapped her and held her against her will. That he was opening up her magic and claimed to have been with her for centuries. Did that make him her hero? Or just crazy?

His pale gray eyes were locked on her and just for a moment, she wondered if he really was here to help her ... or if he may turn out to be a really formidable enemy.

Chapter 16

Women from Sanctuary were waiting on the Virginia side of the river. At least a dozen women, all dressed in black and carrying guns, were spread out just before the tree line, as if prepared to duck for cover fast.

"Finn." A tall woman wearing a heavy dark sweater, black jeans and boots moved toward Finn. Her black hair was short and spiky and her features were taut. In her arms, she cradled an automatic weapon as if it were a newborn. "Good to see you again."

"Yeah." He stepped up and held out one hand. As she shook his hand, her gaze swept the others, lingering briefly on Deidre, then moving on to Shauna with a smile.

"Shauna honey. You look like you've been dragged through a demon portal backwards."

"Been a rough couple days, Chris. Glad to see you guys, though."

Deidre felt like she'd come into a movie too late for the explanations. Everyone else knew the plot and the players and she was standing there blinking like a deer in the headlights. As if the woman knew just what Deidre was thinking, she announced, "I'm Chris, Commander of the Sanctuary Guardians."

"Guardians?"

The woman shrugged. "Security force. Every Sanctuary has one." She paused to give Deidre a knowing smile. "But as the president's daughter, you'd know all about security, wouldn't you?"

"Crap." She'd been so worried about everything else, she hadn't even considered the fact that these people would recognize her.

"Relax." Chris waved one hand at her. "You're one of us. That makes your secret *our* secret."

Nodding, Deidre sighed and let go of at least that worry. After all, whom would Chris tell? The Sanctuary witches? Not like they would be contacting the government anytime soon.

"We've got five for you tonight," Finn said, "plus Shauna if she wants to stay to recoup."

"No, thanks," Shauna piped up. "I'm sticking with you guys."

Nodding, Chris's gaze narrowed on the rescued women, standing apart from the others. Then she called out, "Nora!"

Another woman hurried forward, her blond hair scraped back from her pale face into a ponytail that made her look about sixteen. She too was all in black, but her weapon was strung on a strap behind her back.

"Nobody comes with us, till Nora checks 'em out for transmitters."

"We know the drill," Finn told her. "But they're clean."

"Yeah, we'll just check for ourselves." Chris held that gun a little higher, staring them down, and Deidre was

more than nervous. Traffic still streamed across the Key
Bridge not a hundred yards from them. They were all
standing in the dark on the banks of a river that rumbled
and roared in icy fury.

Chris moved in closer to their group as backup for the
witch heading for the women hoping to be accepted into
Sanctuary. Deidre felt the tension of the moment and
caught herself easing up beside the refugees to silently
offer her protection.

"It won't take long," Chris told them, shifting her gaze
to the men in the group warily.

Joe caught her eye. "It's okay. I'm used to people being nervous around me."

Deidre smiled, but Chris didn't. Her gaze locked on
the tall blond man. "If you'd been hunted by men with
guns, you'd be a little 'nervous' too."

He gave her a half smile and a brief nod of acknowledgment. "As it happens, I have been hunted by men
with guns. Most lately 'cuz I've been saving witches'
asses."

"Point taken," Chris said with a nod. "Tough times for
all of us."

"No shit," Deidre murmured.

Chris's gaze turned to her. "You're one of them, aren't
you?"

"One of who?"

"The chosen."

Her heart jolted in her chest. "What?"

Chris held her gun steady as she shifted for a quick
look at where Nora stood checking out the women.
"Finn and I go back a ways. He told me about you."

"Is that right?" Deidre's gaze turned to him.

"You think there are secrets in Sanctuary?" Chris

grinned and shook her head. "Hell no. Witches stick together. And we all know about the chosen ones."

"Great." Everyone knew all about her. Everyone but *her*, that was. Deidre suddenly felt like she was on display. All eyes were on her and she was torn between the desire to hide and the urge to lift her chin and glare right back. She saw the expressions on their faces. Some were filled with curiosity; others, like Marco and Tony, were suspicious.

"Drop it, Chris," Finn told her in a deep, unyielding voice.

"Look, all I wanted to say," Chris murmured as if understanding the position she'd just put Deidre in, "was to get it done. Okay?"

"Sure." Deidre hunched deeper into her jacket, battling both the cold and the uneasy vibes suddenly spinning around her.

Joe was still watching her thoughtfully, but she ignored it and focused instead on Nora as she swept her open palms over one of the rescued women.

"What's she doing?"

Chris answered. "Nora's gift is manipulating metal."

"Hey, me too."

The other woman laughed. "Good to know. Nora's looking for implanted transmitters. The bastards in the camps have been getting slicker—tagging some of the witches with transmitters in case they get out. Hell, I heard in Alabama last week, they actually *released* a tagged witch and followed her. Eventually, with nowhere to go, she went to a local coven. The feds got them all."

Out of control, she thought. The whole world was out of control. Ten years ago, a woman who hadn't realized she was a witch accidentally killed her abusive ex with magic. She had been the first witch put to the stake. And since then, the majority of people on the planet were determined to wipe out witches.

The worst part was that witches weren't using their powers against civilians. They hadn't intentionally hurt anyone. But fear and raging paranoia had turned even ordinary citizens into rabid vigilantes.

Deidre watched as Nora moved her hands over the women, each in turn. Her palms bristled with energy that anyone close enough could feel, but Nora never touched the women, just hovered an inch or so above their skin while she scanned them thoroughly.

"How we doin'?" Chris asked as the first two witches were cleared and escorted to the waiting van.

"Fine," Nora said, then stopped and looked over at Tony. He gave her a wicked smile and a wink. She chuckled, shook her head, and said, "This one's clear too."

The woman heaved a grateful sigh and scurried across the cold ground to the waiting van. Joe glanced around the clearing anxiously. Shauna stood at the van, talking to one of the guardian witches. Finn watched over the scene while Tony and Marco stood on either side of the rescued witches, protecting them.

Nora cleared another witch, glanced at Tony again and this time frowned a bit in response to his flirtatious smile. "It's weird, but I'm getting—"

Still smiling, Tony shot her.

Blood spatter shot into the air and sprayed across the rocky ground. Nora dropped, dead, before the echo of the gunshot had faded away. Someone screamed. Deidre took an instinctive step forward before Finn grabbed her and pulled her behind him. At the van, the refugees were crying and the guardians had their weapons up and ready to roll.

Instantly, Tony swung his gun barrel around, aiming at Chris. He shouted, his voice carrying over the roar of the river to everyone in the clearing. "Everybody. Drop your weapons. Just stand still. Move and I swear to God, I'll kill every witch I can. Starting with Chris."

"Tony," Joe demanded, "what the fu—"

Deidre looked out from behind the wall of Finn's back, to the van where the women were huddled, clearly terrified. Shauna and the guardians laid their weapons down reluctantly.

Chris moved slightly and Tony smiled. "Don't try it. I will kill you as dead as that bitch." He kicked Nora's body. "If it was up to me we'd kill all of you. But they want you alive."

"They?" Finn's voice came harsh, furious.

Deidre felt the rage pouring off him in thick waves. It sizzled and snapped as it fed off the power he held within his massive body.

"Bureau of Witchcraft," Tony said, then added, "Drop your gun, Joe. I don't want to kill you."

He did as he was told, then straightened as he said, "Never figured you for a traitor, Tony."

"Me?" He laughed. "I work for our *government*. You're the traitor. Big Navy SEAL and what do you do with your training? You help *witches*? What the hell is that?"

"You didn't have to kill her," Deidre said quietly.

"No," he agreed. "I didn't. But it was fun." His gaze narrowed on her and he laughed. "And *you*. You are the bonus of the century. The president's *daughter*? A witch?" Another delighted chuckle came low and deep. "You are gonna get me a fat promotion, sweetie."

A chill of fear snaked along her spine and beside her, she sensed Finn's restrained fury.

"You're not taking her anywhere," Finn told him.

"You can't stop me." Tony looked him up and down and narrowed his eyes dismissively, but Deidre could read the fear on his expression. He used his free hand to pull a cell phone from his pocket. "You're fast, but not faster than a bullet."

"That's where you're wrong." Finn called up the flames and flashed out in a wink. He appeared again behind Tony, grabbed the man's head with both hands and snapped his neck in one easy move. He dropped the body and never looked at it again as he crossed to Chris. "Get the women out of here."

"Well damn," Marco murmured just loud enough to be heard, "that's a handy skill to have."

Deidre looked down at Tony's body and, she was almost ashamed to admit it, felt nothing but relief. Immediately though, a voice in her head took over. He could have ruined her life. Her mother's life. He had *killed* Nora and threatened everyone else. Why shouldn't she be glad he was dead? she argued with a conscience that was suddenly flatlining.

"Can't," Chris was talking to Finn. "There's still one woman Nora didn't check. Hell, one of your own men was compromised. I can't risk Sanctuary."

"She's right," Deidre told him.

"Yeah, she is, so you'll have to do it."

She blinked at him. "How?"

"You said you manipulate metal." Chris looked at her. "Just focus on finding it. Your magic will home in on any metal if it's there. Nora told me it felt like a buzz against the palms of her hands. And silver feels warm.

They tend to use silver in the implants, because it enhances a witch's magic—probably gives their transmitters a boost, too. Open your mind and trust your instincts."

"Okay. I've got no idea how to do that, but I'll try." She hurried over to the woman, who had inched away from Tony's body, and said, "It's okay. I just have to see if you've got any metal on you."

She nodded and turned wide, blank eyes up to Deidre. "Do it. Just clear me so we can get out of here. Before more of them come."

But no pressure. Still, Deidre told herself, shouldn't be too hard. She'd watched Nora do it. All she had to do was let her instincts rule the magic.

She buried all thoughts of Nora's death, of Tony's betrayal and the price he'd paid for it. She didn't let herself think about the cold, dispassionate look on Finn's face when he'd killed a member of his own group. She didn't think about any of it. Her hands shaking, she reached for her magic and swept her hands over the trembling woman in front of her. As she worked, she heard the others talking.

"How long do you think we have?" Chris asked from behind her.

"Not long." Joe cursed quietly. "Nora probably sensed a transmitter on Tony. And if he's been bugged this whole time . . ."

Deidre heard that and her worry grew. If Tony had been bugged, then everyone he worked with would already know who she was. What she was.

She straightened up as she finished checking the woman. She hadn't found a thing, so the woman was either clean or Deidre sucked at the whole testing thing.

Either way, she had done all she could. Deidre waved the woman to the van and as she scurried off, Deidre looked to the small group talking not ten feet from her.

Finn shook his head and said, "He wasn't bugged. I'd have sensed that." He paused and looked around at his group. "Secret's out. You know I'm more than human. So trust me, using magic I would have known if he was bugged. If anything, he probably had a GPS locater on him. The same thing they've been implanting the witches with." He glanced at Deidre as she walked up to join them, then turned to look at Chris and Joe. "Which means they know where we are, but they don't know Tony's been taken out. They could be waiting for a signal from him. In which case"—he paused for a dark smile—"we've got all the time in the world."

Chris slanted a look at the women in the van, awaiting salvation. "But they could also just decide to drop in on us now. Scoop up the people they can."

"Yeah." Finn agreed with a sharp nod. "And that means, we gotta move."

"How long was that guy with you?" Chris asked.

"A week. He came in to replace Jermaine." Joe scowled at the memory. "He probably told his superiors about the tunnels."

"How?" Finn asked, shaking his head. "He hasn't been out of the tunnels since he got there. He was never alone and the rock walls kill electronic transmissions."

Joe smiled. "You're right." He looked at Deidre and shrugged. "Can't tell you how many times I tried to use a cell phone when we first moved in down there and got squat for my efforts."

Finn reached out and dropped one arm around Deidre's shoulders, pulling her in close to his side. "That's the main reason I chose those tunnels." He looked at Chris. "I'm sorry about Nora."

She bowed her head briefly before answering him. "Thanks. Me too. But Nora knew how dangerous the refugee runs could be. We all do what we have to do." She watched two of her guardian witches as they carried Nora's body to the van and laid her gently in the back.

Behind them, the boats creaked and the river roared on. Deidre leaned into Finn, drawing on his strength as well as his warmth. Not too long ago, she had briefly entertained the thought that he might be her enemy.

Now she knew the truth.

He was just what he claimed to be. The warrior standing between her and those who would kill her. But for how long? a voice in her head whispered. He'd come to her out of nowhere—would he go the same way? Was he here simply to train her and leave? Was he going to be a part of her future? Too many questions and not enough answers.

"We have to get the women to safety," Chris said and held out one hand to Finn, then Joe. "Good luck to you and thanks for bringing the women to us. And, Deidre—good luck. You need anything, you come to Sanctuary. Finn can tell you how to contact us."

She hoped she wouldn't need to take Chris up on that, but it was always good to have options. "Thanks."

"Watch your back," Joe said.

Chris flashed him a wide smile. "Always, honey."

They watched as she strode across the ground, shouted, "Fire it up," and leaped into the passenger seat. She lifted one hand out the window as the black panel van disappeared into the tree line.

"Will they make it?" Deidre's whisper was almost lost in the icy wind.

"Hell yes, they'll make it," Joe said. "That woman should have been a SEAL."

"She's going where she needs to be," Finn told him and added, "Which is just what we need to do."

"Got it. What's the plan?"

Deidre deliberately avoided looking toward the spot where Tony's body lay. Instead, she focused on the two men and Shauna as she moved across the clearing to join Marco by the boats.

"Back to the tunnels," Finn told him.

Right now, even the tunnels sounded good to Deidre.

"Get the rest of the team together. Tell them about Tony and ramp up security."

"Right. We'll meet you there." Joe turned to join the others, then paused and gave Finn an interested look. "I'm guessing you won't be needing a ride?"

That's right, Deidre thought. More secrets than just hers had been spilled tonight. Finn had told her his people didn't know the truth about him. Well, that wasn't true any longer.

Finn stiffened. "About that."

Joe shook his head. "Never mind. Don't need to know. Probably better if we don't."

"Right," Finn said with a nod. "Okay then. You, Marco and Shauna head back, meet up with the others. Make sure you're not followed. Dee and I will be there in a few days."

She looked up at him in surprise, but he didn't say anything more.

"We're leaving Tony here?"

Finn looked at the body and his eyes went to pewter

as he answered Joe's question. "Let his masters find their dog."

"Good call. And like I told Chris, watch your back — and hers."

"Count on it."

"See you, Dee." Joe winked at her and ran to the closest boat. He shoved the boat into the water, then jumped in to join Marco and Shauna.

In moments, they were well on their way to the other shore and Deidre and Finn were left alone in the cold emptiness of a clearing stained with death.

"You ready?"

Deidre looked up at him. She knew he was asking her more than if she was ready to leave the clearing. He was asking if she was ready to accept who and what she was. What *they* were, together. And she gave the only answer she could give.

"Yes."

He called on the flames, gathered her in close and flashed them out.

Chapter 17

"**F**ucking dog."

Kellyn kicked the dead hellhound so hard, it flew across the room and slammed into the wall. "Never send a puppy to do a full-grown hound's job," she told herself in disgust.

Walking to the minibar, she poured an ice-cold vodka shot and drained it in one gulp. Not only had the damn hound gotten itself impaled by silver, but it had come straight back to her like it was on a bungee cord. If anyone had followed it . . . They hadn't, of course, but now she would be forced to change hotels again, just in case. Irritation upon irritation.

"Fine. Lesson learned. No more damn dogs." She grabbed the cold bottle of vodka and walked with it to the wide sweep of pale blue sofa nestled on a Persian rug in shades of gold and red.

The hotel was nice, but she was tired of living in them. She wanted her own place. Something, she thought with a smile, palatial. On a cliff, overlooking an ocean. Something with a view.

But she wasn't going to get that until the damn Awakening was shattered. She'd already lost the first two witches. Sneering, she pictured them and their Eternals cozied up inside Haven, laughing at her.

But they didn't matter anymore. She still had time. After all, she hadn't clawed her way out of Hell and possessed the body of one of the chosen witches for nothing. She lifted one hand and checked her manicure. Deep within, she heard the whispered voice of the witch whose body she inhabited. Poor fool was screaming to get out, screaming for vengeance.

"Not gonna happen, bitch," Kellyn assured that small voice. She had trapped her host's Eternal at the bottom of the sea and set herself up to mangle the Awakening and claim the power for herself and she wasn't going to stop until she was successful, damn it.

Taking a deep, cleansing breath, she had another sip of cold vodka. The third Awakened witch was still up for grabs. And, this time, she would have help. Not that she required help or wanted to share in the prize, but desperate times/desperate measures and all that crap.

And certainly this help would offer more reliable assistance than an idiot demon dog who didn't have the sense to avoid a silver dagger.

She had another drink and let the icy slide of the liquor soothe her. Then she refilled her glass and lifted it in a toast to Deidre Sterling, wherever she was.

"Your time is short, witch. Enjoy it while you can."

Traveling by fire was fast, but hard on the nerves.

Deidre lost count of how many times Finn would pause briefly and then flash them away again. All she saw were snatches of countryside, quick peeks at city streets and always the flames flowing up and around her.

By the time he finally stopped, just before dawn, she was dizzy, breathless and more tired than she'd ever been in her life. "Where are we?"

"Northern Maine," he said, taking her hand and drawing her up the stone path toward a small cabin set amidst tall pines and spruce trees. Overhead, the sky was just beginning to lighten to a pale violet. Snow dusted everything, and coated the steeply sloped roof of the cabin. "I built this cabin fifty years ago. No one knows where it is. It's protected by charmed wards. You'll be safe here."

The minute she stepped inside, she felt the stress of the last couple of days drain away. It was small but cozy and luxurious, with rugs covering most of the hardwood floors. Shelves filled with books marched along one wall, windows giving a view of the front yard took up another and on the far wall was a fireplace as tall as Finn. He called up flames on his hand and threw them at the waiting logs in the hearth.

Instantly, a roaring blaze took hold, chasing away the chill in the room and drawing Deidre closer to its warmth. Odd how she was getting more and more used to this whole supernatural world. Either that, or she was so tired she didn't have the strength to jolt in surprise anymore.

She stared into the flames. "Now what?"

He came up behind her and the heat streaming from his body put the fire in the hearth to shame. "Now we start the Mating."

Mating. *Sex.* Her blood sizzled and steamed in her veins. Her core exploded with damp heat and a wicked sense of expectation rose up inside her. Deidre had to fight for calm. Fight to stay rational. Taking a step away from him, she slipped out of her jacket and tossed it onto the nearest chair.

"I'm not saying I'm not interested, because what would be the point? We both know I am." God, was she. Her body was burning, aching. In fact, she seemed to be on the verge of a climax already and he hadn't so much as touched her.

She had never been a particularly sexual person. Not that she was a virgin or anything, but the two men she'd been with in the past hadn't exactly rocked her world enough that she was desperate for a repeat performance.

At least, she hadn't been.

Until Finn stormed into her life.

But so much had changed for her so quickly. She could wield magic and had discovered she was a witch. There were hellhounds. Demons. BOW agents murdering a woman in front of her.

She couldn't trust her own feelings. Not even the desire raking its claws into her. She needed answers before she did anything else.

"What I am saying is that I'm not having sex with you until you *talk* to me. Explain—*everything*."

He shrugged out of his coat and Deidre could only stare. They had both been in the same clothes for more than two days, but she felt like roadkill and he still looked amazing. His black T-shirt stretched across an enormous chest and powerful arms. His black jeans hugged legs that were thick as tree trunks and just as long. His black boots were muddy and he was covered in weapons. If she had any sense at all, she would have been terrified.

Instead, she felt that tingling pulse at her center again and knew that whatever he wanted to do to her, with her, she wanted it, too. She'd never been so torn. Body and mind at war, Deidre was really worried that her body was going to win this battle.

"This is your destiny, Deidre," he said, pale gray eyes locked on her. "You've been heading toward this moment for centuries."

"Destiny?" Deidre shook her head and said, "Y'know, I've been working with witches for years. Maybe I can accept that I'm one of them. But a destiny? To save the world? I don't buy it."

"You know it's true." He cocked his head and stared at her. "Think about it. All your life, haven't you felt as though something was missing? As though you weren't who you were supposed to be? That you weren't complete somehow?"

"How did you know that?" She had never discussed those feelings with anyone. In fact, she had always tried to not even acknowledge them herself. But the truth was, from the time she was a girl, she *had* felt as though her life wasn't right, somehow. As though she was supposed to be doing . . . something else.

She'd spent years looking for that elusive passion that would at last make her feel as if she were complete. As if she had done what she was supposed to do. But she'd never found it. Working with the groups trying to free the witches had been as close as she'd ever come and even then, it still hadn't felt . . . *right*.

Deidre looked up into gray eyes that were growing more familiar than she wanted to admit. "Can you read my mind?"

He snorted a laugh. "I already told you no. I don't have to read your mind to know what you think and feel, Deidre. I have known you for hundreds of years. Your features change in every incarnation, but your mind, and your soul, remain the same."

"You know how crazy this all sounds, right?"

"It's not and you know that. I think you can feel that it's right," he said and she didn't know whether to be comforted or worried.

It was true. As hard as it was to acknowledge, she *did* believe him. But admitting that forced her to take the first step on a road she was still unsure about. Finn was her only guidepost. Through the fear that had been her constant companion for the last few days, the one stable point in her world had been *him.* He irritated her, pushed her, demanded things from her she would never have tried on her own and expected her to succeed.

He'd saved her life and then turned it upside down. She'd been hunted, threatened, challenged and Deidre had never felt more *alive*, and *aware*, in her life. And yet she was also more afraid than she'd ever been, too.

"Okay, say I do believe you. But no more surprises, Finn. I need to know what's happening between you and me and what's coming next. You can start by explaining this Mating thing and *why* we're destined."

"Hell, you're more stubborn in this life than I've ever seen you and that's saying something."

"Flattery's not going to work," she said.

"Fine then. This is about memories," he told her and stopped, folding his arms over his chest. "Your memories are key."

"Memories of what?"

"Us," he said, his voice low, nearly hypnotic as his eyes locked on hers.

"How do I—"

"Open yourself to them, Dee," he whispered. "Open your mind, your heart. Let the past live again...."

The past... Images awakened in her mind. Hazy, indistinct, like photographs left to fade in the sun. There was something almost haunting about them. Tantalizing, as her mind reached to identify them all and came up blank. Frustrating to know that she should know something and be unable to recognize it.

"How is any of this possible?" she murmured, then added quickly before he could speak, "And don't say 'magic.'"

He snorted. "It always comes down to the magic, Deidre. It always has and always will."

She took a long breath and tried to steel herself. She couldn't do a damn thing, make any decision at all until she knew what the hell was going on. It was way past time to find out.

"Tell me more, Finn. I want to know everything."

Scowling, he blurted, "Short version? You're the reincarnation of a powerful witch. Eight hundred years ago, give or take, you and the rest of your coven conjured a spell. You focused your immense powers through a Black Silver Artifact, hoping to open doors into other dimensions. You wanted knowledge. Power . . ."

Deidre shivered despite the heat blasting at her from the hearth and the warmth of him by her side. Memories that *weren't hers* whipped through her mind in a rush of sound and scent and color. More vivid this time. More . . . unavoidable. She clapped both hands to her head as if she could slow the stream of information, but it didn't help. Overwhelmed, she closed her eyes and backed away from Finn until she slammed into the wall behind her. Several books fell from the shelves and clattered at her feet.

He was still talking—just as she'd asked him to.

"We've reunited over the centuries, Deidre. Again and again, I watched you live, age and finally die."

She saw that too, as if he'd conjured the images in her mind. His voice continued, deep, compelling, but she couldn't look at him. Could see only the pictures flashing through her mind, one after another, over and over and over.

Breath coming fast and frantic, she saw herself over the centuries. Different features, hair, clothing, yet she could always recognize herself. How she knew it, she couldn't have said. But it was a bone-deep knowledge that left her shaking. And she saw *him*. Finn. In her life. *All* of her lives. Sometimes as lover, other times as friend. But there. With her. Always nearby.

"I've waited," he said, each word rumbling through the room like the voice of God and sliding along her spine.

Her eyes remained closed, her hands clenching her head as the years washed through her mind, tumbling over each other like grains of sand lost in an undertow.

Trembling, shaking, she heard him whisper, "Longer than you can imagine, I've waited for you. I'm done waiting, Deidre. Our time is *now*. But first, you have to *remember*."

And the force of his voice pushed through the last chinks in the wall in her mind. It peeled back the curtain of time and in a breath, the cabin fell away.

Chapter 18

The wall in Deidre's mind trembled and cracked, and a crystal clear memory spilled through.

They stood on a high cliff edge over a raging sea. Lightning flashed in a black sky and naked women gathered around a pentacle etched into the dirt. Candles burned at each of the five points, flames dancing in the wind. The women—witches—lifted their arms to the sky, their hair blowing and twisting with the wind.

A chant pulsed out around them. Words blurred, but intent was clear. Fury emanated from the men forced to stand outside the circle of women. Eternals. Trying to stop the witches. Shouting in rage and helpless frustration, they sought to reach the women—and failed.

"God . . ." Deidre whispered, as Finn's words continued, painting a picture she didn't want to see—and couldn't help remembering.

". . . it all went wrong." Finn's voice was as dark as the memories still churning in her mind. "A portal opened, but it wasn't to just *any* dimension. It was a Hellgate. You flung it open—you and your sisters—and demons poured through. A battle raged while the coven fought to close the portal. My brothers and I killed a lot of the bastards, but too many escaped into this world." He sighed in remembered frustration. "They're still here, creating havoc, trying to get the gate back open."

"We did that," she said and felt a single tear of deep shame roll down her cheek. If she'd been hoping for sympathy—which she wasn't—she would have been disappointed.

"Yeah."

She opened her eyes to stare into slate gray eyes that churned with frustration and fury.

"We tried to stop you, but none of you would listen," he said. "Now it's your turn to step up and do what you can to fix it."

Unwanted guilt rolled through her, claiming her and she heard herself ask, "How?"

He moved in closer. "By finding the Artifact. After the Hellgate was closed, the coven shattered the Black Silver Artifact. Each of you took a shard and spread out, hiding the pieces all over the world."

Deidre swayed. She remembered that, too. The horror, the fear, the *shame*. She and her sister-witches had turned demons loose on an unsuspecting—and unprepared—world. A shaky breath slid from her lungs as she remembered the horrible days following the opening of the Hellgate. When she had had to face Finn, look into his eyes and realize that not only had she lost the essence of who she was; she had lost her Eternal's respect as well.

She'd lost so much. All of them had. She remembered walking away from her home, her life, *Finn*. Their coven had shattered as completely as the Artifact they had destroyed. Each of them had left Haven, alone. She had taken the Black Silver away to lose it somewhere in the world as payment for what she and her sisters had done.

"Oh, God." Deidre felt an old pain rise up inside her and she fought against it. She didn't want to accept responsibility for something she had done in another lifetime centuries past. This couldn't be her burden to carry. She wasn't that selfish woman who had turned her back on everything she cared about. This was *now*.

Besides, even if she did want to make things right—"I don't know where it is."

"You will," Finn said softly. "Your memories will become more clear. Mating with me will open doors in your mind. The Mating isn't just sex, Deidre. It's the branding of our souls. We Mate and we literally become one."

She swayed, then locked her knees and stood her ground. "Meaning?"

The fire crackled and snapped greedily over the dry wood and the first rays of sunlight began to slide through the windows to lie across the floor.

"Meaning," he said softly, "we accept each other. We Mate and each of us gets stronger. The bond we already share will become unbreakable. We have thirty days to complete the Mating now that your powers have awoken and to find the Artifact and return it to Haven—"

Haven. Another name that drew images into her mind. *Cave walls, etched with the faces of sister-witches through the ages. Mystical symbols carved into walls veined with silver.* Home, she thought wildly. The home that she, in that long-ago time, had lost in a greedy search for power. She shook her head as the information piled up inside her brain and tangled in knots she had no way of straightening out. "Stop. Just—"

"All you need to know right now," he said, taking a different tack, "is that sex with me will strengthen your magic, awaken the memories we need to complete our quest. At the completion of the Mating you'll be immortal and I'll have a heartbeat—giving me a link to humanity—making us the unit we were always meant to be."

"You don't have a heartbeat?" How weird that that was the thing that resonated with her.

"No."

So strange. The most *alive* male she'd ever known and he had no heartbeat. Just another disturbing piece of the magical world she'd been swept into.

"So we have to Mate," she said a moment later, with a slow shake of her head. "But you don't even *like* me and I'm still not sure I completely trust you."

He shrugged out of his weapons harness. He dropped his sword onto the closest table and laid the belt of knives alongside it. Sliding her a glance, he asked, "You think that matters? Our feelings don't count for shit in any of this. It just *is*. It's destiny. Fate. Call it whatever you want to.

"The important thing is the mission we have to complete. Because, bottom line, I'm not looking for a Mate. I don't need a fucking heartbeat. Got along fine without one since the beginning of time."

His flat, empty voice slapped at her as much as the dismissive words. He'd gone to all this trouble to find her, kidnap her, protect her, all the while knowing he had no intention of keeping her? "Then why—"

"We have sex." His features tightened. "We get stronger. We open your memories of the past, find the damn Artifact and then we go our separate ways."

Well, that was clear enough. A surprisingly strong

wave of regret rose up inside her and she dutifully shut it down. She'd had plenty of practice over the years.

After all, Finn wasn't the first man she'd ever known to want her only for what she could do for him. God, she was an idiot. He didn't want *her*. He wanted the witch she had once been. He wanted to use her to complete this quest—but after that, despite any Mating bond between them, he would walk away.

She stared up into pale gray eyes swirling with passions. Anger, desire, frustration. And another memory door opened. One that led her to images of Finn—so many they flashed through her mind with dizzying speed. But always, always, she felt the incredible sexual heat that was swamping her even now.

But that heat didn't touch her soul. Deidre's heartbeat thundered in her chest as she considered everything he'd just said. Her hands swiped up and down her arms, because even with the roaring fire right beside her, she felt cold. So cold she might never be warm again.

"Deidre, take a breath," he said. "You look like you're gonna keel over."

"Feel like it," she admitted. God, what was she supposed to do now? How was she supposed to come to grips with the haunting past and the terrifying present? And the looming embarrassment and disgrace of a destined Mate planning to ditch her.

Deidre stepped out from under his hands. God, she couldn't think. Could hardly breathe. He was looking at her and seeing the woman who had betrayed him centuries ago and how was she supposed to deal with that? And damned if she'd let him know that his rejection of her had torn at her heart.

"I need a few minutes, Finn. To think. To—" To *what*?

She didn't know. All she was sure of was that she needed time. *Ironic.* Since it seemed she had already had centuries to prepare for this moment.

"Fine," he said tightly. "Why don't you go clean up? There's a shower through there."

He pointed and she nodded because she didn't trust herself to speak again. Throughout all of the turmoil of the last couple of days, one thing had been clear to her, despite her fear and confusion. She, Deidre Sterling, was *important* to Finn. He needed her. And that, more than anything, had held her together in spite of everything.

But he didn't *want* her. He wanted the mystical Mate he had to have to complete his mission. The familiar sense of being used was enough to coat the sexual heat inside her with a skim of ice. She couldn't be around him right now and she felt like death warmed over anyway.

She walked away from him, but she felt his gaze on her every moment. His power reached across the room to her as surely as a caress. Deidre shivered and headed toward the doorway like a sleepwalker. Every muscle and bone ached with fatigue—but worse, she felt a sense of . . . loss.

All right, he'd handled that well.

Finn bit off a curse and rummaged through the freezer one-handed as he listened to the phone ringing in Haven on the other side of the world.

"Finn. Did you get your witch?"

"Yeah, Rune, I got her." He scowled at the frozen lasagna. Then he took it from the freezer and set it on the black granite kitchen counter. Closing the freezer with a bump from his hip, he caught the phone between his ear and shoulder and worked the cover off of dinner while he talked. "She's safe. Probably thinks I'm a dangerous lunatic, but what the hell, right?"

Rune snorted. "Wait'll she gets to know you."

"Yeah, that could be a problem."

"What's wrong?"

"What isn't? Some demon sent a hellhound after Deidre."

"*What?*"

"Hellhound. Demon charmed." Just saying it made him want to find the damn hound and wring its neck personally. Oh, and then hunt down whatever demon handled the charm and do the same to it. Instead, he reminded himself, he was nuking frozen noodles. "Damn thing went right through the wall of the tunnel after I threw a dagger into its chest."

"Son of a bitch. They're upping the stakes."

"That about covers it." He read the directions on the carton, punched in the right numbers on the microwave, then stuffed dinner inside. He closed the door, hit START and listened to the machine hum. Leaning back against the counter, he rubbed one hand over his short hair and said, "I brought her to the cabin so we could talk."

"And?"

"I told her everything. It didn't go well."

"Screw talk," Rune blurted. "Get the damn Mating started and find your Artifact before that demon gets even more creative."

"Wow, great idea." Finn pulled the phone from his ear long enough to frown at it. "Easy enough to sit on the sidelines offering advice when your tour of duty's already done."

"Hey, Teresa and I had to face all kinds of crap."

Finn snorted a laugh. "Yeah, a demon bird. Put that up next to a hellhound, I dare you."

"Whatever," Rune muttered.

"Look, I know what I have to do. Just wanted you guys to know that hellhounds have been added to the party."

"And the fun just keeps coming. I'll let Torin know. You need our help?"

"No." Finn pushed away from the counter, stalked across the kitchen and stared out at the brightening sky beyond the cabin. Long ago, he'd cleared a circumference a hundred yards wide all around the structure so no one could sneak up on him unaware. But beyond that perimeter, an ancient forest stood silent as sentinels. "I've got it covered. But you should know I had a traitor in my crew, too."

"Been a helluva night for you, hasn't it?"

"Couple nights," Finn corrected. "And yeah. He's dead, by the way, and I don't think he was able to contact anyone else. BOW planted him, but he got dead before he could be of use to them."

There was more, of course. Like for example the ambush at the jailhouse. There was no way Tony could have alerted the authorities about their planned raid. So someone else had. Which meant, there was *still* a traitor in Finn's happy little band of rebels.

Until he discovered exactly who it was, he wasn't letting Deidre out of his sight.

Rune laughed a little. "Glad to hear it. Keep your witch safe and find that damn Artifact."

"I will."

"Oh, damn," Rune said suddenly. "With all your goings on, I totally forgot our big news. We think we've got a lead on Egan."

Finn stiffened, shoulders going rigid, spine straight enough to snap. Egan. The Eternal betrayed by his Mate. Lost to them until now. "How?"

"Mairi, Shea and Teresa worked a locator spell. They're going to give it another shot to try to narrow down the search parameters."

Everything in Finn wanted to go to Haven. Help his brothers to find Egan. But he couldn't. He was as trapped here as Deidre was. For the next thirty days, they were both locked into an ancient quest with no way out but success. Because failure was unacceptable.

Nodding, he clutched the phone tighter. "Good to hear. Find him, Rune."

"That's the plan. Don't worry about it. You just take care of your part in all this."

"Nag, nag . . ."

He hung up and continued to stare out at the growing daylight. His mind worked, chewing through Rune's news—Egan had been missing for a damn long time and Finn couldn't even imagine what he'd been through. To be trapped at the bottom of the sea, locked into a cage, unable to help himself?

A sympathetic wave of fury rushed up inside him. Hell, even if they got Egan out, there was no guarantee he'd be in any shape to complete his share of this damn mess. Especially since he'd have to trust the bitch who'd locked him up to do it.

Shaking his head, he refocused on the problems facing him at the moment. Finn hadn't said anything to Deidre about the very real possibility of another traitor. He'd figured she had enough to deal with. But the facts were plain. Either that setup at the jailhouse had just been the feds being paranoid—or someone had tipped them off.

And if that was the case, then the traitor was still part of Finn's crew.

But who?

Seriously, this was exactly why he'd steered clear of humanity for centuries. They were too easily swayed by their own passions—lust, greed, revenge, power. Hell, Tony had killed Nora just so he could capture Deidre and get a damn promotion. Who the hell knew what really drove humans? But even as his disgust with the whole damn race of them thickened inside him, he remembered Joe. And Shauna. And Marco and a couple of the others. He didn't believe for a second that any one of them would turn on him and the cause they risked so much for.

So he wasn't going to condemn the whole bunch for the actions of a few. Though it would have made his life easier if he could. Because Finn wouldn't hesitate to slaughter traitors to protect Deidre.

Chapter 19

Scowling, he pushed those thoughts aside even though thinking about traitors was a hell of a lot better than imagining Deidre in the shower. She'd been delighted with the granite and glass bathroom, and surprised with all of the luxury touches he had installed in the cabin over the years.

In his mind's eye, he could see her, naked under the three showerheads, slicking her blond hair back from her face, beads of water rolling in rivulets down her sleek body. Then he imagined her soapy hands, sliding over her skin — across her breasts, between her thighs.

"Damn it." His dick was hard enough to pound nails.

"What's wrong now?"

He whirled around, caught off guard for the first time in — Hell, he couldn't even remember the last time someone had sneaked up on him. Deidre stood in the open doorway, wearing the clothes she'd had on for days. Her blond hair was still damp from her shower though she'd towel dried it enough that waves and ripples were already beginning to show themselves. He realized that until now, he'd only seen her hair in the braid she seemed to prefer. He liked it loose better.

"What's wrong now?" she repeated.

"Nothing." He shook his head, dismissing her concern. Damned if he would admit that he'd been so busy picturing her in the shower he hadn't even heard the water shut off. "Dinner'll be ready in a minute."

She glanced at the microwave, then looked back to him. "Okay then, that gives us time to talk."

"Fine. I'm sure you've got tons of questions—"

"No," she said stiffly. "What I meant was, I talk, you listen. You told me what you need from me. Well, here's what I need. I have to see my mother."

"We've been through this."

"And if you say no," she went on without skipping a beat, "then you get nothing from me. No Mating. No Artifact. Nothing."

What the hell? While he was imagining her naked and willing, she was planning a revolt? He gave her a stony stare, one that had intimidated warriors, enemies and demons over the eons. Deidre didn't even blink. Her blue eyes met his and there wasn't so much as a whisper of retreat in them.

She was drawing a line in the proverbial sand.

"Are you serious? Were you not around earlier? Traitors? Hellhounds? Demon threats and federal agencies on your luscious tail? Did you miss all of that?"

She folded her arms across her chest, unconsciously pushing her boobs higher—or was that a deliberate move to distract him? Well, it was working. His gaze dropped briefly to the swell of those breasts that he wanted his hands on so badly. But a second or two was all the indulgence he allowed himself. Then it was back to meeting her determined gaze.

"I didn't miss a thing," she told him and if there was a quaver in her voice, it was a slight one. "I know exactly what's going on."

"So in response, you lean to blackmail."

"I prefer the word 'deal,'" she said and walked across the room to take a seat at the small table beneath a bay window.

Morning light slid through the glass to lie across her hair and face like a golden caress. She looked more goddess than witch at the moment and that was just more of a distraction for him when he least needed it.

"Look, Finn, I've had a lot thrown at me over the last few days. And according to you there's lots more coming."

He watched her from across the room because he didn't entirely trust himself to get closer. He was on the edge right now. Every instinct he possessed urged him to start the Mating. His dick was hollering at him to get a move on.

But when he looked at her delicate features and read only firm resolve, it was enough to make him pause.

Her gaze locked with his and she lifted her chin. "You're the one who said I'm indispensable on this . . . mission. Well, since I've got the golden ticket, I'm cashing it in."

A part of him admired her for this maneuver. He liked a woman who knew what she wanted and went after it. But it wasn't his job to placate her. It was his job to keep her alive.

"Deidre—"

"I'll settle for a damn phone call, Finn," she said and silently dared him to refuse.

Her blue eyes were fired with so many emotions he couldn't read them all. But front and center was her determination and that was a hard thing to ignore. And even harder to combat.

As if she sensed that she was getting to him, she gave it another push. "I have to talk to her," she insisted. "At least let her know I'm alive."

Finn scraped both hands over his face and up and across the top of his head. He had a feeling he was going to regret this.

"She can't know what you are," he warned, narrowing his gaze on her. "Or, *where* you are."

"Hell, even I don't know where I am," she said on a choked laugh. Then she shook her head. "As for telling her I'm a witch? I'm not an idiot, Finn. I won't do that. Won't endanger her or her presidency. I saw that BOW agent when he looked at me like I was the winning lottery ticket," she said wryly. "No, she can't know. Not yet, anyway."

Her hands moved up and down her arms briskly as if she were fighting off a chill. Since the room wasn't the least bit cool, Finn knew this was a deeper cold seeping through her. In the last three days, Deidre had seen her world collapse around her. She'd been betrayed by a friend, discovered she was a witch and watched Finn execute a traitor. She'd been dragged through tunnels, shot at and chased by a hellhound.

Not hard to understand that shock was finally setting in. But he had to give her points for how she was handling this. Most humans he had known would have been curled up in the fetal position on the floor, whimpering for their mommies. Not his witch.

Deidre dug deep and found strength she probably hadn't even been aware of until now. Hell, she'd even blackmailed him—and done a fine job of it, too.

He blew out a breath as he watched her, his mind racing. Truth was, he didn't want her having anything to do with her old life. As her powers grew and the Mating progressed, she would have less and less in common with the life she had known. Her priorities would change. She would form new loyalties. And being involved with humans could only complicate an already complicated situation.

But could he really expect her to turn her back on her only family? Hell, his heart might not be beating, but he *did* have one. And only a real prick would be able to look into Deidre's blue eyes, shadowed with fatigue and fear and suspicion, and still say no.

Decision made, he walked across the room and dropped into the chair opposite her. Her shoulders squared and her spine went ramrod stiff. She was prepared to fight him on this. She'd already made that clear. So why not throw her a curve and agree?

"One phone call," he said. "But I'm with you when you make it."

Her pleased smile fell away. "Don't trust me?"

One eyebrow went up. "Do you trust me?"

She took a breath and sighing, considered him. "I don't know yet."

"Fair answer." And a pisser as well. He needed her to trust him, but he couldn't just demand it. He'd have to earn it. *Again.* As he had for centuries. Irritation sparked but he pushed it away since it wouldn't do him any damn good.

A cold November wind buffeted the windows and

made them rattle. Inside, the whirr of the microwave was the only sound for several long seconds.

"Call your mother." Finn handed over the phone.

Deidre took it fast, her fingers closed tightly around the cell, half afraid that he might try to snatch it back. But Finn didn't move. He just sat there, watching her. She knew too much about him now to be comfortable under that direct gaze. Too many memories were filling her mind. And in all of them *he* played a starring role.

God, this was a mess.

She looked down at the phone, turned it on and punched in a number she knew by heart. She really wished her mother had a cell phone, but her aides insisted it was too dangerous in these unsettled times—they were too easy to hack into and Cora's enemies were always looking for ammunition to use against her. Deidre cringed at the thought of what they could do with the knowledge that the president's daughter was a *witch*.

The phone rang only once and the White House operator answered.

"Hello," Deidre said quietly. "This is Snowflake. I need to speak to Saber."

A slight inhalation of breath was the only sign of the operator's surprise. Using the code names the Secret Service had given them had ensured that Deidre would be put through as quickly as possible.

"One moment," the operator said.

She half turned in her chair—more to avoid looking at Finn than for any urge to look at the scenery. Though with the first rays of the sun streaking the fresh snow in golden light, she did feel the tightness in her chest loosening up just a little.

Deidre tugged at the ends of her hair, wrapping the

strands around her index finger in a habit that hadn't ended until she had started wearing a braid.

"Deidre?" Her mother's voice came over the line suddenly. "Is it really you?"

"Yes, Mom," she assured her. "It's me."

"My God, where are you? Are you safe? Are you alone? What's *happening*, Dee?"

Guilt and grief erupted inside her and Deidre had to fight back a rush of tears that blurred her vision and turned the view outside into a hazy, impressionistic painting. "I'm fine. Really. I'm sorry you were worried . . ."

"Worried? I've been *frantic*." There was a long pause and Deidre knew that her mother was pacing the confines of the Oval Office. She always walked when she talked, as if she simply had too much energy to remain still for long.

A rush of static filled the phone briefly, then disappeared. "You can't trace the call, Mom," she said. "Satellite phone."

Finn frowned at her and she shrugged. Not her fault her mother's team would instantly try to set up a trace.

"Then tell me where you are! Your Secret Service detail has been scouring the city for you. Dante's team has been working round the clock."

"Oh, God. Tell Dante I'm sorry I left that way—"

"How *did* you leave? They had the building covered and there were no other exits."

"I can't tell you how."

Her mother muttered something very unpresidential. "It seems you can't tell me much. Did you know your friend Shauna is missing, too?"

"Yes," Deidre said. "She's here with me."

"Deidre, don't lie to me. Is this about the RFW? Are you and Shauna in some kind of trouble?"

Oh, if she only knew. "Mom—"

"Deidre, you can't expect me to simply let it go."

"You have to. For both our sakes, you *have* to." She risked a glance at Finn's steely expression. "I don't have a lot of time, Mom."

"Why not?" Suspicion crept into her mother's voice now. "Are you being held against your will? Is someone there with you right now? Are they *hurting* you? Damn it, Dee, tell me where you are. I'll send help."

"I can't tell you because I don't know where I am. But I'm not in danger—" Okay, she told herself, that was a big fat lie. But she couldn't be specific and why make her mother more nuts than she already was? The point of the call was to reassure her.

Finn's scowl deepened and the microwave dinged, letting them know the food was ready.

"Don't worry about me, okay?"

"Of course I'm worried. Dee—"

"I'll be back as soon as I can. I love you, Mom. Just, don't look for me. Please."

"Dee!"

Her mom's voice still ringing in her ear, Deidre hung up the phone and looked across the table at the man who had—for good or bad—become the very center of her universe. His gray eyes were locked on her and his features were twisted into the scowl she knew so well.

"Thanks," she said and handed the phone back to him.

He tucked the phone into his pocket. "So, did talking to her help?"

"Not really," she said with a sigh. "But at least she knows I'm alive. For now."

"Oh," Finn said, standing up, "you'll stay alive. I'll see to it."

"Because of the Mating."

"That's right." He came around to her side of the table, drew her up from her chair and pointed out, "I kept my part of the deal."

"Yeah," she said, looking up at him. "You did."

"Now it's your turn." He bent his head and took her mouth in a deep, desperate kiss.

Chapter 20

"I want everyone on this, Darius. I know Dee is alive, but she couldn't tell me where she was. I believe someone's holding her prisoner."

Cora paced the confines of the Oval Office, facing for the first time a situation where being the first female president of the United States did not bring her any satisfaction. Because it didn't mean anything without Deidre. She had to find her.

"We couldn't run a trace, ma'am. Something was blocking us."

"I didn't expect you could," Cora told him shortly. Who had Deidre? Why? Was she in danger?

"Dante and his men are following every lead, ma'am," Darius assured her. "We've got people on every bus, train and plane connection in and out of the city."

Cora waved her hand as if dismissing their efforts. Nothing had turned up and nothing *would* turn up. Somehow, Deidre and her friend had simply disappeared. Well, Cora wouldn't stand for it. She would use whatever contacts she had to find her daughter.

"If there are no trails to follow," Cora murmured

thoughtfully, "then maybe we have to make the trail ourselves."

"Excuse me?"

She turned to her aide and smiled coolly. "Nothing for you to worry about."

"I know we'll have news soon, ma'am."

"I'm sure you're right, Darius," she said, forcing a smile she didn't feel. "I'm counting on you. And on Dante and the rest, to bring my daughter home." She turned to stare out the wide window over the neatly landscaped yard and the fence separating her from the people she was elected to serve.

Just past dawn and the first of the protesters were already taking up position along the wrought iron fence. Their signs demanded things like WITCHES RIGHTS! or DEATH TO WITCHES! Occasionally there was even one or two protesting taxes—a refreshing change of pace. But mostly, the people gathered outside the White House to demand that their president do something about the magical threat in the world.

She wondered what they would all think if they knew what she was going through. Turning from the window, she walked to her desk and dismissed Darius with a wave of her hand. When she was alone again, she looked around the room, then bent to unlock the bottom desk drawer. She tugged it open and stared at the satellite phone none of her aides knew about.

Picking it up, she dialed a number and made the only call she could.

Deidre met his kiss with a hunger like she had never known.

She still didn't know what she thought of the whole

Mating issue, but she knew that she wanted Finn more than she had ever wanted anything. That's why she had played her only power card available to make that call to her mother. Because she had known that sooner or later, she would surrender to whatever it was that pulled her and Finn together. She couldn't avoid it. Hell, according to him, this was *destiny*.

She knew nothing was solved. Her life was in turmoil and in danger. If nothing else—that point had been made crystal clear over the last few days. And though the man she was with was capable of great violence, she felt . . . safe with him. As if she *belonged* with him. It was more than emotion. More than lust. It was something that had been bred into her bones—or, as he kept insisting, into her genetic memory.

He was familiar in a sea of strange. He was the touchstone that she turned to even when she was furious, which, let's face it, was fairly often. But he was there. Protecting her. Pushing her. Wanting her—if only temporarily.

Didn't matter. For now, it was enough.

His hands swept up and down her back in fast, all-encompassing strokes. Deidre trembled against him, as every single one of her nerve endings leaped to attention. It felt as if her skin was electrified. Like the static buzz you got outside during a thunderstorm—only this was so much bigger.

"Now," he mumbled against her lips and she nodded, unable to speak. Unable to draw a deep breath. Every gasp of air was taken in and released so quickly, she was nearly light-headed. She had been pushed to the very edges of her endurance over the last few days and taking this leap might just be enough to finish her off. And still, she had to do it. Had to ease the ache she couldn't deny.

He gripped the hem of her shirt and whipped it up and over her head. Her damp hair lay against her bare back, making her shiver. But the heat in his big hands chased that sensation away moments later.

In seconds, he had dispensed with her bra too, tossing it to the kitchen floor beside her shirt. Sunlight was streaming into the room, gilding his face, his body, until he looked like some mystical warrior caught out of time.

And, she thought, that's exactly what he was. Flashes of images moved through her mind, and she saw him astride a white stallion, leather armor stretched across his broad chest, his sword singing through the air. A blink and she saw him in a kilt, atop a misty mountaintop, with a cold Scots wind blowing through his waist-length black hair. In the next instant, he was wearing a sheriff's badge in the Old West, his boots worn and scuffed, his pale gray eyes locked on her as she leaned into him.

Century after century he had been there. Near her. With her. Whenever she needed him, he was there.

Just like now.

His hands cupped her breasts and a throbbing ache began at the juncture of her thighs. Damp heat pooled at her core as the ache blossomed into a pulsing need. "Finn . . ."

"I've waited a long time for this." He dipped his head to take first one hard nipple into his mouth and then the other. She arched into him at the tender assault. Sensations too numerous to count dazzled her system and Deidre let her head fall back and her mind go blank.

She wanted only to *feel*.

No thoughts. No plans. No worries. No recriminations or accusations.

For now, there was only Finn—and his mouth on her skin.

His hot breath dusted across her breasts as he nibbled, licked and suckled her. She swayed, her body's demands taking over as she grabbed at his chest, his heavily muscled arms and held on. She wanted to feel everything.

"Have to touch you," she whispered brokenly and tugged at his shirt. He saved her the trouble. Straightening up, he yanked off his shirt, baring that delectable broad chest to her touch. Her palms swept up and down across what seemed like an acre of sharply defined muscles. His abs were so well cut, he might have been carved from bronze. Her thumbnails flicked across his flat nipples and she watched flames erupt in his eyes.

She gasped as he undid the snap of her jeans and shoved them and her panties down her legs. Deidre stepped out of them gladly, loving the feel of the air on her skin and the sensation of his gaze devouring her. *Magic.* She felt it simmering in the air, gathering like a thick, rich cloud around them, twisting tighter and tighter, in an ever-spinning spiral.

Beneath that fiery stare of his, she felt powerful. Suddenly more elementally *female* than she had ever been before. She knew what she was doing to him. Knew that his desire was pumping as thick and hot as her own and the pleasure in that knowledge rolled through her bloodstream like lava.

"First time's gonna be fast and hard." His voice came in a strained whisper.

Her body nearly erupted at the promise.

"Yes," she said, "now, Finn. Now."

He stripped out of his jeans, lifted her up and set her

down on the counter. The cold jolted her, but not enough to dissuade her. Deidre pulled in breath after breath, trying to ease the frantic pounding of her heart, but it was no use. Her body had a mind of its own now and it wanted Finn. *Needed* Finn.

She looked her fill of him, her gaze sweeping across that amazing chest, down those abs — her eyes widened and she gasped. He was way bigger than she would have thought possible. His erection was huge and hard and though her body hungered for it, her mind was smart enough to wonder if they would even fit.

Clearly, Finn saw the doubt in her eyes as she looked at his thick body. He closed one hand around his shaft and she gasped again as he stroked himself. Liquid heat moved through her in a slow slide that assuaged her doubts and fed her hunger all at the same time.

"We were meant, Dee," he said, stepping closer, shifting his grasp to her hips.

She lifted her gaze to his, licked her lips and swallowed past the tremendous flock of butterflies suddenly erupting in the pit of her stomach. His hands at her hips felt so good. His eyes were fire-filled fog. She wiggled closer to the edge of the counter, bracing her bare feet on the cabinets below. She parted her thighs for him and then reached down and wrapped her fingers around his heavy erection.

He hissed in a breath, but his eyes remained fixed on her. Never wavering. The flames in those pearl gray depths continued to flare. She slid her finger across the flat tip of him, smoothing the drop of moisture she found there over his skin and she watched as a muscle in his jaw flexed and twitched as he fought for control.

But she didn't want him controlled. She wanted him

wild and strong and frantic. She tugged him closer and rubbed the tip of him at her core, shivering at the contact. "Here, Finn. I want you here. Now."

Groaning, he reacted instantly, pushing himself inside her in one long, smooth stroke.

Deidre gasped and stiffened slightly as his much bigger body laid claim to hers. She parted her thighs farther, accepting the full, hard length of him. Her body stretched to accommodate him and in seconds, she was tingling with the incredible sensation of having Finn locked within her.

He moved one hand to their joining and rubbed at her core, finding that one amazing spot that sent jolts of something incredible shooting through her body. She rocked into him, loving the feel of his hands on her, of his body laying claim to hers.

She didn't know now why she'd waited as long as she had. She had wanted him from the beginning. Had sensed that they were headed here, to this moment in time. Doubts, fears, plans and hopes all dissolved in the maelstrom of feelings, settling like a fog over her mind.

He touched her again, his fingers moving over her center as he took her both outside and inside, twisting those sensations into an incredibly electric joining.

He rocked in and out of her heat, creating a delicious friction that kindled fires inside her. Again and again, their bodies parted and joined again. Deidre braced her hands on the countertop and moved with the wild, frantic rhythm he set. Her heartbeat thundered in her chest as spirals of completion tightened inside her.

"Good," he whispered. "So good. Let go, Dee. Let go and let me watch you come."

She shook her head, unwilling to surrender to the climax building within. She wanted more. Wanted this delicious tension to go on forever. Staring into his eyes, she locked her legs at the small of his back and pulled him in tight. She wriggled against him, loving the slide of their bodies moving in tandem. Loving the heat and the blistering fight for control she saw etched on his face.

"Come with me," she said breathlessly, sliding one hand up to cup the back of his neck. "Together. We do this together."

"You're killing me," he muttered.

"Not the plan," she countered on a choked-off laugh.

In and out, over and over, he pushed them both higher with every stroke. She felt the first thundering crash of an orgasm and couldn't hold it off any longer. Overpowered completely, Deidre screamed his name and clung to him, pulling him in tighter, higher.

And still he moved within her body. He kissed her then, taking her mouth as he took the rest of her, with deep, even strokes. His tongue and hers tangled together as their bodies melded and became one. Every time he pulled free of her, Deidre moaned and then celebrated when he returned.

Another orgasm shook her and she tore her mouth from his to gasp for air as her body trembled and shook under the onslaught of too much pleasure all at once. And then as she held him, he came, jolting hard against her, groaning as his body filled hers.

Still tingling, still gasping for air, they remained locked together. The silence was overwhelming. The tick of a clock on the wall sounded like drumbeats. Deidre leaned into him, head at his chest and listened to the quiet within him, as well. No heartbeat pounded in time with her own. There was utter stillness inside his broad chest and just like that, she was brought down from the incredible high of their lovemaking.

Would his heart begin to beat now? And if it did, would he cease to need her? No, she thought sadly, he'd still need her around to help him solve his quest. The mission handed down for generations. Once that was done, *then* he'd leave, just as he'd told her he would.

And, now that they'd Mated, she would be immortal. Great, Deidre thought. An eternity of being alone.

Her heart twisted painfully even as the rest of her body celebrated the hum of satisfaction still settling within her.

Finn wrapped his arms beneath her butt, lifted her off the counter and strode from the room, their bodies still joined as if fused together.

Every step he took sent tiny tremors rippling through her body. Miniorgasms that continually set off nerve endings that felt raw and too sensitive. Deidre laid her head on his shoulder and whispered tightly, "No more, I can't. It's too much."

"It's never too much," he told her, dipping his head to kiss the curve of her neck.

Deidre didn't look up when he kicked a door open and stalked inside. She didn't care where he was taking her. His body was still inside hers. He was still hard and though her mind may insist she'd had enough, her body was unconvinced. Those tiny tremors were sliding into need, awakening a hunger that apparently hadn't been the least bit quenched.

He turned, sat on the edge of the bed, and then lay back, holding her on top of him. His sex stirred deep inside and an answering call roared up within her. She gasped and wiggled her hips, taking him as high and as deep as he could go and then nearly purred at the feeling that caused.

He was watching her, his gray eyes hooded, a slight curve to his luscious mouth. When she licked her lips, his gaze locked on the motion and he pushed his hips up so hard and fast, her knees left the bed.

She laughed and lifted both arms. Scooping her hair up off her back, she let it fall around her shoulders and indulged herself by watching the spark of passion glittering in his eyes.

"I don't think I'm done with you," she said softly.

"Happy to hear it," he said and locked both hands at her hips.

But she was in charge now, and braced her hands on his abs, refusing to move. Let him be tortured a little, she told herself and took a moment to finally look around. It was a plush room. The huge bed was covered with dozens of pillows and a deep red duvet that they were now sprawled across. Bare windows gave a view of the outside world, sun washed, clear and cold.

The walls were filled with framed photos of places from all over the world. Paris. Dublin. Edinburgh. Jerusalem. She saw them all. Recognized them all.

And she knew. Knowledge hit her like a fist. She and Finn had lived together in each of those places throughout time. Tiny scraps of memories played at the edges of her mind. Pieces of lifetimes lived and lost. Jagged shards of a memory shattered and only now being set right.

Stunned, she looked from one framed photo to another and realized that she and Finn had a connection that went beyond sex. Beyond thought. All the way to the soul.

Whether he valued it or not.

Whether he was going to walk away or not.

The connection would remain, she thought, turning her gaze back to meet his.

As it always had.

Chapter 21

Finn looked up at his witch and realized that whatever she was thinking, it wasn't making her happy. And he didn't want anything coming between them right now. He'd waited too long for this joining. This was their moment to feel the magics rise up and encircle them during sex.

Over the centuries, they had been lovers, but though the sex had always been off the charts, it had never been touched by magic—because of that one long-ago night. Because the coven had stripped themselves of their power. Now, it was back and damned if he wanted to waste a minute of it.

There would be time enough later to figure out what their next move was. For right now, he wanted her and he could hardly concentrate on anything beyond the needs of his own dick.

"Stop thinking," he whispered, snatching her attention back from wherever it had gone. "Whatever it is, we'll deal with it. *Later*."

"Later." She nodded, took a deep breath and swiveled her hips, grinding her pelvis against his and the twisting friction that started up had him hissing in a breath between clenched teeth.

"That was amazing," Deidre said. "I had no idea the Mating would be like *that*."

In the morning light, her hair looked like spun gold lying across her shoulders. Her skin was practically glowing and her blue eyes, now clear of whatever had been plaguing her moments ago, looked dazzled by what they'd just shared.

He felt the same. Shaken right down to his battered soul. Even now, his body was stirring inside hers as fresh hunger took him over. If he had a heartbeat it would be crashing against his rib cage right about now.

But she had to know . . . "That wasn't the Mating."

Her eyes widened. "Seriously? That was just sex?"

Finn slid his hands over her thighs, up to her waist and smiled when she sucked in a gulp of air. "I wouldn't say that, either. No, even without the Mating vows, sex magic between us is explosive."

"Good word for it," she agreed and twisted her hips atop him and sighed a little at the movement inside. "But I feel stronger," she said softly. "Just like you said I would when we started the Mating."

"You are stronger and so am I." Finn lifted both hands to cover those gorgeous breasts and thumbed her nipples lazily, enjoying seeing her eyes glaze over and her lips part on another sigh. "Between destined couples, sex magic is powerful on its own. Our powers will grow."

She fought for focus and asked, "Then why bother with the Mating at all?"

"Because there's more with a Mating. New powers awaken inside each of us. And, as I told you, Mating creates an unbreakable bond between us. Links us, body, mind and soul. Makes you immortal. Gives me a heart-beat."

"And what do we have to do to earn all of that?"

He dropped his hands from her breasts and laid them on her thighs as he met her gaze steadily. "We join hands and repeat the Mating words to each other. When we've finished, we each feel the heat of the Mating brand burning itself into our bodies."

"Brand?"

He shrugged. "Think of it as a tattoo. It's born of your power and it etches itself onto both of us, showing the world we're a Mated pair. At the end of thirty days, if our quest is successful, the brand becomes permanent." He looked into her eyes and felt the compulsion to Mate with her as he'd never felt it before and Finn fought against the urge. "Mating is much more than sex, Deidre. Basically, we take a vow of loyalty to each other. To trust each other. To let go of the past and accept the future."

She sat atop him, perfectly still. His words hung in the room like a damn banner that neither of them wanted to notice.

"Well, that's the problem isn't it?" she asked and he couldn't help noticing that they were in a weird kind of situation to be having this conversation. "We *don't* trust each other."

He didn't say anything because what *could* he say? Finn knew she didn't trust him and why the hell should she? Her memories were too new to make him anything more than a semistranger who'd introduced her into a world that mostly wanted her dead.

And when her memories *did* return in full, he told himself, she'd have reason not to trust him. Even he didn't want to remember why. Because he'd spent more than eight hundred years trying to expunge that memory from his mind—and had failed.

She was still looking at him and a part of Finn wanted nothing more than to Mate with her now. To take the ancient vows. To feel the burn of her witch tattoo embedding itself in his chest. To be able to stand beside his brothers and their Mates. For him and Deidre to take their rightful place in Haven.

But Haven wasn't in their future. He wasn't going to offer her everything only to have her turn her back on him. Again.

In their shared past, Deidre had never let him all the way in. She'd held a part of herself back from him. Always. As if allowing herself to *need* him would somehow make her smaller. Then, the one night she really *had* needed him . . .

No. He wouldn't let her in that deep again. Her loss had left him hollowed out and empty for too many centuries to endure it once more. He would never be that vulnerable to someone again.

She rocked her hips on his and his dick jerked inside her. If she had been trying to get his attention, that move managed it.

"New powers," she mused, trailing one fingertip across his abdomen. The heat of her touch seemed to sear his skin. "What kind?"

He managed a shrug. "Differs for everyone. Though my Mated brothers tell me there's a mental link between them and their Mates."

"Reading minds?"

He shook his head. "Catching thoughts. Which we could probably do if we tried."

"Okay . . . what else?"

"What does it matter?" he countered.

"Good point." She leaned forward, resting her palms on his chest. Her breasts swayed with the movement and damn near hypnotized Finn. Deidre had always had that affect on him. She was talking though, so he made sure to listen.

"So, would the sex magic alone make us strong enough to be able to finish this mission you keep talking about?"

He frowned, but tore his gaze away from those delectable breasts long enough to think about it. Nowhere was it written they *must* Mate. The point was to open her memories, grow her magic and find the damned Artifact. Mating would help with that, but if they could manage without it . . .

Eyes narrowed on her, he said, "Sex magic will open your powers and yeah, make us stronger. We'd have to work harder to open your memories—"

"Not looking forward to that."

"And sex magic alone won't make you immortal. You need the Mating for that."

She shrugged, and slid her hands down across his abs. "Or your heartbeat?"

His hands tightened on her hips, holding her still when she began rocking again. "Don't need one. Told you that."

"So basically," she said, "neither one of us wants to do the Mate thing, right? So if we don't *need* it, why do it?"

It went against everything they had been striving toward for centuries. His instinctive urge to claim her as Mate was scorching his insides, but he knew how to fight. He could conquer those compulsions. The others would never understand, but Finn didn't really care what they thought of him anyway. This was between him and Deidre. The woman he had waited eons for. And whatever decision they made would be *their* choice and no one else's.

"Works for me." But then he would have agreed to anything when his witch was grinding against him, driving his dick higher and higher inside her.

The heat. The slick, tight feel of her surrounding him. Every cell in his body responded to her on so many different levels he couldn't measure them all. His magic kindled inside him and as she began to ride him, he called on the flames that were his soul, the heart of him, letting it engulf both him and Deidre.

She yelped, startled, and he felt the clench of her muscles. He grinned up at her. "Surprise."

Deidre frantically watched the flames as they danced across her skin, swarming up and down over their bodies like a living cloak. "We're on *fire*."

"And it can't hurt you," he said, smiling as she relaxed into the flames, raising her arms to watch the fire writhe sensuously on her skin. "It will only . . . enhance our magic."

She shook her head, staring from him to the flames, blue, red, orange and green, dancing across their joined bodies, delivering heat and a wicked licking sensation. "It's . . ." She sighed a little, then gasped as the flames danced lower, caressing the spot where their bodies were locked together. "Oh, that's really good . . ."

He shut off the flames in a wink and before she could show her surprise again, he flipped her onto the mattress. Pulling free of her body briefly, he rolled her over until she was facedown on the bed. She pushed herself up onto her elbows and looked back at him through a curtain of silky hair. "Finn?"

"My turn." He knelt behind her, and lifted her hips, his big hands kneading the soft flesh of her behind until she was practically humming in anticipation and pure pleasure.

She wiggled her butt into his touch and gasped when he dropped one hand to her center. His fingers stroked her damp heat, wrenching a moan from her throat as she dropped her head to the mattress. Spreading her legs farther apart, Finn took a long moment to look his fill of her. His erection throbbed with need as his gaze moved over her luscious butt and the hot, sweet core of her.

"Finn, *please . . .*"

"Oh, yeah, Dee." He drove himself into her heat with one long thrust that seated him to the hilt inside her. The glory of it tore a deep, rumbling groan from him. This was what he wanted. What they both wanted and needed. Nothing beyond this moment. Fuck the Mating. They would make do with what they already shared. They would relish it. Revel in it. Take each other as many times as necessary to accomplish what they must.

And sex magic, he knew, would only get better and better every time they came together.

Deidre moaned again and pushed back into him, taking him even deeper than she had before. Finn felt the rush of magic and sensation that erupted. It was like nothing he'd ever experienced before. Hell, he'd been with Deidre many times over the eons, but now was different.

Now was their time. Even without making the Mating vows, the power charging through them was unmistakable.

His hands came down on her hips, holding her steady as he continued to plunder her body. Her soft moans and sighs accompanied the slap of flesh on flesh. Sunlight lay across the bed and them like a blessing as he felt her climax roar through her. Her inner muscles clamped down around him, squeezing, driving him higher and higher as she made that inevitable climb that would end with an explosion of sensation. She shrieked his name, grabbed fistfuls of the red duvet beneath her and rocked her hips to match the frantic rhythm pulsing between them.

In a blinding flash, Finn's release claimed him. He held nothing back. Gave himself over completely to what exploded inside him. The shattering jolt of the orgasm shot from the base of his spine straight up to practically blow off the top of his head.

When it was at last over, he slipped free of her body and lowered her to the bed, where she groaned again, then stretched languorously, making happy little sounds in the back of her throat. "That was . . ."

"Yeah," he agreed, stretching out alongside her, his body, for the moment, content. "Makes you wonder how much better the Mating sex is."

She turned her head to look at him. "Guess we won't find that out."

"No, guess not." His gaze moved over her, her silky skin luminescent in the sunlight, her blond hair tangled and lying across her shoulders and breasts like a soft, golden curtain.

And a part of him wondered if they were making a mistake.

Chapter 22

Dante Dimenticato stared up at Deidre Sterling's apartment building and wondered, for the hundredth time in the last few days, just where in the hell she was. He'd searched every inch of this block several times. He'd hunted for clues, talked to everyone in every damn building on the street and there was simply no trace of her.

She had never returned home from her friend Shauna Jackson's apartment the night she went missing. Which meant she'd either willingly gone somewhere else, leaving behind everything she owned—or she'd been *taken*.

As a Secret Service agent, his main purpose in life was to protect the president and the first family. Deidre *was* the first family and her going missing on his watch was turning out to be a damn nightmare.

An old woman passed him on the sidewalk and gave him a wide berth as she went. Her rheumy gaze locked on him warily and he took a step back, further distancing himself from her to ease the fear he felt coming from her.

He knew what the woman saw when she looked at

him. Short black hair, dark sunglasses. With a hard jaw and broad shoulders, he stood just under six feet four and knew that in his suit and long, black overcoat, he looked damned intimidating. That was the point, though he didn't enjoy scaring old ladies.

Dante glanced over his shoulder at the small park that sat opposite Deidre's town house in the Capitol Hill neighborhood. The grass was brown, the trees nearly naked and the whole area looked as grim as it possibly could on a cold November morning. None of the usual homeless was around and he made a mental note to hunt for them later. Maybe one of them had seen something.

The mic in his ear bristled briefly with static and he reached up to touch it. "This is Dante. What've you got?"

"Squat." Tim Hogan's voice came through loud and clear. "Dante, how long are we gonna search the same four-block radius? Snowflake's gone. Nobody saw her leave. Nobody's seen her since. We're finding *nothing*."

Irritation sparked. "Then we keep looking till we do," he said, his voice a low throb of barely restrained anger. He wasn't going back to the White House to report another day's failure. Somewhere, there was someone who had seen something. And Dante would find them.

"I'm making another pass through the apartment."

"Good," Tim said snidely. "'Cuz the first three times we might have missed a clue."

Dante ignored that. "You head over to the Starbucks where Snowflake's friend worked again. Ask questions. Get people to talk. When I leave here, I'm heading for Shauna's apartment to give it another look, too."

"Right. Fine." A pause and then Tim asked, "What do you think of the rumors?"

"What rumors?"

An icy wind scuttled across the park, rattling tree limbs as it headed straight for Dante. The sky was clear and the sun was doing all it could to beat the November cold into submission, but it was a losing battle as winter stealthily crept up on the city.

"You know what rumors. People are starting to wonder if Snowflake's a—you know."

Witch. At least Hogan was smart enough not to use that word over an open com-channel. There were plenty of people out there skilled enough to tap into any supposedly secure communication system.

"Forget the damn rumors," he said sharply, wanting to cut short all talk like that. "We've got a job to do and we do it. Simple. Understood?"

"Got it. Out."

When the mic went silent, he shifted his gaze back to Deidre's building and headed for the entrance.

The doorman didn't even look at his ID anymore, which was both good and bad. He hated like hell wasting time proving his identity to the same man over and over, but he didn't like seeing security get lax, either. Still, not a problem to address this morning. He headed for the bank of elevators, then stepped into one and rode it to Deidre's floor.

Dante had a key to her town house. Because he was head of her security team, it was imperative that he be able to get to her in case of an emergency. Which, he told himself as he unlocked the door and stepped inside, pretty much described what was happening *now*.

He stepped inside, his gaze going first to the large white tiled hearth that stood cold and empty. The air had that stale feeling a room took on when no one had been around to stir it. Desolation rang inside the neat, completely feminine space. A faint hint of cinnamon hung in the stillness and outside, the wind sighed against the windowpanes, sounding almost mournful.

Great. He didn't need to get poetic. What he needed was to get some answers.

"Where the hell are you, Deidre?" Dante muttered aloud, hoping to dispel the sense of abandonment in the place.

He stalked across the room, a big man in a too-small space, and stopped at the window. There, he peeled back the curtains and looked down on a stark landscape.

Dante ground his teeth together in frustration. He had wanted to give Snowflake a break. Give her a little room. So he had backed off the night she went to Shauna's place—to give the two women a chance to talk. To get out from under the constant glare of Deidre's security team.

A finger of concern jabbed at his heart. He dropped the curtains into place again, then turned to face the empty room. Wherever she was, he hoped to hell Deidre was safe. Because if she wasn't, it would be all his fault.

"I've never had the chance to beat the crap out of a president's daughter."

"Then today's your lucky day," Deidre said, smiling. She circled her opponent, keeping her gaze fixed to his every movement. Corey Davis was fast, smooth and all too eager to prove to Finn that Deidre didn't belong in their happy little band of guerrilla fighters.

A week since the kidnapping. They'd been back in the tunnels for a couple of days now and the cabin in Maine was nothing more than a hazy memory. She almost laughed as that thought skittered through her mind. After all, she had way too many memories to deal with already. Did she really need to be making new ones?

Corey took a swing and Deidre ducked, his right fist plowing past the spot where her head had been. It was close. She felt the fan of the breeze slide past her face.

"Lucky," he said.

And magic, she thought but didn't bother saying. Just as Finn had told her, the sex magic was affecting her. She was stronger, faster and power bubbled in her veins. She felt it constantly, a just-under-the-skin buzz that had become as second nature to her as the color of her own eyes.

She spared a quick look at the small crowd surrounding them in the training chamber. Only Shauna and Joe were smiling. The others still didn't trust her.

Corey stepped to one side, jolted back and threw a punch at her midsection. Deidre turned her concentration back on the fight in time to make a fast dodge to the right. His fist caught her a glancing blow rather than a center hit. She smiled.

"I'll take luck," she told him and dropped, swinging her right leg out and kicking him behind his knee. Instantly, his leg buckled and he went down. Deidre jumped to her feet in an instant, her smile growing wider. "Looks like the president's daughter is cleaning your clock."

Joe laughed and Corey threw the man a dirty look before he got up off the floor and this time, watched her more warily. As if he'd been petting a puppy only to have it bite off one of his fingers, he was going to be more careful now.

From the corner of her eye, Dee caught money changing hands. They were betting on her. Again. According to

Joe and Shauna, they had been cleaning up taking money from the rest of the team who obviously considered Deidre a lightweight.

After three days of training, fighting anyone who called her out just to prove she could defend herself, they obviously *still* didn't believe in her. Well, she was used to that. Her whole life, people had dismissed her. Or worse yet, overlooked her entirely. It was the blond hair, blue eyes, big boobs thing, she supposed. They expected a woman shaped like a Barbie doll to actually *be* a Barbie doll.

Deidre was done with being discarded out of hand. She would earn her way into this group. Prove to Finn and all of the rest of them that she was more than her *destiny*.

She smiled and changed direction unexpectedly, slipping behind Corey and slapping one hand to the center of his back before darting out of reach again.

"Hah!" Joe called out and took a dollar bill from one of the other spectators. "She got you that time, Corey. If she'd had a knife, you'd be dead."

"Yeah?" He never took his eyes off Deidre, but managed to sneer, "And if I had boobs, I'd be my sister."

"And ugly!" Shauna's comment brought hoots of laughter that reddened Corey's cheeks and narrowed his eyes. He was pissed now and Deidre knew she could take him. Anger in a fight shattered concentration. Pushed people into making stupid mistakes. All of those self-defense classes she had taken over the years were finally paying off. She could hear her instructors even now . . . *Keep a tight rein on emotions. Your fear and anger will give your enemy an advantage you don't want him to have.*

Deidre kept that thought in her mind as Corey made a couple of wide swings, then jumped and kicked out one leg at her stomach. She slipped past that maneuver and felt pride well up inside. Oh, she wasn't as good a fighter as most of the members of the WLF—but clearly, she could hold her own. And if anyone tried to pull a gun or a knife on her, she could use magic to whip the weapons out of their hands.

Frustrated that he hadn't beaten her down in the first minute, Corey rushed her, beefy arms up to capture her, the expression on his face pure fury. Deidre had only a second to decide how to handle it and went with her gut.

When he was close enough, she grabbed hold of his shirt and went over backward. She saw surprise flash in his eyes as she planted both feet in his stomach and pushed, flinging him over her head as she fell back. He landed with a crash and rolled up against the tunnel wall. Deidre ended her move with a somersault and stood up, fists raised, feet planted, waiting to see if he'd get up and try it again.

Staring up at her, he shook his head and said wryly, "Chill out, rich-witch. I'm done."

Deidre grinned. Even the insult didn't hurt because she'd beaten him.

From the floor, Corey added, "For *today*. I'll still take you down eventually."

"Sure you will." Joe laughed and walked up to Deidre. Grabbing one of her hands, he briefly held it high. "Winner and still champion."

She smiled up at him, glad she at least had his and Shauna's support. A reluctant smattering of applause rose up and was swallowed by the cold, dank walls surrounding them. Then the team drifted apart and Deidre's gaze swept the entire room.

"He's not here," Joe said, chuckling as Corey pushed himself to his feet and staggered out into the tunnels.

"What?" Deidre looked at him.

"Finn. He's not here."

And hadn't been since early morning when he'd burst into flames and flashed out of the bed they shared in the crystal-studded chamber. She hated to admit, even to herself, that she actually *missed* him.

Maybe it was Stockholm syndrome, Deidre thought hopefully. Maybe since being kidnapped and chased and going on that refugee run, she'd begun to sympathize with Finn and the rest of his group. But even as she considered it, she knew it wasn't true.

It was the man himself. Or Eternal or whatever the hell he was. Even when she fought the attraction, she was drawn to Finn inexorably. She felt the connection between them and it was growing by the day. Heck, by the *hour*. She could sense him when he was close and experienced a near physical ache when he wasn't.

Was it only the sex magic drawing them together? She didn't think so, though the sex really *was* magic, Deidre told herself with an inward smile. No, it was more than that. And more than the memories of lives spent with him that kept erupting unheralded into her mind.

It was, quite simply, *Finn*. He kept this little band of fighters together with the force of his own personality. He was charismatic as hell despite the brusque rudeness he seemed to be known for. He was also strong, fearless and when he looked at her, Deidre felt him staring right down into her soul. It didn't seem to matter that she knew he only wanted to use her. Somehow he felt different from anyone else she had ever known. She . . . cared for him and didn't know how to—or even if she wanted to—stop.

"Deidre?" Joe asked. "You okay?"

"Yeah, I'm fine. Just sort of zoned out. Sorry. So where is Finn?"

"Who knows?" Joe winked at her. "Off saving witches or blowing up BOW headquarters." He shrugged and grinned. "Man made of fire? No telling where he went."

"You seem awful at ease with that," she said, looking at Finn's second-in-command.

"With the things I've seen in my life," Joe mused as he folded up the practice mat and stored it against the wall. "A man made of fire hardly makes the top ten."

Deidre walked across the room, snagged a bottle of water and chugged half of it before looking back at him again. In spare moves, Joe set the room to rights in a few minutes. Deidre had spent a lot of time over the last few days in this particular room off the main tunnel. Like a well-equipped gym, the stone chamber boasted padded training mats, weights, treadmills . . . everything a well-equipped militia team needed to stay in shape.

And she'd made use of all of it.

Joe had even given her a few lessons himself.

"Why are you here, Joe?"

He looked over his shoulder at her and didn't even pretend to misunderstand the question. Straightening up, he turned to face her and stuffed both hands into his jeans pockets. "Short answer?"

She laughed and sat down on one of the folded mats, leaning her back against the wall. "You and Finn with your 'short answers.' You don't have time to actually talk?"

"Not lately," he admitted and strolled across the room to snag a bottle of water himself. Once he had it, he sat on a nearby rock outcropping and took a long drink. "But that's not the only reason for keeping things brief, Dee. You give too much information to the wrong person . . ."

True. These days, it didn't pay to be careless. "Okay, but who am I going to tell? Finn never lets me out of these tunnels and where would I go if I managed to *get* topside?"

"Good point." He tipped his water bottle at her in salute. "Okay, long version then." Leaning back against the rock wall, he stretched out his legs and crossed his booted feet at the ankle.

"I went into the Marines straight from college. Made it through SEAL training and then shipped out." His features tightened and his eyes took on a faraway look as he said, "I did a couple of tours, then got out when things started getting bad at home."

"The war on witches you mean."

"Yeah." He studied the label on the water bottle as if looking for something to say. "See, sounds corny, but my dad raised me to believe in service to country." He lifted his gaze and stared into her eyes. His voice was soft, but filled with a kind of quiet resolve. "And that's what I'm doing. In my own way. This isn't the country I grew up in. We don't imprison innocent people. Or execute women on the suspicion of wrongdoing. That's not *us*. When rule of law no longer applies . . . people have to stand up. However they can."

Deidre's admiration for the normally reticent man skyrocketed. He had risked everything by joining Finn's group. His reputation, his freedom, his *life*. Because if he were found, no doubt those in charge would make an example of a Navy SEAL gone wrong.

Smiling at him, she asked, "How did you meet Finn?"

Tension broken, he laughed, then said, "I was running an op in Boston three years ago. Had a few of my old Marine buddies with me, raiding a prison to free some witches. Imagine my surprise to find Finn already there. He had half the cells opened and he was by himself." Shaking his head in memory, he said, "Impressed hell outta me, I've got to say. Anyway, we got the witches out and my friends and I just stayed with Finn."

Just as she had. Though she hadn't had much choice in the whole thing. "Where are your friends now?"

His smile faded. "A couple are dead. The others are leading small groups like this one. We split up our defenses. Finn wanted guys with some military training to be in charge." He shrugged. "And if we're divided into several groups, the chances of anyone wiping out *all* of us seriously drop."

She got a chill at those quietly spoken words. How sad was it that death was accepted as a matter of course? She remembered Nora, smiling one moment, dead the next and wondered how anyone was supposed to live a normal life under these circumstances. Then, she wondered if she would *ever* live a normal life again.

There had been too many changes in her life already, Deidre thought. She was a witch now and her powers were growing steadily every day. She was living with a group of what the world considered terrorists and actually training to become one of them.

No, normal wasn't even in her vocabulary anymore.

From somewhere down the tunnel, laughter came in a soft ripple, reminding her that though her life was different now, it still went on. Torchlight shone on the walls, sending shadows skittering around the room. Silence fell between them for a long minute or two before Deidre finally asked, "What does your father think of what you do?"

Joe sighed. "He understands. Wishes it wasn't necessary. But he gets it."

Frowning just a bit, Deidre said, "It's nice that you can talk to him."

"Missing your mom?"

Caught, she looked up at him and gave him a rueful smile. "Yeah. I talked to her a few days ago, but . . ."

"I know how you feel." Joe drew up his knees, then braced his elbows on his thighs. Cupping the water bottle between his palms, he added, "But you can't tell her any of this, Dee."

She wanted to argue, but couldn't, since she knew he was right. As was Finn. Funny that Joe and Finn agreed on this subject but it was only Finn she resented for it. "I know."

"It's hard, but necessary." He stood up, then held out a hand to her. She took it and he pulled her to her feet. "If she knew the truth, it could endanger her."

"True," she said and let her gaze sweep around the stone walls that had become so familiar to her. "Doesn't make it any easier, though."

He chuckled and walked toward the curved archway leading to the main tunnel. "Nothing about this is easy, Dee." He paused and looked back at her. "But it's worth it."

She hoped so.

Chapter 23

"That's as close as we can get you," Teresa said, stabbing her index finger at a point on the map.

Rune stared down at the spot Teresa indicated, then looked up at Torin. "Close to Brindisi."

He nodded and dropped an arm around Shea's shoulders. Pulling her in tight to his side, he stroked one hand up and down her arm. "Still a big section of sea to search."

"Smaller than it was," Damyn murmured.

"It's as close as we could get without a focus—something that belonged to Egan. Combining our power," Mairi said, with a smile at her sister-witches, "we were able to narrow the search some. But without a physical connection to our missing Eternal . . ."

"This is great." Damyn came up behind his Mate and wrapped his arms around her waist. "You've all managed to do the impossible. Because of you three, Egan has a chance now."

"You'll find him," Mairi said, staring at the map as if she was once again magically seeing Egan, trapped in his cage at the bottom of the ocean.

"Damn straight we will," Rune pledged.

"Then what?" Everyone turned to look at Shea. "I mean yes, of course we save Egan. But what happens after that? If Kellyn is his Mate and she did trap him, then—"

"We have to find out why," Teresa said and everyone's gaze shifted to her. "While you guys go for Egan, the three of us will work a spell to find out what's driving Kellyn. Why she did this. And *how*."

Mairi nodded. "Agreed." She looked up at her Eternal and smiled. "You three find him, bring him home. We'll find the way to set this right."

The first three witches of the reborn coven looked at each other and each pledged silently to bring their sister-witch to justice. Whatever it took.

Finn flashed into the chamber he shared with Deidre and instantly *sensed* that she wasn't there. Like the crystal-studded chamber he had built for her, this room too, farther along the tunnels for the sake of privacy, boasted magical enhancements. From crystals on the walls and hanging sage bundles to etchings of power symbols carved into the rocks. There was also a damned big bed he'd flashed in down here several years ago. And at the moment, that bed was empty. Hell, it was the middle of the night. Where could she be?

He was raw and frustrated and more than a little on edge. Topside, he'd put in a call to Rune only to discover that his brother Eternals were about to leave on the search for Egan. While *he* was stuck in DC with a witch who was both his Mate—and not.

The sex magic was blistering between them and he'd sensed the changes in Deidre as her innate powers built and matured. But it was taking too long.

He knew damn well they had to Mate for her magic to erupt completely. For her to have access to everything she would no doubt need before this was finished.

It wasn't just that, though. Finn's every instinct screamed at him to claim her. To make her, at last, *his*. Having her so near and yet so far away was driving him a little insane. He'd waited centuries for this. He wanted her—just as he always had, only now that want ran even deeper. In this lifetime, Deidre was a hardheaded, proud, strong woman and just being around her activated every damn one of his protective instincts.

Eight hundred years had passed and now that their time was here, they were both pulling back from what was needed.

"Makes no damn sense at all," he muttered, scraping one hand across his face.

"What doesn't?"

He whirled around to see Deidre, standing in the arched entrance. Behind her, firelight shifted plaintively in the tunnels, gilding her silhouette with a bright light that acted like a damn homing beacon for him. Everything in him was trained on her and when she stepped into the room, his dick stood up and cheered.

"What?"

"You said something doesn't make sense." She walked across the room to the heavy trunk at the foot of the bed and opened it. "What doesn't?" Then she laughed and said, "Cancel that. What *does* make sense lately? Shorter list."

He ignored the banter. "Where were you?"

She glanced at him over her shoulder. "Out dancing."

"Funny."

"Well seriously, Finn, where would I have been except

somewhere along the length of this tunnel?" She shook
her head and bent over the trunk, rummaging through the
clothing he had gone to her place to bring back for her.
"And just how long are these tunnels anyway? I must have
walked miles today with Shauna. She was showing me all
of the storage chambers and then the different routes to
different places in DC and if I had to find my way by myself, I'd be lost forever in this freaking labyrinth . . ."

Finn had stopped listening to her the moment his
gaze dropped to the curve of her behind, nicely defined
by the faded denim of her jeans. Hunger roared inside
him and Finn didn't even bother trying to smother it. Sex
magic would help open her mind to her powers and her
memories. The fact that he simply *wanted* her was just an
added bonus.

He flashed across the room, not wanting to waste any
time. Bending low, he scooped her up in his arms and
when she feebly protested, he took her mouth. Desire
quickened inside her instantly. She wrapped her arms
around his neck and parted her lips to welcome him inside. Their tongues met in a frenzied dance that was familiar and yet new, each time.

Finn tasted cinnamon and woman and witch. And
that heady mix blended in his brain, then headed straight
south. "Gotta have you."

"Yes," she whispered, tearing her mouth free to nibble at his neck. Lips and tongue and teeth moved over
his skin, sending jolts of pleasure ricocheting through his
system.

Magic churned in the air around them, like the bubbles in champagne, constantly rising to the surface.
Power filled the crystals in the walls and reverberated
around the room. Like a resonance chamber, the magics

fed on themselves, burning brighter, stronger, as the sex magic ramped up and kicked simple desire into the realm of raw need.

Finn carried her to the bed and dropped her onto the mattress. He paused only long enough to wave one hand across the doorway, putting up a magical shield that ensured their privacy before turning back to look at Deidre. Her blond hair spilled out around her on the midnight blue duvet and looked like spun gold dust. She licked her lips in anticipation and her breath came in short, sharp gasps. Lifting her hips, she rocked with an internal need only he could fulfill and Finn didn't want to waste another moment.

He snapped his fingers and his clothes were gone in a wink. She frowned up at him. "When do I learn how to do that?"

"You already know how."

"If I did, I'd be naked," she pointed out.

"Draw on your magic," he ordered and heard the tautness in his own voice.

She licked her lips. "How?"

"*Think* yourself naked."

Deidre laughed and the sound filled the crystal-studded room, rippling off the walls to slap back at him with a brush of something almost tender. But he didn't want tender. He just *wanted*.

Steeling himself, he fisted his hands at his sides and silently told his dick to hold on a damn minute. He watched her as she closed her eyes, concentrated, and a moment later, he smiled at her glorious nudity.

"Hah! I did it!" Immensely pleased with herself, Deidre slid her hands up and down her naked body, as if assuring herself that it had actually worked.

Watching her touch herself was the most erotic thing he'd ever seen. Her palms scooped up over her abdomen and to her breasts and everything in Finn stilled. She must have sensed what he was feeling because she immediately shifted the movement of her hands into something slow and seductive. Smiling up at him, she wriggled farther back on the huge bed and cupped her own breasts, thumbs and forefingers tweaking at her nipples.

Finn swallowed hard, but couldn't look away. Those luscious breasts with their rigid pink tips were calling to him—but watching her caress them was mesmerizing. She arched her back and sighed and he gritted his teeth in response.

Over the last few days, Deidre had surprised him with her blatant sexuality. Now that they had made their deal, to avoid Mating but open her memories with sex magic, she had thrown herself into it with staggering enthusiasm.

She was open and eager to try anything and when they came together, every time it rocked his world. She was tormenting him and loving it. And she was damn good at it, too.

"Pleasure yourself," he said, those two words grinding out of his throat roughly as if they'd scraped across broken glass. "I want to watch you."

The scent of cinnamon thickened in the air as her witch power gathered inside her and spilled from her every pore. Every time they came together her power grew. It was a heady aroma, enough to make Finn nearly groan with need.

"Then watch me," she whispered with a smile. Parting her legs, she braced her feet on the bed. Lazily, she slid her right hand down the length of her body until she reached the thatch of blond curls at the juncture of her thighs. Finn hissed in a breath and held it as she dipped her fingers lower, lower. She dropped her left hand down to her center as well, holding herself open for her own touch.

Then finally, she stroked her core and her hips lifted off the bed in response. She tipped her head back into the mattress and sighed as she smoothed the tip of one finger across the swollen bud at her center. He swayed in place and his dick turned to concrete.

"It feels good," she whispered, opening her eyes to meet his gaze, "but it's *much* better with you."

Finn willed himself to stay in place. As if there was a chain around him, holding him to that one spot. His dick ached like nothing he'd ever felt before and everything in him demanded that he take her. Take her *now*. But damned if he wanted this to end just yet.

"More," he ground out, silently congratulating himself on getting his voice to work at all.

"No," she said, "now I want *you*." She rolled over onto her stomach and nearly purred as the cool slide of the silk hit her heated skin.

Damn. He muffled the groan building in his throat as he watched her go up on her knees and wiggle that beautiful behind at him. Deidre looked back at him through a fall of golden hair and whispered, "I want you, Finn. I want you so badly . . ."

"Enough." He practically jumped onto the bed, kneeled behind her and shoved his body deep into hers.

That first, incredible stroke fired them both. She moaned and the soft sounds spilling from her enflamed him. He took her hard and fast, his hips pistoning against hers. She moved into him, arching her back, working her hips, all to take him deeper, higher. There were no soft, languorous touches. No gentle words or slow, mesmerizing foreplay. There was only hunger and the urge to feed it. It was frantic, frenzied and powerful.

They moved in tandem, each of them knowing what the other needed, wanted.

Magic pulsed in the air around them, a froth of power that spilled over their bodies and slipped into their souls. The crystals on the walls hummed louder in reaction. Power sang through Finn's veins and he knew Deidre was feeling it as well. Sex magic was practically devouring them and he couldn't help wondering what it would be like to Mate with her. To feel the burn of the tattoo at the moment of release.

Then Deidre groaned again, grabbed hold of the duvet and held on and Finn stopped thinking. Their combined gasps and sighs filled the quiet air of the chamber as they propelled each other to the staggering climax they knew was waiting for them.

Deidre crested first. She shouted his name and Finn felt her muscles contract around him and that was enough to push him over the edge. He emptied himself into her with a taut groan, and when it was at last finished, Finn lay down on the bed and pulled her in beside him.

Tucking her close, he wrapped his arms around her and listened to her soft, easy breaths as she dropped into sleep, her head on his chest. He snapped his fingers again and the torchlight winked out.

Then Finn lay quietly in the darkness, feeling the beat of her heart echo within his empty chest.

Chapter 24

"Is it day or night?" Deidre asked several days later, sliding the steel of a sharpening rod along the edge of a dagger. The ring of metal whispered rhythmically as she worked. Funny, she thought, how accustomed to this life she already was. Two weeks ago, she wouldn't have had a clue how to freshen the edge on a dagger. Now . . .

"Day," Shauna told her with a half grin. "You should know since you spent all of last night lighting up Finn's world."

Deidre stopped what she was doing and the sudden silence in the room was startling. Appalled, she just stared at her friend. "Excuse me?"

"What?" Shauna laughed, then winced as her injured shoulder gave a twinge. "You think just because your chamber is far away from the rest of us we don't hear anything? Hello? Shrieks of joy carry and tunnels make excellent echo chambers."

"Fabulous." Now that she knew people could *hear* her having sex, Deidre would be more careful about— Oh, no she wouldn't, she thought wryly. What she'd have to do is remember to stuff a pillow over her face or something to muffle her shouts. Because there was no way she could control herself when Finn was touching her. He was like a match to her stick of dynamite and when the two of them came together, it was beyond explosive.

She smiled a little in memory of just how many "explosions" she'd had the night before.

"Okay, now I'm jealous," Shauna muttered. "That smile on your face is really making me miss Max."

Deidre grinned. "Sorry. Well, sort of," she added, unrepentant. "How is Max?"

Shauna's boyfriend, Max, owned a local gym and looked like an advertisement for clean living and weight lifting. The man's only indulgence was a once-daily latte, which is how he had met Shauna in the first place. They'd been together nearly a year and the shine in her friend's eyes told Deidre that the spark between them was still going strong.

"Fine, I guess," Shauna told her with a little sigh. "I haven't seen him in a couple of weeks. He was on a business trip the week before we made that raid on the jail and since then, I've been kind of . . ." She shrugged, then winced again. "I can't go see him until this wound is healed, though, so I've been doing healing spells every night trying to speed things along—"

"I can help if you want." Not that she knew what to do, but Deidre figured she should learn as much about magic as she possibly could.

Shauna grinned. "That'd be great, thanks. We can do a spell when we've finished cleaning the weapons."

Deidre looked around the well-stocked armory. "That could take a while."

"We don't have to do them all. Just the ones most recently used." She looked down the barrel of the sawed-off shotgun she had been working on and nodded, pleased.

"Does Max know you're a witch?"

"Yeah." She smiled a little, dipping her head as if suddenly shy, which was so not like Shauna at all. "He saw me using magic once—stupid, really. Lighting candles before our dinner date. He got there early and—" She shrugged. "At first, I was freaked, but Max was great. Said he loved a powerful woman and it gave him a charge, knowing that I was a witch. He's kept my secret all this time."

What would that be like? Deidre wondered. To have someone know you for who and what you really were and love you anyway? She'd never really had that, she realized. Even her mother's love came with conditions. That Deidre be the "good" daughter. Funny, but since being trapped in the tunnels, Deidre had been more "free" than she ever had been in her life before. No one down here had expectations of her. In fact, most of them still didn't like or trust her. But she didn't have to put on a show in the tunnels. She didn't have to worry about everything she said. Down here, she was just one more refugee from the city above.

Except to Finn, of course. To Finn, she was still a means to an end. He was using her, yes. But Deidre was fair enough to admit that she was using him, too.

Shauna sighed again, laid the clean gun across her lap and said, "I really need to see Max soon. I'm starting to crave him, if you know what I mean. And never mind. You *do* know." Smiling, she snapped the now clean shotgun closed, laid it down and reached for the next weapon on her to-be-cleaned list. Expertly, she ejected the clip of an automatic pistol, then began breaking it down and laying the pieces out on a clean cloth.

"Not easy being a prisoner and cut off from everyone, is it?" Deidre asked, only half joking.

"You're not a prisoner, Dee." Shauna stopped what she was doing to look at her. "And neither am I. It's just . . . safer down here right now. For me, there's the whole bullet wound in my shoulder thing that I can't explain. I don't want Max knowing that I was on that raid. Too much information will just be dangerous for him. For you, the whole damn world is on the lookout for you. Hell, I can't even go back to my job at Starbucks—everyone knows you and I were together the night you 'disappeared.'"

Guilt gnawed at her. For the last few days, all Deidre had been able to think was how much all of this had changed *her* life. How much was being asked of *her*. Not once had she thought about the ramifications for everyone else in these tunnels. Not even her best friend. "Oh, Shauna. I'm sorry."

"It's okay. This is more important than stirring up a Frappuccino for morning commuters." She sighed and looked down, the sharp movement sending the silver hoops at her ears into a wild swing. She dutifully went back to disassembling the pistol and while she worked, she added, "I do miss Max, though. That man can do things with his mouth that should probably be illegal."

"Okay, too much information," Deidre told her.

Shauna laughed. "I had Marco send him a message today, letting him know that I'm all right and that I'll meet him at 'our' spot this weekend."

"Will you be healed enough by then?"

"If you help I will be," she said, wiggling both eyebrows.

"Good." Deidre tested the edge of the dagger. It was

sharp enough, so she picked up another and began running the sharpening steel across it. "So, where's 'your' spot?"

Shauna started cleaning the barrel of the pistol. "It's this sweet little Victorian B and B in Foggy Bottom."

Deidre frowned. Foggy Bottom was a historical neighborhood west of downtown DC. Close to the river, the area got its nickname from the fog and industrial smoke that gathered there. George Washington University took up most of that quadrant of the city, along with expensive private homes, a few select B and Bs and the Kennedy Center. Not to mention the State Department, and the infamous Watergate complex.

And then there was the fact that Foggy Bottom was *way* too close to the rest of the government offices — including the White House itself and the *Bureau of Witchcraft*.

"Shauna, are you nuts?" Deidre stared at her, openmouthed. "Half the government is over there."

She laughed. "Relax, Dee. This isn't the first time I've been to Foggy Bottom to meet Max."

"It's the first time since you and I have been on the news. You just said that the whole world's looking for me!"

"Yeah," Shauna said. "For *you*. Dee, honestly. No one's going to pay attention to me unless I'm *with* you."

Deidre didn't like it, but didn't know how she could convince her friend not to go, either. "You're taking a big risk, Shauna. What if you're wrong?"

"I'm not. But I'm not stupid, either, so don't worry." Shauna winked at her. "Dee, I've been doing this a long time, hiding from cops, feds and anyone else who might want to lock me up or hunt me down. I'm careful, believe me. I'll wear a wig, change up my look. No one will recognize me."

Deidre had a bad feeling about this. But then, she'd had a bad feeling for days. "Finn's okay with this?"

Shauna looked at her and the smile was gone. "He's not my king, Dee. I don't have to ask permission."

Deidre wasn't fooled. Finn was too powerful a presence to this group. Their loyalties were all so tangled together, not one of them would do anything that might remotely put the others in danger. Especially since they had all been hurt by Tony's betrayal.

"But you asked anyway."

"Okay yeah. Fine," Shauna admitted with a short laugh. "I checked it out with him first, since things are so hairy around here right now. But he's good with it. As long as I'm careful and keep to the tunnels for traveling."

Deidre still wasn't happy about this. Going into the heart of the government for a quickie seemed like a really bad idea. She looked up at the rock ceiling overhead and thought about the world above. "Where are we right now? I mean, what's topside from here?"

Shauna looked up too, as if she could see the city beyond the tunnels. "The armory is under Madison and Fourteenth Street. Close to the Natural History Museum and the Holocaust Memorial Museum."

"And *very* close to the White House," Deidre murmured. Her thoughts were racing. She'd had no idea where in the city she actually was. Finn had told her that these tunnels stretched out for miles, running the length and breadth of the city above. His band of guerrillas knew their way around of course, but as far as Deidre knew, she could have been on Mars. Now that she knew exactly where she was though, she couldn't help wondering if she could somehow sneak in to see her mother.

Shauna looked at her. "Don't get any ideas about running home to Mama. Finn would never go for that and Dee, it would be stupid along monumental proportions."

"Probably," she admitted, though she felt a pang of regret. She knew her mother was in a bad spot. And after all of the years of being the daughter who never made waves—creating this tsunami was really starting to bother her.

"Definitely," Shauna said, her features grim, her eyes narrowed.

"I know, okay?" Irritation trumped guilt. "I just don't like putting my mom in this position."

"Yeah, I get that."

They worked in tense silence for a couple of minutes; then Deidre did an abrupt subject change and asked, "How do you keep the days and nights separate down here? After all this time in the tunnels, I feel like a vampire—" She stopped and asked, "Do vampires exist? Finn says werewolves do, but—"

"I've never met a vampire," Shauna told her with a shrug as she ran the cleaning rag through the barrel of another sawed-off shotgun. "But if they *are* real, I hope they're not pretty-white-boy-sparkly-*Twilight* vamps with bad hair. Give me an Angel," she said dreamily. "Or even better . . . *Spike*."

"Agreed," Deidre said with a laugh.

"Makes you wonder, doesn't it?"

"What?"

"Just how many supernaturals out there are biding their time, waiting to see how it goes for witches before they announce their presence."

Deidre thought about that for a second, then shivered. "If that's what they're waiting for, I'm guessing they won't be coming out of hiding anytime soon."

"True." Shauna's voice dropped several notches. "Ten years in the open and witches are an endangered species." She took a breath and said, "Speaking of that, let's see it."

The high-pitched ring of steel on steel halted abruptly when Deidre stopped running the sharpening rod over a dagger's edge. She looked over at Shauna, who was watching her with keen interest. "See what?"

"The Mating tattoo," her friend said as if Deidre was crazy. "You've been with Finn for days and even though your chamber's plenty far from the rest of us, I know what's going on. So let's see it."

Deidre flushed. Amazing that she could be embarrassed by this, but it felt so awkward.

"I don't have a tattoo," she blurted, shifting her attention back to the dagger.

"What? Of course you do." Shauna's voice was filled with confusion. "I know how the Mating works. You and Finn do the deed and get matching brands on your skin, linking you together, preparing you for finishing the mission."

"Just how many witches know this Mating story, anyway?"

Shauna shrugged. "I don't know. I heard it the last time I was in Sanctuary. So . . . why don't you have a tattoo?"

Annoyance flashed. "Because we didn't Mate."

"But you had *sex*."

Deidre glared at her, and the annoyance bubbling inside suddenly exploded. Problem was, she didn't know if she was more annoyed with Shauna or herself. She and Finn had made a deal, but lately, Deidre had been reconsidering. Oh, not that she wanted to be the eternal Mate of a man who didn't actually *want* her. But the part of her that was that long-ago witch craved the Mating. Craved it because she knew it was the only real way out of this mess. The only way to atone for everything she had done.

"Hello?" Shauna sniped. "You had sex!"

"Yes. Okay? We had sex." Repeatedly. God, she thought about the night before and nearly shivered at the memory. The juncture of her thighs went hot and damp and needy and just like that, she was wishing Finn would walk through the doorway and toss her on her back. What the hell was happening to her? "You're the big witch expert. You should know we can have sex and *not* Mate."

"Well, why the hell wouldn't you?" Shauna set down the shotgun she had been cleaning and stood up to loom over Deidre. "Fate of the world not a big enough motivator for you, Dee? Hellhounds, demons and feds after you is just another day at the office?"

Deidre jumped to her feet too, letting the dagger drop to the ground with a soft thump. "This isn't even your business, Shauna. I don't quiz you about your nights with Max, do I?"

"Not really the same thing, is it?" Shauna's dark brown eyes sparked with anger. "What Max and I do together doesn't affect the *world*."

"And this won't either," Deidre snapped. "I'm not risking anything, but I'm not going to bind myself to a man who only wants to *use* me."

"You're insane." Shauna lifted both hands and let them drop to her sides. "Certifiable."

"If I wasn't before, I may be now," Deidre admitted, feeling her own temper spark to match her friend's. "The last few days haven't exactly been a vacation, you know."

"For any of us."

"Okay, true." Deidre shook her head and said, "But as far as Finn and I go, neither of us wants a Mate, Shauna. I'm not holding out on him. He agreed to this, too. We're using sex magic to awaken my powers."

"Not good enough." Shauna paced off a few steps, then spun around and came back again. "And Finn knows it. Hell, Dee, every witch in the freaking world knows it. Our one shot at surviving this . . . extermination is for you and the other chosen to claim your Mates and put that fucking Artifact back together. Seal the demon portal. Destroy the Black Silver. Convince the leaders of this planet that witchcraft can be used for *good*."

"And you think we don't know that?" Deidre shouted right back at her friend. "I've got enough pressure on me right now, thanks very much."

"Pressure?" Shauna just stared at her for a long second or two. "I can't believe you. There are witches all over the earth who would trade places with you in a heartbeat. Did you know that?"

"Yeah, because this is a great gig."

"It *is*." Shauna blew out a breath and whispered, "You have the opportunity to be the hero for a whole race of women. You can save us. You and the other chosen. This is the most important thing that will ever be asked of you and you 'don't want a Mate'?"

Well, now she felt small and stupid and selfish, which was probably the point. She scrubbed her hands up and down her arms and glanced around at the armory. Chests filled with swords, knives, throwing stars and racks of silver bullets lined one wall and along the other, every kind of gun imaginable was stacked neatly, awaiting its turn in the fight. Torchlight danced and swayed across the stones and the constant chill in the air seemed somehow thicker, deeper.

Shauna's voice seemed to echo over and over again in her mind. Specific words resonated more clearly with her than others. *The earth. Extermination. The chosen. The Artifact. Black Silver.* That last one brought another ripple of unease through her as another door to her past creaked open. She could remember channeling her powers into the darkly gleaming Artifact. She could hear the chants of the others. She remembered looking out, beyond the sacred circle of witches to the Eternals, pacing helplessly outside. She searched for Finn's face and—

"Damn it, Dee, you have to do this. For all our sakes."

Deidre snapped out of her memories and right back to this moment in time. She glared at her friend. "Why is my sex life your business?"

"Because your sex life might mean *my* life?" Shauna shook her head and reached out to hug her briefly and just like that, Deidre's irritation drained away.

She and Shauna had been friends for five years. They'd seen each other through bad boyfriends, crappy jobs and a few really awful hangovers. They had a bond that wouldn't be broken by temper—just forged to deeper levels of understanding.

"You think I don't get how freaked out you are about all of this, but I do."

Deidre shook her head. "You couldn't possibly."

Because even Deidre didn't completely understand why she was holding back from Mating with Finn. All she was sure of was that anytime she actually considered being his Mate, something held her back. Some small twist of a memory inside her that cut sharp and deep, then disappeared before she could really *see* it. And she had to ask herself, did she really *want* to see that memory?

Ignoring that, Shauna continued. "But what you're not seeing is that it doesn't matter." She grabbed Deidre's hand and gave it a squeeze. "This has been eight hundred years coming, Dee. It's Fate. Destiny. And you can't just decide you don't want to play."

"I'm doing everything I can," Deidre muttered, even though she knew it wasn't true. She was holding back, not committing entirely to this quest she'd been tossed into. Yes, she wanted to help. She wanted to stop all the senseless killing of witches. But there was a part of her that rebelled against being used—even for a grand purpose.

True, she had come to know him better, and to trust him. She even understood her place in all this. But the bottom line was, Finn still needed her around only for what she could do for him. Just like every other man she had ever known. And Deidre was done with being used.

Besides, it wasn't as if Finn was desperate to Mate with her.

"Not everything."

"Lay off, Shauna." She'd been pushed far enough for one day. Deidre wasn't ready yet to make the kind of full-body commitment Shauna and every other witch expected of her. She didn't know if she'd ever be ready. Maybe that was a huge failing in her. Maybe she'd regret it one day. But for right now, this was what she needed and having her friend jump in her face over it wasn't helping any.

As if sensing that, Shauna nodded and stepped back. Taking her seat again, she picked up the shotgun and got to work. But she wasn't quite finished. "I won't give you any more grief about this for now. But remember, Dee, there's a world full of witches out there, and they—*we*— need you."

Chapter 25

There was a traitor somewhere in Finn's organization. Had to be. He didn't think that ambush on Deidre's first raid had been a coincidence. The guards were too well armed and too damn ready. Tony couldn't have leaked the information, he'd never had the opportunity to tell anyone about the raid and wouldn't have known specifics anyway. Marco had a wife hiding in Sanctuary, so he wouldn't do anything to risk her safety. Shauna had been shot and Joe . . . it wasn't Joe.

Finn knew a real warrior when he met one. And a warrior didn't turn on his team. So that left him where, exactly?

"With too many questions," he grumbled, taking a quick look around the area. He was outside Franklin Square on K Street. Named after Ben Franklin—who Finn had quite liked back in the day—the park was a terraced slope of grass and trees, bare for the winter, and a fountain that splashed fitfully in the cold air.

It was a gray and cloudy afternoon; the icy wind promised snow for later. Discarded newspapers rattled in the wire trash cans and a car horn sounded out in the distance.

The homeless gathered here in the park, for camaraderie or warmth or just to annoy the wealthy residents of the nearby neighborhoods. Most of them camped out beside Commodore Barry's statue, which meant they weren't close enough to Finn to notice when he flashed out to the tunnels below.

His exceptional eyesight scanned the tunnel and found it empty. Most of the team had gone topside. Finn wasn't happy about it, but he couldn't force them to stay in the tunnels. The time was coming, of course, when the tunnels would be their only safe refuge. But for now, he supposed they should blow off steam while they could.

Joe had gone to visit his father two days ago. Shauna was off spending the night with Max, and Marco and a couple of the others were in Sanctuary, visiting family kept there for their own safety.

Locking people away to keep them safe. Hell of a world, Finn thought, remembering all the times he'd seen the same kind of persecution rise up and take over. The Inquisition came to mind. When the church had perfected torture. But that was just one of the many times people had turned on each other in the name of fear.

Shaking his head, he realized that after centuries of keeping his distance, he was being drawn deeper into the humans' world. He actually *cared* about these witches and the people who were trying so hard to save them.

"Sucker," he muttered. His footsteps echoed in the tunnel as he stomped along the well-worn path. He glanced into the empty chambers he passed and kept going. Instinct was guiding him now and those instincts were leading him to Deidre.

He felt her presence like a soothing balm against an ancient wound. Every thought centered around her. His body ached for hers, continuously. She had become *essential* to him in the last several days. He wasn't even sure how it had happened—especially since he had been so determined to simply complete the mission and then walk away.

Now, walking away from her felt a more impossible task than finding that damned Artifact.

Scowling at his own thoughts, he followed the curve of the tunnel and stopped dead at the entrance to the chamber he shared with Deidre.

"It's a disguise."

"Yeah," Finn said with a short laugh as his gaze swept her up and down. Damn. Gone a few hours to reconnoiter and when he comes back, the woman he knew looked completely different. "I guessed that."

The long blond hair that he loved to wrap around his hand was hidden beneath a short, spiky black wig that made her features look almost elven. Silver hoops flashed at her ears, winking in the torchlight. She wore black jeans, a dark green GWU sweatshirt and a pair of boots. She looked like a college student out for a night-long pub crawl. The dark glasses covering her eyes seemed silly inside the tunnels, but he got what she was going for.

"The question is, why the disguise?"

She pulled off the sunglasses and twirled them by one earpiece. Her blue eyes fixed on him. "Because if I don't get out of these tunnels for a while, I'm going to snap, Finn."

His smile disappeared and he shook his head once.

"You could at least hear me out."

"No way." He stepped past her into their chamber and shrugged out of his long black leather coat. The cool air on his skin tempered the heat raging inside him. "It's safer down here."

"I'd be even safer *dead*," she said. "But I don't want that, either."

"Don't even say it." Because the thought of Deidre hurt or dead pumped mindless rage through his arteries. He couldn't watch her die. Not again.

She took a deep breath and blew it out again in a rush. "Sorry. But, Finn, I need to get out. Breathe air that doesn't taste like damp rock. See the damn *sky*."

He felt her turmoil. Heard it in her voice. Tension rolled off of her in waves that slapped at him and every instinct he possessed. He knew she was safest in the tunnels. But he also knew that caging Deidre wasn't the way to earn her trust or her cooperation.

She never had done well in enclosed spaces. Through the centuries, if given a choice, she had always chosen to live away from crowds, out in the open. In the mountains, at the beach, in a forest. Even when she had lived in the city though, she had taken every opportunity to be out in the open because seeing the sky, the trees, fed her soul. So being in these tunnels for extended periods was like being shut away in prison for her. No wonder she wanted to get out.

Didn't mean he had to like it, though. "Whose idea was the wig and"—he waved a hand at the outfit—"all of this?"

She grinned and turned, letting him get the full effect. Pretty impressive, he had to admit. If his body wasn't magically linked to hers, if he didn't *feel* her presence, he might not have known her. That damn wig made the biggest difference. It changed her looks completely.

When she was facing him again, she said, "It was

Shauna's idea. She took me to the room where you store all the extra clothing and the disguises you keep for the team. Fascinating, really. Anyway, she was getting ready to go meet Max and I thought—"

She kept talking. Rambling, words speeding up in her rush to convince him to let her go aboveground. He looked at her and felt something inside him turn over. Her eyes were sparkling with excitement and her mouth curved in a smile despite the fast flow of words erupting from her.

Desire curled low and hot in his belly. He was instantly hard and ready for her, body aching with a need only she could assuage.

He smirked inwardly at just how bad he'd become over the last few days. Finn remembered all too well how he'd laughed at his brothers when their Mates had run them in circles. He'd watched as they'd made what he considered stupid decisions all because they wanted to please their witches. Now it looked as though he owed his brothers apologies.

Because damned if he wanted to be the one to wipe the excited gleam from her eyes. To end that smile that tugged at his nonbeating heart.

Hell, he knew what she was feeling, trapped down here. And she'd done well up till this point. Hadn't bitched or complained. Hadn't demanded special treatment. Hadn't even asked to contact her mother again since that one little slice of blackmail.

She was throwing herself into learning combat techniques, focusing her magic and opening her memories. She had done everything demanded of her—but for the Mating. And he couldn't fault her for that, since he had argued to skip the Mating as well.

His chest ached now, as badly as his dick. And if he didn't know better, he'd swear his heart was actually twisting. The thing was, the more time he spent with her, the more he actually wanted to Mate with Deidre. He hadn't lied when he told her their destinies were entwined. His soul burned to become a part of hers. To join their very essences in the most profound way possible.

To keep her from dying and leaving him again.

But Mating would do more than help in their search for the Artifact. It would also open up all of her memories. And he didn't really want her remembering that one last night.

Eight hundred years and still that memory made him ashamed and furious. Everything in him yearned to take her as his Mate now; she'd become so much a part of him that the thought of losing her tore at the frayed edges of his soul. But he didn't want to risk Deidre remembering that last night—not until he'd had time to prove to her that she wasn't the only one who had changed and grown over the centuries.

So, though he wanted her—he couldn't have her. Not completely.

"Come on, Finn," she urged, walking toward him, a hopeful look in her eyes. "Give a little."

He shouldn't. But he knew he was going to.

"What'd you have in mind?"

Excitement bubbled around her. He could practically see it in the air. "A movie? No, scratch that. Don't want to be inside. A walk in the park? Go see all of the Christmas lights?"

Finn surrendered to the inevitable. He couldn't stand against her. Never had been able to except for that one time and look where that had gotten them.

"If we do this, we wait till night to go. Easier to stay unnoticed at night. You stay by my side the whole time," he said tightly, "and when I say it's time to go, we go. No arguments."

She crossed her heart and then held up three fingers in a well-known Girl Scout salute. "Absolutely."

"Fine. We'll go tonight."

Deidre threw herself at him, wrapping her arms around his neck and holding on tight. She buried her face in the curve of his neck and said, "Thanks, Finn. I owe you."

His arms came around her and he held her close. "Damn right you do."

She pulled her head back and grinned up at him. Her blue eyes shining, she asked, "So, what will we do until it's time to go topside?"

Instantly, his body went even harder than it had been—something he would have thought impossible until Deidre. "I've got a few ideas about that."

"Can't wait to hear them," she said and kissed him.

Chapter 26

"Oh, God, I've missed you," Shauna said on a satisfied sigh. She stroked one hand across Max's incredibly defined abs and tipped her head back on the pillow to look at him.

Candlelight flickered from the bedside table. Max's dark skin gleamed like onyx and his brown eyes were soulful as he gazed at her. "I've missed you too, babe. Took you long enough to call this time."

She shifted on the bed, hooking one long leg over his muscled thigh as she leaned across his chest. "I got injured a while back. Had to wait for it to heal before I could come see you."

"Injured?" He frowned and dragged the tips of his fingers down the length of her spine. "What happened?"

"It was nothing," she lied, loving the feel of his hands on her. His body was pumping out heat and the slide of cool sheets against her skin was a sexy contrast.

She loved this place. It was where she and Max had made love for the first time and just being here rekindled all of those sparkly feelings she'd had for him from the beginning. The walls were a soft green, oak furniture shone with polish and the rag rugs beneath the four-poster bed were colorful and bright. Everything about the B and B warmed Shauna to her soul. Being here with Max just made it all that much better.

After doing a healing spell with Deidre every afternoon for the last few days, the weekend couldn't come soon enough for her. Shauna had dressed and hurried to Max as fast as she could. In their room at the B and B, she had found him, naked and ready for her. God, she got chills just remembering that first orgasm when he'd backed her against the wall and taken her with his talented mouth. Now, two hours into her R & R, Shauna wasn't nearly finished with the man she loved so desperately.

"I don't like you being hurt, honey," he told her and pulled her up along his body so he could kiss her deeply, thoroughly. "I hate that witchcraft has put you in so much danger."

She looked at him and smiled. "It's who I am, Max."

"I know," he said, sliding one hand down to cup her behind. "And I want you to know, I'm really sorry about this."

"About what?" Frowning, Shauna fought the tingle of danger beginning to spread inside her. This was *Max*. She loved him. Trusted him. "What're you talking about?"

He sat up abruptly and drew her with him. Pinning her to the wall of his chest with the ironclad strength of one heavy arm, he reached for the bedside table and opened the drawer.

Shauna watched every move as fear galloped inside her, pushing her heartbeat into a frantic rhythm that threatened to choke her. The candlelit shadows flickering across his face turned Max into a stranger. Something was wrong. Seriously wrong. He wasn't acting like himself.

And now that the sexual buzz was being buried under a ton of *oh-shit*, she realized that he had been acting sort of weird since she got there. Nervous. Jumpy. Really unlike him.

Oh, God.

She squirmed against him, not willing just yet to use magic against him. This was her lover. The one person in the world she trusted more than Deidre. How could she use her power to hurt him? "Let me go, Max."

In response, his arm tightened around her, making drawing breath an Olympic sport. She didn't want to hurt him, but she couldn't let him hurt her, either. Reaching deep for her magic, she called it up, focusing everything she had on the simple matter of breaking free of him.

Her chant came soft and low. "*Power fly and spirit soar—*"

"Oh, no, you don't, little witch!" He pulled a white gold chain out of the drawer and when she struggled to escape his hold, he dropped it over her head.

Instantly, a cold, draining sensation opened up inside her. The magic that had been at her fingertips moments ago was gone. Gasping, Shauna felt her power slide away, disappearing into a black hole opened up by the white gold searing her skin like dry ice.

She was trapped as much by the delicate chain of magic-killing metal as she was by Max's strong arm around her. She looked up at him, knowing that hurt and denial shone in her eyes.

"Aw, now don't look at me like that," he said with a slow shake of his head.

Her brain seemed to be racing despite the fact that her soul felt as if it were dying. Suddenly, she understood how that ambush on the raid had happened. She had told Max about their plan, so sure she could trust him. He must have informed the feds and . . . "Oh, Max . . ."

As if reading her expression, he said, "I'm sorry about you getting shot. That wasn't supposed to happen."

This couldn't be happening. She knew him. Loved him. "Max, let me go."

"No can do, babe." He kissed her forehead and she shivered.

"Why?" she asked, as he pulled a syringe from the bedside drawer. "Why, Max?"

He bit the protective cap off with his teeth, jabbed her upper arm with the needle and pushed the plunger home. Only then did he look at her. "Why? I'm losing my gym, Shauna. Got too far behind on the payments and they're gonna take it from me. I can't let that happen."

"But—"

"You're a witch, babe," he said with a shrug. "You know how much money I'm getting for you?"

"No, Max . . ." she said, hearing her own voice like a faraway whisper. Money. He was getting money for her. He was turning her over to the feds. To Doc Fender.

Pain and fear blossomed inside only to be swallowed by the drug overtaking her. "But I loved you."

"Love you too, babe." He stroked one hand across her short hair and even slipping into unconsciousness, she tried to move away from that traitorous caress. "You'll see. Fender will drain the magic out of you. Then we can be together again."

No.

Then Max kissed her one last time and the world went dark.

Christmas lights were everywhere.

Sparkling white, multicolored, they shone from every bare-branched tree and draped across light poles and storefront windows. The air was clean and cold and a light dusting of snow drifted down from the black sky.

In short, Deidre thought, it was *perfect*.

Walking down Constitution Avenue with Finn at her side, Deidre felt almost normal. Well, until she concentrated on the buzz of power drifting from his hand to hers and back again. She glanced up at him and briefly studied his profile.

His features were hard and tight. His gaze was constantly shifting, examining their surroundings, wary of attack. Worry rippled through her briefly, but Deidre fought it into submission. Finn would protect her. And she wasn't exactly helpless anymore, was she?

"What're you thinking?"

"Just that it's great to be outside again," she said.

He nodded, then looked away, scanning the area. And seeing that fierce look on his face reminded Deidre that they weren't just any couple enjoying a winter night. They were in the heart of the government, surrounded by enemies.

She should probably feel guilty for talking him into this outing, but she just couldn't. It was great to be outside. In the world. She felt as if she could breathe again.

For a Saturday night, there weren't many people out. Of course, since the whole witchcraft thing had come to light, federal agencies had really cracked down—asking for IDs, making random arrest sweeps—not to mention the early curfews. It was enough to convince most people to stay home at night.

Still, down the block, a small crowd of people was lined up outside a club. Cars streamed along the road, headlights blazing a trail through the darkness and from somewhere close by, a Christmas carol droned in Muzak format. Their stroll was taking them toward the National Mall and Deidre cringed a little inside.

"Is it safe to be this close to the White House?"

He shot her a sidelong look. "Probably not."

If she'd been hoping for reassurance, she would have been disappointed. Thankfully, she'd been around Finn long enough to know that he would, at least, be honest with her. So now she felt on edge and a little less giddy about being outside in all the icy fresh air.

Her gaze, too, swept the area, taking in the occasional pedestrian, the snow-covered limbs of the naked trees and lamplight sifting through windows to paint the sidewalks in bars of golden light. This was her city. She knew it well. And now, she was looking at it through a stranger's eyes. A trickle of unease spread along her spine.

If she had to make a run for it right now, she wouldn't have a clue where to head. She didn't even remember where they'd come up from the tunnels. Idiot, she told herself. Way to protect yourself. But the sad fact was, Deidre had been so thrilled to be getting *out*, she hadn't been thinking about getting back *in*.

She looked back over her shoulder as if expecting to see a neon sign reading THE ENTRANCE IS HERE, blinking on and off. Naturally, all she saw was more snow, more Christmas lights and a lone man, walking head bent into the wind.

Frowning, she glanced up at Finn. "So, where's our chamber in the tunnels from here?"

"Why do you need to know?" His hand tightened around hers. "Planning an escape?"

Irritated that he could still assume she was ready to bolt even after she had told him she understood the need for secrecy, she snapped, "Yes, Finn. That's why I went to all the trouble to find a disguise and talk you into bringing me out here. Because I'm an escape artist." Shaking her head, she whispered, "Haven't I earned some trust yet?"

Silence stretched out for a long minute as if he was considering her question carefully. And that only spiked Deidre's irritation. He had to *think* about it?

"You have," he said finally.

"Wow, thanks." She shook her head and tried to pull her hand free of his, but he only held on tighter. "I really appreciate the vote of confidence there."

"I trust you," he said again, turning his head to look down at her. "But I know what it's costing you to stay away from your family. To stay hidden."

"And you believe I'll make a break for it?"

"Can you honestly tell me you haven't thought about it?"

Hmm. She could lie and remain the injured party, or she could admit the truth and realize that he had good reason to have a little doubt.

"Okay fine," she blurted, the tension in her shoulders relaxing a bit. "I did think about it. But then I realized that going to my mother would only make her life harder, so what would be the point?" Shaking her head, Deidre huffed out a breath and said, "You said we've got thirty days to complete this quest, right?"

"Yeah. Well, less now."

Deidre nodded. "Then I can't risk getting caught, can I? So you're stuck with me for the duration."

She tipped her head back and stared straight up. She couldn't see stars for the clouds, but it was enough for her to know they were up there. The wind rattled tree limbs, making an eerie clicking sound that had her hunching deeper into the jacket she had found in the tunnels. "For right now, I can't go to my mother. And unless the witch situation changes dramatically, maybe I'll *never* see her again."

Oh, Deidre didn't like the sound of that, but it was the only way she knew of to keep her mother safe and clear of the charge of harboring a witch. If the truth came out, her presidency would end in a scandal that would make Nixon's look like a college prank gone wrong.

But that wasn't the worst of it by any means. Deidre had done a lot of thinking about this over the last several days and she knew darn well that not only could Cora Sterling lose her reputation and her position as president—she might even be looking at prison time.

If the truth about Deidre came out, there would be conspiracy theorists determined to prove that Cora had known all along about her daughter. That it was the reason she had run for president in the first place and why she had been so "lenient" on the witches.

No. The White House was definitely out of bounds.

"Our chamber is below E Street, under the Spy Museum," Finn said.

That surprised a short laugh out of her. "Oh, that's perfect."

"I thought so," he mused, one corner of his mouth

tilting into a half smile that Deidre didn't see nearly often enough.

His whole face changed when he smiled. He looked less predatory. No less dangerous, but somehow more . . . approachable. Which was probably why he didn't smile more often.

"Thanks for telling me."

He shrugged, as if trusting her with the location of their lair was no big deal—which she knew was a lie.

"I know this is hard for you."

"For you too, I'm guessing," she said. "I mean, we're stuck together waiting for the right memory to pop into my head—we spend hours every day talking about the Artifact and the past and still I haven't found that one memory I need so badly."

"We need," he corrected.

"Fine. The point is, I'm no closer to knowing what I did with the Artifact shard all those centuries ago and meanwhile—"

"Meanwhile, we free witches. We train. We do everything we would have done with or without the Awakening."

"Awakening," she repeated and that word stirred memories into a blur of images and scents and sounds. She was walking in DC, her Eternal at her side, and yet she was also in Scotland, then Paris, then Jerusalem.

She rubbed her forehead and he saw it. "The memories are still scrambled?"

"Yes. It's confusing as hell," she admitted and heard the surliness in her own voice but was unable to stop it. No matter how often they talked about the past, she couldn't force the memories into linear fashion. They came twisted and jumbled as if now that the door to the past was open, everything she had ever done was anxious to be noted and recalled. "They're my memories, but they're not me, you know? My own life is starting to blur with those other women's lives and sometimes, I can't see the line dividing them anymore."

"Reincarnation's a bitch all right," he said.

"Are you laughing?"

"Hell no," he assured her, though she was pretty sure she saw his lips curve.

"Whatever. The point is, how am I supposed to sift through centuries of memories to find the *one* that we need?"

He dropped her hand, then wrapped his arm around her shoulders, pulling her into his side. Deidre sighed a little as she molded herself to the tall, muscled length of him, amazed as always that she seemed to fit perfectly against him.

"Don't tell me," she muttered. "The answer is magic."

He snorted. "It always comes back to magic, Dee. It's who we are. *Why* we are. Magic lives at our cores. There's no escaping it. No pretending it doesn't exist."

"I did pretty well for the first nearly thirty years of my life."

"No, you didn't," he said, glancing down at her as they walked along the serene winter splendor of the National Mall. "You were always different from everyone else. You knew it. You felt it. You just couldn't put a name to it."

He was right. Just as he had been before when he first reminded her of all the ways she had felt ... disconnected, most of her life.

"You have to open yourself to it, Deidre."

She leaned her head against his shoulder and immediately felt a bright burst of desire flash inside her. She breathed into it, relishing the low-down stir of something wicked and delicious. The man was addictive. She couldn't seem to get enough of him. Ever. Sex with him only made her want more. And right now, she wanted him badly.

"Open myself to it," she echoed. "I thought that's what we've been doing almost nonstop. Don't think I could get more open."

"Yeah," he said and held her tighter, as if feeding on her desires. "Sex magic is working, but it's not as strong as the Mating, so you have to focus your energies more fully on the target."

"Easier said than done, since I don't know what that target is," she reminded him. "I mean, every once in a while, I'll get an image of the Black Silver." She frowned as she tried to draw that picture up in her mind. It was hazy, indistinct, but everything in her recognized it.

Gleaming in moonlight, its black curves and intricate knots made the dark metal seem almost alive. It bristled with power, with promise.

Briefly, the present fell away.

Chapter 27

The past wrapped itself around her. The sounds of their footsteps became nothing more than a muffled counterpoint to the memories of lifetimes lived and lost. She knew where they were. Somehow her subconscious kept her walking and talking in the present while her mind drifted to another time, another age. They cut across the grass surrounding the Washington Monument, lit up by spotlights that made it glow like a beacon from heaven in the night. On the other side of them was the Ellipse, where the national Christmas tree glittered under a barrage of thousands of multicolored lights.

Used to be that the tree wasn't lit before December. But Cora had changed all that when she took office. Now the tree was electrified the first week of November — the thinking being that maybe in the time of witch hunts, a little extra peace-on-earth goodwill to men couldn't hurt.

In the distance, the White House stood, squat and sure of itself, bathed in lights bright enough to make it shine like a nova. Inside that building, her mother waited and worried. But there was nothing she could do about that, so Deidre deliberately turned from the sight and focused her mind inward, trying desperately to pin down the elusive memory that meant everything to them.

"I can see the Artifact in the center of a pentagram. And I see a battle," she said, voice soft, memories already fading. "But I haven't seen the damn piece of the thing that I supposedly hid."

He stopped dead beside one of the bare trees, turned her to face him and wrapped his big hands around her shoulders, then looked deeply into her eyes. "It's all there. In your mind. Lost in time, all you have to do is remember who *you* were then. Concentrate on bringing forth that lifetime. Remember her and all you did and thought and said and felt."

Deidre grumbled, "Well sure, why didn't I think of that?"

"I didn't say it was going to be easy," he reminded her, his voice a low rumble.

"No, you didn't. And it's not. How'm I supposed to—"

"You have to stop fighting it. Stop pretending that the woman you were is separate from you. Once you've accepted that long-ago life and reclaimed her, you'll remember."

Looking into those amazing gray eyes of his, swirling now with magic and secrets, she could almost believe him. But doubts were still racing through her mind and the task felt impossible. "I'm trying Finn. I really am. But that long-dead woman is as foreign to me as a stranger on the street. I'm not her."

"No, you're not," he said, voice deepening as his gray eyes swirled pewter. "No more than I'm the same Eternal who lived in those times. We all change, Dee. We all grow and all of the other touchy-feely crap psychologists today talk about until you want to hack off your ears to avoid listening to them anymore."

She smiled ruefully. That was the Finn she knew. Crabby, irritable, impatient.

"But the point is, no matter how much you change, there's still that core of you that remains." He eased his grip on her slightly. "Your soul is *you*. Through however many lifetimes you live, that soul stays with you and somewhere inside, you know that."

"Yeah," she admitted with a brief nod. "I guess I do. So maybe the truth is, I don't want to remember the woman I used to be. She doesn't exactly sound like a fabulous human being."

And *other* memories worried her, she reminded herself. That elusive piece of the puzzle that both fascinated and repelled her, like a storm, brewing in the distance.

"None of us were perfect." Finn hugged her. "But that long-ago witch? She had her moments."

"Then why don't you just tell me where she—I— might have hidden it? Save us both some time."

"Don't you think I would if I could?" He gave her a shake that convinced her he was as frustrated by all of this as she was. "I don't know what you did with the Artifact shard you were entrusted with."

"Just great." She broke free of his grip, though she missed his hands on her.

Shaking his head, he told her, "My memories of that time can't help you."

"So, we're back to square one."

He gave her that half smile again and Deidre swore she felt her toes curl. Then that smile disappeared, his entire body went on red alert and he yanked her behind one of the stark skeletons of a cherry tree.

"What's—"

"Quiet." He slapped one hand over her mouth and she got the message fast.

Deidre nodded and peeled his fingers off. Looking at him, she mouthed, *What is it?*

Scowling, Finn lowered his head until his mouth was beside her ear. He held up one hand and said, "Take it, hold on tight, focus your magic and look out over the Reflecting Pool."

Confused but willing, she threaded her fingers through his and felt the instant pulse of connection burst into life between them. She delved deep, drew on her magic and stared at the long, narrow strip of water between the Lincoln Memorial and the Washington Monument. The water was still but for a ripple of movement caused by the wind. Lights shone on the surface and the stark outline of the Washington spire lay like a shadow across the water.

"What do you see that I don't?" Her voice was less than a whisper. Hardly more than a breath.

He increased his grip on her hand until her fingers throbbed in time with her heartbeat. "Wait for it."

Deidre concentrated, drawing on her newfound magic more deeply. She felt it building inside her and she opened herself to it, allowing the ripples of power to rush through her veins. Like supernatural carbonation, it sizzled and popped along every inch of her body. It was a dizzying yet triumphant feeling, knowing that she was at last capable of commanding her magic. She stared hard at the Reflecting Pool and where a moment before there had been only darkness, now Deidre saw a ribbon of color snaking along the pool. Soft shades of gold and orange flared briefly, then faded, only to reappear again farther along the way. It was beautiful, yet every instinct she possessed screamed *danger*.

And it was heading right at them.

"Oh my God, what is that?"

"Demon trace energies."

His breath was warm on her cheek, but couldn't combat the icy-cold ball of dread that single word had dropped into the pit of her stomach. "Demons? Here?"

As she watched, that swirl of color kept moving, drawing closer and closer to them.

"Yeah." Finn pulled her away from the tree and gave a quick look around, assuring himself that they were alone. "Demons in DC. What better place for 'em, if you think about it."

"What do we do?"

"Follow it," Finn said, already moving after the energy patterns. Deidre wasted no time falling into step behind him. Fear dried out her mouth and made her palms damp. She didn't have a clue what she was supposed to fight with or what she would do with a demon if she did manage to capture or kill it. But she figured it was time she learned.

Finn moved like a shadow. If she didn't know where he was, he would have been hard to spot. Thankfully though, it was late enough that not many people were wandering around the darkened President's Park. They followed the demon to the Ellipse, where a short white fence enclosed the grassy area. While a ring of elms encircled the Ellipse, only a solitary Colorado blue spruce— now glittering with Christmas lights—stood within the fenced boundary.

Finn jumped the fence, then waited for her to follow. Deidre took a step and stopped. She looked over her shoulder and Finn whispered, "What're you doing? Come on."

"I heard something." She wasn't sure what. A quiet *crick* of sound, as if someone had stepped on a twig, snapping it in two.

"Move it," he snarled and headed off after the demon.

Right. Demon. More important than noises. She held on to the top rail of the fence and swung her right leg over. Then something grabbed her from behind, dragging her back and away from the fence. She took a breath to scream, but an arm wrapped around her throat and squeezed. She could hardly see Finn, as he blended into shadows, following his quarry.

What the hell? Demon? Witch hunter? Fed? All these thoughts and more flew through her mind in an instant. Then all questions were answered.

"Gimme your money."

The words came fast and low and Deidre's heart slid back down into her chest. A *mugger?* Sure, it was scary, but an everyday, run-of-the-mill mugger? On her list of terrifying entities, a mugger was down so low, she hadn't even considered it. Hell, with what she had been afraid of, this was practically a *relief.*

He kept a tight hold on her neck, and patted one hand up and down her body as if looking for a wallet or anything else he could steal. Fury suddenly eclipsed surprise and relief. With everything already going on in her life, Deidre wasn't going to be the victim of a random thief. She didn't plan her next move. She simply reacted.

Grabbing hold of the thick forearm pressed across her throat, Deidre planted her feet, bent in half and pulled, flinging her would-be attacker over her shoulder to land on the snow at her feet. She was panting for breath and her heart was thundering in her chest when Finn bolted back across the fence to join her. The mugger struggled to his feet and Finn took a step toward him.

"No," she said and moved in herself. Now that she got a good look at the guy, she could see that he was the man she'd seen wandering behind them on the sidewalk earlier. He'd only waited for them to separate, however briefly, before attacking the one he thought would be the weak link.

Well, she wasn't. Not anymore. Her self-defense courses would have helped her out here anyway. But after days of training with Joe and the other members of Finn's group, Deidre was confident, strong and too damn tired of being attacked.

"Stupid bitch," the man murmured. "I only wanted your money."

"But it's *my* money, isn't it?" He came at her again and she swung her right leg out, catching him in the abdomen with her knee. Breath wheezed out of him and he bent over, arms wrapped around his middle. Before he could straighten up for another try at her, Deidre hit him again, this time with both hands locked together. She slammed her fists down on the back of his neck and he dropped like a dirty stone.

She was breathing heavy, but if anyone had asked her how she was feeling at that precise moment, she would have said that she felt *great*. She'd taken a stand, done what she had to and shown not only herself but *Finn* that she could be counted on in a crisis. All in all, she owed the mugger a big thank-you. Not that she would give it to him.

"You okay?" Finn asked after a long minute while

Deidre stood over the mugger, staring down at him in triumph.

"Yeah." For a second or two, she considered what had just happened. A week ago, she might have been a weak noodle about now, wanting to swoon quietly in her room while she slugged back a couple of glasses of wine to recover. Now, she just felt . . . energized.

How quickly things could change, she thought, tearing her gaze from the mugger to look up at Finn. "You know, I'm really good."

"Oh," Finn told her with a slow, approving smile, "you're way better than good."

Chapter 28

Shauna woke up in a cold white room.

She was strapped to a table that was leeching warmth and strength from her body at a dizzying speed and she knew. It was made of white gold. Swallowing hard, she tried to move, but her naked body was strapped down tight. She lifted her head to take a look at her situation and nearly wept. Though the straps across her body were canvas, the shackles attached to her wrists and ankles were white gold. Like the table. She wouldn't be able to escape their grip and lying here naked, like some sacrificial lamb, told her that escape really was her only option.

Shauna almost laughed at the skimpy white towel someone had tossed across her, covering her from boob to groin. As if the thing she'd be worried most about in this situation was her modesty.

Her brain was still foggy, but bits and pieces were coming back as she pulled in one breath after another of the medicinally scented air. *Max.* He'd done this to her. He'd made love to her, then drugged her and brought her ... where exactly?

Shauna's eyes wheeled to the left and she saw a metal tray covered with different medical instruments. A counter held a sink, a paper towel dispenser and a black phone. She glanced around the rest of the room quickly. No windows to the outside world, but there was a glass partition between this room and another, filled with chairs arranged in stadium seating.

Not good.

If people sat in those chairs to watch a show ... then *she* was going to be the entertainment.

"Doc Fender," she whispered brokenly.

This had to be his lab. Where he experimented on witches. Where he tried to drain their powers and—*Oh, God.* Max had turned her over to a madman who was going to kill her—but not before torturing her first.

Terror wormed its way into her heart. She was choking on a knot of desperation in her throat and a single tear escaped the corner of her eye and rolled into her hairline. No one knew where she was. No one would even miss her until tomorrow when she was due back in the tunnels. Max had chosen the perfect time to betray her. There would be no rescue coming. There was only her and her will to survive.

When the door opened, she jerked against her restraints and shot a wide-eyed stare at the man stepping into the room.

Tall, with a full head of flyaway gray hair and blue eyes hidden behind round glasses, Dr. Henry Fender didn't *look* like a psycho. In fact, he had a kind smile, an Old World charm and a soft voice that practically begged you to trust him. The whole country thought of him as a miracle worker. No wonder that Max had believed Shauna would simply come here and leave without her magic.

Fender had built up an entire organization around the idea of stripping magical abilities safely. The Seekers treated him as a prophet, showing them the way to rid the world of dangerous magic. The only problem was, it couldn't be done. The public never knew that Fender tortured and killed the witches brought to him. Though they probably wouldn't have cared if they did know. After all, what was one more dead witch in the grand scheme of things?

And now, Shauna was going to be that dead witch.

"I won't tell you anything," she said, through chattering teeth.

Doc Fender gave her that patented smile, smoothed one hand over her forehead and said, "My dear. Of course you will."

Her heartbeat kicked into a hard gallop in her chest as she looked up into his eyes and saw . . . nothing there. Just emptiness. And she knew, deep within her, that she would never be strong enough to survive this man's attentions.

Though it did her no good, Shauna fought the restraints again, feeling the roughness of the canvas straps dig into her stomach and thighs.

"Now, now," Fender said, leaning over to pick up a scalpel off the nearby tray. He held it up, admiring the sweep of the miniature blade and allowing the overhead light to glint off the sharp edge. "No point in trying to get away, my dear. We both know you can't. Don't put yourself through the misery of disappointment."

As opposed to the sheer terror of torture.

"I am sorry that we're meeting here," he said with a sigh and a long look around the small, sparse room. He shook his head in sad disappointment at his surroundings. "My personal lab is far better equipped for the work you and I have to do today. But having you turned in was such a surprise, I'm afraid we'll simply have to make do with what's available."

Oh, God.

He gave her a proud smile. "I want you to know that all of my instruments are crafted of the finest white gold. Only the best is good enough for my work. The blades, of course, are stainless steel—much easier to hone a razor's edge."

Shauna couldn't tear her gaze from that scalpel as Doc Fender turned it hypnotically.

"Don't do this," she heard herself whisper.

He smiled gently. "Let's begin."

Chapter 29

"**D**o I really need to know how to make a bomb?"
They were back in the tunnels and sitting on a
bench in the armory. Deidre could admit, at least to herself, that she was becoming more comfortable down
here. At least, it was safe. She didn't have to be on guard
for an attack every minute. Yes, it had been nice to go
topside and breathe in some fresh air—but that trip had
also reminded her that she didn't belong in the real
world anymore.

This was her world now. These tunnels. Their chamber
with the crystal-studded walls and the oversized bed.
And, most importantly, this man. Her Eternal.

Her gaze locked on his as he leaned over a small table
littered with metal pipes, cotton batting and anything
else the well-equipped terrorist might need.

He looked at her and quirked an eyebrow. "Don't you
want a well-rounded education?"

She quirked her eyebrow right back at him. "De-
pends. Are these magical bombs?"

"If we could do it that way, we would. But no. These
are just your everyday pipe-bomb explosives."

"Then thanks, but I'll pass."

"Shauna knows how," he teased.

Deidre laughed at his attempt to use her recently honed competitive spirit to get her agreement. He was sneaky, she was discovering. And something of a smart-ass as well. It was weird, but she had started to enjoy her time with Finn. She hadn't expected to be anything but miserable down here in these godforsaken tunnels. But he was hard to ignore. And hard to avoid forming an attachment to.

After the incident with the mugger last night, she'd sort of had a come-to-Jesus moment. Oh, she'd known about the magical danger and the feds and witch hunters and every other damn thing in the world that wanted to kill witches.

But last night, a simple, ordinary mugging could have gotten her killed. Deidre never would have finished this quest. Never would have accomplished a damn thing that really *mattered*.

It all could have been over in an instant. Not because of supernatural forces, but because life sucked sometimes. Because you could be fine one minute and dead the next and there were no guarantees about any of it.

Long after they'd left their mugger behind, battered yet alive, and returned to the tunnels, Deidre had lain awake in Finn's arms. Sometime during the night, she'd realized she wasn't ready to die. There was too much she wanted to do. To set right. She wanted to complete this task of atonement—not because she felt any sympathy for the witch she had once been and all of her bad choices. But because she owed it to the world to do what she could to save it. Especially since she had been one of the women to set all of this misery into motion.

And if that meant facing memories she would rather leave buried in the past, then that's what she would have to do. She was strong enough. She believed that, now.

Plus there were all the women like her who were locked away in prisons. The little girls who grew up scared to be who they were. Someone had to help them. Someone had to fight for them. Like Joe had told her, when things got bad, people had to stand up, however they could. Deidre was ready to do that.

With her head on Finn's chest, she'd listened to the silence—the absence of a heartbeat—and had asked herself if they were doing the right thing in not Mating. If they had just done what they were meant to do, she might have all of her memories by now. By holding themselves back, were they risking too much? The world? Those doubts were still with her. She looked at him now and wondered if he regretted their choice to be together and yet separate, as much as she was beginning to.

While she watched, Finn picked up one of the pipes and carefully twisted on an end cap. Rebuilding their supply of explosives was taking a long time, she thought, as he checked the interior of his homemade explosive and carefully attached the fuse. She tapped her fingers against the tabletop until he glanced at her and frowned.

"Not a good idea during bomb-making class," he pointed out.

She hated the idea of having to use explosives to accomplish their goals. But what choice was there? Some of the places they had to infiltrate were so well guarded, there was no other way.

"Right," she said and felt suddenly antsy. As if she had to move. Do something. Be somewhere. She wasn't sure what had prodded the sensation, but it was real and it was growing inside her.

"What're you planning?" Finn asked, suddenly wary.

She tipped her head to one side and nervously twined a stray lock of hair around her finger. "World domination?"

He nodded sagely but couldn't quite hide the hint of a smile at his mouth. "I like a woman with goals."

"Yeah?" She leaned forward, cautiously bracing her forearms on the table. Glancing at the three completed pipe bombs, she took a breath and held it. This probably wasn't the best time to be having a talk about Mating. But her insides were jumping and a whisper of worry was beginning to thread itself through her body. So the sooner they talked about this, the better.

The sex magic had been great, but her memories weren't coming any more clear and Deidre knew they were running out of time. She knew what they had to do. They had to become Mates in the truest sense of the word. Open her magic. Complete this quest. So, with her goals clearly in mind, she said, "I've been thinking . . ."

"*Finn!*"

Joe's shout splintered the quiet.

Finn bolted up off the bench and was at the arched doorway of the armory chamber before Deidre had scrambled hastily to her feet.

Joe raced around the corner of the tunnel, skidded to a stop on the rocky ground and raked his gaze quickly over Deidre before pinning Finn with a steely look. "Shauna's been captured."

"*What?*" Deidre stepped up closer to Finn and stared at Joe as if he were speaking Greek. Shauna? Caught? How? She was with Max.

Torchlight from the tunnel highlighted Joe like an ever-shifting golden shadow. His features were tight, worried and fear snaked through Deidre in response.

"Heard it on the news," Joe told them, scraping one hand across the back of his neck.

"How?" Finn demanded and his voice was a low rumble of sound that seemed to roll through the room like a clap of thunder.

Joe flinched and blew out a breath. "Heard she'd been turned in by a 'concerned citizen.'"

"Max," Finn muttered.

"No, he wouldn't do that to her. He *loves* her," Deidre argued, and both men gave her the kind of pitying looks reserved for those who still believed in Santa. God, if they were right, poor Shauna. Not only captured, but betrayed by the man she loved.

Betrayal.

Something stirred inside her. Memory? Still, she pushed it away for later.

Finn demanded, "Where's she being held?"

Right. The most important part, Deidre told herself, wrapping both arms around her middle and holding on. They couldn't save Shauna if they didn't know where she was. And they *would* save Shauna.

"Called an old SEAL buddy," Joe admitted. "He's got connections high up and less than popular sympathies," he added wryly.

Meaning, Deidre concluded, Joe's friend wouldn't turn on him as someone had Shauna.

"He checked it out for me." Joe paused. "It's not good Finn. She's at BOW. With Fender."

"Son of a bitch," Finn muttered and glanced at Deidre. She saw the worry in his eyes, tangling with pure fury, and she knew her eyes looked the same. Those earlier ripples of foreboding and worry came back in a rush and this time, they were nearly staggering. Her heart felt like it was being squeezed by an ice-cold hand and every breath shuddered in and out of her lungs as if it would be her last.

Fender.

My God, even her mother worried about Fender and had tried repeatedly to shut him down. But he was practically a national hero. This year, he had even been named *Time* magazine's Person of the Year for his work against the supernatural.

"Good news is, he's here in the city," Joe was saying. "He hasn't taken her to his lab in Virginia, so they're close enough that we can move faster."

"That's the only good news," Finn said. He looked from Deidre to Joe and added, "Gather the group. You'll have to go topside to contact them."

"On it." Joe took a step and stopped. "We'll need a plan."

"We'll have one," Finn assured him and Deidre heard the determination in his tone. "Get everyone back here by nightfall and tell them to be ready to go."

"They will be." Joe was already headed down the tunnel to the closest exit.

"Be here in the armory by five," Finn called after him.

Joe lifted one hand in acknowledgment, but didn't slow his pace. When his footsteps were hardly a whisper of sound, Deidre spoke up, demanding, "Why are we waiting? Why not go after her now?"

He turned to look at her and in those pale gray eyes, flames of fury danced. "Because we go in with the best chance of getting her out. Broad daylight, the guards are heavier, too many pedestrians out on the street and too easy for us to be spotted." He walked to the far wall, picked up a bag and started stuffing it with guns, knives and throwing stars.

"Shauna . . ." Deidre whispered her friend's name and tried to imagine how terrified she was. How scared she must be that no one would come for her. That she would die in captivity at the hands of a madman.

"We'll get her," Finn said.

Deidre looked up at him. Tall, broad shouldered, he was a walking wall of muscle. She'd already learned he was single-minded, unwavering from his goal once set on a course. If anyone could get Shauna out of the clutches of BOW, it would be Finn.

But even superheroes needed *all* of their strength.

"I was going to talk to you about this earlier, Finn, but there's no time now to slide into the conversation smoothly. We have to Mate," Deidre said, determination flooding her. It was the only way. They needed every ounce of their magic and strength they could gather before they went after Shauna in a few hours. "It's time, Finn. Time to accept who and what we are. You said it yourself. I have to open myself to acceptance. No more hiding. No more avoiding."

Finn's gaze flickered in surprise.

"We're strong enough to do this as we are, Dee," he told her.

"Maybe," she allowed, walking closer to him. The slide of her shoes across the pebble-strewn ground sounded like a crowd shushing her. But it was well past the point of being quiet about what she was feeling, thinking. Now was the time to speak up. "But what if we're not? What if by holding back, we risk everything?"

He dropped the bag, letting it hit the dirt floor with a solid thud. Turning to face her, his features were unreadable and his eyes shifted and swirled with impossible shades of pewter and silver. "What's changed? Why now?"

"It's not just now. I was thinking about this before, too." Deidre laughed. "Besides, *everything's* changed, Finn. Me. You. My memories aren't coming fast enough. You said we've got thirty days and nearly two weeks are gone already. We're no closer to ending this 'mission' than we were when we started." She took a step closer, and then another one. "People are *dying* all around us and now Shauna's been captured."

Close enough to touch him, she was still surprised when he reached out and grabbed hold of her shoulders. He could move so fast, he was hardly more than a blur of motion. His hands on her sent heat washing through her and Deidre swayed with the impact of his body's energies mingling with hers.

"I'm right about this and you know it."

He didn't want her to be right. That was clear enough from his expression. Emotions chased each other across his features. Confusion, eagerness, reluctance, they were all represented and still he didn't let her go. His fingers dug in more tightly until she felt the press of each individual fingertip, right through the long-sleeved shirt she wore.

"The Mating ritual is forever, Dee," he said, gaze locked with hers. "Once started, it can't be stopped. And there's no going back to undo it."

She shivered as his words sunk in. Excitement? Worry? She wasn't sure and it didn't matter. "I understand."

"Do you?" He snorted, let her go and turned away from her long enough to reach up and shove both hands across the top of his head. Whirling back around, he glared at her. "We'll be joined for eternity, Dee. Always linked. Each of us always aware of the other and never really whole unless we're together."

She licked her lips and pulled in a long, deep breath. Right now, that all sounded pretty good to her. She'd already made this decision. Lying in his arms in the dark, she had realized that she wanted more from Finn. She wanted everything. She wanted the Mating not just for the strength it would bring her, but for the sense of one-ness she would share with someone else. Even the man who right now looked as if he would prefer being any-where but there, with her.

"Why are you against it, Finn? What happened in our past that makes you so anti-Mate?"

He laughed again but there was no humor in the sound.

"Aren't you the one who told me that our feelings didn't count for shit in all of this? That we had to become Mates for the sake of destiny?"

Shaking his head, he muttered, "I don't like having my own words thrown back at me."

"If they're not worth hearing, then maybe you shouldn't say them in the first place," she snapped and moved in on him again. "You called this our fate. Said we owed it to the world to do this."

"Yeah. I also said I didn't *want* a Mate. Remember that?"

Pain slapped at her, but she ignored it. "That's not news to me, Finn. No one has *ever* wanted me. Why should you be any different?"

"Dee—"

"But you do *need* me, whether you want to admit it or not."

"That's the problem," he snapped. "I've always needed you. And not once in eight hundred years have you ever returned the favor."

The look in his eyes had her backing up. Not from fear, but from a bone deep sense of . . . *shame?* What the hell did she have to be ashamed of?

"You're talking a good game now, Deidre," he said, and now it was him closing in on her. His gaze was fixed on hers. His jaw was tight and every word he spoke sounded as if it had been forced out. "But bottom line? We don't work as a team. Never have. Never will. Neither one of us is big enough to bend. We're both too blindly committed to going our own way to ever become the kind of Mates destiny had in mind."

Firelight threw shadows across his face that shifted and pulsed in a weird kind of dance that made him look fierce one moment and tender the next. It wasn't fair, she thought, him having access to all of the lifetimes they had spent together—when she had only bits and pieces of the past.

She didn't like knowing that his memories weren't good ones, either. Didn't bode well for what she was hoping to recall. But that was then and this was now.

"Well, I need you *now*. And we'll become the only kind of Mates we can be," she said simply. "We do what you said in the beginning. We Mate. We do what we have to and then, if we prefer, we go our separate ways."

He just stared at her, silence thrumming in the air until it was almost a presence. Another living, breathing being in the room with them.

After what felt like forever, Finn shook his head. "There are risks you don't know about."

"Then *tell* me!"

His gaze darkened, those soft gray eyes of his becoming more like dirty fog with chips of darkness swirling in their depths. "If we don't complete this quest—find the Artifact—by the end of thirty days, return it to Haven?"

She shivered at that word. "What? What happens?"

"Our souls die. No more rebirth. No immortality. It's over. Final. End of the fucking line." He stared at her, his mouth flattened into a straight, grim line. "Get it now? Mate and succeed, big prize. Mate and fail—oblivion."

Chapter 30

For a second, Deidre didn't know which seemed colder — that possible fate, or Finn's voice. Just when she felt as though she was getting to know him, to understand him, he threw her a curve ball and she was clueless again. He had to know, just as she did, that the Mating ritual was all important now. That they *needed* whatever strength they could get. Yet he was still pulling back. Almost as if he was trying to keep her from taking this step. As if he didn't want her to remember everything she had to. *Why?*

Staring up at him, she admitted silently that everything he had said put a new spin on the situation. But it didn't change anything, either. Without the Mating ritual, she would eventually die anyway. And meanwhile, she wouldn't be strong enough to do what she had to do. Shauna's life was at stake here. Not to mention the fate of the world.

"Then we don't fail," she said and hoped her voice sounded stronger than she felt at the moment.

"Just like that," he said flatly. "Shauna's captured and you're ready to hostage your soul to destiny?"

"I'd already decided to do it. Last night, after the mugger, I realized that we *have* to do this, Finn. I could have died right then, game over. We can't afford to risk failure. Whether you want me as your Mate or not."

"It's not about want," he told her, shifting his gaze to sweep the interior of the room as if searching for something. Finally though, he looked back at her and his eyes were burning now, flames shining at her, mesmerizing her.

Desire etched itself into his features and she felt his heat reaching out for her. Her heartbeat jolted into high gear and raced so fast, she felt it like a wild fluttering in her chest.

"I *do* want you," he admitted, reaching for her again, pulling her in close. "And I don't want you risking the death of your soul for this."

"It's my risk to take," she said, though that part made her insides quake.

"Damn it, Deidre." His arms came around her and like steel bands, tightened until she could hardly draw a breath. The tension in his big body radiated from him to her and back again. His hands swept up and down her spine, as if he couldn't touch her nearly enough.

"You *do* want me," she whispered and slid one hand up his back to the base of his neck. Her fingertips smoothed over his neatly shorn hair, then dragged across his skin.

He hissed in a breath, then gave her a brief, punishing kiss that had her blood boiling and her mind swimming. When he lifted his head again, his gaze locked to hers. "I do, damn it. That's why I don't want you to do this."

"That's why we have to," she said, suddenly feeling the calm that always came when she made the right decision. It was done. The worrying over. The questions, the doubts, the hesitation. And now that she knew which road they had to take, she didn't want to waste another minute.

She pulled out of his arms and snapped her fingers. Instantly, her clothes disappeared and Deidre smiled at him.

"You're getting way too good at that," he said, gaze moving over her in a hungry sweep that took in every inch of her body.

In response, Deidre concentrated, murmured a few words and waved one hand at the ground. Silken blankets and pillows popped into existence, their rich, lush colors in stark contrast to the rest of the room.

"You're sure."

"I am," she said and sank to the blankets at her feet.

He got rid of his own clothing a second later and dropped to her side. Pulling her into him, he pressed her body to his and Deidre sighed at the sensation of her skin brushing against his. The hard, muscled wall of his chest radiated heat and drew her touch like metal filings to a magnet.

She touched him and he caught her left hand in his right, threading their fingers together, connecting their bodies.

"Finn?"

He shook his head, glanced at their joined hands and instantly, flames erupted across their skin. Red, yellow, orange, blue licks of fire moved over their hands, between their palms, along every finger.

Deidre's breath caught in her lungs. She couldn't look away from the fire that burned without heat, searing the two of them together, into a single powerful unit.

Energy flowed from her palm, along her arm and down into her body. Deidre felt it like electrical sparks, igniting every cell, charging every square inch of her.

"Deidre," Finn said, calling her attention back to him. "It's still not too late. We can stop now and walk away from destiny. We don't owe that bitch anything."

"No," she agreed, lifting one hand to cup his cheek. "But we owe each other. We owe the *world*."

He seemed to consider her words before finally nodding. "Okay then. Deidre, do you accept me?"

Shadows crept closer and the fire on their joined hands seemed to burn brighter, bolder.

"Yes," she whispered, her gaze never wavering from his. "I accept you."

"And our past?"

A shadow flickered in his gray eyes, then disappeared again. Memory tugged at her before slipping away.

There was still so much hidden in the recesses of her own mind. She hadn't remembered nearly enough, but she had recalled enough to know that this was her quest as much as it was Finn's. She knew that their only chance to complete their task was to do it together. To trust each other. To let the past lie dead and buried and to take from it *only* what they needed to build a future.

"Yes," she said, nodding. "I accept our past, too."

The flames crawled along her arm now, moving across her skin in flashes of brilliance that dazzled the eye and burned in her heart with a matching intensity.

"And our future?" Finn's next question came quickly.

The future, Deidre thought, staring into his eyes. Until Finn, her future had been nebulous. She hadn't known what she would do. Who she would be. She had been simply an extension of her mother and that wasn't nearly enough. Now, she was terrified, motivated, stronger than ever and wildly in lust with an immortal being who had convinced her that she could do *anything*.

It didn't matter now, what the future held, failure or success. All that mattered was that Deidre was determined to meet it. To do all she could to not only survive, but to *succeed*.

"Yes, Finn. Our future, too."

The fire spread farther and she felt the first tugs of what felt like threads wrapping around their joined hands. She couldn't see anything, but those fragile, mystical strands wrapped tighter, holding them together, binding them at what felt like a cellular level.

"Do you take me as your Mate? To stand beside you? To do battle with you and to put right what once went wrong?"

At those words, magic swept through the air. Like nothing she had experienced before, it swarmed around her head, dove into her body and danced along her skin. Heat simmered inside her, bristling with newfound strength. The eternal flames erupted with a rush of sound and color and the air in the armory sang with the promise of things to come.

She felt alive, powerful, and instinctively knew that *this* question was the most important one of them all. She didn't have to look into Finn's eyes to know it. She *felt* it.

"Yes, I accept you as my Mate," Deidre answered slowly, carefully, wanting him to know that with every word, she was making her vow to him. To destiny. "I accept the responsibility of my role in this. I accept your help in the battles to come and will count on you to help me undo the wrongs of the past."

The flames dancing on their joined hands flashed so brightly, she was forced to turn her head against its brilliance. The flames died an instant later, winking out of existence as if they'd never been. And at the same time, Deidre felt a stinging burn in the center of her palm and she jolted in surprised pain.

The burn raced up her arm, down into her chest and centered behind her left breast, where it exploded again into a fiery sensation that stole her breath and made her sway in Finn's grip.

"What was that?"

He let go of her hand and grabbed her hips. Lifting her high, he then set her down firmly, pushing his hard, thick erection deep inside her.

Deidre gasped at the invasion and arched into him, wriggling slightly to feel more of him, to take him deeper, higher within.

"It's the Mating brand," Finn said, lowering his head to take her left nipple into his mouth. His tongue and teeth and lips worked her sensitive skin until she writhed in his arms, squirming uncontrollably as she rode the crest of a desire-filled wave unlike anything she'd felt before.

"Brand?" She frowned, licked her lips and said, "The tattoo?"

"Yeah." He raised his head, and urged, "Look at it."

Deidre wrapped her arms around his neck and glanced down at her breast. There, just above the dusky pink areola, she saw a dark red mark. Looked sort of like a burn. "That's it?"

"No," Finn said, leaning forward, to lay her on the blankets. "It's just the beginning. I'll have its match on my body. It marks us as a Mated pair. A team."

She looked at the top of his breast and saw the same mark she carried. Deidre touched it and he groaned. She smiled up at him. "I *like* it."

He rocked his hips against hers and she shivered. "I like *this* too."

"Damn straight," he muttered and launched into a frantic pace, driving in and out of her body with a need that was desperate, all consuming.

Deidre lifted her legs and hooked them around his waist. Her bare heels dug into his butt, pulling him in tighter, deeper as she moved with him. Matching her body's movements to his, she met him stroke for stroke, gasp for gasp.

Sex magic was nothing compared to this, she thought wildly as new bundles of nerves were lit up and exploded inside her. Tingles of expectation became a wave of orgasms that left her screaming his name and holding on to him as if he were the only stable point in the universe.

Again and again, she came, her body splintering, sealing itself and coming apart again. Brighter, faster, magic swirled and desire burned. Her body shook, quivered as she gasped for air and wept for more. He shouted and emptied himself into her over and over again. And still they weren't finished. It was as if awakening their magical bond had released something primal in them. Something so rare and wild that it couldn't be contained.

And as their bodies Mated, their souls were entwined and somewhere along the way, Deidre and her Mate became one.

Chapter 31

Not having to breathe was a big plus.

And still Rune hated being underwater.

Fully dressed, none of them had bothered with diving gear. They didn't need it for survival and what would be the point? Once they got out of this Belen-forsaken ocean, they'd use their magic to dry off and change clothes.

But the longer they were down here, the less likely it seemed they'd ever finish this job and get out. He, Torin and Damyn had been searching the bottom of the Adriatic for hours. Splitting up to cover more territory, they were determined to not leave this place without Egan.

But finding a solitary cage with one Eternal trapped inside was turning out to be a hell of a lot harder than he had thought it would be. Which was saying something.

Fucking fish everywhere were creeping him out. These bottom-dwelling fish were damned ugly, too. Give him a demon or a witch hunter and Rune was ready to do battle. Fear never entered into the equation. But down here, in the persistent, murky darkness, things kept bumping into him, sliding along his skin and he didn't like it.

A big damn fish swam too close to his face and Rune

lifted one hand to bat it away. But because of the water, his movement was so slow, the fish gave him a look that said if it had a middle finger to show, it would be flipping it to Rune.

Damn, if Egan didn't kill his Mate after all this, Rune might, for putting all of them through this.

The darkness and the pressure of the water were wrapped so tightly around him, it felt like he was moving through wet cement. His immortal eyesight plumbed the blackness with no problem, but it was damned cold at this depth. When Damyn joined him, Rune shook his head, silently letting the other Eternal know that he too had come up empty. A flicker of movement caught the corner of his eye and Rune turned his head to see which fish he'd have to avoid next.

Instead, he felt a hard jolt nearly knock him off his feet. He grabbed Damyn's arm, then pointed.

Damyn's eyes lit up. They headed for the cage, a darker spot among the shadows. Egan's arms were waving from between the bars and Rune had the first good feeling he'd had since they had started this trek. If Egan were rational enough to know a rescue operation when he saw one, then maybe he wouldn't be too far gone.

Rune's steps were slow and plodding and Damyn, right beside him, moved the same. Irritating as all hell that they couldn't flash underwater. But, the water kept their innate flames from taking hold, smothering the magic they needed to maintain them. Which must have only added to Egan's misery over however long he'd been trapped down here.

Damyn mimed about going to find Torin and Rune just nodded as the man moved off and was swallowed by the shadows. As he got closer to the cage, Rune could see his old friend's gray eyes shining like beacons in the darkness. Rune wouldn't be able to just wait for the other two Eternals to reach him.

He had to concentrate on getting Egan out. As he hurried forward, Rune pulled the hacksaw he had brought along with him from the belt on his jeans.

The first explosion at BOW headquarters lit up the night with sound and light. The old building at Thirty-second and G streets shook like a snow globe in the fist of an angry child.

Deidre and Finn were through the tunnel entrance beneath BOW before the last of the reverberations had faded away. They came up in a long-unused basement. Dust streaked the white tiled floor and cobwebs in the corner of the ceiling attested to its "forgotten room" status. Stacks of metal shelving went along three walls and a heavy steel door stood between them and the hallway.

Finn smiled grimly. Metal doors wouldn't be a problem. Nor would locks. Deidre's power was growing like nothing he'd ever seen before. Since they'd begun the Mating ritual that afternoon, even *he* had been stunned at the changes taking place in her. His brother Eternals had told him stories, of course, about how their Mates' magic had increased. But they'd talked about almost incremental changes.

With Deidre, it was more of a powerful eruption. As if the magic inside her, once free of the bonds restraining it, had blossomed all at once. Now that power was going to help them reach Shauna.

Finn looked at her. Her blue eyes were sharp, focused. Her blond hair was scraped back from her face into a long braid that lay against her back. She had used her magic to create a black sweater, jeans and boots and she looked like a beautiful commando. Finn got hard just seeing her like this. She was, he told himself, a hell of a woman.

"Get it open," he told her, looking behind him as Marco and two of the others crawled up the tunnel entrance behind them.

Deidre didn't waste a minute. She turned to the heavy door and flung one hand toward it, stabbing her fingers. Instantly, the sound of locks sliding free grated in the air and the door swung wide in welcome.

"Hot damn," Marco muttered and gave another man named Sam a high five.

"Yeah, Rich-witch comes through," Corey said.

"Cut the chatter. Just move." Finn looked at all of them, then carefully checked the hallway before waving them out after him. Not bothering to keep his voice low, since most of the BOW security would be out dealing with the explosion Joe and his team had set off. They'd placed the bombs as they always did where they could create maximum chaos with a minimum of human damage. He reminded them all, "We've got the specs on the building. We know where to go. We get Shauna and we get out. Mission over."

Deidre was practically vibrating with energy beside him. Her magic was surging and her self-confidence shone in her eyes. She was amazing. Beautiful. Strong. And damned powerful already.

"Okay, let's hit it." Finn led the way, Deidre right behind him. Marco, Corey and Sam followed after.

Their footsteps pounded on the white tile floor and bounced off the acoustic tiles overhead. Fluorescent lighting flickered unsteadily and the hush in the place

was damned eerie—especially in the wake of the first
pipe bomb exploding. The home of the federal agency
that tracked and captured witches felt cold and sterile.

They raced along the corridor, made a right and faced
another steel door. Another explosion shook the building and this time alarms sounded, a whining siren that
punched holes in Finn's ears, but made him smile. He
knew every able-bodied guard in the place would be
concentrated on the "attack" at the front of the building.

Joe and his team were creating a hell of a diversion.

Dee walked past Finn to the door. She fired up her
power and flung it at the steel door with confidence. In
response, locks clattered free again and this door too
opened at her command.

Marco whistled.

Finn led them down another hallway just like the first.
Empty white walls, scarred white floors, flickering light.
According to the specs and the information from Joe's
buddy, there were still two more doors and about a mile
of corridor between them and Fender's makeshift lab in
the basement.

The next two doors, Deidre opened as they approached and Finn held up a hand to silence his group.
If a few of the guards had stayed behind, no point in
warning them that Finn's group was coming. He waved
them to slow down.

Sure, adrenaline was a rush, but humans had to be on
their toes when dealing with the feds or it would be their
last rush.

"It's there," Deidre looked up at him, then pointed
down the narrow hallway. "Last door down the third hall,
just like Joe said."

Finn nodded. "Marco, Corey and Sam, you guys be

ready. We're going in to get Shauna—and shoot anyone who gets in the way."

The men smiled grimly and Finn knew he could count on them. Not one of them was a traitor. They'd all lost family to the witch hunts and Marco's wife and daughter were still hiding behind the shield of Sanctuary. Their loyalty was unswerving and at that moment, he loved them like brothers.

Deidre lifted one hand to send a wave of power at the last door. Finn caught her hand and closed his fingers over hers. "Open it and step aside, Dee."

"I can help."

"You already have."

She wanted to argue. He saw it in her eyes and in the way she clenched her jaw as if she was physically fighting back the words trying to get out. But thankfully her concern for Shauna overrode her natural tendency to buck authority. Especially *his*.

"Fine." She looked over her shoulder at the others. "Here we go."

"Get it done, witch," Corey murmured.

Finn held his sword in one hand and a gun in the other. He preferred the sword, but he was a man of his times— willing to use whatever he had to get the job done.

The door opened, Deidre moved aside and Finn went in first, dipping to the right. Sam came in behind him, heading left and Marco went in last, keeping low.

A single gunshot sounded and Sam went down. Finn swung his sword in the next instant, catching the guard across the midsection and the man dropped, dead before he hit the floor. Marco went to Sam, putting pressure on the shoulder wound while the other man grunted and tried to get up.

Finn was aware the moment Deidre stepped into the room but he didn't stop as he crossed the narrow room in three long strides, avoiding the white gold table and the icy feel emanating from it. A medical tray had been upset and instruments were strewn across the floor, lying in puddles of fresh blood that splashed across the white tiles and one of the walls. Finn hissed in a breath of raw fury.

Shauna's nude body, crumpled near a cabinet, lay in a pool of her own blood that was so fresh, it was still running in rivulets across the gleaming tiles. Her arms and legs bore witness to the torture she'd undergone before dying—long slices where dried blood had congealed. Two of her fingers were broken and her lip was split as well.

"Gods damn it!" Finn noted her hands still cuffed together in front of her and wanted to rip the building apart with his bare hands. Tear it stone from stone until nothing but crumbs of mortar remained.

"Shauna?" Deidre's voice cut to the heart of him. He didn't want her to see—

"You're far too late to save the witch." A deep voice spoke up from the far corner.

"Who the hell are you?" Marco demanded, standing up, putting himself between the injured Sam and the stranger.

A gray-haired man with kind blue eyes and round glasses never even glanced at Marco, instead his gaze went straight to Finn and stayed there as he answered, "I'm Dr. Henry Fender."

Fury washed through Finn. *Here* was the notorious torturer. Here was the man who had heard the dying screams of thousands of women—witch and human alike. This was the bogeyman of young witches' nightmares. The thing that went bump in the night.

Fender walked out of what looked like an observation room and took up a position behind a narrow white gold examination table on the far side of the room. Every cell in Finn's body went on red alert. The old man had a reputation for terror and pain that stretched around the globe. Just went to prove that danger didn't always *look* dangerous.

Deidre barely glanced at the old man. Instead she walked up to Finn, looked past him and gasped as she stared down at Shauna's body. He felt her pain like a white-hot stab to his gut. He wanted to comfort her, but now wasn't the time. "Dee—"

She whipped her head around and her blue eyes were alight with a murderous rage as she glared at the doctor. "You killed her."

"I most certainly did not," Dr. Fender disagreed, smoothing the lapels of his tweed jacket before leaning both hands on the table in front of him. "I had great hopes for her and she deprived me of my work." He frowned in disapproval at the dead woman, crumpled on the floor. "Silly bitch grabbed a gun from one of the guards. We had released her from her bonds in preparation for taking her to my base lab for further testing. But"—he shrugged—"she shot herself to avoid talking." He peered at them through round glasses. "Talking about *you* I would imagine."

Deidre made a move toward him. Finn grabbed her and pulled her back. "Stay away from that table."

Even from across the room, Finn was aware of the cloying sensation of the white gold. He didn't want Deidre any closer to it than she was right now.

"Ah, yes." Doc Fender looked from Finn to the others in the room before shifting his gaze back to Deidre. "Don't want a witch so new to her power to be drained. You are a witch, aren't you, my dear?"

Marco pulled the hammer back on his gun. The sound was as sharp and stark as a gunshot would have been.

Fender ignored the implied threat. "You're fairly glowing with power, my dear. I could help you. I could—"

"You bastard." Deidre made another stilted move to get at him.

"Dee—"

A single gunshot exploded into the room and Fender dropped, a hole in his chest. Marco spat on the body. "My wife and baby girl are forced to live in Sanctuary because of people like you, you *dick*." Then he looked at Finn. "Enough talk already. Fucker dies. Now. Besides, it's time to motor."

"You're right," Finn said with a satisfied nod as he gave the torture master one last look. If he felt a little disappointed that he hadn't been the one to end the monster, he put it aside. As long as the prick was dead, who cared who killed him? "Right about all of it. Grab Sam and go. We're right behind you."

Sam was already on his feet, swaying and a hell of a lot paler than usual, but standing. Marco handed his friend a gun, then slung Sam's arm around his shoulders and helped him back down the hall.

Another explosion from outside rattled the walls. Finn smiled grimly. Joe was putting everything he had into it. Then he looked at Deidre and the poor semblance of a smile faded. She was staring down at Shauna and as he watched, the sheen of tears in her eyes froze over.

"We gotta go," he said softly.

"I know." Deidre went down on one knee, kissed her friend's forehead and when she stood up again, she faced Finn coolly. Her eyes glinted with chips of ice. "I'm a *witch*."

"Yeah?" He didn't know where she was going with this, but judging by the hard edge in her eyes, he was going to like it.

"And I'm done being a good girl, Finn." She squared her shoulders, lifted her chin and whispered, "Marco's right. Fuckers are *all* gonna die."

Pride swelled his chest and a swift, hard jolt of something even more personal, more intimate cut at his heart. Deidre Sterling had just officially claimed him, body and soul. But now wasn't the time. He grabbed her hand and headed out and as they raced back down the empty corridors the way they had come in, he promised, "They're all gonna pay, babe. Starting tonight."

Chapter 32

The WLF hit an internment center two hours later.

They left Sam in the tunnels, under the care of Tracy, a former nurse. Then they loaded up on ammo and hit the tunnels again. Coming up at Massachusetts and Seventh streets, they organized fast. In the center of Mount Vernon Square sat what had once been the home of the Washington Historical Society. A Beaux Arts building originally built by Andrew Carnegie in 1902, for the last four years, the stately old white stone building with leaded windows had housed the local internment center.

In the middle of the night, it looked quiet. Damn near serene. Snow covered the ground and there were no recent tire marks marring the snowy circular driveway. Lamplight shone from three or four different windows, but the guards wouldn't be expecting an attack. And the skeleton night shift was rarely as alert as those on daylight hours.

Deidre looked up at the beautiful building and all she felt was a cold revulsion. Here, they kept suspected witches under lock and key until they were ready for the kangaroo courts that would sentence them to torture, prison or death. No one was ever found innocent of all charges. And once you had been locked up at Internment Central, you never went home again.

In the shadows, Finn nodded to Joe. Joe gave a thumbs-up to the teams waiting for his signal. Two bombs went off almost simultaneously, blowing out huge chunks of the building at both ends. The rattle of bricks and mortar hitting the ground was counterpoint to the blast wave that had Deidre's ears ringing.

Before the dust settled, their small army of well-trained guerrillas rushed through the gaping hole left behind in the north wing. They'd hardly entered the building before the gunfire erupted as guards tried to intercept them.

Deidre stayed on Finn's heels. She wasn't scared. Wasn't second-guessing herself. Didn't feel guilty for her first real act of domestic terrorism. She knew the WLF was careful to avoid killing if at all possible. But as for the building? This place and all the others like it had to go. These women had to be freed. What was happening to them was *wrong* and Deidre was determined to do whatever she could to protect the innocent.

Joe shot the first guard to get in their way, leaving the man on the floor, clutching his right leg, and they kept running forward, pushing ahead. Most of the night shift guards were still stumbling around in shock, so that gave the WLF the few necessary seconds to cross the widest part of the hall.

The black-and-white tiled floors thumped beneath their feet as they ran toward the stairs that would take them to the second-story holding cells. The old building had been renovated countless times and changed hands just as often over the years. Tall columns looked stately and elegant, even with guards hiding behind them firing off what sounded like hundreds of rounds of ammunition.

The WLF scrambled for cover.

Someone shouted in pain and Deidre winced even as she reached for her magic, felt that now familiar burst of power and then held up both hands. Her magic swelled from her, pouring from her fingertips into the open room and, instantly, she *halted* the rest of the bullets in midair. She exhaled with a rush and smiled to herself. It was getting easier. She had more control. She had more confidence in her own abilities.

She was becoming the powerful witch she had been once before, long ago. And at that thought, Deidre hoped to hell she made better decisions this time around.

With a flick of her fingers, she let the metal projectiles drop to the floor with a loud clatter sounding like rocks rolling down a mountainside.

Finn grinned at her, flashed across the room and grabbed one of the guards by the neck.

The federal agents in their black and gold BOW uniforms were all stunned. They'd thought they were safe here in their little fortress. They hadn't been expecting a frontal assault and none of them was prepared for *real* magic.

"Which of you wants to die for your cause?" Finn's furious shout rang out loud and clear and seemed to echo in the huge room. He gave the man in his grip a hard shake that had the guy gasping for air and clawing at the strong fingers wrapped around his throat.

When the feds hesitated, Deidre fisted both hands, and every gun the guards held was yanked out of their grips and the barrels turned on them menacingly. Oh, she wasn't going to fire the guns at them, but they didn't know that.

They got the message. One by one, they knelt on the floor and slapped their hands on top of their heads. Deidre kept them there by maneuvering their weapons to follow their every move.

"You guys okay?" she shouted to the rest of their team.

Marco called back, "Yeah, we're good. Katie's arm took a hit."

"It's a flesh wound," a feminine voice shouted from behind a toppled oak table. "Huh. I always wanted to say that."

Deidre choked off a laugh and found herself grinning at Finn. He nodded, dropped the guard he'd been threatening and ordered, "Pick up their weapons. Tie them up—if they try anything kill 'em."

"On it, boss," Joe yelled and, with four of their men, sprinted across the tiled floor, carrying plastic zip ties for their prisoners' wrists and ankles.

In the distance, Deidre heard the wail of a siren and knew they didn't have much time. Even with the city's emergency-response teams split between here and BOW, cops and fire trucks would be here all too soon. As if hearing her thoughts, Finn used his magic to appear at her side, wrapped his arms around her and then flashed them both to the second story.

As they disappeared in a pillar of flame, Joe laughed and asked an astonished guard, "Were you *really* thinking about fighting *him*?"

Upstairs, what had once been an elegant hall with dozens of small cells for private study had been turned into an open area, then outfitted with two dozen smaller cages. Only four of them boasted white gold bars. Apparently, BOW didn't have a never-ending supply of cash.

As her powers grew, so did her aversion to white gold, though. Deidre wanted to steer a wide berth around those particular cages. While silver enhanced a witch's magic, white gold—because it was a man-made alloy filled with all sorts of different elements—acted in the opposite way. White gold could drain the power from a witch, leaving her weak enough that she couldn't fight her attackers.

Which, she told herself, was probably exactly what Fender and his bunch had done to Shauna. Her spine stiffened and tears that wanted to seep from her eyes were instead turned into chips of ice filling her bloodstream. Shauna wouldn't want *tears*. She'd want Deidre to save these prisoners and that's just what she was going to do.

Women crowded the bars, all of them stupefied and excited, yet afraid to hope for the rescue that looked as if it was on hand. A rush of sound rose up from the women, all talking at once, pleading, shouting, some praying.

"Free the ones you can," Finn ordered and set off toward the four protected by white gold.

Dee didn't want to leave him. That alloy would affect him as much as her, but she knew time was slipping by too quickly. She sprinted down the length of the hall, starting in the back of the long room.

Waving one hand at the lock, she heard the metallic swish and clank of gears turning. Then the door swung open, the young witch inside stepping free with a stunned smile on her face. Just like the others, she wore a white gold chain around her neck, designed to keep witches docile. They'd have to get those chains off, but it could wait.

"That was . . . amazing," the girl said.

"Yeah, I know." Deidre grinned. "Help me with the others."

One by one, they freed them all. Young women, girls hardly more than children and one woman who looked about a hundred and ten. All of them sitting on what was, in essence, death row and all of them now free. But for the last four behind the white gold bars.

"Oh God," one of the women whispered, "you can't manipulate white gold, can you?"

"No," Deidre agreed, stepping up to Finn because she could see the tightness in his features. He had tried to pick the lock, then when that failed, he'd attempted to use brute strength to rip the door open. But it wasn't working and the proximity to the white gold was beginning to drag at him.

"I know where the keys are," one of the women whispered hesitantly, then dipped her head as if ashamed of speaking up.

"Where?" Deidre looked at her. Long brown hair, dirty and stringy around her pale, narrow face, the woman met her gaze with bruised brown eyes and fought back tears.

"The guard's break room. Down the hall. I saw them there when they—" She shuddered and another woman stepped up to drape her arm around her.

"They've been taking Crystal in there every night. If she says the keys are there . . . they are."

Finn nodded grimly, clearly understanding exactly what the woman had gone through and why she hadn't spoken up. Deidre knew why, too—she hadn't wanted to admit to herself what had happened in that room with the guards. Hell, it was a wonder Crystal was walking and talking after being treated like little more than an animal for who knew how long.

Bastards, Deidre thought. Not enough they had to lock women away, but they had to brutalize them, too. For one brief, fierce moment, she wished she had turned those guns on the guards downstairs and killed them all. It would have been more justice than any of these women had seen.

"Stay here," she ordered and looked at Finn. "I'll be back."

"I can flash there faster," he argued.

She shook her head, alarmed at the paleness of his skin and eyes. Working with the white gold was draining him and she needed him as strong as possible. "No, just . . . get away from the white gold."

"For God's sake," a witch behind those gold bars screeched, "get us the hell out of here!"

"Working on it," Dee shouted and took off at a sprint.

The freed witches gathered around Finn. Dee looked at all of them as she ran back to them, keys in her hand. A rush of something she'd never known before filled her, heart and soul. This was *it*. This was the place she had been looking for all of her life.

Here, she belonged.

She mattered.

She made a difference.

With the WLF. With *Finn*, she had found the home she'd always longed for. How weird to realize that in the middle of a life-and-death situation.

"Yo, boss!" Joe's shout from downstairs punched into the air. "Emergency teams getting closer! Gotta bolt!"

"Go," Finn ordered the women as he grabbed the keys from Deidre. They hesitated, but he shouted, "Friends are waiting downstairs. We'll get you out but you have to go now."

He turned to the first white gold lock, jammed the key in and turned it. The door opened and the captive witch sprang free. She ran, grabbing one of the other women as she went and that was enough to get the rest of the nervous, terrified crowd moving.

"Headed to you," Deidre called down to Joe.

"On it!"

Sirens wailed, coming closer, sounding like banshees announcing imminent death. Another white gold lock sprung and one more witch was hurtling down the stairs. The last two opened just as easily and when the final two witches were running to freedom, Finn grabbed Deidre and yanked her in close to him.

"*You* were incredible." His pale eyes shone with pride and hunger and something she couldn't quite identify.

Her heart turned over as she realized that just maybe, Finn felt more for her than he was willing to say.

She laughed, threw her arms around his neck and kissed him hard and deep. When she came up for air, she found him grinning at her like a loon. It was the widest, most sincere, most joy-filled smile she had ever seen on his face. And it went right to her heart and seared itself there forever.

"Like Joe said," Finn told her, grabbing her hand and threading her fingers through his, "gotta bolt."

He called up the flames to engulf them and Deidre asked, "Are you sure? You're okay?"

"I'm great," he assured her. "Let's flash downstairs and get those women to safety."

Deidre nodded, clung to him and laughed aloud as living flame erupted over their bodies.

Then together, they vanished in a pillar of fire.

Chapter 33

Deidre worked like a dog to help settle the refugees into temporary chambers set up in the tunnels. Marco and Tracy went for food and Deidre made sure all of the women had plenty to eat and a change of clothes from the WLF stockpile.

Finn watched her and was impressed as hell. She never stopped moving, never stopped reassuring the women who were balancing on a high wire between elation and fear. Released from their cages, the women were still in lockdown mode—uncertain about how to act, what to say. Their fears were ingrained and would take years to overcome.

Deidre told them about Sanctuary and promised they would all be taken there in a couple of days. Finn watched as she assured them that the tunnels were safe and smiled when she promised they were even cozy once you got used to them.

He figured she was making that part up, but it had helped the women so that was good enough for him. His heart broke a little as Deidre held the youngest girl in the group while she cried for the mother who had been killed by their jailers.

And finally, Finn had left Deidre and gone to help Joe in the armory. There was cleanup to get done and lists made of ammunition they needed to replace. By the time he was finished, he headed back to their chamber and found Deidre there, curled up on the bed, sobbing as if her heart were being torn from her chest.

Instantly, he gathered her up close, wrapping his arms around her and holding her while she grieved for Shauna and all the others like her.

He didn't speak. He simply gave her the comfort of his presence, hoping it would help. What could he say, after all? That everything would be okay? A lie. And unworthy of her.

"Why would Max do that to her?" Deidre whispered, face buried in his chest. Her fingers curled into his shirt and held on with a death grip. "She loved him. Trusted him."

"I know," Finn said softly, running one hand up and down her back in slow, smooth strokes. It cost him to bury the temper raging within him. But Deidre didn't need his anger.

Shaking her head, she gulped for air and released him long enough to swipe her tears away with her fingertips. More fell to take their place. "She told him she was a witch and he used it against her." Her features fierce despite the tears, she said, "She told him everything about herself. She probably—"

"—told him about that first raid we took you on?" Finn finished for her, a bitter taste in his mouth with the words.

"Yeah."

"That thought occurred to me too," he said, voice

grim, eyes narrowed. "Shauna trusted him, so of course she would tell him. There's my spy."

"She wasn't a spy!" Defensive of her friend, Deidre's eyes flashed and temper spiked a rush of color in her cheeks.

"No," he said, deliberately cool and patient. "She wasn't. She trusted a man who claimed to love her. She was my friend too, Dee."

It took a moment, but her features dissolved into a mask of misery again and she laid her head on his chest with a fresh bout of soul-deep tears. His own unbeating heart ached for her as he held her tightly, letting her pour out her anguish and pain. Her body shook with the racking sobs and her voice was raw as she cried and talked and cried some more. He held her through it all. For her he would be a rock. Patient. Stoic. Loving.

That word hit him hard and even as he accepted the truth of it, Finn rejected what it meant. An eternity together wasn't what he had signed on for. Besides, she was expecting him to leave when this mission was complete.

His arms tightened around her, soothing, giving comfort and taking it as well. Finn stared up at the crystal-studded ceiling above them and told himself that Shauna had known the risks. That fighting in the WLF was a choice they all made and that they had sworn to give their lives if they had to in order to protect others.

But she hadn't signed up to be betrayed.

Deidre's breathing evened out and her sobs dissolved into tired sniffles. Her body relaxed against his and soon he knew she was in an exhausted sleep. He kissed her head and gently rolled to one side, laying her on the mattress with the utmost care. His hand lingered for a moment on the curve of her cheek and his heart shattered further at the silvery tracks of tears across her skin.

She'd had too much taken away from her lately and, in response, she'd given of herself and now she had lost something irreplaceable. Deidre would recover, he knew. She was strong and she knew the stakes. So she would pull herself together and carry on—but there would always be a piece of her heart missing. A piece torn out by betrayal.

And that, Finn wouldn't stand for.

He didn't want to leave her. It tore at him to think of her waking alone and reaching out to find him gone.

But there was something he had to do and it couldn't wait. Kissing her gently, he eased off the bed, covered her with the midnight blue duvet, then checked his weapons. When he was ready, he flashed out of the tunnels.

Kellyn jolted straight up in bed. Morning sunlight crossed the room, reaching for her. But it wasn't dawn that had awakened her so brutally.

It was something else.

Something *wrong*.

She reached down inside herself, listening for the witch trapped inside her own body and found her there, screaming for release. Nodding, Kellyn smiled. At least she was still in control of this body. She'd waited too long and come too far to lose now.

So then, what was it?

Naked, she climbed out of bed and crossed the luxurious room until she reached the French doors leading onto a terrace. Below her, the city hummed with life, with purpose. Above her, a cold November sky shone a brilliant blue. She shivered, but it wasn't from the cold.

It was, she thought, the feel of one of her spells breaking. An enchantment had come down somewhere in the world and the chill snaking along her skin was the result. A sort of inner radar, letting her know that all was not as it should be.

"Fat lot of good it does me to know *something's* wrong, but not what, exactly." How the hell could she be expected to fix it if she didn't know what *it* was?

A moment later though, she decided to not worry about it. Things were moving too fast here. She and her partners were almost ready to claim their prize and damned if she'd let anything else interfere with something she'd waited centuries for.

"Screw you, universe. Do your damndest. You still won't stop me."

The storm raged all around them.

Lightning flashed across a black sky, spearing toward earth in a tremendous display of the gods having a temper fit. Thunder roared like a caged beast straining to get out and the wind rose up off the sea, tearing at the women's hair, flinging it into a wild tangle around their heads.

Yet for all the ferocity of the storm, the candles set at the five points of the pentagram carved into the earth remained lit. The flames didn't so much as waver, despite the tempest.

The witches of the last great coven stood in a sacred circle around the pentagram, skyclad, their nude bodies buffeted by wind and rain. Magic sang in the air as they lifted their voices together into a sonorous chant that demanded the attention of the gods. Demanded that they be given the full range of the powers once promised them.

And at the center of the pentagram they circled was the Black Silver Artifact, the focus of their magic on this night. They each concentrated on the complicated tangle of Celtic knots that gleamed darkly in the intermittent light from the heavens.

Deidre felt the wind tug at her hair, brush against her skin. Then the kiss of rain fell, softly at first, then harder, colder, slapping her like tiny needles thrown down by their goddess, Danu. She shivered, but remained resolute.

The sisters had agreed on this course of action. They had learned all there was to know, and they hungered for more. Hungered for the worlds beyond this one. The worlds denied them by jealous gods, protecting their power and domains from any usurper.

That ended tonight.

She picked up the chant, letting her voice soar with her sisters. They invoked the old ones, the wise ones. They called on the power of night and the magic of the stars. They resisted the pull of the moon, as the moon served Danu and wouldn't help them in this task.

Deidre chanted and while she did, she remembered her battle with Finn. How he had tried to take her from here. To keep her from joining with her sisters. To leave the coven incomplete on its most important night.

Tossing and turning in her sleep, Deidre moaned, reached across the wide bed for Finn and couldn't find him. She sighed once in loss and returned to the past . . .

Finn shouted that she was foolish. Blind. That he was here, and he loved her but she wouldn't need him. Wouldn't need anything beyond her sisters and their relentless quest for more power.

But Deidre did love him and so she told him. Facing down her lover, meeting those swirling pewter eyes that looked like molten silver when he was inside her. She told him then that she would need him tonight, when the spell was cast and the portal into the next world was open. Then she would need him by her side and they would have all that he wanted them to have.

And in the tunnels, Deidre wept.

The chanting swelled and magic pulsed from one witch to the next in the circle. The candle flames leaped three feet high with a whoosh of sound that seemed to take all the air from their lungs. The Black Silver hummed, electrified by nature and magic, and behind it, a portal opened.

Deidre rejoiced. This is what they had worked for. This is what they had earned. She looked outside the circle to the Eternals pacing in their frustration to get within the sacred circle. She searched for the one face she longed to see. Ached to see.

Finn wasn't there.

Then the Hellgate swung wide, and demons emerged in a chorus of shrieks.

Chapter 34

A white Ming vase with copper-red detailing of lotus blossoms hit the wall in the Oval Office and splintered into a thousand delicate shards. Once a gift from the premier of China, it was now brightly colored trash.

"YouTube?" Cora Sterling faced her aide, Darius, and gave her temper free rein. "Someone put a fucking video of Deidre participating in the internment center raid onto the Internet?"

Darius kept his distance. Ever a wise man, he had learned when to speak and when to shut up. Usually, Cora liked that about him. Today it was an irritation.

"Well?" she demanded. "Who did it?"

He cleared his throat, folded his hands in front of him and braced his feet as if expecting an even bigger storm in a moment. "One of the guards who were taken down. It seems that before they were tied up, instead of firing his weapon, this particular guard used his phone to make a video of the assault. And apparently, the video clearly shows—or appears to show—Deidre using magic."

Cora's vision went red around the edges and danced with black spots. She couldn't speak. She could hardly breathe. Her heartbeat sounded like a bass drum in her ears and even swallowing was damn near impossible. How the hell had this happened? Why weren't her ministers of security on top of this? Didn't they screen every damn piece of video some moron uploaded to the Internet?

"Don't we have *laws* against this?"

He whispered something and she turned on him like a snake. "What was that?"

"I'm sorry, ma'am," he said, keeping a wary eye on his president. "But the First Amendment still stands. Congress hasn't passed its revocation yet."

"You can't be serious!" She stalked around the perimeter of her office, frustrated, furious. "They were supposed to have that on my desk last week."

"The holidays are coming and—"

She whipped her head around, glared him into silence and put a tight rein on the temper already out of control. She had to remember who she was. What she was. "Do you think I care about the holidays? This country is in danger every damn moment. With free speech still a way of life, people are inciting riots. They're posting blogs and Web sites calling for more executions."

She took a long, deep breath and remembered the most telling argument she had had for "temporarily" dispensing with the First Amendment to the Constitution. "For the public good, we must censor our own people. They're terrified and helpless. At the mercy of those who would use fear to win their arguments."

"I understand, ma'am, and I sympathize—"

"I don't need your pity, Darius," she snapped. "Only your obedience."

"Of course." He dipped his head in obeisance and she felt a little better.

"What's been done about this guard who posted the video?"

"I believe he's on unpaid leave from his unit pending investigation."

She simply stared at him. It boggled the mind, it really did. "Unpaid leave? That is his punishment from his superiors?"

"For now, ma'am," Darius murmured.

"No, that won't do." She walked calmly, coolly, to her desk and deliberately sat behind the stately *Resolute* desk, used by so many presidents before her. Instantly, Cora felt restraint flood her system as she put things into perspective. One video. How much damage could it have done?

"Have you pulled the video, Darius?"

"Yes, ma'am. Homeworld Security pulled it this morning."

"After how many viewings?" she asked quietly.

He frowned, swallowed and winced before admitting, "Two million and change."

"Two *million*?" Cora reached for her calm again, drawing on her years of practice. Her hand fisted around a black onyx pen and squeezed until her knuckles were white. She took deep breaths, willed her heartbeat back into a normal rhythm and at last, conquered her demons long enough to say, "Two million people saw my daughter wielding magic."

"Yes, ma'am. It showed her controlling weapons, stopping bullets in midair and being . . . transported by a man made of fire."

"Sweet mother of all that's holy," Cora muttered. Shaking her head, she took a breath and said, "Obviously, the video was doctored. Special effects these days are so tremendous they can fool people into believing anything. Fine, fine. I'll take care of this. Set up a press conference for day after tomorrow. Don't want to rush this or we'll look worried."

"Shall I call your speechwriters in?"

"No, I'll be speaking from the heart. The people will see me and believe me," she said confidently, not sure whether she was reassuring Darius or herself. "If we wait to give the speech, it will give everyone time to think about what they've seen and heard. They'll know that I've given the matter much careful consideration. And they'll believe me when I speak to them."

She would do what she had to to protect her daughter. To see that her plans for this nation weren't sidetracked.

"Yes, ma'am," Darius said and turned to go.

"And, Darius," Cora said, swiveling in her chair to look out over the White House lawn. She saw her aide's reflection in the bulletproof windowpanes and speared his gaze with hers. "The guard who took the video? Speak to his supervisor immediately. I want his employment terminated."

"Yes, ma'am. I'll see to it personally."

He left and Cora was alone. She stared out at the lawn, the protesters out beyond the fence that protected her from the American people and at the city beyond them. Somewhere out there, her daughter was frightened and in the hands of a terrorist.

She had to get her back.

Max had already counted his money three times.

He'd been up all night and now, in the early morning, he still couldn't seem to stop touching the lovely piles of green in front of him. He'd made neat stacks of hundreds, then he'd spread them across the coffee table like a beautiful green tablecloth. Then he had stacked them again, running his fingers over the crisp bills, counting the ways this was going to get him out of trouble.

"I'll pay off the gym. Maybe get a new car," he told the empty room. "Hell, I can do whatever I want, now."

He jolted and leaped to his feet when a pillar of fire appeared in his living room, just inches from him. The flames winked out and Max was staring up into a pair of cold gray eyes.

"Who the hell—*what* the hell are you?"

"Something you never should have pissed off," Finn told him. He lifted one hand, sent the bills floating to the floor, then stabbed one finger at the closest pile. Flames leaped from his hand to the money and Finn relished Max's shriek when the bills burned and curled, sending tendrils of smoke upward.

"Cut it out, man," Max shouted, dropping to his knees briefly to pat out the fire. "That money's *mine*."

"I know it's yours, you little prick." Finn's gaze took him in and dismissed him as a worthless pile of shit.

Max saw the look and made the mistake of getting tough. He got to his feet, bunched meaty fists at his sides and said, "You can't come in here and—"

Finn unleashed his sword and the hissing sound silenced Max instantly. His gaze landed on the long, wickedly curved blade that shone in the sunlight pouring through the window.

"Just a minute, man. We can talk. I mean, uh . . . what's the deal?" He backed up until he slammed into the wall; then he looked around, terrified, realizing he was trapped. The only way out was through Finn and that was never going to happen.

He licked his lips, wiped one hand across his broad face and asked, "This is about Shauna, isn't it?"

"Give the dick a prize." Finn watched realization dawn on the bastard's face and enjoyed the fear that sparked in his eyes. "I'm here because you betrayed Shauna. For *money*."

Max swallowed hard, ran one hand over the sweat beading on his forehead. "She's gonna be okay. They'll take the magic out of her and—"

"She's dead." Finn watched the words hit home and he saw, in Max's eyes, that despite the expression on his face, the man wasn't surprised. He had known exactly what he was doing. He'd sold Shauna, knowing she'd die. He just hadn't expected to join her.

"No, I didn't mean for that to hap—"

Finn had had enough. He sent his sword through Max's middle with one quick blow and the big man just stared at him in disbelief. Pulling his sword free, Finn watched, unmoved, as Max dropped to his knees, hands clutching his belly, where blood spilled out over his fingers to drain onto the floor.

Calmly, Finn wiped his sword blade on the couch, then resheathed it.

"But—"

"Shauna's dead," Finn said again. "And now, so are you."

He called up the flames and flashed out.

Alone, Max fell forward and died with the smell of money in his lungs.

"Where were you?" Deidre was wide awake and waiting for Finn when he appeared in their chamber.

Frowning, he said, "I went to see Max. He's dead."

"Good." Deidre spat the word. "But that's not what I meant. Where were you back then? When I needed you?"

Finn sucked in air like a drowning man. It was here then. The confrontation he'd been dreading. She finally had the memory of that night and he couldn't keep the truth from her any longer. He had hoped that somehow she would regain every memory but that one. He shrugged out of his coat, dropped his sword and knife belt on a table, then turned to face her.

She looked, he thought idly, much as she had then. The features were different, of course, but there was a prideful tilt to her chin and the promise of retribution in her eyes that was damned familiar. Her magic was shimmering around her in an aura bright enough to light up the chamber, but those eyes looked cool.

"I was in London."

"Why the hell were you there?" she countered. "Every other Eternal was right there that last night. Trying to reach their witches. Trying to stop us. But you—"

He shoved both hands across the top of his head, then glared at her. "How the hell was I supposed to know you would finally *need* me?" he snapped the words out, as furious with himself now as he had been eight hundred years ago.

"I looked for you," she said and her voice was almost wistful, tearing at Finn like knives.

His gaze snapped to hers. "You think I don't know that? That I haven't known it for eight hundred fucking years?"

She didn't even blink at his tone. At what had to be an expression of frustrated fury on his face.

"You've haunted me, Dee," he admitted in a growl

that scraped at his throat as the words escaped. "Through time, I've carried you with me. I relive that night over and over again. In my mind, I change things. I do it differently. I'm there, with you when crap rained down on all of us." He blew out a breath. "But the reality is, I can't change it. I can only regret it."

She scrubbed her hands up and down her arms. "Regrets? I just lived through the reenactment and I can tell you, I've got plenty to regret." Turning her gaze up to him she said, "But you did come to me that night. You were there ... finally."

"This is damned infuriating, defending myself over an eight-hundred-year-old argument."

"Yet, you think you need defending."

"Of course I do. Why the hell do you think I didn't want to Mate with you *now*? Because I wasn't there when you needed me. When you finally called for me—I wasn't there. I've lived with that for centuries, Dee. Not something I'm proud of."

Finn's teeth ground together. He didn't like thinking about that night. Hated remembering that the one time she had ever needed him he hadn't been there for her.

Back then, he'd hungered for her like a damn madman. She'd been ethereal. Elusive. She gave him her body and withheld everything else. Her heart. Her soul. She had kept him at arm's length always, insisting on going her own way. Then, it had frosted his ass. Now, he admired that same trait in her. So who really had been the one with the damn problem?

Like a blanket had been pulled from his eyes, Finn saw the past as it had really been. Not as his own damaged pride and fury had painted it all these centuries. He'd wanted her to be less than she was so she would need him. When he should have been at her side, proud of her strength.

God, what an idiot.

"Yeah," he finally said. "I did come back to Haven that night. I felt your fear," he muttered, reliving those moments when cold had dropped over him and he had known that she was in trouble. "I got back as fast as I could. The battle was already engaged. You were—"

"Wounded," she said for him.

"Yeah." He nodded and swallowed hard. "Blood pouring down your arm, dripping onto the ground and when I saw you hurt—I lost it." He closed his eyes and let it come back. "I tore through demons to get to you. To protect you. To make up for not being there when you needed me."

"You saved me."

"No. I couldn't save you from yourself. You and your sister-witches jump-started a damn war with Hell that night and none of us could talk you out of it."

"I know—"

"But I'm going to save you now, Dee," he said and reached for her. Yanking her close, he looked into her eyes and knew that the love he'd had for her back then, as deep and rich as it had been, didn't even come close to what he felt for her today. "I never saw it until now, but your strength was what bothered me. Your confidence, your abilities, seemed to ensure that you would never need me. I let my own pride dictate what I did back then.

"This time I will for damn sure *always* be there when you need me."

"But," she said softly, "it's not enough for me, Finn. You say I never needed you, I only wanted you. Well, now, you don't want me, you just need me. To complete your mission or slap a Band-Aid on the past." She poked him in the chest with her forefinger. "Well. I've been needed and used all my life. For politics or to look good or to be the right friend at the right time. I'm tired of being *needed*. *Used*. No one has ever *wanted* me, Finn. Just for me. Deidre Sterling."

"Maybe it's karma's way of kicking my ass, twisting this all around like she has," Finn muttered. "Making us each feel what the other had so long ago. Hell, need. Want. To me, they're the same thing. I need you. I want you. Not for what you can give me but because I'm not whole without you." He cupped her face, his thumbs tracing across her cheekbones. "You're *it*, Deidre. Didn't want you to be. Thought I was long past the hunger for you. But it's more than that now. You're air to me. Magical, mystical."

He shook his head, his gaze moving over her features like a caress. "I thought I could walk away from you. Mate and then leave. Well, screw that. Damned if I'm going anywhere and you can just learn to live with it."

"How can I believe that you're not just trying to some-how salve your own conscience for what happened cen-turies ago? I want you to want *me*. Not her—not that witch I was so many years ago. Not what I can do. Just *me*. Deidre Sterling. And you don't."

He laughed quietly, slid his fingers into the soft hair at her temples and forced her to meet his gaze. "Now you're the crazy one. You're not listening to me, Deidre. I want you more than I've ever wanted anything. You've be-come the very center of me, Dee. Without you I've got nothing. With you, I've got everything."

She trembled a little and he read wariness in her eyes. "I want to believe that."

"You can," he insisted, never breaking his gaze. "Because I swear to you—if it comes down to a choice between your life or saving the world? I choose you and fuck the world."

She took a breath, held it, then laughed. "That's really insane, you know."

"Shoot me, I'm a romantic."

Deidre laughed and leaned into him. "No, you're not. But apparently, that's okay with me."

He wrapped his arms around her, felt his own little corner of the universe slide into place. "So are we good?"

She looked up at him. "We're way better than good."

"You keep throwing my own words back at me."

"I have an excellent memory."

"I'm getting that." He kissed her forehead. "So, besides remembering what a dick I was, did any other memories pop up? Like what the hell you did with that damned Artifact?"

"Sort of," she said, frowning.

"What's that supposed to mean?"

"Yeah," she said wryly. "A romantic. That's you."

"Deidre—"

"I don't know what it means. I saw myself—her— whatever, leaving Wales. She was headed for London. That's all I've got so far."

Finn bit down on his own impatience. It was not helping. "It'll come."

"In time?"

"We still have more than a week. We can do it. We *will* do it." He reached down and peeled back the edge of her shirt. His fingers moved across the tattoo inching its way across her skin. A ribbon of linked chain was forming around her breast and would soon wrap under her arm and around her back.

His mark.

Damn, he was still a medieval guy, he supposed, because the thought of her wearing his brand made him hard as stone. He wanted to claim her again and again, revel in the knowledge that she was his.

"Guess we'd better try to open more memories." He picked her up and headed for the bed.

Chapter 35

A howl of rage and pain shrieked through the sage-scented air of Haven.

Teresa cringed and looked across the table at Rune. "We can't just leave him in there alone."

Rune didn't like it any more than his Mate did. Bringing Egan back to Haven had been their only choice. Locking him up was the only sane maneuver left to them.

Frowning, Rune admitted, "He's better off alone right now, Teresa. Egan's half mad with rage. I don't trust him around you or the others."

She dropped an uneaten cookie onto her plate. "So what? We get him out of one cage and put him in another?"

"It's not a cage," he grumbled, pushing away from the table.

Another howl sounded out, filled with pain and misery and so much fury it raised the hairs on the back of Rune's neck. He swung out an arm and pointed off down the hall toward Egan's room. "Did you hear that? Hell, Teresa, he's hardly done more than that since we got him out of that damn cage at the bottom of the sea." His voice dropped and his shoulders hunched as if distancing himself from the pain his brother was feeling. "I've known Egan for centuries and the Eternal sitting in that bespelled room? *That's* not Egan."

"Of course he is," Teresa argued, going to him to lay both hands on his forearms.

Just the feel of her touch was enough to soothe him, Rune thought and thanked Belen, Danu and any other god that had had a hand in bringing them together.

He dropped his forehead to hers and inhaled the familiar scent of her. "He's not who he was," Rune corrected. "And what about his Mate? You haven't discovered anything about Kellyn yet."

"No," Teresa muttered, clearly frustrated. "She's been charmed or she's cast a spell on herself. It's as if she's drawn a blanket over her head, keeping us from seeing what's beneath it. But we'll get there."

"I know you will."

"See? You have faith in us, so have faith in Egan. He's hurt and angry and who the hell can blame him?" She wrapped her arms around him and held on. "But he's still Egan. Once his mind realizes that he's truly free, he'll come back to us. You'll see."

Rune wanted to believe her, but the madness in Egan's gray eyes had chilled him to the bone. It had been days and Egan was no closer to regaining any semblance of self. He was still the raging, infuriated beast they'd pulled from the water.

And Rune worried that that was all he would ever be.

If that was true, then the Awakening was over and the world was in deep shit.

*   *   *

"We've got trouble."

Finn and Deidre looked up from the map of the city they had been studying. Her head was spinning from all the new information, but she had a much better understanding of exactly which tunnels went where in the city now.

As the days passed, she and Finn were more and more the team they always should have been. Her heart was full and her soul more at peace than she ever would have believed. Even living a life on the run, hiding from federal agents, local cops and everyday citizens, couldn't take away the satisfaction of knowing that she was doing what she was supposed to be doing. With the Eternal she had always been meant for.

But their little interlude was over and the world was once more interfering. Joe was standing in the archway, torchlight shifting shadows across features that were tight with resignation.

"What kind of trouble?" Finn asked and Deidre was amazed again at just how quickly her Eternal could go from relaxed lover to deadly warrior mode.

Joe walked into the armory, holding a small computer tablet. He tapped it on as he came closer.

"We get Internet down here and not phone service?"

"No." Joe looked at her and shook his head. "This isn't live. A friend downloaded what I'm about to show you and I loaded it up onto the tablet. It's not good."

Finn scowled and said, "Just show us."

He did and Deidre went cold as she watched the raid at the BOW internment center play out on the screen. She saw herself holding her hands up, turning weapons around on the agents and flicking bullets to the floor as if she was dismissing lint from a black coat. Then she watched as Finn approached and flashed her out of the room.

All of it caught in living color.

Her heart actually sank. "What the—"

"One of the guards apparently used his cell phone to make a video of the raid. Never saw the bastard do it, either."

This was definitely not good. If it had been up on the Internet . . . "When was it posted?"

Joe met her gaze. "It went up right after the raid."

"That was *a week* ago."

"Yeah. The feds pulled it but . . ."

Pulling it wouldn't have helped and she knew it. Something like this went viral in a matter of minutes. No telling how many people had watched her perform magic. Watched her and Finn disappear in a column of fire.

"Oh, God." Deidre looked up at Finn, saw the closed expression in his eyes and wondered what he was thinking. Her own feelings were fragmented, shattered into a million different emotions.

In a weird way, she was almost proud as she watched herself perform magic. But the reality was, she'd been exposed. This video had probably been around the world several times already. She'd put her mother in a terrible position and she couldn't even imagine what was going on in the White House right now as a result of all of this.

God. It had been weeks since she'd read a newspaper or seen a news program. Life in the tunnels was so separate from everything, she may as well have been on Mars.

"Like I said, the feds took the video down," Joe was saying. "Claimed it was being used to foment fear and violence."

Great. Now Deidre was going to be the poster child for witchcraft. Fabulous.

"Taking it down doesn't mean anything," Finn said. "Hell, we're proof of that. We're standing here watching it *after* they pulled it."

"Yeah," Joe said. "And there's more."

"What's *left*?" Deidre countered and appreciated the arm that Finn dropped around her shoulders.

Amazing, but since beginning the Mating, accepting him and who they were together, Deidre felt stronger than she ever had before. She knew her place in the world. She knew what was important and what was just clutter.

This was important.

"My friend also recorded something else." Joe's eyes were soft with sympathy as he looked at her. "You're not going to like it."

Nodding, Deidre said only, "Play it."

Finn stood beside her, his body as tense as she felt. She leaned into him and lifted one hand to lay it atop her left breast, where her Mating tattoo was still growing. It gave her strength. Completed the connection to Finn that she had a feeling she was going to need.

Joe called up the next file and turned up the sound.

It was the White House press room and Deidre held her breath. Her mother walked to the podium, surrounded by frowning aides and Secret Service. She recognized Darius and in the background, Dante.

"Thank you for coming," her mother said, looking directly into the camera. "I have a brief statement and I will not accept questions."

Murmurs of disapproval rumbled through the room, but Cora Sterling only stiffened her spine and lifted her chin. Deidre knew that look. Her mother had been pushed to the brink and she was calling on every ounce of her fierce will to get through this.

Guilt nibbled at the edges of Deidre's mind and she winced. God knew what her mother had been going through the last week. What people had been saying to her. Both houses of Congress were probably up in arms and oh, she didn't even want to think about what the press had been saying.

Deidre knew all too well that some of the senators and congressmen were pushing for a repeal of the First Amendment. To temporarily get rid of free speech in an attempt to put a lid on the witch situation. With every fruitcake in the world going on blogs or simply standing on street corners trying to foment riots, some people thought the only way to calm everyone was to curtail what was being said.

Deidre didn't think she could live with herself if she turned out to be the reason the Constitution was stomped into oblivion.

"As most of you know," Cora began, her words coming fast, clipped. "My daughter, Deidre, was kidnapped two weeks ago. But for one short phone call, I've had no contact with Deidre since. I've prayed every night for her safety and I thank all of you who have joined me in that.

"Recently, a disturbing video was on the Internet. It showed Deidre wielding magic. Appearing to take part willingly in a raid at a BOW internment center."

The reporters in the room took a collective breath— and so did Deidre. She reached for Finn's hand and he curled his fingers over hers.

"The world's newspapers, television news stations and Internet sites are now insisting that my daughter has not been kidnapped by terrorists at all—that she *is* a terrorist. I cannot tell you how harmful such lies are. The pain they have caused me personally and the damage these lies have done to the fight against cruelty to witches is immeasurable. So let me say this plainly," Cora told them all, her gaze moving steadily over the reporters hanging on her every word. "The video is a fabrication," Cora said flatly. "The White House has investigated, brought in experts to examine the original video and they have assured me that it has been doctored.

"Deidre's kidnappers have altered the film to make it seem as though she has become one of them. As if she herself were a witch."

"What?" Deidre murmured.

"Shh," Finn urged.

The reporters in the press room began muttering to each other and the sound grew into an angry buzz, as if a swarm of killer bees had just dropped into the room.

Cora held up one hand for silence and instantly got it.

"These people are holding my daughter. She's in danger. And now they're stripping away not only her freedom, but her reputation." A solitary tear tracked down Cora's cheek as the camera zoomed in to capture the poignant moment.

"I promise you now, as your president, as Deidre's mother, I will stop at nothing to find my daughter and bring her captors to justice. Thank you."

The room erupted with questions shouted from the reporters. Camera flashes sputtered from every corner. One of the White House aides stood at the podium shouting for quiet as Cora turned, and surrounded by Secret Service personnel, left the briefing room.

Joe turned the tablet off and the sudden quiet was overwhelming.

"Oh my God. I don't believe this." Deidre's heart

ached. All she could see was the tear her ferociously controlled mother had allowed to slip past her guard. The
guilt that had nibbled on her earlier began to chow down
in earnest now.

She had always had a complicated relationship with
her mother. Cora wasn't the warmest human being on
the face of the planet. And her goals and dreams had
always taken precedence. But Deidre loved her and
knowing that she was causing her mother not only personal anguish but professional pain was a hard thing to
live with.

"Dee," Finn said, his voice slicing into her thoughts
with the finesse of a freight train. "You can't go to her."

"I know," she said, even though her mind was racing
with the notion of doing just that. The least she owed her
mom was to show her she was all right.

"I mean it." He jerked his head at Joe in a signal to get
lost, and when they were alone again, he turned her to
look at him. "I know what your mother means to you,
but you cannot go to the White House. It's just too dangerous. Whoever told your mother that tape was doctored is lying to her. Which means there's someone
around her who can't be trusted."

"Yeah," she admitted, "I thought of that, too." She
wrapped her arms around herself in a futile attempt to
stave off the cold swamping her.

Funny, but over the last couple of weeks, she'd actually adapted to the chill of the tunnels. Acclimated to the
taste of dampness flavoring every breath. She hadn't
been really cold in days. She was now.

"You can't go to her."

She snapped a look up at him. "You said that already.
God, Finn. Give me a minute here, okay?"

"I know what this is doing to you," he said, pulling her in tight and closing his big arms around her. "If I could change it I would. But my first priority is your safety, Deidre. Something's not right with this and until we discover who's behind the lies, then I don't want you anywhere near the White House."

He might be used to giving orders, but Deidre wasn't as accustomed to taking them. She knew he was only looking out for her, but she was a damn adult. Not to mention a powerful witch. She could take care of herself and she didn't appreciate being told what the hell to do. Or maybe it was just that her insides were jumping with fear and worry for her mother.

She clung to him, relishing the warmth and safety he offered, but even as she held him, Deidre knew she wouldn't be able to let this go. Someone had lied to her mother about that video. What if they planned to do more than lying to the president? Deidre couldn't live with herself if she found out too late that her mom had been in danger and she'd done nothing to help. She had to see her mother—whether Finn approved or not.

Chapter 36

A few hours later, Finn and Joe were ready to do some recon for their next raid. One of Joe's friends had told him about an execution planned for the following week in Alexandria, Virginia. The internment camp there was getting crowded, so the theory was to dispose of the troublemaking witches and it was a win-win for everyone.

The WLF would be making another raid to save those doomed witches and they needed the intel they could get only from an up-close-and-personal visit to the site. Of course, finding the Artifact was still the most important thing to Finn and Deidre both. But until they did that, there were women to protect.

"Do you want to come with us?" Finn asked as he strapped on his knives and sword.

"No," Deidre answered, but smiled. Even discounting his unreasonable protective streak, they'd come a long way if he was willing to include her on a recon mission. "I'm going to help Tracy inventory the medical supplies. We're running low on just about everything."

"Right." He nodded, came to her and kissed her as if

her lips meant his life. When he finally let her go, he looked down into her eyes and said, "I know you're still thinking about the video and your mother. We'll figure this out, Dee. Together. Meanwhile tomorrow we'll go topside so you can at least call her again."

"Okay, thanks. Now, go do your job and don't worry about it."

He stared at her for a long minute and Deidre forced herself to maintain her smile. Wouldn't do for him to suddenly decide that Joe could do the recon without him. Deidre just needed an hour or so. She'd be back long before Finn. "Just go with Joe. Tell me all about it when you get back."

He nodded, shrugged into his black coat, then with one last kiss, flashed out of the tunnels.

The minute Finn was gone, she grabbed her own jacket and pulled it on, then yanked the note she'd written to Finn out of the pocket and laid it on the bed. Then she ran from her chamber and hurried down the tunnel in the opposite direction of Tracy and the inventory she'd lied to Finn about. Deidre made one brief stop at the supply room where they kept everything they might need on missions—not to mention the extra clothes and bedding they needed for the witches they rescued.

Back in the tunnels, she ran, her boot steps pounding out a frantic rhythm that matched her heartbeat. She knew her way around now and her main concern was to get as far away from everyone else down here as possible before she could chance using one of the exits.

She knew this was a risk. But Deidre couldn't get the image of her mother out of her mind. Cora didn't look well. She had lost weight and frankly, the loss of control that had allowed a tear to be seen by the world was so unlike her mother that Deidre was terrified for her. Then there was the chance that whoever was lying to Cora was also a danger to her.

Deidre really did hate going behind Finn's back, but she had to make sure her mother was all right. Besides, if there were a traitor in the White House and he pulled three dozen guns on her—Deidre would disarm him and still be back before Finn. Back in time to tear up the note she had left for him—just in case. She wasn't a complete idiot after all and in case something went wrong that she couldn't handle, Deidre wanted Finn to know where she was.

Deidre stepped into the real world near the corner of Pennsylvania Avenue and Fourteenth Street in Pershing Park. Thankfully the tunnel entrances were well concealed. Deidre went topside behind a cluster of winter bare trees very near the now quiet waterfall. The adjacent pond was frozen over and a couple dozen people were out skating on what was the city's favorite ice rink every winter. She watched them for a second or two and felt just a little envious of the skaters. Then she remembered why she was there. Everyone was so busy having a good time, no one noticed the woman in black sneaking farther away from the crowd.

When she was sure she was alone, she pulled the cell phone she'd snatched from the supply room out of her pocket, and made a call.

A man answered, and she whispered, "Darius, it's Deidre. I need to see my mother."

"We've got her." Shea stood outside Egan's room in Haven. It was small, but comfortable with a bed, a couple of chairs and plenty of books. Oh, and the magical barrier across the entrance, preventing him from leaving the room.

He had finally stopped pacing and shouting the night before, but he looked, well, terrible. Shea couldn't blame him, but she didn't blame the other Eternals for wanting to keep an eye on him, either. Though he was getting control of his raging emotions and fury, he still didn't look quite . . . sane.

Egan stalked toward the doorway and came up short when he hit the charmed barrier Shea, Mairi and Teresa had constructed to keep him confined. A sizzle of sound and a burst of light when he hit it told Shea their spell was still working fine.

"You found Kellyn?" His voice sounded scratchy and raw and no wonder, after days of shouting.

"We did." Shea turned to watch the others approach. Torin walked up beside her with Rune, Teresa, Damyn and Mairi right behind them. "It took everything we had, but we found her. With all of our power combined, we were able to peek past whatever spell or charm it was that was hiding her. Finally."

"Where is the traitorous bitch?" He slapped both hands to the doorjamb and leaned as close as he dared without coming up against that wall of magic.

"She's in Washington, DC," Teresa said.

He pulled in a breath that swelled his huge chest to massive proportions. "Then let me out of here and I'll go find her."

"There's more, Egan." Rune spoke up next and his voice sounded grim.

"I don't need more," the Eternal with the raging eyes insisted. "I just want to find the bitch and make her pay for what she did to me."

"And what about the Awakening?" Mairi asked.

"What about it?" His hostile gaze snapped to hers.

"You think I want to *Mate* with her? After what she did to me?" Egan's voice got louder and rougher. His dark skin flushed with rage again and his closed fists beat against the wall beside the barrier. "I was down there for *months*. Cold. Hungry. Alone. Couldn't use magic. Couldn't escape. You expect me to forgive her for that?"

"Yeah, about that," Teresa told him, with a glance at her sister-witches. "It wasn't exactly Kellyn who trapped you in that cage. There's more going on than you know."

Egan's gaze narrowed as she talked and with every word, his pale gray eyes darkened until they were the color of storm clouds about to explode with lightning.

Darius sneaked her into the White House and hustled her upstairs to the residence quarters. Leave it to Darius to know how to get her into her mother's quarters without being seen. Truth be told, Deidre had never liked Darius much. She found him a little creepy. But tonight, she was glad for the help.

She stepped into the green room, her mother's favorite parlor on the second floor. Deidre knew it well. Pale green walls, silk-covered furniture and an oil portrait of George Washington. Deidre walked forward, then stopped dead. Cora wasn't alone, damn it. A young, pretty woman with spiky black hair and eyes almost as dark sat in one of the French provincial chairs. *Damn it.* She had wanted a few private minutes with her mother.

"Deidre, thank God," Cora said, pushing up from the sofa to face her. "Where in the hell have you been?"

"It's a long story, Mom," she said with a sidelong glance at the other woman. "And one I'd rather tell you in private."

Cora waved her hand. "Don't be foolish. Kellyn is . . . a friend. She has every right to be here."

Deidre's spidey sense started tingling with the voltage of an electric chair. Something was *seriously* wrong here. Her mother wasn't weeping and worried. In fact, Cora looked more annoyed than anything else. Kellyn was watching Deidre as if she were a bug under a microscope and Darius . . . had just locked the door.

Holy crap, what had she walked into? Was Cora in trouble? Was *Deidre?* "Mom," she said, inching farther from Darius while keeping a wary eye on Kellyn, "I just wanted you to know I was okay, but I can't stay."

"You're not going anywhere." Cora shook her head and sneered at her. "Now, take off your shirt."

"What?" Deidre looked from her mother to the other two people in the room and back again. Was it her imagination or did her mother look suddenly . . . different?

"You heard me, Deidre." Cora's voice was crisp, impatient. "Take off your shirt before I have Darius do it for you."

Fear exploded inside her and Deidre knew she was in deep shit. Something was happening here and she didn't know what. She never should have come here without at least telling Finn. Because now she was on her own. "What's this about?"

"Oh for chrissakes," Kellyn muttered. She stomped across the room on needle-thin high heels and before Deidre could blink, had ripped the front of her T-shirt open, tearing the bra beneath it as well. She was a hell of a lot stronger than she looked.

Deidre's Mating tattoo was displayed and Kellyn applauded.

Shocked and acting purely on instinct, Deidre pulled

back her right arm and punched Kellyn dead in the face. The other woman staggered back, stunned for a second before coming at her again.

"Kellyn, that's enough."

She whipped her head around to glare at Cora. "The bitch *hit* me."

"Watch who you're calling bitch, *bitch*." Deidre grabbed the edges of her torn shirt together, hiding the marks on her skin. Too late, of course. Bag open, cat gone.

"It doesn't matter," Cora said, a pleased glint in her eye. "All that matters is she's finally Mated." Shaking her head, she looked her daughter up and down and then waved Darius closer to Deidre. "My gods, I thought this day would never get here. I have waited your entire, pedestrian life for this moment."

Deidre's breaths came short and sharp. She had slipped into the *Twilight Zone* without even realizing it. She tried to keep an eye on all three of the people in the room, but frankly, it was her mother that had her riveted. This was Cora Sterling as Deidre had never seen her before. She was a stranger with the light of fanaticism in her eyes.

"Mom . . ."

Cora shuddered. "All I want to hear from you is the location of the Artifact, Deidre."

"The—" Another shock in a series of them.

"Artifact." Cora rolled her eyes. "Yes, I know about it and I want it. *Now*."

Deidre's brain raced to compute all of this new and startling information. Her mother knew she was a witch? Knew about the Artifact? The tattoo? How?

"Swear to the gods, if she doesn't start talking, I'm going to beat the living shit out of her," Kellyn said idly.

Deidre shot another look at the woman and this time, her dark eyes were completely black. No iris. No white. No pupil. Just unrelieved black, like the tar pits she'd seen once as a child. And Kellyn's eyes looked just as flat and treacherous.

"You'll have your chance," Cora told the woman. "Darius, tie Deidre up. Can't have her slipping away."

"I don't think so, Darius," Deidre said and flung out one hand. She snatched his gun from his hip and whipped it through the air to point at her mother. God, how had this happened? She was holding a gun on her own *mother*. With magic.

"I'm out of here," Deidre said. She had to get to Finn. Have him help her figure out what was wrong with her mom. Find a way to save her.

"How much more of an idiot can you possibly be?" Cora said with a smirk that said she wasn't worried in the least about that gun. "You can't get out of here, Deidre. Every guard and Secret Service agent on the premises has been aware of you from the moment Darius escorted you inside."

Deidre flushed. She really was an idiot. She had thought she would be safe coming to see her mother. The woman who had always protected her. The woman who had *cried* on national TV over her daughter. But the woman Deidre was facing now was not the mother she knew. And fear crept up her spine in icy spike heels.

Her only hope was that Finn would get back to their chamber early, find her note and come after her. *Finn*, she screamed his name in her mind and knew that it wouldn't do any good. She hadn't once picked up a stray thought from him, so why would he be able to hear her silent cries?

"Have you realized yet you have very few options?" Cora studied her. "Tell me where the Artifact is, Deidre. Now."

In a burst of brilliant light and the color of living flame, Finn flashed into the room and pulled Deidre in tight to him. His steely eyes swept over the three people in the room and Deidre took her first easy breath in an hour.

Cora didn't take long to recover. "Eternal, this changes nothing."

"It gets her away from you," he ground out, keeping one eye on Darius. Deidre wanted to tell him that she thought Kellyn was the real danger there, but didn't have the time.

"I'm done playing nice," Cora told him, batting aside the gun still hanging in the air. "Deidre, you give me that damned Artifact or I swear to your god, I will kill every witch in this country."

Finn was through talking. He called up the flames and flashed himself and Deidre to the tunnel entrance in Pershing Park. They didn't speak until they were safely belowground and when they were, Deidre threw herself at him. "Oh my God, Finn. What was that? My mother was—I can't believe this."

She burrowed in closer, grateful to be alive and back with Finn. Terror still crouched inside her, but with his arms around her, it was bearable. "How did you find me?"

"We got back early. Saw your note. Thank Belen, I can track you through the power of the Mating tattoo," he admitted, making Deidre more glad than ever that they had actually begun the Mating.

Then Finn scowled down at her. "What the hell were you thinking? Why would you risk yourself like that?"

She stilled. Was he really worried about her? Or was he more concerned that she stay alive to complete their task? "I should have thought. With the Awakening here and the Artifact still to find . . ."

"Fuck the Artifact and the Awakening," he murmured, holding her tighter, closer, his arms flexing around her until she could hardly breathe. "I told you. Give me a choice between the world and you and I'll choose you every time."

Deidre sagged into him. He did care for her. Did want her. And he'd just saved her from— "I'm sorry. I really am," she said, tipping her head back to look up at him. "I thought she was in danger. I had to see my mother, Finn, and I knew you wouldn't go for it."

"Damn right."

"Yeah, well," she said, pushing away from him and tugging at the edges of her shirt. "As it turns out, you were right."

"This was almost worth it just to hear you say that," he muttered and yanked off his coat. Draping it over her shoulders, he asked, "What the hell happened?"

Deidre pulled his coat around her, grateful for the warmth of his body that still clung to the supple leather. "I don't know. My mother was . . . *different*. I've never seen her like that. And the other woman? Her name was Kellyn and she had black eyes, Finn. Completely black. She was stronger than she should have been, too. Ripped my shirt and bra in two just to get a look at the Mating tattoo."

"Kellyn." He muttered a curse so vile, Deidre blinked. "She's supposedly an Awakened witch. She trapped her Eternal in a cage at the bottom of the sea."

"Okay." Deidre swallowed hard and felt jittery with

the rush of adrenaline that was still pumping through her system.

"Dee, there's something else."

The wary tone in his voice should have given her a warning, but nothing could have prepared her for what he said next. "Your mother. I'm not sure she's human."

Chapter 37

"**A**re you crazy? Of course she's human. She's my *mother*."

Finn looked down at her and felt every protective instinct he possessed roar into life again. As long as he lived, he would never forget that moment when he had *felt* Deidre's fear hit him with the force of a sledgehammer. It had slammed into him.

He'd left Joe in Virginia and had flashed to her, following the supernatural homing beacon of her tattoo. He wasn't even surprised to find she had gone to see her mother. Deidre wasn't a woman to be cowed by anyone's threats or warnings. Of course he was angry that she'd put herself in danger. But what he'd sensed in that room changed the whole damn ball game. She had no idea what she was dealing with now and he had to make her understand.

Wiping one hand across his mouth, he took a breath and said, "Her body may be human, but I sensed an 'other' presence in her."

"Other?" Deidre's eyes narrowed. "What does that mean?"

"I don't know," he admitted and that worried him. The feeling had come and gone so quickly, it was as if someone had hit a light switch, shutting down his ability to sense magical beings. Which made him wonder about the other two in that room.

Especially since he knew that one of them, Kellyn, was already suspect. He hadn't picked up any sense of wrongness from her though, which told him she had to be working a protective spell of some kind.

"You're wrong," Deidre said firmly with a shake of her head. "I grant you there's something off here. Maybe she's being blackmailed. Or she's bespelled or . . ."

She couldn't come up with an explanation and he knew it. Nothing her mind provided would explain why the mother she knew had been all too willing to attack her to acquire the Artifact. The fact that the president *knew* about the Artifact—and Deidre's connection to it—told him she was much more than she pretended to be. Finn only had to wait until Deidre could admit that truth to herself.

"I need to contact the other Eternals. Tell them where Kellyn is." He glanced up at the tunnel exit above their heads. "But not from here. We're too close to the White House. They'll have every cop in the city out looking for us."

"My mother won't—" She stopped talking, bit her lip and stared at him defiantly.

"Come on," he said, wrapping her close and calling up the flames. "We'll get back to our chamber and go up from there."

She held him as he flashed them out, but Finn felt a new distance between them and it bothered him more than he cared to admit.

*   *   *

"She's a demon," Rune said.

Finn had the phone on speaker so Deidre could hear as well. After all, her mother was somehow in this up to her neck and unless he convinced Dee that she was now the enemy, this wasn't going to go well.

"Kellyn's a demon?" he repeated, gaze locked on Deidre's wide eyes.

The cold November wind sighed down the alley they stood in, rustling discarded papers and rattling a paper cup along the damp asphalt.

"Possessed by one, anyway." Rune sounded pissed off and tired.

"How the hell is that possible?" Finn argued hotly. "If there's a demon around, I should be able to spot trace energies."

"Yeah, well. Seems the blanketing spell she was wrapped in was like nothing known before."

"Then how'd you find out it was there?"

"Teresa and the others did an enhanced spell." He paused. "They channeled some of their power through the Artifact shards here in Haven and—"

"They *what*?" Finn's shout startled Deidre enough that she jumped, then scowled at him. Lowering his voice he demanded, "Are you guys nuts? This whole thing started with spells focused through the Artifact."

"Yeah, we know. It was a risk." Rune paused a moment and said to someone in the room, "I'll be there in a minute." Then to Finn, he said, "Look, we've got plenty of problems here to deal with, the main one being Egan. He's like a starving pit bull trying to break his chain. He gets loose and the damage count's going to be unbelievably high."

"That's no reason to mess with that fucking Artifact again."

"Don't you think we know that? Torin, Damyn and I argued against it and lost."

"Just like old times," Finn mused, remembering how the Eternals had tried to stop their witches eight hundred years ago. His gaze locked on Deidre. Her scowl deepened.

"You could say that," Rune agreed. "This time it was different. They needed the power boost to get through whatever shield was protecting Kellyn from them. They did it. The real Kellyn is shut up somewhere inside her own body and a demon's at the steering wheel."

"Fan-fucking-tastic."

"That about sums it up," Rune muttered. "So if Kellyn's hanging with Cora Sterling, you gotta wonder if there's a surprise inside the president, too."

"Oh my God," Deidre murmured as the possibilities clicked in.

Finn was as rocked by this news as Deidre. "So how do you want us to handle Kellyn?"

"You take care of the Mating and find that damned Artifact. We'll take care of Kellyn." Rune blew out an impatient breath. "Believe me when I say it's number one on our agenda."

"Right. Good luck."

"Back atcha," Rune said. "We're all gonna need it."

The next few days were tense. Everyone in the WLF was feeling the pressure. Cops, BOW agents and the MPs, Magic Police, were all over the city. Random checks on IDs were the order of the day and the rumors were that martial law was on the horizon.

Since Joe was off visiting his father for a couple of days, Finn and Deidre were topside, doing recon on a small holding center in Oak Hill Cemetery. He could have done it alone; he just didn't like the idea of leaving Deidre by herself. Too many things were unsettled. He'd spent most of his time the last few days just trying to get through to her. The woman's head was as hard as that Black Silver they needed to find so badly.

Just inside the Thirtieth Street entrance stood a red-brick Italianate building once used as the living quarters for the cemetery's superintendent. Built in 1850, it was stately, beautiful and right now being used to house four accused witches before they could be transferred to BOW headquarters.

With the snow falling and light shining through leaded glass panes, it made a picture more suitable for a Christmas card than a holding tank for witches. Redbrick gateposts stood a few feet apart, with black, wrought iron fencing in between. The two evergreens flanking the arched front door were dazzled with Christmas lights.

"When will we hit it?" Deidre asked, huddling deeper into her coat.

"We'll wait for Joe to get back. A couple of days."

She nodded and Finn ground his back teeth together. This was how it had been between them now for three days. A polite coolness. Distance even when they were wrapped around each other, pushing the Mating into completion.

The hell of it was, he *missed* her, damn it.

Missed the connection he'd found with her and he wasn't about to let it go. "Deidre—"

"If you're about to tell me that my mother is a demon, don't bother."

It had been this way for days now. Her denying what she had seen and heard with her own eyes and ears and him pushing for her to deal and move on. Anger sparked inside him. He'd been patient, for Belen's sake, and look where it had gotten him. Exactly nowhere. It was past time for a damn confrontation about this and he was done waiting.

"Well," he demanded, "have you got a better explanation for what's going on?"

"No." She stuffed her hands into her pockets and turned her back on the gatehouse. Staring out over the cemetery, her gaze swept over ancient tombstones, spires of granite and marble and simple flat markers, all placed there to remember the dead. "But how can I accept what you're saying? If I do, then I have to ask myself for how long? Has she been a demon my whole life?"

She turned her head to look up at him and he saw pain in her eyes and he ached for her. But at the same time, she *had* to work through this.

"Was nothing I knew real? Was it all an act, played out by a creature who was just waiting for me to get this damned tattoo?"

He grabbed her and held on. She was stiff and unyielding against him for a long moment, but he kept holding her and eventually, she leaned into him. "Finn, if my mother has always been a demon, then what does that make me?"

"It makes you Deidre Sterling," he said firmly, tipping her chin up until her gaze met his. "A witch of awesome power. Lover of an Eternal. Holder of a secret that can save the world. It makes you just exactly who you have always been. Never doubt it."

She took a deep breath and blew it out, watching it

cloud into cold vapor in front of her. "None of this makes sense," she muttered. "I've been trying to work through it for days and none of it makes sense."

"Yeah, I know. And I promise you, we'll find out what happened to your mother. But right now—"

She rubbed her forehead and whispered, "The Artifact's more important."

"None of this will mean a damn thing if we don't find that gods-damned piece of Black Silver, Dee."

"You think I don't know that?" She pushed one hand through her hair, long and loose around her shoulders. "It's like the memories just stopped coming. I haven't had one since—"

"—you were nearly captured by your mother."

"Yeah." Her mouth worked as if she were chewing on something bitter until finally she said, "I haven't gotten anything clear since—"

"London. I remember." He snorted. "Funny, I could never get you into the city back then. Guess that's why the night of the spell I went there." He stroked one hand up and down her back, soothing both of them with the touch that sparked their magic and the connection simmering between them. While he talked, Finn looked at his own memories of long ago. "I was in a pub by the docks. The ships were preparing to sail and all I could hear was the creak of the wood, the sailors cursing each other and the slap of the water against those huge hulls."

"Finn!" She swayed and grabbed him. Her hand clutched his arm and through the fabric of his leather coat, he felt magic and heat push into him in a wild rush. "Oh, God."

"What is it?"

"When you described that scene, I got an image in my

mind." Her eyes were wide and she stared straight ahead, though he knew she was looking at a scene long dead and buried. "A ship. It had two masts."

"Tell me."

She shook her head and concentrated. "I went up the gangway and slipped on board. God, the smell. Dead fish, old whiskey and unwashed men. I was sick. Sick at heart and my stomach kept churning with what we had done. The piece of the Artifact I was holding was dead. Flat. As if the spell had used up its magic and left it empty. But I knew it wouldn't last."

Her hand slid down his arm to his hand and she threaded her fingers through his, holding on as more of the past unfurled inside her mind.

"You put the Artifact on a ship?" His voice was low, urgent.

Finn watched as she frowned, working through memories that had been clouded for centuries. He couldn't imagine what it was like trying to sift through so many images looking for only one specific picture of the right time and place.

"I could only think to get it out of England. Away from us. Somewhere safe," she said, words tumbling from her mouth in a rush. "I used magic to mold the Black Silver into a plaque, with the name of the ship . . . *Marguerite* scrolled across it. Then I spelled the captain." She smiled slightly. "He didn't want me on his boat. Women were bad luck on a ship . . ."

Finn snorted. Men were always calling women bad luck, when the truth was much simpler. Men who couldn't *get* a woman made up superstitions to explain why they didn't *want* one.

Her palm to his, Finn felt the heat of the Mating tattoo spreading across his skin, climbing up his back and knew she was feeling it too. As her memories came, fast and rich, unspooling through her mind, the Mating brand became more complete. Magic pulsed and breathed all around them. Snow fell, the wind blew and somewhere in the distance, a siren wailed.

Her voice was soft, almost lost in the sigh of the wind. "I used magic to convince the captain the Black Silver plaque was his. That it was a gift from a patron. Precious. To be protected."

Finn's heart lurched. If the captain had taken that plaque with him on his travels, who the hell knew where it had finally ended up? It could be anywhere now. Hell, if the ship had sunk, as plenty of them had, back in the day, the damn thing was at the bottom of a very deep ocean.

"Deidre—the sea captain took it with him?"

She lifted her eyes to him, horror for what she'd done clouding her blue gaze. "Yeah, he did. I watched the ship set sail the following morning. God, I gave that magical time bomb to him. Who knows what the Artifact did to the man when its power woke up again?"

Frustration crouched inside him, but he heard the misery in her voice and responded. "No, Deidre. You did the only thing you could to—"

"Dump my problem off on someone else?" she interrupted. Turning away, she stomped off a few paces, then whirled back to face him. "I was supposed to get it somewhere safe. I could have buried it or hidden it in a cave or something, I don't know! Instead, I handed it off to some poor guy who didn't have the slightest idea what he was holding." She slapped both hands to the side of her head and asked, "What the hell kind of person was I, anyway?" Her gaze snapped to his. "Why the *hell* did you give two shits for me?"

Okay, he'd tried understanding. He'd tried patience—which really wasn't one of his strengths—and he'd tried being kind. Time to pull the gloves off. "You want to be a martyr," he told her, voice as cold as the snow swirling around them, "go for it. But leave the weeping and wailing till after we're done."

She hissed in a breath. "Bastard."

"Always." He stalked to her side and caught her when she would have darted away. "You thought you were perfect in your past life? Is that it? Because *nobody's* perfect, Deidre."

"Not everybody's an evil, selfish bitch, though."

"More than you might think," he countered with a grim smile. "And I'm damned if I'll watch you tear yourself apart over things a different woman in a different time once did."

Shaking her head, she said, "Nice try. But you told me yourself that this soul? It's the same one I carry through lifetime after lifetime. So she was me. I'm what's left of her."

"Wrong. You're what's *become* of her. There's a difference." He paused. "And I wish to hell you'd stop throwing my own words back at me."

Furious, she tried to pull her hand free, but he held on. "You're not *her*, Dee. Let it go. Her mistakes aren't yours. Don't you think you're paying enough for what she did? Haven't we both paid enough?"

A long, simmering moment passed before the tension in her body drained away. She turned her face from his to look out across the cemetery again. Gaze locked on her, he waited for her to find her balance again. To reclaim who she was and let the wrongs of the past slide away.

Snowflakes lay on her hair, her eyelashes and drifted around her like pieces of a cloud. His heart clenched in his chest. Everything he had said was true. He had cared for her in that long-ago time. Loved her as much as he was able.

Deidre, he loved beyond all reason.

"It's not going to be easy finding out what happened to a thirteenth-century sailing ship," she said at last.

He smiled when she turned to face him. "We've got a name. The *Marguerite*. We'll find it. We'll use magic. Call the others and get them to do a combined spell—"

A phone rang shrilly and Finn scowled. "What the hell?"

Deidre reached into her coat pocket and pulled out her cell phone. Holding it flat in her palm she stared down at it as the ringing continued, the screen flashing with an incoming call. "I grabbed it from the supply room. I've been carrying it whenever we go topside, just in case my mother—"

Finn took a huge breath and held it until he thought his chest might explode. But he thought he understood now. It wasn't that she didn't believe her mother wasn't human. It was that she *couldn't* believe it. The truth simply didn't compute—and maybe it never would unless she faced the woman down again and learned the facts firsthand.

"Is that her calling?"

"No," she said, as the phone stopped ringing and a small green light began to blink. "It was Dante. My Secret Service protection. He's left a voice mail."

Chapter 38

This meeting was probably a huge mistake, Deidre told herself an hour later. But what choice did she have, really? She glanced up at Finn, beside her. Tall and strong, he had been at her side through all of her lifetimes. She knew that for herself now, had remembered a lot of their combined past. He was her warrior. The one who stood between her and danger. The one who held her at night and made her laugh and cry and stirred anger so hot inside her she could hardly breathe.

He was, in short, *everything*.

They had found a way beyond their shared past to a future that looked amazing—if they could pull this off. Finn was the other half of her. The piece of her personal puzzle that made everything else feel right.

She wore his brand on her chest, the links of that ribbon of chain now scrolling completely around her breast, under her arm and halfway up her back. The tattoo seemed to burn with urgency when he was near, as if reacting to the matching brand on his skin. Deidre burned, too.

Even now, in the quiet darkness of the National Mall,

surrounded by the granite and marble reminders of this country's glories, she wanted him. She would always want him, Deidre knew, with a hunger that would never be satiated. Instinctively, she reached for his hand and his fingers wrapped around hers and squeezed.

The Korean War Memorial was haunting even in daylight. But at night, like now, Deidre always half expected the larger-than-life statues of a squad of men in full battle gear to come alive. A thin dusting of snow covered them. Small spotlights shone on their faces, creating shadows that seemed to waver in the wind. The sheet of black granite comprising the wall to one side of the memorial was sandblasted with the faces of the fallen. Figures were staggered, as if they were approaching the wall from the mists of time to peer out at the country for which they'd sacrificed everything.

She shivered.

Finn misread the gesture. "You can head back to the tunnels, Dee. I'll meet with this guy alone."

"No," Deidre said. "It's not the meeting, it's this place. It's always affected me like this. This memorial is more heartrending than any other place on the mall. At least for me." She sighed. "No, you can't meet him alone and we can't ignore it. He said he wasn't comfortable speaking on the phone. And he obviously thinks this is important enough for us to meet. So like it or not, we have to find out what Dante has to say."

"Fine." Finn nodded and let his gaze scan their surroundings again. "But one wrong move from him and we're gone."

"Agreed."

Dante's message had been short and to the point. There were things Deidre had to know. Things he couldn't say on the phone. He'd promised that he would be here, at the memorial, every night at midnight until she came.

Yes, it was a risk to be here, as Finn had pointed out immediately after listening to the Secret Service agent's message. Even now, there could be a whole crowd of feds hiding behind trees and bushes and monuments, just waiting for the signal to pounce.

But Deidre didn't think so. She'd known Dante for three years and she trusted him. Then again, she'd known her mother her entire life, and look what had happened there. So there was always the chance that she was wrong about him. A scuffle of sound came to her and she stiffened, turning with Finn to face the agent approaching them. She only hoped she could *still* trust Dante Dimenticato.

"I didn't think you'd come," he said, stopping when he was just a few feet from them.

"Won't be here long," Finn assured him, keeping a tight grip on Deidre's hand. "So make it count."

She squeezed his fingers hard and spoke up. "Dante, what's going on? What's happening with my mother?"

He looked around, as if assuring himself no one else was near. The wind kicked up and fluttered the edges of Dante's coat. "Nobody knows. The cabinet's being shut out. She fired her advisors and she's closed down diplomatic relations with at least a half dozen countries."

Stunned, Deidre could only stare at him. Fear balled into a cold, tight knot in the pit of her stomach. Her mother, whatever else she was, had always been a good politician. She had kept her friends close and had always maintained lines of communications with her enemies. Hearing this was akin to being told that her mom had taken to flying around the interior of the White House on a broomstick. It was *that* unbelievable.

"What?" she asked when her brain stopped spinning. "That can't be right."

"I know what it sounds like." He shrugged deeper into his black overcoat. "Your mother's out of control, Deidre," he said simply. "She's on the verge of signing an order to rescind freedom of speech. Says she's doing it for the good of the country, but I don't know about that."

"This can't be happening," Deidre murmured.

"And, she's holding a press conference by the end of the week. She's going to threaten to kill a witch a day, *every* day, until you come to her."

"Oh my God." Deidre's whisper was lost beneath Finn's low-pitched growl.

"Worst part?" Dante mused, "She'll have the backing of most of Congress and the majority of the population. Witches *will* die, Deidre."

"Did she send you here?" Finn demanded, loosening his grip on Deidre's hand to take one menacing step toward the other man.

"No." Dante laughed, but backed up another foot or two. Snow swirled in a sudden gust of wind and danced between the two men like fairy dust. "Don't expect you to believe that, but no. She's only talking to Darius these days. He's the only one allowed into the Oval Office. Hell, she hasn't even spoken to the VP in *weeks*."

"What do you expect Deidre to do about it?" Finn asked.

"Don't expect anything," Dante admitted, then shifted his gaze to her. "But I thought you should know what's coming."

"What's wrong with her?" Deidre murmured, not really expecting an answer. Her mother's friend, Kellyn, was possessed by a demon. Was it possible her mother had been, too? Or were there even *worse* things out there to worry about?

"That's what I want to know." Finn moved closer, frowning the nearer he got to the other man. Dante stepped back again, as if determined to keep distance between them. "And I think you have the answers. What the hell's going on?"

"I said what I came to say." Dante told them. "What you do with it is your choice. If you need me," he added with a glance at Deidre, "call."

"Just a damn minute," Finn said as the other man turned and moved quickly down the path until he was swallowed by darkness and the falling snow.

Shaken by this latest information, Deidre moved up beside Finn and asked, "What is it?"

"There's something . . ." He shook his head and scowled at the retreating man.

She looked after Dante too, but saw only the darkness and the still falling snow. "What are you talking about?"

Scrubbing one hand across his jaw, he said, "For a split second, I got that sense of 'other' again. Then it was gone."

She jolted and looked up at him. "You mean like what you felt about my mother?"

"Yeah, but different." He was still staring into the night as if he could see past the trees and the snow and the monuments, right into the heart of the man who had just left them. "There's something off there. Wish to hell I knew what it was."

There were a lot of things Deidre wished. First and foremost being that her world would right itself and begin to make sense again. But since that wasn't going to happen anytime soon, she steeled herself for what was to come.

"It doesn't matter," Deidre said, and waited until he turned to meet her eyes. "You know it doesn't."

She had known the moment Dante had told her about Cora's plans. As if the last few weeks had been leading her directly here, there was no other path to take. No choice at all, really.

Ever since Finn had flashed her out of the green room in the White House, Deidre had fought to find a reasonable explanation for what her mother had done and said. She'd argued with him, and resented him for relentlessly pushing her to face the cold, hard truth.

But there were no excuses for what Deidre's mother was doing.

Whether or not Cora Sterling *was* her mother, she had to be stopped.

So it didn't really matter anymore, did it? Remembering the cold, dispassionate look on her mother's face as Cora had ordered Darius to tie Deidre up, she came to grips with her new reality. Old loyalties were set aside. She and Cora had never been close and now she was almost grateful for that emotional distance.

Because she had a feeling that the only way to stop Cora would be to kill her before she tried to do the same to them.

Of course it wasn't easy to kill the president of the United States.

Even if she was an "other."

"If Cora Sterling is really planning to execute women just to get my attention," Deidre said sadly, "then you were right, she's *not* my mother."

"Dee—"

She shook her head, dismissing his sympathetic tone. God, if he offered her kindness or pity now, she'd crumble just when she most needed to be strong. "We can't let her get away with that, Finn. Not if we can stop her."

He pulled her in close and wrapped his arms around her. Deidre felt his strength and was buoyed by it. Whatever was coming next, she would be able to handle it if he was there with her.

"I know," he said, words muffled against her hair as he kissed the top of her head. "We're going back to the White House. But first, we need a plan."

Chapter 39

Back in their chamber in the tunnels, Deidre turned to Finn and pulled his head down for a long, hungry kiss. After meeting with Dante, all she'd been able to think of was getting back here. With Finn. In the last three weeks, this chamber had become home. This tunnel familiar ground and the members of the WLF her surrogate family.

The place she had once considered a trap now surrounded her with welcome, with the comforting sensations of safety and love.

"Hey," he said, lifting his head to look down at her, "we'll figure it out, Deidre. We'll find the Artifact. We'll end this. And we'll keep your mother from killing more witches."

"I know," she said, walking backward to the bed. "I know we will, Finn. But this is all so horrible. Before I can face all of that, I need you. I need to feel you with me."

He snapped his fingers and they were both naked. She loved the way his magic sizzled and burned all around him like an aura only she could sense and feel. His Eter-

nal powers grew along with hers. She already knew
about the traveling by fire, the ability to sense danger
and coming threats. She knew he was strong and practically invulnerable and she knew that his powers would
continue to evolve now that they had Mated.

Deidre sighed and he smiled, running his fingertips
along the curve of the chain tattoo that was branded into
her skin.

Deidre closed her eyes and held her breath as he
traced each link of that chain tattoo with his fingers, his
lips, his tongue. She swayed into him, but locked her
knees, so she wouldn't topple over under the sensations
he caused.

When he touched her, the world fell away. The past,
the present, even the still hazy future that might spill out
in front of them . . . it all disappeared and there were
only the two of them in the universe.

The magical crystals embedded in the walls hummed
with the energies they were picking up from the Mating
magic building between Finn and Deidre. She felt the
reflected power bristling along her skin even as her insides lit up. This is what she had needed so desperately.
This was what her soul, her body had hungered for.

With Finn's hands and mouth on her skin, she felt
power bubbling inside and knew that anything was possible.

He toppled her onto the bed, and she fell backward
eagerly, opening her eyes to him, lifting her arms to hold
him. But he shook his head and whispered, "No. Not
yet."

Deidre tensed as he slid along the length of her, letting his mouth blaze a trail down her stomach, across her
abdomen to the thatch of blond curls at the juncture of

her thighs. "Open for me, Dee," he whispered and she was helpless to resist—even if she had wanted to.

He shifted position, kneeling between her thighs, then scooped his hands under her butt and lifted her off the bed. His strong fingers gripped her behind as he lowered his mouth to cover her.

She gasped and arched her hips into him as he took her, his tongue and teeth tormenting her until the spiral of need within her tightened beyond bearing. Deidre reached for him, and held his head to her, reveling in the wildness of his touch, in the magic bursting in the air around them.

When her climax came, she shouted his name and at the same time, she felt the burn of her Mating tattoo sizzle. While her body rocked through the waves of pleasure only he could give her, Finn laid her down on the mattress and pushed himself deep within her.

She held him, moving with him, keeping pace, pushing him harder, faster, deeper until neither of them could have said where one of them ended and the other began. And finally, when his body erupted into hers, the aching burn of the Mating tattoo seared them both and the last door in Deidre's mind opened.

"You can sense the Artifact?" Finn looked up and down the darkened street while Deidre focused her magic.

"Yeah," she said. "I do. I just can't ... *place* it. But I know that Artifact's here. In DC." She looked around at the night, as if expecting to see a sign that read HERE I AM, COME GET ME.

"It's more than we had yesterday," Finn told her in response to the irritation in her voice. After making love the night before, something inside Dee had clicked "on."

Her soul fully awakening, the ancient pull of the Black Silver . . . who knew what it was, exactly? But she had suddenly *felt* the Artifact's presence.

They hadn't nailed it down yet, but they were closer than ever now and they would get it done. He wouldn't lose her. Not to death, not to oblivion and sure as shit, not to her mother.

This was a risk, Finn thought. But one they had to take. Like Deidre, he couldn't allow innocent women to be killed if they could stop it. Since her awareness of the Artifact had opened up the night before, he and Deidre had done nothing but discuss this plan. Though neither of them liked it, it was their only option.

If they stalled while they located the Artifact, women would die. Neither of them could live with that.

With Joe still off visiting his father, Marco was in charge of the group creating a much-needed diversion. Finn and Deidre waited in the shadows until the first of four planned explosions rocked the night. Then, smiling grimly, Finn flashed Deidre to a long-unused tunnel beneath the White House.

Forgotten for more than a hundred years, most of the narrow passages were blocked from falling rock and dirt, forcing Finn to flash them past blockade after blockade. The dank tunnels had been lost to history and it was only because Finn had spent so much time in and around the city, exploring, that they knew of them at all.

Hard to believe that the current residents knew nothing of this piece of the past. But then, most people looked to the future, not to what had come before. And these half-collapsed tunnels wouldn't have seemed like a security threat to them even if they had known.

Finn flashed her into an unused storage room in the

basement of the White House itself, then pulled Deidre close.

In the distance, they heard another explosion rattle the city and Deidre looked up at him, a twist of a smile on her face. "That's two. The State Department building may never be the same."

"Yeah, but it should draw most of the feds and cops over there," he whispered, "keep them out of our way."

She looked up at the ceiling as if she could see through the plaster and wood straight through to the room where her mother waited. "What'll we do when we see her?"

"First," he promised, "find out what the hell she is."

Deidre winced and he was sorry for it, but damned if he'd risk her life for Cora Sterling. Whoever or whatever the president was, it was Finn's job to neutralize her before she could do more damage. "Where will she be this time of night?"

"Her living room. She has a glass of wine while she watches the late news."

He nodded, remembering the sketch Dee had made for him of the president's private quarters. He knew exactly where they were going. He was just in no hurry to put his woman in the line of fire.

"You ready?"

"Yeah." She didn't look ready, but she threaded her arms around his waist and held on as he flashed them to the residence.

"Now!" Cora's voice shouted the order the moment Finn and Deidre appeared in the living room.

An icy cold drape of white gold fell across Finn, capturing him in the power-draining mesh of a specifically designed net. Deidre was ripped from his hold. A soft, sibilant sound whipped through the room and Deidre

cried out. Finn's gaze snapped to a man in a corner holding a small crossbow, already notching another arrow
into the slot. Beside him, Deidre staggered with another
cry—that's when Finn saw the white gold arrow jutting
from her left shoulder.

He howled in fury and fought like a madman to be
free of the white gold netting that had effectively neu-
tralized him. He couldn't get out. Couldn't call on his
magic to flash out and couldn't reach Deidre. It was a
nightmare. The president's aide stepped in close and
threw a hard punch to Finn's midsection, adding insult to
injury.

Still struggling against his bonds, Finn glared through
the minuscule links of the white gold netting. Cora, Kellyn, Darius, Dante and two other men were in the room.
A new burst of fury nearly blinded him. *Should have
killed Dante when he had the chance.* And he saw Deidre,
crumpled on the floor, face pale, eyes wide with pain and
shock.

"No guns to manipulate this time, sweetie," Cora said,
stepping in close and looking down at her daughter.
"The white gold in that arrow should keep you . . . coop-
erative."

"Mom—"

Cora ignored her and strolled over to stand beside
Finn. "Did you really think it would be so easy?" Shaking her head she added, "I sensed your presence the moment you were on the grounds. You cannot defeat me."

"Get this fucking net off me and we'll see about that,"
Finn challenged.

She reached down, cupped his chin in her hand, grinding the white gold chain against his skin, driving that icy
cold deep inside him. Her eyes flashed with banked

power and the otherworldly presence he had felt before washed over him in a thick, dangerous wave. Finn had been a warrior for centuries, but he had *never* lusted for a kill as he did at this moment.

"You killed Henry Fender," she murmured, features taut. "There will be payment for that."

"Get these chains off me, you can try it yourself."

She smiled. "Another time, perhaps." Cora straightened up, flicking her fingers at Finn in a dismissive gesture. "Take him away. Make sure he suffers. Then lock him up until I decide what to do with him."

"Mom, what are you doing?" Deidre's voice was thin, reedy with pain and the cloying pull of the white gold embedded in her body.

Darius and two others moved in on him, leaving Dante standing in the background behind Cora and Kellyn. Finn *would* get out and when he did, they were all going to die.

Then Kellyn crouched beside Deidre with a hypodermic. The needle jammed into Deidre's arm and she slumped bonelessly to the floor.

"DEIDRE!"

Chapter 40

Deidre woke up in a cell with white gold bars. The arrow was gone from her shoulder, but a white gold chain lay around her neck, sending that sweeping arctic sensation through her body, dampening her power. She sat up on her cot and pushed her hair back out of her eyes. The room smelled of disinfectant and made her nose tingle with every breath. Her vision was blurry—thanks to whatever they had shot her up with—and Finn was nowhere in sight.

Finn. Memory rose up and she saw him, struggling against his bonds, his captors. She remembered Darius and Kellyn and her mother—and she remembered Dante, there in the room with her enemies.

"God, I'm an idiot," she whispered, taking a long look around her cell. She'd convinced Finn to trust her Secret Service agent and look where that had landed them.

Okay, enough self-pity. Now it was time to find a way out.

A door opened and Kellyn walked in. "Finally."

Deidre stood up. She was still a little wobbly and the white gold around her neck made her feel weak, but she would face whatever came next standing on her own two feet.

"Thought you were going to sleep forever," Kellyn mused, moving close enough to drag her fingertips across the white gold briefly. She shuddered, rubbed her fingers together as if to wipe away the chill, then stepped back. "Honestly, you witches and the white gold thing. How do you stand it?"

"*We* witches?" Deidre asked, gaze locked on her enemy. "You're one, too."

"Oh, this?" Kellyn waved one hand up and down her own body. "This body's just a rental. See." She wandered the close confines of the room while she talked, her needle-thin heels tapping relentlessly against the white tile floor. "Thanks to you bitches, eight hundred years ago I slipped out of Hell. I do owe you a big *thanks* for that, but maybe later."

"You're a demon."

"Wow." Kellyn's eyes went wide with pretended amazement. "Nothing gets past you, does it?" She sighed. "Yes, I'm a demon. Spent the last several centuries hanging around, having fun, waiting for you and your sisters to start the Awakening. Then, I hopped a ride on one of the chosen and"—she shrugged—"here I am."

Didn't make sense. But then what did, lately? "How did you know who Kellyn was? No one knows who the chosen ones are. Not until they're called."

"Oh," Kellyn told her with a slow smile. "Your mother knew. Well, *mother* isn't really the word for her."

Her mother knew? Had known all along? That meant—

"Shut up, Kellyn."

Deidre watched Cora enter the room, followed by

Darius and Dante. Her gaze narrowed on the man she had thought of as a friend, but he looked impassive, as if betraying her had meant nothing to him. Slowly, Deidre looked back at her mother. "What do you want from me?"

Cora gripped the white gold bars in both hands and squeezed. Her blue eyes were dark with shadows and her mouth was tight. "I should think that would be obvious, Deidre. I want the Artifact."

She shook her head. "Are you a demon too?"

"I'm something you can't even conceive," Cora whispered and her features blurred, shifting, as if the very bones in her body were unstable. They reformed themselves in a blink and she was once again the woman Deidre had always known.

Thinking fast, Dee knew she couldn't give this woman the Artifact—with its power, she would be unstoppable. She could turn the world into a graveyard—and probably would. The only way out of this then, Deidre told herself, was to find the Artifact and use its dark power herself to stop them.

She had enough of her memories to know that it was a dangerous move. That the Black Silver would spark dark energy inside her. That she would have to fight against it with everything in her. But there was no other choice. If she stayed locked down here, with white gold around her neck, she would never be able to escape them. Would never find Finn—wherever he was—and she would never defeat the woman watching her now with a reptilian gaze.

"So what's it going to be, Deidre?" Cora asked pleasantly. "Do you give me what I want, or do I hand you over to a torturer and get the information that way?"

"I'll find it," she whispered, looking from Cora to Kellyn and then to Dante. Shifting her gaze back to her mother, she said, "I can sense the Artifact's presence. But I can't do it with this chain around my neck—or with these bars so close to me."

Cora frowned and Kellyn shook her head. "Oh no, don't be stupid," the demon snapped. "She only wants out so she can escape."

Cora studied Deidre's face and then slowly shook her head. "She's not that foolish. She knows I'm holding her Eternal. And even immortals will die if you take their heads . . ."

Deidre swayed under that mental image, then lifted her chin defiantly. She wouldn't let them see how scared she was, not anymore. If she was going to die, then she was going to go out fighting—just as Finn had taught her. "How do you know about Eternals? What *are* you and what did you do with my mother?"

Laughing now, Cora said, "Foolish child, I *am* your mother. I've been in this body for decades. I *chose* this body because I knew it was destined to give birth to you."

Sickened, Deidre couldn't say anything. She could only look at the woman in front of her and wonder how she had never once seen past the façade that Cora had presented for all those years. Seemed impossible now, but the proof was looking right at her out of eyes that seemed both familiar and strange.

"You possessed her."

"I *stepped* into her," Cora corrected. "Oh, not like my little demon friend over there. She's got her witch trapped inside her own body clamoring to be free."

Deidre winced at the image.

"But when I took this body, I separated the soul and sent it wherever tiny spirits like hers go. This body is mine. For now."

"How? How did you know that she would give birth to me?"

"Are you under the mistaken impression that I've come to illuminate you in some way? I haven't." Cora leaned forward, putting her face next to the bars. "Enough questions. Just know that I can kill your Eternal with one command. Don't fuck with me."

A mindless, all-encompassing anger roared through Deidre and shook her right to the bone. But she couldn't show any of it. Had to do exactly what her "mother" had taught her to do all those years. Put on a stoic face. Let no one see that you're worried. Funny, now she needed that advice to fight the very woman who had given it to her.

"I understand," she said. "I'm accustomed to being used by you. Now, if you want that Artifact, get me the hell out of this cage."

"You're crazy if you do this," Kellyn snapped.

"We've come too far to stop now," Cora told her, never taking her gaze from Deidre. She waved Dante toward the cell and Darius lifted the small crossbow he'd already used on Deidre once.

Cora warned, "We'll have white gold arrows aimed at you every moment. You'll be under our control. You try *anything* and your Eternal dies."

Deidre nodded and let her gaze stray to Dante. He managed to avoid her accusatory stare though, as he waited for his orders.

Cora straightened up, met her gaze for a long moment, then nodded. "Do it."

Chapter 41

Finn now had a taste of what Egan had endured. Draped in white gold chains, he was secured to a wall, unable to move or flash out. Unable to reach Deidre, unaware of what was happening to her. Unable to fight back against the two men currently beating the crap out of him. No wonder his friend had lost his grip on sanity.

He lunged forward, the manacles on his wrists digging into his flesh, white gold burning him with an icy cold. Rage rolled through him like a damn freight train. The flames that were such a part of him were buried beneath the magic-killing metal and the men in front of him knew he was powerless.

The chains rattled ominously as he pulled and yanked at them. And still they didn't budge from the stone wall at Finn's back.

"Big bastard, ain't he?" One of the men said, drawing his right fist back for a punishing blow to Finn's jaw.

"Yeah, but it's not doing him any good, is it?" His partner countered with a crushing fist to Finn's abdomen.

Narrowing his eyes on his attackers, Finn blinked blood from his vision and glared his fury because that was all they'd left him. His broad chest ran with blood, since the white gold was hampering his natural healing abilities, his face throbbed incessantly and if he'd had a heartbeat, it would have been racing.

A single-minded chant repeated over and over again in his mind. *Deidre* . . . Had to get to *Deidre* . . .

A door across the room opened and both of his attackers turned to look.

Joe walked in and Finn felt a short, painful jab that had nothing to do with physical pain. His *friend? Here? Was Joe a traitor?* Working with the president? Fresh fury and agony swamped him. There would be retribution for this—he swore it.

"Who the hell are you?" One of Finn's captors demanded.

"None of your damn business," Joe said. Then he shot both men with a single shot to their heads. Before they dropped, he was on his way across the room.

Finn choked out a laugh. "You had me worried there for a second."

"Yeah, well . . ." While Joe found the keys on one of the dead men and unlocked Finn's manacles, several more men, wearing dark suits entered the room.

Finn flinched, but Joe reassured him. "It's okay. They're friends."

Finn wasn't so sure but with his hands free and the white gold chains shoved off of him, he felt a slow swell of his power returning. The wounds on his body began to heal, but there was still too much white gold in the room for his strength to come back fully. That would change though, as soon as he got out of here. He had to find

Deidre. He focused on the connection they shared through the Mating tattoo, but couldn't feel her. Either she too was surrounded by white gold or she was—

No. She wasn't dead. *That* he would feel. The emptiness would crush him. The flames that were such a part of him lay dormant beneath his skin, struggling to get free.

An older man walked toward them, leaving the others who had come in with him to hover near the doorway.

"Finn," Joe said with a smile, "I want you to meet my father, Samuel Rooney. The vice president of the United States."

The instant the white gold chain was off her neck, Deidre felt the pulse of her power rush back in, filling her veins, her muscles, every inch of her body. It hummed inside her and she felt . . . good.

"Get on with it," Kellyn snapped, arms folded across her meager chest. She stood under the North Portico, in essence the White House front porch, watching from what she probably thought of as a safe distance. If Deidre had her way, Kellyn would never be safe from her.

Two Christmas trees, lights blinking cheerfully, flanked the double-door entrance to the White House. Cora dismissed the two guards usually on duty. She had Darius and Dante with her and apparently didn't want any other witnesses to what would happen next.

Deidre glanced briefly at Dante. He gave her a slight, barely perceptible nod and she frowned, wondering what the hell that was supposed to be. An apology for turning traitor and betraying her? If so, it was a pitiful attempt.

"Do you sense the Artifact or not?" Cora demanded.

Late November cold seeped through Deidre's clothes and turned her breath to vapor. She ignored everyone around her, closed her eyes and reached out with her magic. She concentrated solely on the feel of the Black Silver. It had only just begun to call to her in the last day or so. Like an oil spill on her soul, blackness swam toward her. The dark energy pouring from it hummed inside her like a tempting lure. *Use me. Be with me.* The pull of it was mesmerizing and Deidre was now forced to open herself to it completely.

"There." One whispered word and the atmosphere on the porch ignited.

"Where?" Cora bit off the word.

"Follow me," Deidre said and headed down the steps into the cold, dark night.

"Vice president?" Finn repeated, looking from his trusted second-in-command to the man standing beside him. There was a startling resemblance.

Samuel Rooney held out one hand to him. "My son wanted to tell you before," he said. "But I insisted he keep my secret."

Finn looked at the man's hand but didn't take it. "Why?"

"Because he's had doubts about Cora Sterling for years," Joe said, irritation plain in his tone. "Just recently, she's gotten worse and Dad was worried. Damn it, Finn, we just saved your ass. Doesn't that buy us at least a little faith?"

Nodding finally, Finn shook the vice president's hand, then released him.

Samuel Rooney met his gaze steadily. "Cora Sterling is unstable. She's threatening world leaders, letting alliances fall apart and about to declare martial law." His jaw clenched, he added, "I love my country and I'm willing to do whatever I can to save her from destruction. So, I wanted to tell you in person, that you will have my full support if you can bring Cora down."

A simmering moment of silence passed. Finn glanced at Joe, then told his father, "That's the plan."

Deidre allowed the pull of the dark energy to lead her down across the north lawn. She walked along the circular drive that led to Pennsylvania Avenue. She passed the circular pool and fountain, dormant now for winter and when she came to the wrought iron gates at the end of the drive, she stopped.

Her blood was humming with energy, dark and light. She clung to the light and followed the dark.

"Open the gates!" Cora's order was obeyed instantly and the creak and groan of cold metal sounded like the screams of dying souls.

Dante, Darius, Kellyn and Cora followed Deidre, staying right on her heels as she hurried across Pennsylvania Avenue, empty of cars. There wasn't a soul around. It had to be after midnight and with the curfew in force, people didn't risk arrest for late-night strolls.

They were alone, the small group of enemies, the only sound in the stillness, the crunch of their feet in the snow.

"Where the hell is she taking us?" Kellyn murmured.

No one answered, least of all Deidre. She wasn't even thinking about those who followed her now. All she could concentrate on was the burn of the dark magic sliding through her system. Her lungs were tight, making each breath more difficult than the last. But her steps were sure as she led those behind her into Lafayette Park.

The seven acres of greenery and trees, directly across from the White House, was known, along with the Ellipse, as the President's Park. In their winter glory, the trees were bare and it was a world of dark and light, white and gray and shadows crept quietly all around them.

Deidre didn't hesitate. She walked faster, every step bringing her closer to the dark energy dragging at her, teasing her senses. She heard those behind her scurrying to keep up and didn't care. All that mattered now was the Artifact and how she could use it to free herself.

If she could resist the dark, sensual lure that had snared her and her sister-witches in that long-ago time.

She stopped dead in front of the statue of President Andrew Jackson astride a rearing horse. The sculpture was bronze and had been in this spot since 1853. A dusting of snow covered the statue and the moon suddenly appeared from behind a bank of clouds to pour down a silvery light that encompassed the statue and the small crowd of people in front of it.

"Well?" Cora demanded.

"It's there," Deidre said, lifting one arm to point. "The plaque. That's the Artifact."

"What?" Kellyn scoffed and snorted dismissively. "Out in plain sight all this time and we never felt its presence?"

Deidre whipped her head around to glare at her. "It wasn't meant for *demons* to find."

Kellyn's eyes narrowed and she took a step forward. Cora stopped her with one raised hand. Then she turned to Darius and ordered, "Pry it loose."

He handed his crossbow to Dante. Picking up a huge rock, he slammed it against the plaque methodically, hoping to knock it from the stone, but nothing happened.

Deidre smiled to herself. The Black Silver was thrumming in the air, sending waves of power at her in silent welcome.

Someone must have brought the Black Silver from Europe long after she handed it off to that sea captain. How it had landed here, in DC, reforged into a plaque for a favored president, they would never know.

"Not coming off, ma'am," Darius finally admitted.

Cora scowled, looked at Deidre and said, "Get the damn thing and hand it over if you ever want to see your Eternal again."

Lies, Deidre thought. Cora had no intention of letting her or Finn live beyond tonight. So all that mattered was keeping Cora from taking the Artifact. Deidre walked up to the statue, laid one hand on the plaque and, instantly, the Black Silver became liquid. It released its hold on the stone and poured itself into Deidre's waiting hands, where it reformed itself into the Celtic knots she remembered so well.

Dark power sang inside her and she rocked with the force of it. Closing her eyes, she took a breath, savoring the feel of something so primal, so . . . dangerous.

"Hand it over." Cora's voice, short, sharp.

A column of living flame erupted in the darkness and when the fire died away, Finn and Joe were standing there, guns pointed at Cora.

"She's not giving you shit," Finn told her.

Chapter 42

Darius sent a white gold arrow at Joe, but he dropped out of the way and fired his weapon, knocking Darius over. Dante moved in behind Deidre, and Kellyn screamed, "You stupid bitch! I told you to kill him!"

Cora turned on her, but Kellyn laughed wildly and blinked out of existence, teleporting away from the scene.

Furious, Cora grabbed Deidre just before Finn reached her. She held a ceramic knife to her daughter's throat and said, "One step, Eternal, and I'll slice her open in front of you."

Deidre *knew* her mother was about to kill her. And since the knife wasn't metal, Deidre couldn't magically get rid of it. The dark power she held so tightly urged her to use it. To free herself and damn the others. But she wouldn't. Wouldn't give in to the tempting urges she had once surrendered to.

She looked at Finn and tried to say everything she needed to say in that single glance.

Finn stopped dead. His gaze met Deidre's and he felt again as powerless as he had in that damn holding room. He had tracked Deidre here through their shared tattoo and had brought Joe along as backup, to help take back the witch he loved.

Now though, he was caught. If he flashed out, Cora would kill Deidre before he had a chance to reappear and grab her.

Deidre's hands were cupped around the Black Silver protectively, as if terrified to let her mother so much as touch it. Deidre's eyes glittered dangerously and darkened with the force of the energy pulsing through her from the Artifact. She was in danger from more than just Cora. Behind Finn, Joe moved carefully to one side, easing closer to Darius. Finn did the same, only he went the other way, one incremental step at a time.

"Who the hell are you?" he demanded, meeting Cora's gaze. "What are you? Demon? Dark angel? Sorceress?"

Cora laughed and hitched Deidre closer, the knife's edge digging into her skin and sending small rivulets of blood along the long white column of her neck. Everything in Finn fisted.

"You idiot," Cora snarled, flicking her glance between him and Joe. "I'm sister to your god, Belen."

That news hit Finn like a rock wall.

"I see you know nothing of me. Lost in time, my brother and I," she muttered darkly, her gaze swinging wildly between Finn and Joe as words spewed from her mouth and the knife at Deidre's throat dug in farther. Bitterness colored her tone and madness glittered in her eyes. "We should have been worshipped. But no. Belen shunted us aside in his race for glory. He thought only of his lover, Danu—*we* should have been first with him. Then Belen and his bitch created the witches. And you Eternals. And with that creation, my brother and I slipped even farther into the background."

Finn shook his head. What the hell was he supposed to do with this? And where in the *fuck* was Belen when his sister was running around murdering witches?

"Who's this *brother*?" Finn snarled.

"Who *was* he, you mean," she shot back. "Henry Fender was my brother. I felt his life end when you killed the body he wore and his spirit was lost—he was one with that body as I am with this one. We risked everything, even our immortality, for this. We became vulnerable the moment we took these bodies and you *killed* him. And now, you'll feel it when I kill this bitch."

Good to know, Finn thought fiercely. Kill the body, kill the god.

Deidre struggled, still holding on to the Artifact and Finn knew she was trying not to be overcome by the dark magic. But if it meant her life, then damn it, he *wanted* her to use that Black Silver.

"Take them out," Cora snapped.

Finn felt a hard slam of shock as Darius erupted into a pillar of flame. His smile for Finn was dark, deadly and promised pain.

Seeing the look on his face must have amused Darius because he sneered, "Our goddess masked our energy signature so you wouldn't discover us, but the Forgotten have been here all along, Eternal. And we will take back what should have been ours."

The Forgotten. Damn the capricious gods who paid no attention to the very beings they created. How could his god not have even fucking noticed that his rejected Eternals were trying to stop the Awakening?

Then Dante too was covered in flames and the two men flanked the president, protecting her. Joe was no match for two immortals and Finn couldn't fight them, the president *and* save Deidre.

As if she were reading his mind, Deidre whispered, "I love you. I'm sorry we failed."

"Hand it to me," Cora warned.

Finn shook his head, silently telling Deidre to hang on to the damned Artifact. If they were meant for oblivion, then they would meet that fate together. He called on the flames and as he did, Dante laid one hand on Deidre and she stiffened in response. Seconds ticked past, flying and crawling all at once.

"Get out of here, Joe," Finn ordered.

"Screw that," Joe said.

"Here!" Deidre lifted the Artifact, so that Cora would have to move the knife away from her throat to grab it. Of course she did. With a satisfied sigh, Cora let Deidre go, grabbed the Artifact in both hands and smiled down at it as if it were a long-lost lover.

Cora sighed, sliding her fingertips across the shining Black Silver. "Finally, it's mine," she crooned, backing away from all of them. "Nothing can stop me now. Belen will pay for what he did. You'll all—"

Finn flashed to Deidre, grabbed her and flashed back to a safe distance. She was protected from the creature who had been her mother, but the Artifact wasn't. They couldn't allow Cora to have it. Couldn't—

"What the— No!" Cora lifted horrified eyes to Deidre. "What's happening—" She dropped the Black Silver to the snow at her feet and it shone like a stain on nature. *"You!"* She turned a vicious gaze on Deidre. "You did this. To me. To *me!*" Her body trembled and quaked as if she were being shaken by the hands of the gods themselves.

"You think you've won." She gasped for breath, fought for it. "But you've won nothing. There's worse than me out there. And they won't stop until you're all dead."

Finn tightened his grip on Deidre as Cora convulsed. Then she let out a piercing, blood-chilling scream and exploded into dust. Her ashes scattered across the Black Silver still gleaming darkly in the moonlight.

Finn whipped around to face the Forgotten, but it was too late. Darius flashed out and was gone. Only Dante remained and Finn headed for him, wanting nothing more than to pound the Forgotten Eternal into the ground.

But Deidre caught his arm. "No, don't. He's the reason I'm alive. He asked me to trust him one last time and told me to give the Artifact to Cora."

"Why?" Finn asked the question and if he didn't get a good answer, he'd kill the Eternal where he stood.

"Because not all Forgotten are out to destroy the Awakening," Dante said. His flames blinked out and he was just a man, standing in the snow beside the dust of a fallen god.

"Some of us seek atonement, just as you do. Belen created us first, and for a time, we thrived. But we were filled with our own power and created so much chaos . . ." Dante shrugged in acceptance. "Belen had no choice but to cut us off. He discarded us in favor of your kind. And, some of us took it better than others," he added ruefully with a glance at the spot where Darius had been only moments before.

Joe walked up to join them and took a stand on the other side of Deidre, his plan to protect her obvious from his stance.

Finn was withholding judgment on this Eternal, but he *had* saved Deidre. "How did you know what the Artifact would do to her?"

Dante smiled. "Belen himself told me. He knew what

his sister had done and wanted me prepared to save the Awakening. He couldn't turn to any of the Eternals—it was part of the atonement spell cast. He and Danu are forced to stand back and allow you all to succeed or fail on your own. But he *could* call on those few Forgotten who still believe in him." He bent down and picked up the Artifact, then tossed it to Finn. "Call it a loophole. Anyway, since the witches created the Artifact against the wishes of Danu and Belen, the power locked within it is repellent to the gods. The Black Silver reacted to the god-link within Cora's assumed body. Her own spirit was as repelled by the energies as Belen or Danu's would have been."

"Thank you," Deidre said.

"Yeah." Finn nodded. "I owe you."

Giving Deidre a slight bow, Dante then looked at Finn and said, "No, you don't."

"Where are you going now?"

Dante shrugged again. "Not sure. But I'll be around." Then he called on the fire and flashed out.

"Well, there's something you don't see every day," Joe said quietly. "Unless you're *us*."

Finn laughed and pulled Deidre in close. He didn't think he would ever be able to hold her tight enough, near enough to make up for those moments when he had come so close to losing her. The Artifact burned in his hand, dark power swirling, but it was weak, as if being in Cora's grasp for even such a short time had drained some of its energy.

Curling his fingers around the damn thing, Finn released Deidre, but kept her hand firmly in his. He wasn't ready to stop touching her just yet. "Are you all right?"

"I am now. I was tempted by the Artifact," she admitted, "and I'm in no hurry to hold it again, but I don't think it has the pull on me it once did."

"According to their Mates, your sister-witches had a harder time resisting its pull."

Deidre looked up into his eyes. "We're all different, Finn. Our hearts, our minds, our souls. And that's a good thing, right?"

"Yeah, it is." He shifted his gaze to where Cora had died only moments before. "Will you be all right with what happened here tonight?"

Deidre followed his gaze. "I will. She wanted us dead, and we won. So yes, I'll be all right. But the president's dead, Finn, and we don't even have a body to prove it. What're we supposed to do now?"

A slow smile curved his mouth. "I think Joe might have an idea about that."

"Joe?" Deidre asked.

"Joe Rooney, son of the vice president," Finn said.

Judging by the look on her face, Deidre was stunned. "I thought VP Rooney's son died overseas three years ago."

"The reports of my death were greatly exaggerated," Joe told her, then shrugged. "Dad wanted me to be able to stay undercover in case he needed me. He never trusted your mother."

Deidre glanced again at the spot where Cora had died. "Smart man. Why don't we go see him?"

An emergency meeting was called at the White House. VP Rooney broke the news of the death of the president to her cabinet and was given the oath of office by the chief justice. After that, the cover-up began. And no one did cover-ups like DC. The press was told that an autopsy was performed by newly sworn President Rooney's personal physician and it was deemed that Cora Sterling had died of a heart attack.

The country went into mourning and nations around the world sent representatives to attend the state funeral.

Deidre and Finn met with President Rooney and his staff two days before the funeral. Ostensibly, she was there to offer good wishes to him. In reality, they were there so that Finn could check to make sure there were no more "others" hanging around.

Once that visit was over, President Rooney faced Finn in the Oval Office. "Well?"

"They're all clear," he said, then added, "Unless there's another goddess wandering around masking their power. But what're the chances?"

The president didn't smile, just shifted his gaze to Deidre. "I want you to know, I'll do everything I can to stop the persecution of witches. And I'm issuing a pardon for the both of you and the other members of the WLF. You can return to your normal lives."

Deidre shook her head sadly. "Mr. President, until every woman and witch is released from prison or from the fear of imprisonment and execution, there is no 'normal' for any of us."

"She's right," Finn said, pulling her in close to him. "And you should know, the WLF isn't going anywhere. We'll be here, working to free every last witch on the planet and we won't stop until it's done."

"Change will come, but it won't be fast. Or easy." Finally, the president gave them a rueful smile. "I'm not surprised you'll continue to fight. And I suspect my son will be joining you."

"Yeah." Finn grinned. "I know he will."

Deidre laughed as Finn called up the flames and flashed them out.

Chapter 43

Haven welcomed them.

The moment they arrived in Wales, Deidre had felt a surge of peace, of warmth. It was as if her soul had come home, at last. She had never been there before—at least, not in *this* lifetime—but she recognized Manorbier Castle and could have found her way through the grounds blindfolded.

Meeting her sister-witches and discovering an instant kinship was balm to a heart still bruised by the betrayal of a mother she had once loved. With pride, she wore the coven's traditional floor-length toga, baring her left breast—and her Mating tattoo—to the world. She had found her place. With Finn. With the WLF at home. And here. At Haven.

"It's an odd thing," she said, leaning back against Finn. "Being here, *belonging* here."

They stood in the ceremonial chamber. Across the room from them burned three fire cages, each of them containing a shard of the Artifact returned to Haven by the witch who had once hidden it. Deidre stared at the cage where she had placed her piece of the Black Silver and felt as if everything had finally been righted.

There were other pieces of the Artifact still out there of course, Deidre thought, flipping her long braid over her shoulder. There were more Eternals and more witches still to Mate. Still to accomplish their tasks. But with the help of Danu, Belen and those who had already succeeded, the coven would eventually complete their atonement. She just knew it.

"It's strange for me too." Finn kissed the top of her head and wrapped one arm around her middle, holding her to him. "Back in the day, none of the Eternals were ever welcomed into Haven." He stopped and looked around at the intricate carvings on the rock walls veined with silver. "It's nice."

"Yeah." She tipped her head back to look up at him. "You'll notice, we're back in a cave. I'm getting to be really comfortable underground. What's that say about me?"

He grinned. "It says you're going to love my cave in the Mexican desert."

Deidre laughed and turned in his arms. "It figures you've got another cave somewhere."

"That one's got a hot tub. Underground spring. You'll love it."

Truthfully, she thought, as she stared up into her Mate's eyes, she would love it anywhere as long as he was there with her. Haven would always be here, waiting for them. A safe place. The home of her heart, her soul. The place where the trouble had all begun and where it would finally end.

She laid one hand on his broad, bare chest and felt the steady beat of his heart. "Are you used to that yet?"

He covered her hand with his, pinning her there to the beat of his heart, to the Mating tattoo that bonded him to her. "No. Not really. Feels good, though. How are you dealing with immortality?"

"Weird to think about it," she admitted. "But more time with you is a very good thing."

"Agreed." He lifted her chin with his fingertips and kissed her.

"Oh, man," Rune called out as he and the others entered the dining chamber. "I don't need to see that."

"Close your eyes then," Finn growled and finished kissing Deidre before he broke away and smiled.

Watching his brother Eternals with their Mates, Finn felt hope for the first time in a long time. But as Egan walked into the room behind the others, that hope was dampened slightly.

According to the others, Egan was beginning to deal with what had happened. But when Finn looked into those gray eyes, he saw nothing of his old friend there. Only the eyes of a hunter.

Mairi, the once and future High Priestess of the coven, spoke up into the suddenly charged silence. "Deidre, if you're ready, we'd like to try the location spell now. We need to find Kellyn."

"I'm ready," she said, stepping from the circle of Finn's arms. "But you should know, she's not going to be easy to catch. And she's dangerous."

Egan spoke up before anyone else could. "All you guys have to do is locate her. I'll take care of the rest."

"Egan"—Torin's voice held a warning—"this isn't just about you and Kellyn. What happens to each Mated pair affects us all."

Egan snapped him a hard look. "You spend a few

months at the bottom of the ocean and then we'll talk. For right now, she's *my* witch. And I'm going to find her."

Finn and Deidre flew back to DC in time for the funeral. Thank God the Mating was complete and her powers were under her control so they could take the jet Finn owned to fly back and forth from Haven. If she were still in the Awakening, her magic would have been too unstable to risk flying. She could have brought down the plane. And after hearing her sister-witches' stories, Deidre really hadn't wanted to spend days on a boat.

It was, she thought, too bad that Finn couldn't yet flash them across the ocean. The distance was too great. But as his powers grew with their Mating, who knew? She smiled to herself. Maybe one day.

They would return to Haven again, soon. Though their fight to save witches was in DC, their spiritual home was in Wales. Besides, Deidre thought, Finn needed to be with his brothers so they could all help Egan. She worried about the Eternal and almost pitied Kellyn when he finally found her.

Still, Deidre knew that with their Mating complete, their task accomplished, they were now stronger than ever. And would only get stronger still as time passed. Together, they would help Egan heal and recover. Just as they would help free accused witches.

They were together, as they were always meant to be. There was just one more thing that had to be done and then she would slide out of public view and return to the tunnels. To the fight.

The world looked hazy and dark through the filmy black veil of the hat she wore. With her features hidden from the curious, Deidre stood among the crowd and yet apart from them. Apart from everyone but the Eternal at her side. Standing tall and proud beside her, Finn wore a magically conjured dark suit and still looked every inch the warrior. Her hand in his, their magic pushed back and forth between their bodies, riding the permanent link that connected them.

An icy wind blew, but the sun was shining and the streets of DC were crowded with people who had come out to say good-bye to Cora Sterling. Deidre felt their stares. Felt their sympathy. But it all rolled over her without leaving a mark.

She had said good-bye to her past already and now all she wanted was her future. She imagined the television reporters were busy cataloging the procession and she saw the flash of cameras documenting everything. But she didn't care about any of that. Not anymore. The cortege began to roll toward Arlington, and Finn and Deidre began their own journey, walking hand in hand down the long road ahead.

"This is Margaret Johnson, reporting from the funeral of President Cora Sterling. The late president's daughter is marching behind her mother's coffin, bravely walking hand in hand with a man who is, according to rumor, her fiancé. As Deidre Sterling hides her tears behind a veil, we can only wish her well."

And beneath her veil, Deidre smiled.

"They took my mom away last night."

Shea Jameson wanted to lock her classroom door and walk away. It was the only sane thing to do. But the tremor in her student's voice pulled at her. The day was over at Lincoln Middle School and the hallways should have been emptied. Shea knew because she always waited until everyone else had left the building before she headed home. She made it a point to avoid crowds whenever she could. As a teacher, she was faced with classes filled with kids every day, but they didn't bother her. It was the parents of those children that worried her.

She looked down at Amanda Hall and sympathy rose up inside her. Shea had heard the rumors, the whispers. She'd watched as the teachers had reluctantly protected Amanda from those who only yesterday had been her friends. And she knew that the girl's situation was only going to get worse.

"Ms. Jameson, I don't know what to do."

Her heart broke for the petite blond girl leaning against a row of closed lockers in the empty, quiet school hallway. The child's face was streaked with tears, her blue eyes swimming with them. Her arms were crossed over her middle, as if she was trying to console herself, and when she looked up at Shea, stark misery and panic were stamped on her small features.

She wouldn't be able to turn her back on the girl, despite the risks, Shea thought with an inner sigh. How could she and still live with herself?

"I'm so sorry, Amanda." She glanced over her shoulder to be sure there was no one near. Not a soul was around, though, and the silence, but for Amanda's soft sniffling, was deafening. The beige walls were decorated with posters announcing the coming Fall Festival and Shea's gaze slid away from the drawings of cackling wart-encrusted witches burning at stakes.

The small hairs at the back of her neck stood straight up and she could have sworn that there was someone close by, watching her. A shiver of something icy slid along Shea's spine, but the halls were still empty. For now.

She shouldn't have stopped, a voice in her mind whispered. Shouldn't have spoken to the girl. No one knew better than Shea that there were spies everywhere. That no one was safe anymore. If someone should see her talking to this child now, her own personal nightmarish circus would begin again, and there was no guarantee that this time Shea would survive it.

But how could she walk away from a child in desperate need? Especially when she knew exactly what Amanda was going through? Shifting her books and papers in her arms, Shea dropped her free hand to the girl's shoulder and tried to think of something comforting to say. But lies wouldn't do her any good and the truth was far too terrifying.

If Amanda's mother had really been taken, she wouldn't be coming back. In fact, it was probably only a matter of time before the authorities came to snatch up Amanda as well. And that realization pushed her to speak.

"Amanda," Shea asked quietly, "do you have anyone you can stay with?"

The girl nodded. "My grandma. The police took me there last night. Grandma didn't want me to come to school today, but I did anyway and everyone's being so mean . . ." She shook her head and frowned in spite of her tears. A flash of anger dazzled her damp eyes. "My mom's not evil. I don't care what they say. She didn't do anything wrong. I would know."

Shea wasn't so sure of that. These days, secrets were all that kept some women alive. But even if Amanda was right and her mother was innocent, there was little chance she'd be released. Still, what was important now was Amanda's safety. The girl had already learned one harsh lesson today—*don't trust anyone*. Her friends had turned on her and soon everyone else would, too. Once word got out about her mother being taken, the girl would be in danger from so many different directions, she'd never find shelter.

"Amanda," Shea whispered fiercely, "don't come back to school tomorrow. Go to your grandmother's and stay there."

"But I have to help my mom," the girl argued. "I thought you could go with me to the principal and we could tell her that my mom's not what they think. Mom's the president of the PTA!"

Shea winced as the girl's voice rose. She couldn't afford for anyone to see them. Couldn't risk being seen helping the child of a detainee. Leaning down, she caught Amanda's eye and said, "Your mom would want you to be safe, wouldn't she?"

"Yeah . . ."

"Then that's the best thing you can do for her."

"I don't know . . ."

"Amanda, listen to me," Shea said, her words coming faster now as the creeping sensation of being watched flooded back into her system. "There's nothing we can do to help your mom right now. The best thing for everyone is for you to leave here and go straight to your grandmother's. Okay? No stops. No talking to anyone."

"But—"

A door opened down the hall and Shea glanced toward the sound. Her stomach pitched with nerves as she spotted the school principal coming out of her office. Lindsay Talbot's eyes narrowed as she noticed Amanda and Shea huddled together, speaking in whispers. Instantly Ms. Talbot darted back into her office.

"Just go, Amanda," she said, giving the girl's shoulder a quick squeeze. "Go now."

The girl picked up on the urgency in Shea's voice, nodded briefly, then turned and ran down the hall toward the back door. Once she was gone, Shea took a deep breath, steeled herself and walked in the opposite direction. Her heels clicked on the tile floor as she neared the glass wall of the school's office. The front door was only a few feet away and the sunlit afternoon shone like a beacon of safety. She was leaving, no matter what, she thought, but she had to know what Ms. Talbot was doing.

Shea glanced through the office windows in time to see the principal hang up the phone. Then the woman turned around, met Shea's gaze and gave her a cat-about-to-eat-a-canary smile.

Just like that, she knew it was over.

All of it.

Shea had been happy here. For a while. She enjoyed spending her days with the kids. She had convinced herself over the last year and a half that she'd finally found safety. That her normal behavior, her gift for teaching, was enough to prove to everyone that she was nothing more than she claimed to be. A sixth-grade science teacher.

But as she met Lindsay Talbot's harsh stare, she felt the old familiar stir of panic. Fear rushed through her, churning her stomach, making her hands damp and drying out her mouth. She had to run.

Again.

She let her papers fall to the floor in a soft rustle of sound, then tightened her grip on her shoulder bag and raced for the front door. As her hand pushed the cold steel bar, she heard Lindsay Talbot call out behind her, "You won't get away. They're coming."

"I know," Shea murmured, but she ran anyway. What else could she do? If she stayed, she would end up with Amanda's mother. Just one more woman locked away with no hope of ever getting out.

Outside, she squinted at the beam of sunlight that slanted into her eyes, and took the steps down to the sidewalk at a dead run. She dug into her purse as she turned toward the parking lot, blindly fumbling for her keys. Her only hope was to be gone before the MPs arrived. It would take them time to find her and in that time she would disappear. She'd done it before and she could do it again. Dye her hair, change her name, find a new identity and lose herself in some other city.

She wouldn't go back to her apartment. They'd be expecting her to, but she wasn't that stupid. Besides, she didn't need anything from her home. She traveled light these days. A woman constantly on the move couldn't afford to drag mementos from one place to the next. Instead, she kept a packed suitcase in her car trunk and a stash of emergency cash tucked into her bra at all times, on the off chance that she'd have to leave in a hurry.

A cold wind rushed at her, pulling her long hair free of the knot she kept it in. Slate gray clouds rolled in off the ocean and seagulls wheeled and dipped overhead. She hardly noticed. Parents were still milling around out front, picking up their kids, but Shea ran past them all, ignoring those who spoke to her.

Her car was at the far end of the parking lot, closest to the back exit. She was always prepared to run—to slip away while her pursuers were coming in the front. She was sprinting now, her heart hammering in her chest, breath rattling in her lungs. She held her keys so tightly the jagged edges dug into her palm.

The soles of her shoes slid unsteadily on the gravel-laced asphalt, but she kept moving. One thought pulsed through her mind. *Run. Run and don't look back.*

Her gaze fixed on her nondescript beige two-door compact, she never saw the man who leapt out at her from behind another car. He pushed her down and her knees hit the asphalt with a grinding slide that tore open her skin and sent pain shooting along her legs.

His hands reached for her as a deep voice muttered, "Gimme the purse and you can go."

Absently, she heard voices rising in the distance as parents saw the man attacking her. *Oh, God, not now,* she thought as she turned over and stared up into the wild eyes of a junkie who desperately needed money. She couldn't deal with this now. There was too much attention on her.

He pulled a knife as if he sensed she was hesitating. "Give me the money *now*."

Shea shook her head, and when he reached for her again, she instinctively lifted both hands as if to push him off and away. But she never made contact with him. She didn't need to. A surge of energy suddenly pulsed through her and shot from her fingertips. As a *whoosh* of sound erupted, the man in front of her erupted into flames.

Shea stared up at him, horrified by what was happening. By what she'd *done*. His screams tore through the air as he tried to run from the fire. But it only fed the flames consuming him and as his shrieks rose higher and higher, Shea staggered to her feet, glanced down at her hands and shuddered.

That was when she heard it.

The chanting.

Over the sounds of the dying man's cries, voices roared together, getting louder and louder as she was surrounded. One word thundered out around her, hammering at her mind and soul, reducing her to a terror she hadn't known in ten years.

She looked up into the faces of her students' parents as they circled her. People she knew. People she liked. Now, though, she hardly recognized them. Their features were twisted into masks of hatred and panic and their voices joined together to shout their accusation.

"Witch! Witch! Witch!"

Shea fought for air as the mob tightened around her. There was no way out now. She was going to die. And if the crowd didn't kill her, then the MPs would take her away when they arrived and she would be as good as dead anyway. It was over. The years of terror and dread, the hiding, the praying, the constant worrying about survival.

"Stop!" she shouted, her voice raw with horror at what she'd done. At what they were about to do to her. "I didn't do anything!"

A useless argument, since they'd all seen what had happened. But how? How had she done it? She wasn't a witch. She was just . . . her. "If I had power, wouldn't I be using it now?"

Some of the people around her seemed to consider that and their expressions reflected worry. It was not what Shea had been after. If they were worried about their own safety, they'd be just that much more eager to kill her.

Her head whipped from side to side, desperately looking for a way out of this. But she couldn't find one. In the distance she heard the wail of sirens that signaled the MPs' imminent arrival. And the Magic Police weren't going to let her get away. They might save her from the mob. On the other hand, they might stand back and let these everyday, ordinary people solve their problem for them.

Frantic, she stumbled back as the crowd pushed in until she realized they were herding her closer to the burning man stretched out on the asphalt. Heat from the flames reached for her. The stench of burning flesh stained the air. Shea looked from the dead man to the crowd and back again and knew that whatever happened next, she deserved it.

The fire suddenly erupted, growing until hungry licks

of orange and red flames leapt and jumped more than six feet high. Someone in the crowd screamed. Shea jolted. Black cars with flashing yellow lights raced into the driveway and then screeched to a stop. Men in black uniforms piled out and pointed guns, but they were the least of her problems now.

Flames reached for Shea. Engulfed her. The roar of the quickening fire deafened her to her surroundings. She screamed and looked up into a pair of pale gray eyes reflecting the shifting colors of the flames. She felt hard, strong arms wrap around her, as a deep voice whispered, "Close your eyes."

"Good idea," she answered, then fainted for the first time in her life.

ABOUT THE AUTHOR

Regan Hastings is the pseudonym of a *USA Today* best-selling author of more than a hundred romance novels. She lives with her family in California.

CONNECT ONLINE

www.reganhastings.com
facebook.com/reganhastings
twitter.com/maureenchild

ALSO AVAILABLE
from

Regan Hastings

Visions of Magic
An Awakening Novel

In the ten years since magic has reemerged in the world,
witches have become feared and hunted. For weeks Shea
Jameson has been haunted by visions of fire. When she
unintentionally performs a spell in public, she becomes
one of the hunted. Her only hope is Torin, a dangerously
sensual man who claims to be her eternal mate.

**"Magic, passion, and immortal warriors—
this fabulous new series has it all."**
—*New York Times* bestselling author Christina Dodd

Available wherever books are sold or at
penguin.com

"Like" us at facebook.com/ProjectParanormalBooks